Gerswin scanned the screen, studying the eight devilkids, all stretched on the febrile flooring. The cots were empty. Five young men, three women—the result of six months search—waited like the caged animals they resembled.

Eight. Were eight all there were, or all he and Imperial technology could find and drag from Earth's ruins? Gerswin took a deep breath.

"Hold these, Harl." He handed the weapons belt to the technician, and palmed the portal release.

"Ser! You can't go in there! Clerris and N'gere are still recovering! Those—they're—"

"Savages?" Gerswin said. "I know. That's why this is my job.

"You forget—I'm one of them." He eased inside the portal.

L. E. MODESITT, JR.

VOLUME I OF THE FOREVER HERO

DAWN FOR A DISTANT EARTH

A TOM DOHERTY ASSOCIATES BOOK
NEW YORK

This is a work of fiction. All the characters and events portrayed in this book are fictitious, and any resemblance to real people or events is purely coincidental.

DAWN FOR A DISTANT EARTH

A Tor Book
Published by Tom Doherty Associates, Inc.
49 West 24th Street
New York, N.Y. 10010

Cover art by Wayne Barlowe

ISBN: 0-812-51613-3

First printing: January 1987

Printed in the United States of America

0 9 8 7 6 5 4 3 2

For Lee,
    my first fan and critic,
        who kept grabbing for the pages
            before they left the typewriter.

I

In the west wing of the tower of time, abandoned as it is by the keepers of the clock, lies an ancient key. Not an impressive long steel shaft is this key, but a small volume, a compendium of pages enameled against the ravages of the decades and the centuries.

The book has no title, no preface, no table of contents, nor any title embossed on its black spine, nor even printed pages evenly matched and marching end to end.

What is it, you ask?

That question must hold for another. The other question? What is the tower of time? For there are no towers left on Old Earth, only the rambling farms, the sweep of grass, the ramparts of the west mountains, and a few score towns nestled into their restored places in history. There is only a single shuttle field . . . without a tower.

This tower of time rears backward into history, not into the dark starred nights that are so cold to one used to the light-strewn nights on planets that once belonged to the Empire. Backward into history, you say? How far?

Far enough. Back to the time when purple landspouts raged the high plains, back to the time when boulders fell like rain, and when the devilkids were the only beings who dared to run the hillocks outside the shambletowns. . . .

Yes, that far. Back to the days of the Captain. . . .

The Myth of the Rebuilding
Alarde D'Lorina
New Augusta, 4539 N.E.C.

(⭑ II

Step . . . pause . . . listen. Step . . . pause . . . listen.

The boy crept through the thin bushes and scattered patches of ground fog toward the shambletown wall. The leathers of his tunic were ripped, and the thonging where the skins were joined was loosening. The rain stung his skin, as the chill wind froze the droplets before they struck.

Overhead, the thick clouds were barely visible in the gloom that passed for twilight.

Most of the torches on the shambletown wall had blown out and would not be relighted until the wind and rain abated. That would not be long. Beneath the west mountains, on the high plains east of the shambletown, the rains seldom lasted. Nor did the purple furies of the landspouts usually penetrate into the hills and gullies.

A single torch by the gate flared back to light, and the boy ducked behind one of the few grubushes left near the walls, just below the outcropping of old brick, powderstone, and purpled clay on which the shambletown had been raised.

In the gloom downhill from the wall, he would not be seen. Even if a sharp-eyed guard did sight the small shadow created by the torches, that darkness would be blamed on a skulking coyote, or even a king rat scuttling for his hole.

The boy's left leg hurt, still stiff from his encounter with the she coyote. He needed food, better food than he could grub from the plains and the hills, food without the poisons that the wild plants springing from the sickly soil carried.

Most times he could eat the yuccas and needle pears, but the coyote wound and its infection had lowered his body's ability to digest the wild food.

He froze behind a thicker grubush and peered through the scraggly leaves at the wall. Too high—more than twice his height, and even with a healthy leg, beyond his reach.

2

That meant the Maze. He had known that from the beginning, but had hoped . . . He shivered, but there was no escaping the need for the cleaner food that lay beyond the shambletown wall.

Tightening his grip on the jagged blade he carried in his left hand, he dropped farther down the hillside and edged eastward, bit by bit.

Slide . . . pause . . . listen. Slide . . . pause . . . listen.

The pattern was nearly automatic, his ears straining for the click and scrabble of the rats, or the pad and click of a foraging coyote seeking a shambletowner out alone after dark.

The scattered grubushes grew more thickly as he neared the tangled mass that comprised the Maze. While they never crowded closely enough to provide a thicket or a constant cover, their numbers and sharp leaves and twigs slowed his progress. He checked each before sliding toward it to insure that no rat lay concealed there, no female coyote on the prowl for hungry cubs.

At last, the Maze towered above him.

He stopped, letting his breathing smooth. He sniffed, the thin nostrils in the narrow nose dilating to catch the scents nearby, and those from the Maze.

Crouching by one hole, he edged away as he caught the pungent odor of rat, all too fresh. A second entrance he rejected for the musty smell that indicated neither rat nor the air circulation necessary for an access to the less closely guarded eastern wall of the shambletown.

A third and fourth hole were each rejected.

A fifth was too low and reeked of land poison.

Click, click, scrabble.

The blade flashed. The rat darted—but not quickly enough.

The rat's purpled gray coat was scarred, streaked with silver.

The boy nodded. The rat, half the height to his knee, had been slow. Not sick, but old.

He left the carcass. While the hide might have been useful, only the shambletowners had the ability to turn it into leather. The meat was inedible, even for him.

Checking the hole from which the rat had emerged, he rejected it, and continued his slow movement along the Maze.

Deciding that none of the lower openings were likely to

provide the access he needed, he switched his attention to the higher holes.

At last, he located a promising entrance, slightly above his head, but with easy handholds. He climbed to the left side, to avoid appearing in front of the dark opening. He let his nose test the scents, catching the mixture of free-flowing air, overlaid with the scent of shambletowners and their excrement, and the faint hint of omnipresent rat.

Blade in hand, he eased into the Maze, his hawk-eyes dilating farther to adjust to the gloom that was darker than the blackest of the clouded nights.

From behind him, he could hear the wind whistle as it shifted more to the north.

The passage branched, one dark pit stretching below, from where the scent of rat oozed upward, the other darkness twisting leftward, away from the shambletown. With the slump of his shoulders that passed for a sigh, he silently took the left opening, which, as he had hoped, again forked.

From his right came the definite smell of shambletown, although he could detect a gentle incline which bothered him. The last thing he wanted was to pop out high on the Maze wall in clear range of the shambletown guards and their slings.

Two more branches and he squatted just inside an exit overlooking the eastern wall of the shambles. He was higher than he would have liked—more than a body length above the wall and three body lengths above the uneven clay expanse between the Maze and the wall. His exit was to the north of the small eastern gate and the majority of the torches.

He shifted his weight to relieve the nagging ache and the pressure on his left leg and studied the wall. He would have to slip over the wall roughly opposite his vantage point. Unlike the northern wall, which was higher, the eastern wall, behind the bulk and protection of the Maze, also sloped outward as it dropped to its stone base. The slope might be just enough to let him make the climb quickly.

By now, it was as dark as it would get. The frozen rain pelted down in a desultory *click, click, click* that might cover any noise he made climbing down to the clay.

Only a single torch by the gate was lit, and the boy decided that the sooner he moved the better.

With a single fluid motion, he slid out of the hole and let his bare feet search for the outcroppings he knew were there, careful to let the bulk of his weight rest upon his good right leg. That brought him within two body lengths of the hard ground.

Ears, eyes, and nose all alert for rats, coyotes, or shambletown guards, he began easing himself down the Maze's rough surface as quickly as he could.

The animals avoided the freezing rain when they could, as did the shambletown guards, and he reached a position under the wall without an alarm being raised.

Again . . . He stopped and listened, straining to hear, to see if he could sense anyone on the far side of the wall. Had he judged his position correctly, once over the clay bricks he would be opposite a narrow lane leading deeper into the lower shambletown.

No sound came from beyond the wall—just the *click, click, click* of the frozen droplets hitting the hard surface.

Flexing his fingers, toes, he sprang, scrambling quietly to the top, the abrasiveness of the sandpaint giving his extremities just enough purchase to support the effort.

He vaulted over—and down onto a covered clay barrel.
Boom!

Even as the sound of his impact on the empty container rumbled down the cleared area next to the wall toward the guard post, he was dashing for the alley.

"Hear that?"

"Storm, stand?"

"No storm!"

The boy did not stay to hear the debate between the two guards, but slunk down the narrow alleyway deeper into the dark, sniffing and listening.

He sought an empty dwelling. In all those he had passed, he could sense shambletowners mumbling to each other after their evening meal. Either that or sullen silence.

Dark was the shambletown, lit but by a few ratfat torches set behind salvaged glass, and by the dim glow from deep within the claybricked homes.

Another alley lane, across a wider street and to the left, beckoned. The boy darted a look, then melted back into the gloom as two figures trudged down the street, not looking to either side. The muted clanking told him they were the replacement guards for the eastern wall, and he shrank farther into the darkness.

Once they disappeared from view, he skittered across the dimly lit thoroughfare, such as it was, and vanished into the darkness again, more like a rat than a boy.

Three dwellings down, he found a likely place. Like all the others, at this time of night the window was sealed with a patched hide cover, but there were no sounds from within, and not even the faintest touch of heat radiating from the hide.

He looked up and down the alleyway, then raised his sharp and jagged blade. One cut . . . two . . . three . . . and the bottom flap of the hide was free.

A glance under the hide and inside told him that no one was within. He needed no further encouragement to scrabble up the flaking sandpainted wall and through the narrow aperture.

The enclosed space was small, just two rooms plus the alcove used for food preparation and cooking, and the flat shelves in the now-covered front window that contained the plant beds.

As he saw the plants, despite the smell of excrement used as fertilizer and the musty smell of unwashed shambletowners, saliva moistened his mouth.

He checked the cooking area and found a small bin with three shriveled and raw potatoes. He took a bite from one, forcing himself to chew it slowly. One swallow of the mealy substance was all he could take, although the taste told him it was free of landpoison.

While he finished chewing, his eyes surveyed the two rooms. In the sleeping room was a single pallet wide enough for a man and a woman, centered on a raised clay platform. In the clay brick alcoves behind the platform where there should have been a few tunics and personal belongings, there were neither.

In the main room were only a table woven from grubush branches and two matching stools.

His eyes darted back to the pallet made of ground cloth, newly pounded into shape, and with no scent of shambletowner to indicate it had been used.

The boy padded over to the largest plant flats, but only sprouts broke the surface. On the far left was a narrow flat with older plants. He sniffed, and could detect no landpoisons. Then he pulled a single leafy stem and attached bulb from the damp soil. Wiping it on his tunic, he studied the rounded white bulb and narrow leaves.

Finally, he nibbled on a leaf. While slightly bitter, the taste was better than yucca. Next, he took a nip from the bulbous part. Nearly tasteless, it was crisp and swallowed easily.

He could have wolfed down the entire plant on the spot, but he knew that that much food that quickly, even poison-free food, could cause his guts to rebel, and he contented himself with a series of small and careful bites.

Leaving the remainder of the bulb by the flat, he retreated to the sleeping quarters and slashed a section off the unused pallet, carefully cutting it to keep one corner of the bottom double-thonged section intact as a bag. After bringing his makeshift bag across the nearly pitch dark room to the slightly lighter area behind the leather hide front window cover, he began to pull out the bulbous vegetables one at a time until he had a small heap.

He shook his head. While he would have liked more, he could carry only so many. If he stayed, he ran the risk that the shambletowners would find and kill him, as they had his parents.

He hoped what he could carry would be enough to get him through the weakness. If not, he would have to come back, and that he scarcely wanted to do.

Every concentrated scent in the shambletown, every odor from the Maze, was an assault, an assault that made it difficult for him to concentrate fully and increased the danger of being discovered.

After loading the bag, he gathered it and tied it shut with a piece of leather cut from the rear window cover. Then he used another loop to hang it around his neck and under his tunic. That left his hands free, although it created a bulging outline—a dead giveaway were he seen. There were no fat people on the high plains . . . anywhere.

A check of the back alley indicated no passers-by, and he eased himself out through the narrow window and onto the uneven stone pavement with only a slight scratching and muted thump. He replaced the window cover as well as he could.

Retracing his steps up the back lane, he came again to the single street he had crossed, and, again, he checked both ways, listening carefully, before he slid across into the darkness of the other side.

Whussshh!

Instants before the cudgel struck, he saw it and tried to drop away, away from the flat-faced man who hammered it toward his skull.

Hands grabbed for his thin arms.

Fire burned down the side of his face, but even as his knees buckled his own blade slashed at the four legs around him.

"Fynian! Hold devulkid! Hades! *Eiiiii!*"

The boy whipped the knife from leg level toward the man with the cudgel, his legs recovering and supporting his spring. Though off center, the jagged edge ripped a thin cut in the underside of Fynian's left arm as he brought the cudgel around for another attack.

The fingers grasping him loosened, and the boy broke clear, avoiding the deadly club, and scrambled behind both men, running, regardless of the noise and the growing pain in his left leg, full speed toward the wall.

"Devulkid! Devulkid!"

"Devulkid!"

Still clutching the blade, his bag thudding against his chest, he pounded across the open space before the eastern wall and leaped onto the clay barrel just ahead of the two pursuers and a wall guard. Without slowing, he scrambled up and over the rough bricks to slide to the bottom of the wall with a thump, his left leg buckling under the impact.

His breath hissed from the pain of the fall, but he lurched to his feet and half ran, half scrambled the distance to the Maze, where he began to climb. Halfway up toward the hole, his fingers slipped as an old brick snapped in two under his weight, and he skidded down, the rough-edged rubble abraiding his already injured left leg, which collapsed again as his feet hit the purple clay.

Fssst!

Another wall torch flared into flame. Then a third, and a fourth.

The devilkid ground his teeth against the pain from his leg and scrambled up the Maze toward his escape hole, forcing himself to make sure the handholds were firm before trusting his weight on them.

Crack!

A slingstone plowed into the rubble next to him, shattering a brick. The chips stung his uncovered right shoulder.

He forced himself upward toward the narrow hole that he knew the large shambletowners could not and would not fit into.

Crack!

Another slingstone shattered under his feet.

He could see the hole just above him, could scent the odors he recalled from his entry and squirmed the last body length to it.

Crunch!

"*Ooooo!*" The involuntary exclamation was forced from him, expelled by the force of the slingstone that had hit his side as he had twisted inside the dark passage.

"Got devulkid, Fynian!"

Now it hurt not only to use his left leg, but his left side was bruised.

He slid farther down the winding way and behind an ancient beam to catch his breath.

While an occasional slingstone rattled part way down the hole, he could tell from the outside sounds that the shambletowners were not about to chase him tonight, not with the still-freezing rain, and not into the higher Maze holes. Not this time.

He rested. But before long, he began to pick his way back out of the Maze. He had to be clear of the shambletown, well clear, before the lightness of dawn.

Fynian, the broad man, he would remember.

(* III

Screens. Screens and their images were what dominated the bridge. Every console on the *Torquina*'s bridge had at least three, and each was tied to an accompanying seat that doubled as an accel/decel couch, despite the fact that such usage had never been required.

The main screen displayed the image of a planet, a planet swathed mainly in clouds, except for occasional clear spots over the oceans. The *Torquina* swung in an almost geocentric orbit to allow the sensors and data relays from the exploratory torps maximum analytical time.

Some of the officers and techs watched. Some paid no attention. Some looked periodically.

The data flow centered on a single console with but four screens, in the innermost corner of the bridge. Had the captain wanted, he could have duplicated or monitored the flow. He did not so choose.

The Imperial Interstellar Survey Service officer facing the console continued to juggle the inputs, often manipulating two screens simultaneously.

"What does it look like?" asked the engineering officer who stood behind her.

"Worse than you can imagine. Worse than I'd believe. Some are still alive. Don't see how."

"How can you tell?"

"Patterns. Patterns. Look." She pointed to the top screen in front of her. "See the square here? That's built on top of the ruins. Then there's the background heat. Wouldn't be there if it were deserted."

She shook her head, and her short red hair fluffed out above the silver and black of her watch uniform.

"Background contamination is high."

"How high, Lieutenant Marso?" asked the captain from the command console across the bridge.

"Until we get the sampling data back, Captain, I can't

10

provide figures. There are areas of widespread erosion and a total lack of vegetation in places where by all rights there should be trees, or at least grasses, especially by some of the streams and rivers. First class ecological disaster, ser."

"We knew that," commented the engineering officer. "We knew that before we came."

Lieutenant Marso ignored the comment, not even turning her head in his direction.

"Any hopeful signs?" pursued the captain.

"Some. Some signs of habitation. Mainly in the high plains areas and places where there is drainage. Sedimentation areas look the deadest. I can't tell about the oceans, although they should have been affected last and should have been the first to recover."

"Place will never recover. Like Marduk," observed the chief engineer.

"It's not like Marduk. Nothing at all lives there. Here you can see some recovery."

"A few savages, a few thousand square kays where they can eke out a minimal survival. That's recovery?"

The ecologist bit her lip and shifted the image from screen three to screen four, bumped four into memory store, and took the latest torp data on screen three.

As the temperature data began to register, she frowned, then checked the parameters again.

"Trouble, Lieutenant Marso?"

"Not exactly, Captain. But it's cold, a great deal colder than the old records would indicate. The ice caps are larger, and the high plains temperature, where it should be mid-summer local, shows a high of less than ten degrees Celsius. Even taking into account unusual variations, that's more than twenty degrees below either the old records or our modified projections."

"Recovery!" snorted the chief engineer under his breath as he clumped from the bridge back to his own control center. "Recovery indeed."

Lieutenant Marso's fingers continued to flicker over the console controls as the data in her files built, as the ship's torps continued their transmissions, and as the purple landspouts traversed the continent beneath.

The captain waited, and the *Torquina* crept along her surveillance orbit.

(✱ IV

First, to the south of the small wilds and east of the Maze was the shambletown square, purple-gray clay hard-packed over the jagged rubble of the buried city. Around the square was the shambletown itself, a mass of old stone and clay brick structures threaded with winding ways. Last, around the shambletown were the walls of clay brick painted rough-smooth with sandpaint and backed with walkways for the handful of guards.

East of the shambletown was the Maze, that jumble of toppled buildings of the ancients that crowned the long ridge top, and to the west, below the space cleared by the shambletowners, rising from scattered grubushes, was a marble hulk, once domed, that had been a capitol.

As for the Maze . . .

The boy darted from it, from grubush to grubush beneath the northern edge of the smooth shambletown wall, until, at last, he could see the cracked and tumbled walls of the old structure.

He rested more weight on his left leg than his right, and when he walked, he limped. The limp was less pronounced when he ran. Even in the dark his blond hair glinted, as if with a light of its own, to match the hawkish brown-flecked yellow of his ever-searching eyes, eyes that also seemed to glow in the darkness.

"Hsssst . . ."

His eyes tracked the sound, his body turning. As he saw the plume of dust rising on the downslope to his right, he checked the wind direction, then relaxed.

The breeze was still blowing toward the mountains and would carry the chokeplume down into the clay-filled rubble that spread across the valley.

The area had been spared the worst of the landspouts and the concentration of landpoisons had kept the scavenging down,

12

but little enough was left of the old city, little enough that few would even have recognized the desolation for what it had been.

The blond boy let his eyes trace the faint outline of what others could not see at all in the night, from the jagged and sand-scoured peaks of the west to the flattened hills to the north and the rolling plains to the east. The ground fog was building in the depressions, gathering its own poisons as they sifted from the poisoned ground, and though the swirls caused by the joining of mountain and plains winds could not be seen, the boy could sense them, as he always had.

"*Fssst!*"

A new torch flared on the shambletown wall.

"Devulkid!"

"Where devulkid?"

The jumble of voices registered in his ears, echoing and rumbling off the rubble of the Maze, off the rough-smoothed walls of the shambletown. To both the north and the south, the Maze dwindled into low mounds, sometimes little more than humps of clay and sand and brick. From the larger mounds protruded here and there rusted or black metal beams twisted into shapes never designed by their makers.

The thin and golden-haired boy darted a look back over his shoulder, as a gate began to creak open.

The oily smell of torches wafted toward him, ahead of the pursuers who still gathered their courage, but who had waited for him to return.

Taking a last look over his shoulder at the puddle of light outside the shambletown wall, the hawk-eyed youth began to trot to the east toward the diffused and yet-to-appear glow in the sky that would be all that usually represented the sun.

His breath left a ghostly plume that faded into the darkness and into the beginnings of the ground fog.

The leader of the shambletown pack carried a long staff and lumbered to the edge of the downslope just above the point where the last vestiges of the chokeplume trailed away. He looked northward into the darkness and raised his head as if to scent out the interloper.

A second man joined him, carrying both cudgel and torch.

"See devulkid?"

"No. Think went wilds?"

"Too smarmy."

The two turned toward the east. To their right was the higher mass that rose into the Maze, and ahead were the rough hummocks through which their quarry had departed.

"Track out?"

"East, then south," offered a third man.

"South, back to desert," affirmed the man with the cudgel.

"More than desert. Ships."

"No ships! Never ships! Ships brought the death!" The first man laid his staff across the arm of the second. "Never!"

The leader shook his head at the unseen devilkid and pointed his staff back at the gate from which they had emerged.

"Back!"

The wind blew the steam of his breath, like a chokeplume, down the hillside toward the river of groundfog that wound its poisoned way toward the north along the thin trickle that had been a river.

Then he turned and began to retrace his steps toward the shambletown, the oasis of hoarded warmth and frugality that represented the only order left on the high plains.

The second man flexed his sore arm and lifted the cudgel, looking eastward into the darkness.

"Gram saw him. Me. Devulkid." He spat at the ground and made the hope sign in the air.

In turn, he dropped his head, turned, and plodded after the other two as they retreated behind the safety of their wall.

 V

Build with honest iron; build with stone; build with wood. If you cannot build with those, do not build.

For while what you have built may last, while it may tower into the night skies and mirror the sun by day, you cannot afford the cost.

And, in time, your children will grub for their lives in the wilderness, or pay their sustenance to the warlords, if they survive at all.

Jane-Ann D'Kerwin Nitiri
Philosophies of Rebuilding
Scotia, Old Earth, 4011 N.E.C.

(* VI

The boy loped across the after-dawn dimness south of the shambletown and north of the windridge toward the hill cave that served as home.

The hide bag he had taken some days earlier from the shambletowners bumped against his chest under the worn, frayed, and ripped tunic that once had been left unattended by a careless owner. Inside the bag, itself held in place by the pressure of the tunic and the loose thonging around his neck, were a handful of the reddish fruits that grew on one scattering of hills south and east of the shambles. The hills were far enough from the shambletown, nearly onto the rolling plains, to discourage casual foraging and open enough to keep the rats from exposing themselves to the coyotes.

The boy had been lucky. Although his battered blade was sharp and his reflexes quick, his leg was not fully healed. But he had not had to test them during the night's trip to the fruit trees.

He feared the foraging parties of the shambletowners far more than the coyotes. The four-footed beasts often traveled alone, almost never in packs, and preferred to avoid him unless they were close to starving.

The towners took whatever they could find from wherever they found it, but avoided foraging at night and generally stayed close to the foothills and the higher ground where the landpoison was less intense.

The boy's eyes never rested, flicking from one hummock to another, from one patch of grass to the next, from one grubush to the one behind, as his untiring and uneven steps covered the ground between him and his cave and the relative safety it offered.

His ears strained for the telltale rustle of a coyote returning to its den, or for the hiss/squeal of a rat, and his eyes periodically checked the clay for the even rarer trace of a firesnake.

16

WWWHHHeeeeeee!!!

The intensity of the whistling sound jolted him to a stop, and he covered his ears to block the pain. As the intensity dropped, he uncovered them and tried to localize the source. He sensed that it had started above the clouds and had crossed nearly overhead.

He dropped behind the nearest grubush and waited, waited until the whistle dropped to a whispering from the direction of the hills.

A brief glint of sunbright light flashed—again from the west—and was gone.

The silence was deeper than before as he trotted toward the hills and the light and the whispering sound that had died to nothing. The source of the noise and glare was on his way back, and anything that noisy should have frightened off anything likely to bother him.

Though not counting his steps, he had gone beyond what numbers he knew, far beyond, when he saw the silvery arc above the grubushes.

He slowed his trot and began to slip from bush to bush, from bush to hummock, and from hummock to bush as he angled toward the object that had dropped from the sky.

The smoldering grubushes, the charcoal smell mixing with the faint odor of grubush oil, both told him of the heat the object had created. His feet told him of the rumbling in the clay underfoot, and his ears could sense vibrations he could not hear.

As he neared the silvery object that towered higher than a shambletown wall, he slid behind a mound of clay that reeked of old brick and corroded metal. Beyond the mound, the bushes and other cover were too sparse for a safe approach, not to mention the steaming ground heat.

He waited, but the whining and the vibration did not stop.

Finally, the golden-haired boy peered over the mound again at the source of the sounds. After looking at the shining mass of metal, he blinked. Though the whining sound had not changed, a section of the metal wall had peeled back, and a ramp had been extended.

Thud.

He could feel the force with which the ramp settled onto the ground, and flattened himself as well as he could behind the mound, trying to keep himself above the ground fog while not letting the plume of his breath show in the increasing light of dawn.

He shivered, wondering what the metal machine on the desert plain meant. Was it one of the ships that the shambletowners always talked about?

Ships. He shrugged and snorted faintly, ignoring the white plume that trailed behind him. Always there were the ships that would come to save them. Even his parents had wondered. But no ship had come to save them from the shambletowners.

If the metal machine was a ship, or from the ships, would it spend the time to save anyone, devilkids or shambletowners?

The whining sound stopped, and the boy peered back over the top of the mound.

Rrrrrrrrrrr.

The sound echoed across the emptiness as a smaller object positioned itself on the top of the ramp and began to move down toward the ground, tracs clanking on the metal of the ramp.

No sooner was the armored tractor clear of the ramp than the whining began again as the ramp lifted and began to retract.

The tractor began to roll directly toward the mound which shielded the boy.

He scuttled sideways to another mound that barely covered him, but he could tell from the sound that the tractor had shifted direction and still headed toward him.

He looked left, then right, for another cover, making a quick dash to the left, scampering as low as he could, even breathing the ground fog that caught in his lungs like fire.

The roaring increased, louder, and he darted a glance from his hiding place.

Once more, the tractor had switched directions and was headed toward him, now less than a hundred body lengths away from him.

He ran, ran as fast as he could, with the practice of years and the spur of fear.

The pitch of the roaring increased, and the armored tractor increased its speed.

Could he make the gully he had passed earlier, the dry one where the poisons and fog were thinner?

He turned directly east and increased his stride.

In turn, the tractor's roar increased.

Although he refused to look back, concentrating on avoiding the grasp of the grubushes while staying ahead of the machine, he knew that the gap was narrowing, bit by bit.

His breath came raggedly, and the cold air he inhaled tore through his throat, burning like fire. His breath plumes trailed him like banners as he felt the ground begin the gradual rise before the drop-off that was the gully ahead.

Thrumm!

He felt a tingling sensation as something sleeted past his left shoulder, but refused to stop, forcing his legs to keep moving. He could see the drop-off just ahead.

Thrummm!

The strange energy barely cleared his head as he ducked just before the sound. Only a handful of steps remained to the gully.

Thrummm!

He tried to duck and twist, but the blackness rolled up around him, and he could feel himself falling even as it did.

⟨* VII

Corson paused outside the portal. As the chief engineering officer, he had the absolute right to enter any duty space on the ship, but he still hesitated. Marso had the kind of tongue that could strip flesh from bone.

He frowned, then squared his shoulders and keyed the portal with his own code, the one that overrode all but the captain's locks.

"Nooo!"

Corson saw the streak of blond, bent, and spread his arms. *Thud.*

Even at nearly two hundred centimeters and one hundred ten kilos, he was staggered by the impact and set back on his heels. But he refused to let go of the snarling figure that pounded at his midsection and sent kneecaps toward his stomach.

Corson shifted his grip into the patterns he had learned too many years before at the Academy and finally fumbled until he had immobilized the smaller figure.

It had to be the boy that Marso's tractor had stunned down on the surface.

He carried the still-squirming youngster back into the combination sick bay/laboratory.

Marso stood there, leaning on the console with her right hand. The scratches on her left cheek still glistened with the dampness of just-applied quick heal.

Corson did not miss the dark smudge beneath her left eye that would likely become a black eye.

His own eyes widened as he took in the snapped straps on the stretcher that had brought the youngster up from the surface with the shuttle.

"How did . . . ?"

"Damned if I know!" snapped the ecologist. "I came in to check him again, and he jumped me. Then you came blundering along and almost let him get away."

"I . . ." Corson closed his mouth and tightened his grip on the boy, who seemed stronger than most men he had ever dealt with.

"What do you want me to do with him? Your young man here?"

"He's not that far along yet. No sign of puberty, not overtly, and the initial readouts support that."

Marso replaced the quick heal back in the cabinet and reached for a pressure syringe.

"What's that for?"

"Put him under for linguistics. I'd like to be able to talk to him. Then maybe so much force wouldn't be necessary."

"Talk you now," muttered the boy. His accent was odd, but clear and understandable.

"How did he learn Panglais?"

"He didn't. Panglais is a derivative from simplified Anglish. The maps indicate his ancestors spoke Anglish."

"Why ship take me?" asked the boy, still twisting to see if he could escape.

"To see if we could help you."

"Help devulkid? Snort fog!"

Corson raised his eyebrows.

"What does he mean?"

Marso pushed a stray strand of hair back off her forehead. "I suspect it's a rather direct way of saying he doesn't believe us."

"Devulkid believe none."

"He thinks he's a devilkid. What does that mean?"

Marso frowned, but did not look directly at the chief engineer.

"There may be some veracity in that assumption, particularly if the metabolic analyses taken while he was unconscious are fully accurate."

Corson shook his head. Marso had never engaged in scientific doubletalk. Then he nearly smiled. She was trying to clue him without alerting the young savage.

"That much capability for physiological prowess?"

Marso nodded.

"What want devulkid?" interrupted the youth with another squirm that nearly broke Corson's grasp.

"Devilkid needs better talk," offered the engineer.

"Devulkid talk good."

Marso edged nearer the squirming figure, pressure syringe ready.

Corson turned slightly to his right to make Marso's effort easier, carrying the boy with him.

"*Ouggh*," he muttered with a wince as the devilkid's heels crashed into his leg.

Marso slapped the syringe against bare flesh.

The boy convulsed as if a current had passed through him, and it took all of Corson's strength to hold him.

"Hold him!"

Corson said nothing, but glared at the red-haired officer.

By the time the young savage had collapsed, Corson's arms ached, and his back felt stiff and sore.

"Where do you want him?"

"Back on the stretcher. I'll plug him in there, but that won't hold him for more than a standard hour or two."

"What?"

He'd seen the dosage she'd injected, and it would have laid him out for days.

"Corson. He may be a devilkid indeed. He's not too far from full growth, but the muscular and skeletal development indicates he'll be capable of taking you apart with one hand. If we're wrong, and he's less mature than I think, he could be a physical superman, but I don't think the readouts are that far off."

"What about brains?" the engineer asked drily.

"Hard to tell. Probably no genius, but bright enough. Be difficult to tell what cultural retardation has done to his innate capabilities, if anything."

Corson stretched the slight frame out on the pallet. Marso used three sets of straps before adjusting the headband and contacts.

"Whew! Could use a little freshening."

"No survival value," snapped the ecologist.

Corson looked over the boy's face. Even unconscious, he did not appear relaxed. A residual tension centered around the closed eyes, and there was a sharpness to the nose uncommon to a mere boy.

"Is that all he is? Just another specimen?"

"Given time, given some education, he might be human.

Right now, he's more like the proverbial wolf child, though I'd bet on him rather than on the wolves. I wonder if he really is a child."

Corson frowned and rubbed the middle of his forehead with the thumb side of his clinched fist.

"You just said he was."

Marso continued to work, sitting at the console and adjusting the feed to the headset.

"I said there was no sign of puberty and the associated developments. Those could be delayed because of environmental conditions, diet, who knows what. The other indications are that he may be older than twenty standard years. Brain scan patterns show more than a child's development."

Corson switched his attention from the lieutenant to the child/man/??? and realized that the unconscious figure's lips were moving.

Marso followed his gaze.

"That's a good sign. Shows verbalization ability is present. The sooner we're on the same wave length the better. Once he gets proper medical care and diet, I don't think brute force, other than sheer imprisonment, will keep him anywhere."

The chief engineering officer turned to leave.

"Let me know if you need help, brute force variety. I question whether your specimen believes in sweet reason, particularly on the wave lengths you have in mind."

"We'll see."

He could feel her eyes boring into his back as he thumbed open the portal and continued his inspection of *H.I.M.S. Torquina*, the newest of the Service's survey vessels, and dispatched for that reason alone to begin the preliminary survey of Old Earth, otherwise known as Terra, that would precede the clean-up pledged by the newly crowned Twelfth Emperor.

(* VIII

The first tests of the jumpshift were the drones. They returned unharmed.

The first full-scale test followed with a fusactor-powered in-system inertial driver. It did not return. Nor did the five ships that followed. The small drones continued to function superbly. Their jumpshift was powered with stored energy.

Finally, the UNSRF team theorized that the shift itself might have disoriented the fusactors. In response, they built a ship that was little more than an immense assembly of energy storage cells within a cargo shell. It jumped and returned, with scarcely an erg left.

The next step was another jumpshift, this time including a shut-down fusactor. The ship returned, but the magnetic storage bottle for the hydrogen starter had shrapneled the power room into shredded metal.

Interstellar travel had arrived, but no equipment that relied on the use of electrical or magnetic fields to generate power was able to survive the trip, and the jumpshift did not operate except in the corridors outside the main system gravitational fields.

No independent power generation equipment light enough to carry between the stars has ever been developed, nor was research pushed in that direction after the development of the Cardine molecular energy storage system . . .

Notes on the Jumpshift
Fragmentary text
Old Earth [Date unknown]

 IX

He turned in the straps, testing his strength against them. While the straps were more than adequate to hold him, he could tell from their give that he could squirm free in time.

The headset bothered him, but not so much as the headache it had created. So many words . . . and so many possibilities.

His eyes swam, and he waited, thinking.

". . . so you're awake . . ."

The woman stood on the other side of the room looking at him.

"Yeh."

"I'm Lieutenant Marso. I don't know your name. Would you like to tell me?"

"Tell what?"

"I see. Let's start more slowly, and less directly." She frowned and was silent for a moment.

He knew what she wanted, but the words had no reality, no more reality than a shambletowner running the high plains.

The woman began to point at objects, naming each in turn. With each name he found a link in his own mind, and some of the confusion began to sort itself out.

After she had pointed to everything within the compartment, she went to the dispenser and poured herself a drink of water.

He could scent the moisture.

"Would you like some?"

"No. *Yuggg!*"

"This is not like the water on . . . where you live." She drank it. "Try some."

She let him smell the glass and dribbled some on his lips. He licked them. The water was nearly tasteless, except for a faint bitter odor and the hint of metal, both far fainter than the landpoisoned water of the plains.

He liked the smell of her better. Clean. Warm, like the

flowers of the yucca. Not like the grease of the shamble-towners.

"Would you like some?"

"Yeh."

"Yes," she corrected.

"Yes," he mimicked, because she wanted him to, and because there was no reason not to.

She set the cup on the high table beside the bed where he was strapped. After that, she pulled a metal object from a sheath attached to her wide belt.

Thrummm!

He winced at the sound, but watched as the fire from the object struck the floor.

"I am going to let you sit up. If you move toward me, I will use this. Understand?"

"Stand."

He thought he knew what she meant. She was afraid of him, but the blackness thrower would keep him away. He shivered. Still . . . she was a woman. Perhaps . . . later.

Holding the thrower in one hand, she did something underneath the bed with her other, stepping back quickly afterward.

He could feel the straps loosening and began to sit up slowly. Taking the cup in both hands, he sniffed the water again. His nose confirmed that it was safe to drink.

He sipped and waited. After a time he sipped again. The water was clean. Finally, he drained the cup and set it down.

"Are you hungry?"

He looked at her blankly.

"Do you want to eat?"

"Yes."

She tapped her fingers on the surface beside her, not taking her eyes off him, one hand still holding the weapon.

"Lieutenant Marso here. Need some finger food for our guest. I'd keep it bland and as natural as possible."

"Natural?"

His eyes widened at the voice from nowhere, but he said nothing.

"He has a well-developed sense of taste and smell."

"Do what we can, Lieutenant."

"All I can ask. Thank you."

The boy watched. She acted like the headman of the shambletowners. She talked to nothing, and someone answered. He must wait, but he was good at waiting, and listening.

✶ X

MacGregor Corson frowned.

Should he follow through with his impulse? He looked down at the impromptu motor chair he had built. What if he were wrong in his assessment?

He shrugged. Then there would be no problem.

The ecologist had left the devilkid's quarters inside the sick bay, sealed the locks, and headed for the mess.

If she only understood what she would not . . .

He shrugged again and let his long and heavy strides carry him down the passageway to the sealed cabin. Marso was jealous of her prize, and had set the seals herself. But they had been the engineer's first.

No one else had been in the exterior corridor, nor in the sick bay itself, not surprisingly, since the orbiting ship was in stand-down condition while the techs and their monitors gathered the necessary data.

As he reached the sealed portal he pulled the small kit from his belt pouch and touched the analyzer tips to each side of the plate. The first series of pulses was strictly random. The second built on the reactions to the first.

Marso had thought out the combination well, but he still solved the pattern in six sequences. The portal stood ready to be opened, once he touched the access panel.

The analyzer went back into his belt pouch, and he replaced it with a nerve tangler. The weapon ready, he touched the plate, tightened his finger on the firing stud.

His guess had been correct.

As the portal irised he could see the streak of blond, and he triggered the tangler.

The slim form thudded to the decking halfway through the portal. The boy's legs were twitching uncontrollably from the nerve jolt, and his brown-flecked, hawk-yellow eyes threw anger at the big engineer.

Corson did not touch the devilkid, but used his free hand to drop a loop of cord around one ankle. Then, tangler ready, he dragged the boy back into the cabin, sealing the portal behind them.

He leaned against the portal, waiting until the youngster dragged himself into a sitting position.

"All right, devilkid. Let's get a few things straight." He eyed the black bulk of the hand-held tangler. "This is a nerve tangler. If I use it enough, your heart will stop. You die. You understand?"

"Stand. I stop." The tone confirmed the young savage's understanding.

"That's right. Now . . . do you want to go back to where we found you? Or better yet, back to the shambletown? Isn't that what you called it?"

"Not shambletown."

Corson studied the boy, realized that in the few weeks aboard the *Torquina* he had changed, more than having gone from a dirty savage to a clean one, or from a scarcely verbal scrabbler for survival to a youngster who could understand most of what the crew said.

Corson nodded to himself. He suspected Marso had been right about diet, and that the ship's food was speeding up, or allowing the return of, physical maturation.

Subtle things, like the look the boy gave Marso when she wasn't paying attention, a bit more heaviness to the jawline, more muscular development across the chest, all were signs of physiological change.

But the devilkid was still a savage, still a danger, mostly because he did not understand the basics of what *any* society was. And Corson was going to have to teach him before it got any later, Marso be damned.

"The shambletown. That's where you'll go if you don't learn." He glared at the youngster. "First . . . keep your hands off Lieutenant Marso."

"Hands off?"

"Devilkid!" snapped the engineer. "You may be the toughest, meanest, strongest animal in the universe, but you hurt *anyone*—anyone!—and I'll tie you in knots with this and leave you in shambletown. You understand?"

There was no response. Corson saw the boy's legs were no

longer twitching, and that he was drawing them underneath himself slowly.

Corson fired—twice.

"*Ayiii!*"

The devilkid lost his balance and tumbled onto his side. Slowly, slowly, he righted himself. Outside of the one exclamation, he had uttered no cry.

Corson's palms were perspiring. The shocks he had directed at the youth would have left even an Imperial Marine totally incapacitated for at least a standard hour. All that they had done to the savage was paralyze his legs, which was where the engineer had aimed. The peripheral effects normally left most people stunned or incoherent, not to mention the pain that went with the withdrawal.

"Get this straight, little man," he growled. "You can hurt me. You can hurt the lieutenant. So what? There are one hundred men and women on this ship. One hundred. There are more than one thousand ships where we came from." He lifted the weapon. "And this is a small tangler. That means you don't hurt people."

"Don't hurt people," repeated the youth.

Corson wondered whether he really understood, but decided to go on with his plan. He snapped the tangler in half, separating the butt that contained the power cells from the half that contained the barrel, neural focusing and trigger. Both halves went back into his belt pouch, since he was bending the regulations to even carry such a weapon within the ship.

Then he palmed the exit stud and reached down, hesitating only momentarily, and lifted the youth.

Corson could feel the devilkid stiffen, but offer no other resistance as Corson carried him through the portal and lowered him into the improvised motor chair.

"Now, we're going to see the ship. All of it. Along the way, I'm going to try to make you understand why you have to behave, why you can't attack people. Force is important, boy. But brute force and strength won't beat a nerve tangler. And it won't beat a ship. It won't beat a thousand ships."

As they came to the main portal from the sick bay, the engineer tapped the access panel and guided the chair through. He wondered if he should have strapped the devilkid in.

"Corson! What are you doing?"

He sighed and turned toward the sharp voice. If only Marso had taken her time at the Mess.

"I'm giving him a guided tour of the ship. If you would like to come, you're welcome, provided you don't interrupt—"

"But he's not—"

"Marso . . ." The engineer's normally gruff voice deepened into a tone that would have frozen even the captain.

The lieutenant stiffened.

"We'll be back within two standard hours."

"How did you get him to agree?"

"It took some considerable doing. But I think he understands."

"Devilkid understands," the blond youth affirmed.

"Understands what?" clipped the ecologist.

"Devilkid one. Ships many."

Corson felt his own jaw drop open. He hadn't expected understanding so quickly, and he doubted the boy was sophisticated enough to offer a deliberate lie about an abstract proposition.

"That's right, Mr. Engineer. He's bright. Very bright."

"Then he should enjoy the tour, Lieutenant Ecologist."

"He might at that." The red-headed lieutenant stepped aside as Corson keyed the chair.

Corson watched his charge's eyes follow the ecologist and felt his heart sink.

He was doing his best, but if Marso encouraged the boy (who wasn't likely to stay one much longer), what could he do? He shrugged, though he didn't feel like it.

"Let's start with the bridge, young man."

He could feel her eyes on his back as the two of them headed up the passageway, the whine of the chair scarcely audible above the gentle hiss of the ventilation system.

⟨* XI

"Why start so high? So far inland?"

"Because it won't do any good to start any lower."

"Run that by me again."

"The chemical contamination is so high that you have to clean the land and the watersheds from the headwaters down. Otherwise—"

"—the rivers and the winds just recontaminate what you've cleaned."

"The rivers. We can't control the winds. Not until we can restore ground cover, get some trees in the high watersheds."

"You're talking centuries."

"Probably longer. We don't have accurate maps of the topography, nor any detailed analyses of the compounds poisoning the land. And Istvenn knows what they did to the ground water."

"What about the oceans?"

"A quick scan indicates they've got some buffering ability, but there's too much in the way of sulfur compounds. Balanced flora/fauna population, but too thin for my liking. But they'll recover long before we can reclaim the land. We'll have to set up a handful of extraction plants for the worst toxic hot spots on the continental shelves. Projections indicate that would do it in the worst cases."

"What about the future?"

"Hard to say, but I'd recommend against any disruption of the soil. Has to be an agricultural economy, if we even get that far, for dozens of centuries."

"You make it sound so cut and dried."

"Hardly. The theory's easy enough. So are the techniques—in theory. But in practice? No. That won't be easy. You can't manufacture anything in this system, and that means a massive resource drain for the Empire. This Emperor may allow it, but this project will need work for the lives of more than a few emperors. Just can't be done in less than centuries and billions of creds worth of equipment . . . Maybe it can't be done at all."

(* XII

"You need a name."

"Have name. Devulkid."

The lieutenant shook her head, short red hair fluffing out with the motion. "That would not be acceptable and could certainly cause problems."

"Problems?"

"Difficulties, hard places."

The blond-haired young man wearing the unmarked tan shipsuit wrinkled his nose, as if at the smell of landpoisons.

"Hard places with name?"

The lieutenant smiled faintly. "It does sound strange when you put it that way. But you need a name, at least two names."

"Two names? One person?"

"Call it the Empire's way of doing things. Like the ships, like the uniforms."

"Two names for one person?" repeated the devilkid.

"Some people have three names," admitted the lieutenant.

"Three names?"

Lieutenant Marso nodded.

"How many names for you?"

"Three. Jillian . . . K'risti . . . Marso."

"The big man has three names?"

"Major Corson? Two, I think. MacGregor Corson."

"Why two names?" asked the blond youth again, as if the lieutenant had yet to answer the question.

"Look. If you want to go to the transitional school, if you want a chance at going to the Academy, you have to have two names. Any two names. You can have three if you want, but you have to have two."

"School needs two names for devilkid?"

"That's right. Both the transitional school and the Academy, if you make it that far, require two names. Two names and a number."

"Number?"

"Don't worry about that. Once you decide on the names, we'll use them to get you your imperial I.D. number. That won't be a problem at all."

The devilkid frowned as he sat uneasily in the ship swivel across from the lieutenant.

"Devilkid choose names. Empire choose number?"

"Right."

The curly-haired blond pursed his lips, but said nothing.

"Did your parents ever give you a name?"

"No name." His tone was more abrupt than before.

"I could read you some names and see if you like them."

"No."

"All right. But you'll have to choose something."

"Gerswin? Means what?"

"I called you that when you whistled that strange little melody. A gerswin is a music-maker, a wild singer, sort of like a dylanist, but the power is mostly in the music and not in the words."

The devilkid looked back at the Imperial lieutenant blankly.

"Gerswin means music, like your whistling," she repeated.

"MacGregor? That means?"

"Once it meant 'son of Gregor.' Now it has no special meaning."

"Corson means?"

"Son of Cor," the lieutenant answered uneasily.

"The big man, the major? Two fathers?"

Lieutenant Marso laughed. "Some would say he had none. But, no. He has just one father. Sometimes, names are chosen because people like them. They like the way the names sound." She frowned momentarily. "You have several days before you have to choose. Now that you've passed the initial screening tests, the transitional school will give you other tests, tests with more words."

"*More* words?"

"More words," affirmed the woman. "That is, if you want to learn more. If you don't want to go back to the shamble-town."

A shadow crossed the young face.

"Learn . . . means not to go back to shambles?"

"Learning means much more than that. The more you learn, the more you can do. If you can make it through the transitional school, then you could go to the Academy—"

"Academy means learn more?"

"If you can."

"Devulkid learn. Learn everything."

 **XIII**

In "Warfare, Basic Theories of [4/C, BC W-101]," Gerswin's console was in the third row, second one from the far right aisle.

The instruction hall itself was similar to all the others, with identical consoles with the identical gaps into which unidentical cadets placed their identical bridge modules, incidentally recording their presence while allowing them direct access to their individual data banks.

The thirty fourth-classers stood beside their consoles, waiting at standing rest for Gere Yypres Gonnell, Major, Retired [Disability], I.S.S., who was listed as their professor.

"Ten'stet!" rang the tenor voice of the section adjutant.

Gerswin stiffened with all the others, exactly in key with their motions, although he could have easily beaten them into position.

"At ease," squeaked an amplified voice.

Gerswin watched the instructor's podium and the figure who moved behind it with jerky steps.

"Please be seated, Cadets," the squeaky and raspy voice added.

Gerswin sat, but wondered. He could see the shimmering metal bands around the professor, could see that while the professor's throat moved, his mouth barely opened.

"For those of you who have not met me, and that may well be all of you, I am indeed Major Gonnell, otherwise referred to as 'old-gonna-hell,' 'old metal bones,' or other endearments less flattering. This is the class technically referred to as 'Warfare, Basic Theories of.'"

A raspy sound like tearing patch tape followed.

"Excuse me, but subvocalization is not perfect."

A clanking sound followed.

"All of you are supposed to have read chapter one of the text. Knowing the Academy and the idealism with which you all approach your studies, you all have."

An intake of breath that would have been laughter at any non-military institution punctuated the otherwise silent instruction hall.

"The title of the course is incorrect. A more accurate description might be 'A Few Guesses as to Why Societies Fight.'"

Gerswin tabbed in the new title, noting that few others did.

"A standard hour a day for four months is totally inadequate for those of you who survive the institution to practice the profession, but I hope to make a small dent in your ignorance and to let you know how little you really know, in the hopes that you will at some future time be inspired to actually learn the subject."

The metal figure swiveled as if to survey the hall.

"Cadet Culvra, what does Adtaker mean when . . ."

"Cadet Hytewer, describe the Empire in the terms outlined by Hyrn . . ."

Gerswin noted most of the questions, but few of the answers. From the pace of the inquiries from the professor, he began to understand why the major had gotten the reputation he had.

"Cadet Resia, you have just asserted that wars are caused by scarcities. If that were true, would not all warring between systems be non-existent?"

Cadet Resia did not answer, but kept his square face directly pointed toward the major.

"Come now. We have had wars between systems. I have some personal experience which I doubt is a fiction." At that, he raised a metal-bound arm. "Yet the costs of building jumpships, the energy costs of jumping with stored power, the relative abundance of raw materials in all but the most crowded systems—all these would indicate that scarcity could not be a motive for war except in a limited number of systems, say perhaps a dozen. Those systems, however, lack the knowledge and resources to build a jumpship space force."

"That doesn't prevent others from occupying them," observed a red-haired young woman in the first row.

"While I was prodding Cadet Resia, I will accept that observation, Cadet Karsten. If your interjection is true, then scarcity and weakness prompt others to war over the least desirable systems. Is not that the logical outcome of your observation?"

Gerswin frowned. If what the discussion was leading to actually followed, then war could only be fought for non-economic reasons.

"Would anyone else care to comment?" asked the major.

Gerswin looked down, finally pressing the red stud.

"You have a comment, Cadet Gerswin?"

"A question, ser. If wars aren't fought for material gain, does that mean that there are other logical reasons for war? Or material ones?" he added.

"The original question assumed there was a distinction, if you please, between wars within systems, and wars between systems. Are you questioning that distinction?"

"Yes, ser . . . I mean . . . no, ser . . . I mean . . ." Gerswin closed his mouth.

"Would you like to clarify what you mean, Cadet Gerswin?"

"Yes, ser."

"Please do so."

"Ser, I wasn't going to question the distinction. Not sure now. Text indicates costs of war almost always outweigh the gains. Doesn't say that, but the numbers seem to—"

"What numbers, Cadet Gerswin?"

Gerswin repressed a sigh. "Looked up military budget differentials, reconstruction costs, death benefits . . ."

"I'll accept that for purposes of discussion. Are you saying that the costs to even the victor outweigh the quantifiable benefits?"

"Yes, ser."

"Aha. Cadet Gerswin is suggesting that since the costs of war outweigh the benefits, no wars have a logical basis. A novel approach. Any takers?" Major Gonnell surveyed the hall again, his metal support skeleton swiveling him from side to side. "Any dissenters?"

Another sweep of the room followed.

"I see. Cadet Gerswin's suggestion is so novel none of you have considered it. Very well, your first submission, due in five days, is: 'Wars Have No Logical Basis.'

"The submission must be a proof, although documented anecdotal material may be used, and you must take a definite position. Any submission which fails to support *or* refute the illogicality of war will be failed."

The major surveyed the class once again before concluding in his rasping squeak, "Section dismissed."

"Ten'stet!"

The cadets snapped out of their seats to attention as the major departed.

(*   XIV

"All hands! All hands! Stand by for jump! Stand by for jump!"

Gerswin laid back in his couch, made sure the webbing across his chest was tight, although there was scarcely any chance that it would be needed. As a second class cadet, he had no permanent duty assignment. Consequently, he had no station from which to watch the jump.

Only Tammilan had managed that, and only because the *Fordin*'s number three navigator billet was unfilled. The missing officer had stepped in front of a lift loading a cargo shuttle less than an hour before orbit break. While the emergency releases had stopped the lift in time, not all of the weapon spares had been securely fastened, and the junior navigator was now recovering from multiple fractures in the I.S.S. medical facilities at Standora Base.

Gerswin waited for the blackness that filled the ship during the jump itself, that and the accompanying distortion. Supposedly, the jumps were instantaneous, but the longer the jump, the longer the subjective feeling of blackness and disorientation.

While Gerswin had been on a jumpship before the *Fordin*, this tour was his first trip since learning enough to understand what a jump really was. The upcoming jump was only the third since the cadets had boarded the *Fordin* off Alphane, using the Academy's shuttles to reach the cruiser.

The battlecruiser was headed for quarantine duty in the New Smyrna system, along with two other cruisers and two corvettes.

"Jump!"

BRrrinnngggg!!!!

The jump alarm seemed to stretch out through the darkness like an organ reverberating in slowtime.

With his third jump, Gerswin could see that the blackness

was not uniform, but a swirl of differing blacks, as if each had a different shape and depth.

Just as suddenly as the darkness had dropped over the colored plasteel corridors of the cruiser it was gone.

Gerswin unstrapped, checked his uniform, and scurried out of the closet-like room he shared with Tammilan. Since he was now assigned to the Gunnery department that was where he headed, down the corridor to the spool and in two layers to the central spoke.

No sooner had he entered the Gunnery operations center, with its spark screens and representation plots, than a voice boomed out.

"Cadet Gerswin!"

"Yes, ser."

"What is the maximum effective range of a Mark II?"

Gerswin braced himself. Lieutenant G'Maine, the junior of the three Gunnery officers, always tried the question on unwary cadets, or so Tammilan had told him.

"There is no effective range for a Mark II, ser, since there is no Mark II, ser."

"A smart cadet. Tell me, Mr. Gerswin, the difference between the calibration technology used in the tachead rangers and the EDI detectors."

Gerswin wished the lieutenant would quit booming out questions, but he remained at attention beside the detector console.

"Tacheads have no rangers; calibration is independent and based on mass detection proximity indications. EDI tracks are actually a flow ratio compared against background energy flows."

"A really smart cadet! Can you tell me, Mr. Gerswin, the power flow managed by this center at full utilization?"

"No, ser."

"Why not?"

"Because I don't know, ser."

"And why don't you know—"

"Lieutenant, would you spare the cadet for a moment? I have some rather menial and less intellectually demanding tasks for him."

Gerswin was glad someone had rescued him, though he did not recognize the voice. From the corner of his eye he caught a glimpse of the uniform, which seemed to be that of a major. If so, it had to be Major Trillo, the chief Gunner of the *Fordin*.

"Certainly, Major."

Gerswin waited.

"On your way, Mr. Cadet Gerswin."

"Yes, ser."

"And, Lieutenant," added the Major, "I also need a word with you after Cadet Gerswin is dispatched."

The lieutenant nodded, his blocky face bobbing up and down.

"Mr. Gerswin, don't stand there like a statue. We've all got things to do. Get on over here."

"Here" meant to the main console, which was a quarter of a deck high and at one end of the narrow room overlooking the banks of screens.

Gerswin stepped up.

Major Trillo was short, only to Gerswin's shoulder level, square, with shoulders broader than his, deep violet eyes, and short, black curly hair. Her voice was velvet over frozen iron.

One tech stood near her control seat, and the major looked, merely looked, and the tech retreated to the main operating screen level.

Gerswin was impressed. He felt more secure with the Lieutenant G'Maine's of the I.S.S.

"Gerswin, I can't blame you, but it's not smart to make your senior officers look stupid, even when they behave like robomules. You must have known what G'Maine would do. You had the answers down pat. If you'd played a little dumber, G'Maine could have crowed and been delighted to teach you all he knows, which isn't that much.

"Now, I'll have to make him responsible for teaching you more than he knows or he'll make everyone's life miserable. So . . . if you don't learn everything he has to teach you and more, it will go in your record under lack of adaptability. But I don't expect that."

Unexpectedly, the major sighed. "Maybe it's better this way. I have an excuse to force him to learn more. But it takes more of my time, and I have little enough of that anyway. So put it all down to experience, and don't do it again. Do you understand?"

"Yes, ser." Gerswin nodded.

"Understand, Cadet Gerswin, I am not opposed to your knowing more than your superiors, nor to learning anything and everything you can. I am opposed to junior officers flaunting such knowledge when it is totally unnecessary. Do you understand that?"

"Yes, ser."

"Further, young man, if you breathe a word of this conversation to anyone, I will insure that you spend the rest of this cruise on maintenance detail and that there is a half-black on your cruise file."

Gerswin swallowed, swallowed hard. A half-black amounted almost to a bust-out. A half-black with a year to go at the Academy—only two had ever graduated with a half-black, only two in the last century, according to the rumors.

"Yes, ser."

Major Trillo smiled, and the smile was friendly.

"If you understand, you've learned more from this encounter than some officers learn in an entire career."

Her voice hardened slightly. "For the past week, the ES section has been promising to reclaim the contents of the repair and recycle locker and take back the material. Would you please gather it all together—all the junk in bin ER-7 over there—and take it down to the E-section senior tech, Erasmus.

"On the way back, stop by the Mess and bring back two cafes, one liftea, and whatever you would like."

"Yes, ser."

"And don't mind Erasmus. He'll grouse."

The major switched her attention from the cadet to the screen, effectively dismissing him.

Gerswin found a snapbag two bins away from the one labeled ER-7 and carefully placed in it all the mysterious pieces of the transequips and solicube segments.

He wondered if the major saw through his carefully cultivated facade, if she read the contempt he tried to avoid displaying when he ran across Service types who fancied themselves great warriors. Most wouldn't have lasted a night on the high plains.

His lips quirked as he thought about the major. He had no doubts that she would have survived anywhere.

At the Academy he had avoided cadet rank, had tried to blend into the middle of the class. He had been successful, except in the physical development classes. Even there, he'd minimized his strength by concentrating on skill-oriented combat forms, or on learning and mastering the range of energy weapons.

His reflexes made him number one in unarmed combat. He could usually beat the instructors, when he tried, but he made certain that he never won all the time. Instead he worked on learning new techniques until perfected, at which point he began to learn a new repertoire.

He shook his head and concentrated fully on placing each component within a separate insulated section of the carrying case.

Finding E section was harder than he had anticipated, since it wasn't listed except by spoke and frame number. He had to retrace his steps twice before he knocked and stepped inside.

Grouse wasn't exactly the word Gerswin would have used to express the tech's outburst.

"That malingering she-cat knows I have no use for this despicable pile of misbegotten droppings from the devil's offspring! And she sends an innocent to the slaughter, knowing full well how I feel!"

Gerswin's eyes nearly popped out of his head.

Never had he heard anyone discuss a major in the I.S.S. that way in public, let alone a technician who hadn't even a commission. Even if Erasmus was a senior tech—and Gerswin couldn't tell that because the man's white tech suit, contrary to regulations, had no insignia, not even his name—Erasmus should not have discussed a senior officer so candidly.

Gerswin said nothing, certain he had failed to understand something.

Finally, he spoke. "Will that be all, Senior Technician Erasmus?"

"Will that be all, Senior Technician? Will that be all, Senior Cadet? Is it not enough to have been given sewer sweepings, the remnants of proud equipment, without as much as a by-your-leave? Do they think that good equipment springs full-blown from the heads of gods? Will that be all indeed?"

Gerswin tried to hide the beginnings of a smile.

"And you, would-be officer, smirk upon what you see as the rantings and ravings of a demented technician. Do you also smirk at the equipment upon which your very life rests? Do you?"

The cadet had to take a step backward to avoid the long probe the technician waved in his face.

"Do you?"

"No. Not at all."

Erasmus looked at the carrying case in Gerswin's arms.

"Ah, well. Bring it in. We'll do what we must." The technician shook his head sadly. "But the sheer effrontery, the sheer underhandedness! At least she did not send that bonehead, the one with the skull so thick and so empty that not even a laser would have any effect."

Gerswin repressed another smile. To hear Lieutenant G'Maine so described by someone else was a pleasure.

"And you, Mr. Cadet Gerswin by your name plate, what do you think?"

Theoretically, second class cadets outranked even senior technicians, but in practice, Gerswin had known from his devilkid days, things didn't always conform to theory.

So while Gerswin theoretically did not have to respond to Erasmus's questions, he swallowed his smile and did.

"I don't know enough to make an intelligent answer."

"Wish more had the nerve to admit what they didn't know. But you did not answer my first question. Your life rests on technology, on equipment like that." His probe jabbed down at the bag Gerswin had carried in. "Put it on the work bench next to the console."

As Gerswin did, the technician's questions continued.

"That equipment carries your life, and yet you do not understand it, except how to use it? Is that not so?"

"Right now, you're right. I don't."

"Will you ever? Don't answer that. You might answer honestly and disappoint me. Or you might answer honestly and fail to live up to what your answer promises. Or you might lie. Not much chance that you'll ever really understand technology. Not if you become the standard I.S.S. officer."

Erasmus sighed. "That's why you have technicians. To keep you running. Don't forget it, Mr. Gerswin. Don't forget it."

"You make a strong case, Senior Technician."

"Damned right, Cadet. They put up with my 'peculiarities' because I can repair anything in this Emperor's Navy. But I'm right anyway. And don't you forget it."

Gerswin didn't know what else to say. If he used the formal 'will that be all?' Erasmus would think he had been merely half listening.

"Would you like me to convey anything else to Major Trillo, generally?"

"Ha! HA! HAAA!" Erasmus laughed, then stopped. "You're cautious, Cadet. But you're learning. She wouldn't take official notice, and no sense putting you on the spot. Besides, we understand each other, she and I do."

Even the chuckling stopped.

"That will be all, Cadet. Keep listening. It's worth all the cubes and lectures at the Academy."

Despite the feeling that he had suffered a mental bombardment, Gerswin found his feet leading him back to the wardroom, where he picked up two cafes and two lifteas, not that he particularly liked liftea, but the tea was far better than the oily taste of the cafe, which reminded him all too strongly of landpoison.

Once back inside the weapons center, he saw Lieutenant G'Maine standing between him and the main console, which seemed vacant except for a single tech.

Gerswin walked straight to G'Maine.

"Lieutenant, did you want cafe or liftea? The major asked me to bring some on my way back, but I don't know which you prefer, ser."

"Appreciate it, Cadet. I prefer cafe. So does Lieutenant Swabo, but the major likes liftea."

G'Maine took a cafe and turned away without another word.

Gerswin searched for the major, located her in the far corner, the missile center, with Lieutenant Swabo.

Once he made his way there he stood, holding the tray, waiting to be noticed, as the two women conferred about something with gestures toward the small plot in the center of Swabo's console.

Without looking up, the major said, "Cafe for the Lieutenant, liftea for me."

Gerswin placed the beverages in the holders on the consoles and retreated to a corner folddown where he sipped his own liftea.

$\overbrace{}^{\ }$ * XV

Ding! Ding! Ding!

With the sound of the third bell the captain's face appeared on all the screens on the *Fordin*, and her voice echoed through all the passageway speakers.

Gerswin looked over Lieutenant G'Maine's shoulder to get a view of the skipper. He had met Captain Montora once, when he had been formally introduced by the executive officer after he had reported from the Academy.

She looked as crisp now as she had then, short and bobbed blond hair in perfect place, ice green eyes steady into the screen, square jawed, smooth olive skin. A closer study might have showed the hints of age—the slight shadow and fine lines around the eyes, the sharpened nose, the lines in the otherwise smooth forehead.

"This is the captain. Shortly, we will be changing course and jumping for Newparra. This will be a two-jump trip. Once in-system, we will become the nucleus of the quarantine battle group.

"While a full backgrounder will be available through the ship's infonet, for those of you who have not participated in a quarantine action before, our job is to isolate the system from any outside contact and to keep any system ships from departing until a new government can be recognized by the Emperor.

"We will be joined initially in this action by the *Krushnei*, the *Saladin*, and the *Kemal*. Before system entry, you will be ordered to alert status.

"That is all."

As the screen blanked, Gerswin looked up to the raised deck and to Major Trillo, the Gunnery officer.

"Ten'stet!" The major's voice cut off the rising murmurs of speculation.

47

"All Gunnery officers and cadets, report to the main console here immediately."

Gerswin tagged along behind Lieutenants G'Maine and Swabo as the three of them trooped between the consoles toward the major.

"Relax." The major gestured vaguely in a circular motion. "I don't believe any of you except Lieutenant Swabo have participated in a quarantine action. When we're done here, you all, and especially you, Cadet Gerswin, need to call up that backgrounder and to review the Imperial articles of quarantine. Study them, if you need to. If what I recall of Newparra is still current, this could be one of the nastier quarantines you will ever see.

"Now . . . We're not organized for full round the clock operations, but you've all seen the combat roster. For the first few days, however, I intend to double the officer count. There will be two officers on duty at all times. For these purposes, Cadet Gerswin will be included on the duty roster as junior gunnery officer. To balance his inexperience, he will be paired initially with me. Chief Technician Alvera and Sub-Chief Gorta will head the duty techs.

"Senior Lieutenant Swabo will act as Gunnery officer in my absence."

The major waited for the duty pairings to sink in.

Lieutenant G'Maine frowned momentarily, with a puzzled expression following almost immediately.

"You expect some action, ser. When Newparra has been part of the Empire for so long?"

"This is the third quarantine of Newparra, Lieutenant. That may well be a record. The government has been a compromise between radical Christers and Istvennists. By definition, a quarantine is called when no one government controls the entire system. Unfortunately, while the overall level of technology is moderate, the government has maintained nearly twenty jumpships of all classes."

Gerswin kept himself from nodding. While the jumpships were not supposed to be armed, a revolutionary or embattled status government could certainly do so.

"The Empire has always taken a strong stand against revolutionaries being able to export their ideals or wars or to import weapons and other support. That's why we have quarantines. But none of this should be news to any of you. Read the backgrounder. Then I'll answer questions.''

Ding!

The screen chime punctuated the major's last sentence.

"All hands! All hands! Ten minutes until jump. Ten minutes until jump."

The major nodded, then concluded, "The first duty tour will be Lieutenant Swabo and Lieutenant G'Maine. If this lasts as long as it probably will, in time we'll go to the one in three roster, with Cadet Gerswin as back-up."

Gerswin understood, he thought. Until the major had the chance to settle G'Maine and him down, she and Swabo would be keeping a close watch to insure neither went off half-blasted. But the major also knew that a four on, four off routine was too fatiguing to be effective beyond a few days.

"Dismissed."

Gerswin hurried back to the closet that doubled as his cabin to ready for the jump.

Tammilan was not there, probably relishing taking the jump at the duty station of the absent third navigator.

As Gerswin strapped in, the screen chime rang again.

Ding!

"All hands! All hands! Stand by for jump. Stand by for jump."

The blackness and dislocation seemed longer this time, but his experience was so limited Gerswin had no idea whether the subjective feeling meant anything at all.

The second jump was less than ten minutes after the first, and, if anything, seemed to last longer than the earlier jump.

Gerswin wondered if every jump seemed to take longer than the previous one, despite the indoctrination materials which had indicated that the objective and subjective time of jump was constant. Not for him, they didn't seem constant.

After the second jump toward Newparra, he unstrapped and sat up. There was no reason he couldn't go back to the Gunnery operations center, although he didn't see why he needed to, either. He wasn't hungry, and he'd already missed more sleep than he'd intended on this cruise. All he could do as the *Fordin* headed in-system was to get in the way.

Yawning, he stood up and undressed, leaving his uniform laid out. Then he climbed back into the bunk, and, as a precaution, loosely adjusted the restraining webs.

For a time he stared at the flat underside of Tammilan's bunk before drifting into sleep.

Tammilan tiptoed in several minutes later, as he was about to drift off. She did not stay, but merely picked up a clean uniform and left. Gerswin did not look over at her, but wondered why she was so secretive about her actions. The entire ship knew she spent more time with the number two navigator than in her own quarters, but who cared? That was her business, and if she hadn't been a cadet, the official cabin arrangements merely would have been changed.

He thought he woke twice with the lurching of a sudden course shift as the grav-field generators compensated for the stress, but with no announcements following in either case, he went back to sleep.

After waking in the still-empty cabin, running himself through the tiny fresher, dressing, and grabbing some fruit and cheese from the open snack table in the Officers' Mess, he made his way back to the Gunnery operations center for his first watch with Major Trillo.

Gerswin slipped behind the console next to the senior tech, Alvera, with only a nod from the departing G'Maine.

Alvera, a small man with jet black hair and eyes and a jerkiness to every movement, jabbed at the screen.

"Cadet. Here's the status. Inbound from exit corridor two." His thin index finger pointed to a green blip on the representational screen. "Here. Comm is running sweep and comm screen analysis. Nav has pulled deep EDI traces. Results came in about ten minutes ago. Solid contact shows in red. Conditional contact in amber. One of ours in green. Understand?"

"I think so."

Alvera pointed to the small screens to the left of the larger representational screen. "Top is punch laser. Energy available. Second shows tachead status and support data. Third is hellburners."

The senior tech looked directly and pointedly into Gerswin's eyes.

"Got that?"

"Yes."

"Fine. Unless something looks wrong, you do nothing.

Nothing, understand? My techs make sure these figures are right. You're the back-up to the major. You should know every number on these screens, what they mean. You don't. You might learn. I'll try and teach you."

Gerswin did not smile at the man's nervous energy, but instead nodded his head thoughtfully.

"I think I understand. You and your techs provide all the inputs. The major recommends to the bridge. I watch. If something looks strange, unless it's an emergency, I ask you or the senior tech. I keep quiet until I understand what it all means."

"That's right, Cadet." Alvera nodded. "Learn now. Some day you'll be the one making those recommendations, or, maybe, having to act on them. Better know what they mean."

Gerswin nodded once more and began to concentrate on the representational screens, which showed a series of red blips around the fourth planet, Newparra itself, and two red blips circling the third planet, with a lone red blip around the sixth planet, the inner of the system's two gas giants.

The blip closest to the *Fordin* was amber, outside the seventh planet, with a vector indicator showing an outward course that would intersect the *Fordin*'s path in roughly a standard hour. A standard hour?

Gerswin's fingers touched his own comp screen and keys.

The screen confirmed that if the amber blip was a ship, it would intersect the *Fordin*'s path in one point three standard hours.

"Did we shift course for intercept?"

Alvera nodded. "About one stan ago."

Gerswin inclined his head toward the representational plot. "How accurate is that? How many don't show?"

"Good question. Right now, we couldn't pick up anything under corvette size unless it was on full-drive or talking wide-band to the universe."

A green light winked in on the top side of the board, across the system from the *Fordin*, then was jumped inward abruptly as the techs made the real time adjustments.

"How many exit corridors does the system have?"

"Not much dust here. Two that are almost particle free. If you don't mind the skewing and the extra energy costs, no absolute need for corridor use."

Gerswin frowned. The only way to control system entrance
or exit realistically would seem to be by an orbit patrol of
Newparra and the industrial centers on the third planet, and on
the two major moons of the sixth planet. But, if the *Fordin*, as
the heavy of the quarantine squadron, took station off Newparra, that left two search cruisers and two corvettes to cover
the rest of the system.

Glad he didn't have to decide the positioning of the Imperial
ships, he returned his full attention to the screens, noting that
the amber blip approaching the *Fordin* had become a red blip
with a notation symbol beside it.

Rather than ask Alvera what the symbol meant he tried to get
an answer from his own screen, but stopped after two
unsuccessful tries at asking the system for a coded symbol that
neither appeared on the keyboard nor in answer to the standard
inquiries.

"Chief . . . how do you interrogate for the symbols beside
the blips?"

Alvera chuckled. "Can't get there unless you've already
been there. Right?"

Gerswin shrugged.

"Ask for SKS. Stands for 'screen key symbols.' Follow
with 'Gun' or you'll get the Nav and Comm codes as well. The
symbols will all display on your work screen, along with the
working subscript. That's what you use for your inquiries.
Simple enough."

Gerswin dutifully followed the instructions and discovered
that the approaching blip was listed as a "system heavy patrol"
with class two armament—tacheads and punch lasers. That
brought up another question.

"Why the puzzled look, Cadet?"

"System patrols don't carry jumpdrives. Non-Imperial
jumpships don't carry weapons. No one knew when we were
coming. That means that patroller was on a jump exit course
before he knew we were inbound. Either that or he has
jumpdrives."

"He knew *someone* was coming. Manual for quarantine
actions are no secret. Imperial force has to get to main system
planets at max speed. Means clearest corridors. Delay means
more to clean up."

"They'd try a direct attack against a battlecruiser?"

"No. They know that some incomers are cruisers. That's an even match. If they can blow a cruiser or the corvettes, then that buys them time before we can fully cover the system, until our torps reach the fleet commander. We lose ships, that means the captain will have to take more drastic action."

Gerswin let Alvera's comment pass. What drastic action could the Captain take, besides destroying the patrollers and whatever other craft the isolated and embattled system government had managed to arm and retain?

By now his ears were beginning to sort out the verbal messages coming from the comm link of the console, words mixed with static and garbled transmissions.

". . . stand off between Satanists and Brotherhood on Demetros . . ."

". . . Gabriel to Archangel Michael . . . successful, divert Gyros . . . Satanists hold Gyros and Janus . . ."

". . . *norstada cin trahit . . . Gyros stadit . . .*"

". . . negative diversion this time . . . negative . . ."

". . . have no lucifer for Demetros . . ."

". . . *fiela cor Gyros, cor Janus . . .*"

". . . EDI standing wave . . . heavy battlecruiser . . . Imperial . . . presume Imperial presence . . ."

". . . Gabriel . . . negative diversion . . . understand battlecruiser . . ."

". . . unleash Cherubim on north coast. . . . North coast . . ."

Another green blip pinged into existence in the jump corridor outsystem behind the *Fordin*. That made three out of the four comprising the Imperial quarantine squadron.

Gerswin studied the representational screen, then the three green dots upon it. Three ships. Just three ships? Where were the corvettes?

He checked the closure on the Newparran patroller and found that the closure time had dropped to less than thirty minutes.

"Cadet Gerswin, Chief Alvera, give me a weapons spread proposal for target one." There was no mistaking the voice of the major.

Gerswin turned to Alvera and raised his eyebrows. He'd done proposals at the Academy, but was the major serious?

"Like this, Cadet. Patroller characteristics under sub-

script . . . here . . . armor, screens, power max. Then
factor the profile, closure rate, and acceleration . . .''

"Acceleration?"

"Acceleration. Don't teach that at the Academy. Acceleration takes power. Less power for screens. Too much acceleration and you can't shift from gravfield to screens without losing
control. Some ships have limited shunt capability. Bigger the
ship, less shunt capacity. That's why the battlecruiser is the
biggest effective single action ship."

Alvera's fingers danced across his controls, and then touched
a stud.

"Hit accept, Cadet."

Gerswin touched the stud, and a duplicate of Alvera's
proposal lined up on his work screen.

Gerswin studied the recommendation for a moment. Alvera
had suggested using six tacheads spaced in a bowl-like pattern,
whose detonation would be preceded by a series of quick-
spaced bursts from the punch laser. No hellburners, obviously.

The cadet pulled his lips together as he tried to follow the
tech's reasoning. The actual energy that could be diverted to
the laser would scarcely dent a corvette's screens, let alone the
heavier ones carried by a patroller.

"Understand the tacheads, Chief. Why the laser? Energy
level wouldn't break his screens."

"Not the purpose. With his profile against ours, no laser
could make a physical impact. The laser bursts are powerful
enough to blind him for six–seven seconds. That forces him to
move, but he'll have to move blind, and the tacheads are
spaced on the most probable computed evasion tracks.

"Odds are that no local system government would be able to
pull together a complete crew experienced enough to handle
the course changes. They'll have to trust their AI, and that's
what the tacheads are programmed against."

Alvera touched the stud to transmit the recommendation.

"Cadet Gerswin, do you concur in the chief's recommendation?"

"That is affirmative, Major."

"Chief, what delay factor did you compute for reaction time
to the first laser?"

"One point five standard seconds."

"Too quick for a crew that will be short-handed or

inexperienced. Run it at two point five for the inner spread and angle it back to four point five for the outer."

Alvera nodded.

"Will do, Major."

Gerswin watched as the chief made his corrections.

"Looks good, Chief. Set the spread for execution from the command console."

"Stet, Major. In the green."

The noise level in the already quiet Gunnery operations center dropped further, and the silence, unbroken except for a faint humming, stretched on and on.

"Ten until contact. Program running."

Gerswin looked down, was surprised to find his fists were clenched, and forced himself to relax them. The shipboard version of a fight was so dispassionate, so far removed from the jagged blade and the threat of a king rat or a she coyote on the prowl. Here, his fate was in the hands of so many others. . . .

The background scent of fear, faint enough not to reach the awareness of the others, acrid, lingering, began to fill the center. To Gerswin, even the ventilation system seemed to stop, while the air hung heavy over the screens and consoles.

Cling.

"Laser punch on. Burst one."

The lights in the center dimmed momentarily, flickered, then remained at the lower level.

"Burst two."

On the representational screen, the green blip that was the *Fordin* sprouted a yellow lance that crept toward the Newparran patroller only slightly faster than the *Fordin* did.

Gerswin detected the gentlest of shudders in the battle-cruiser's frame.

"Burst four."

"Tachead spread one away."

"Burst five."

"Spread two away."

"Burst six."

"Three away."

Ding! Ding! Ding!

"All hands! All hands! Evasive maneuvers! Evasive maneuvers! Remain at stations! Remain at stations!"

Gerswin glanced over at Alvera, discovered the tech was studying the screen, his hands resting on the edge of the console, unmoving.

". . . *fiela Gyros . . . cor Janus . . .*"

". . . Imperial target . . . heads away . . ."

The whispers from the comm monitors took on an added loudness in the comparative silence of the center.

". . . *fiela Janus . . . nir nulla trahit . . .*"

"Imperial EDIs outsystem . . ."

". . . releasing and commencing beta . . . evasion . . ."

". . . diversion when appropriate . . . when appropriate . . ."

The lighting level dropped further, to emergency levels, and the gravfield dropped toward the null point before surging momentarily to almost two gees, then dropping to a stable one gravity.

Through it all, Gerswin kept his eyes on the representational screen, watching as the simulated punch laser impacted the Newparran patroller's screen image, and as the images of the tachead bursts began to blossom on the screen, and as the course line of the *Fordin* veered left, then angled back.

The red blip that had represented the Newparran patroller flared brightly, then vanished.

"Target termination complete," announced the major as the gunnery lights returned to normal.

As the former devilkid watched the silent kill of who knew how many men and women, he shook himself, almost like a wet coyote, but he continued to watch the screen. The *Fordin*'s course line again shifted, this time toward the sixth planet, presumably for the two satellites rather than for the gas giant itself. Better the sixth than the seventh, which was a third of the way around its orbit from the Imperial battlecruiser, reflected Gerswin.

Since there were no blips, hostile or otherwise, he wondered about the reason for the course switch.

In the meantime he noted that the fourth green blip, the *Krushnei*, had appeared on the system farside, outsystem from where another Newparran patroller raced toward the *Saladin*. The *Kemal* remained out from the *Fordin* and remained on a more direct in-system course.

Less than two standard hours since he had come on duty, and the *Fordin* had been attacked and had destroyed the attacker. After thinking a moment, he corrected himself. The *Fordin* had simply attacked and destroyed the unnamed Newparran patroller which had tried, unsuccessfully, to stop the Imperial quarantine.

He pulled at his chin. Even before contact, the two ships had been poised to destroy each other.

As he wrestled with the implications, he continued to watch the representational screens, to listen to the comm bands and to wait as the *Fordin* began to slow in her approach to the nearer satellite.

"*Pleutfiere, Empire sur transit Gyros . . .*"

"New Jerusalem, Faust has struck. Michael has been cast down. EDI tracks indicate course shift . . ."

"*Trahison! Couvrey des plaques! Comprennez? Des plaques de Janus et de Gyros . . .*"

". . . *norstada nil . . . premiere . . . Gyros . . .*"

"Cadet Gerswin, Chief Alvera. Specs for maximum surface damage on Gyros, centered on the landing traps and the linear accelerator."

"Stet," answered Alvera.

Gerswin said nothing. He looked sideways at the tech, whose movements were slower now, not quick or jerky.

"Hellburner?"

"Not much else. Not enough sealing power in a tachead. Probably take an above surface burst, about five kays. Maybe two. Depends on terrain and separation."

Gerswin opened his mouth to ask why, but remembered his earlier conversation with the major and shut his mouth without saying a word.

"Good thought, Cadet," murmured Alvera in a voice low enough not to be heard beyond their consoles. "Good thought."

Gerswin sighed silently and began to run the problem off on his own console. As he finished, he saw Alvera was waiting.

"Let's compare."

Gerswin shrugged and studied Alvera's solution. Both had recommended two mid-class burners with a five kay separation and a three kay burst height.

"Looks about the same," he commented to Alvera.

"About identical." Alvera raised his head and touched the transmit stud.

"Cadet Gerswin, do you concur?"

"My solution is identical to the chief's, Major."

"Do you concur?" There was an edge to the velvet voice.

"Yes, ser."

Gerswin and Alvera sat side by side, neither looking at the other nor talking, but silently viewing the screens and the symbols as they changed.

Gerswin listened to the intermittent transmissions whispering from the comm link, like ghosts about to flee at morning light.

The *Fordin* shuddered faintly, once, twice.

"Burners away."

This time the representational screen showed nothing, nothing except the number two followed by a single symbol, both next to the disc labeled "Gyros."

Gerswin shifted his weight, beginning to feel stiff after nearly three hours hunched before a single console.

"Cadet Gerswin, prepare the specs for a similar interdiction pattern for Janus. Key seven for background. Chief Alvera will verify before you transmit."

"Yes, ser."

Another set of hellburners? For what? Another dome and burrow mining and heavy industry settlement on an isolated satellite? For perhaps five thousand, ten thousand people?

Despite his deliberate pace, the equations were easy. Three hellburners—there were two lines of steep hills separating the landing traps, the accelerator, and the comm complex—at a height of one point five kays.

Alvera nodded.

Gerswin transmitted.

"Do you concur, Chief Alvera?"

"Yes, ser."

Gerswin listened as he waited for the *Fordin* to complete her creeping approach to Janus, or for his watch to end. But the comm bands were less active now, only a distant garbled whisper or so.

". . . got . . . Michael . . . out Gyros . . ."

". . . *fiela* . . . *trahit* . . . *Demetros* . . ."

The blinking of a green blip caught his attention, and he

concentrated on the representational screen. The blinking green was the *Saladin*. Had been the *Saladin*, Gerswin realized as the light flared red and white and vanished, to be replaced with a subscripted line at the bottom of the screen.

"Major said this one would be nasty," muttered Alvera.

Gerswin did not even shake his head. He didn't pretend to understand. If the Christers had control of most of the ships and the government, why were they attacking Imperial quarantine vessels? And why was the captain searing the launch and port facilities on Janus and Gyros when they belonged to the Istvennists, who weren't attacking the Empire?

The *Fordin* shivered three times, so slightly that Gerswin doubted whether anyone else noticed, wrapped as they were in their own concerns and the interest in the fate of the *Saladin*.

"Burners away."

He checked the time. Not too long before Lieutenant G'Maine was due to relieve him.

The course line on the screen changed again, showing the *Fordin* returning toward the original in-system destination.

Gerswin noted that the red dot that had totaled the *Saladin* was still headed out the system jump corridor toward the incoming *Krushnei*.

Given the lag times, they might not know the results of that confrontation until he was back on watch. He shook his head. In-system maneuvering time took so much longer than the between-system jumps.

"Cadet Gerswin, ready for relief?"

G'Maine's hearty voice startled Gerswin. He hadn't expected so burly an individual could move so quietly, or, perhaps, he had not been so aware as he should have been. Perhaps his skills were slipping in the confined ship environment. He'd have to work on that.

"Ready for relief, ser."

Gerswin stood and vacated the console.

"You stand relieved, Cadet." G'Maine smiled. "From what I've heard, you had quite an indoctrination."

"Yes, ser." Gerswin nodded. "Also told me how much I don't know."

"Good healthy attitude. See you in four." G'Maine swiveled into position to study the console and the screens.

"Cadet Gerswin?" The voice was the major's.

"Yes, ser."

"Would you join me? I'm on my way to the Mess. No seating arrangements during alerts, and I'd like to go over your performance."

Gerswin wondered what he'd done that merited evaluation. Some of his skepticism must have been communicated to the major.

"Mister Gerswin," she commented in the antique form of address, "you did well, much better than anyone would have expected. Mathematically, your last solution was better than mine or the chief's." Her eyes raked over him, and despite the fact that he was a shade taller than she was, he felt momentarily as though she were looking down at him.

"Let's go. I'm starved."

Gerswin matched her quick, short steps.

The Mess, predictably, was half full. The major piled her tray high and launched herself toward an empty square table at one side of the narrow dining area. She left the other side for him.

"Sit down. You like the fruits and vegetables, I see."

Gerswin nodded and pulled his chair into place.

The major took three large mouthfuls of a mixed cheese and meat dish that looked like synthleather covered with glue. Gerswin had avoided it for his fruits, vegetables, and a thin slice of meat that hadn't seemed to smell too artificial.

He sipped at a glass of water, ignoring the metallic tang that was unnoticeable to anyone else.

Tammilan walked in, smiling, between two junior navigators, both lieutenants, saw Gerswin, and grinned. Both eyebrows went up, and she shook her head in mock-disapproval.

In spite of his glumness, Gerswin returned the smile.

"Friend?"

"Roommate. In name only."

"You seem down."

"Private thoughts?" asked Gerswin.

"All right. Provided it's nothing illegal, or that I would be forced to enter on your record."

"Nothing like that." Gerswin shook his head. "No. I just don't understand. From all the backgrounders, the comm freqs, everything I can pick up, the Newparran Christers control the ships, or most of them, and most of the government. But they're the ones sending patrollers to blast the quarantine squadron. Then we sear off two moons to seal off the Istvennists, who haven't threatened us. There must be a reason, but I can't figure what."

The major packed in another three mouthfuls before answering. While she was solid, she didn't seem overweight, and he couldn't believe how she kept that way with her food intake.

"Gerswin, what do you know about the Christers? Or the Istvennists? Or Newparra?"

"Not much beyond the background and the comparative religions course at the Academy. Christers are fundamentalist believers in a single god. Istvennists believe in their own god above all others, but within a context of total personal religious freedom."

"Carry those trends to their logical extreme, and think about it. That would explain the way the Empire has had to act." She drained half a glass of a purple punch in a single gulp. "Christers believe they are the only true believers of the only true God. They are fanatical achievers in anything and everything, and they usually end up in disproportionate numbers in government and business. Both their government and their businesses are honest, but cruelly so, and without much compassion. Less than twenty percent of Newparra is Christer, but they control the government. They passed a law to require religious prayers in all institutions of learning and another law to forbid voluntary euthanasia—in which the Istvennists deeply believe as a matter of personal choice. Then they blocked genetic improvements as unnatural, despite the fact that the majority of Istvennists come from a weak genetic background.

"I won't go into a more detailed blow by blow, because I don't know all the details, but the upshot was that the Istvennists called for elections to throw the Christers out of government, and the Christers refused to leave and seized the government and control of the major weapons systems of the small military. The Christers saw it coming and managed to smuggle in some high tech equipment before the Empire quarantined the system, and Christers from all over the Galaxy are dying to get help to their brethren here.

"The Christers can't win over the long run without outside help because the numbers are against them. The Istvennists claim they should have outside aid to shorten the inevitable result and reduce the loss of life, and, besides, the Christers cheated on the quarantine."

"Imperial policy is simple. This is a local system matter and will stay that way. You have a revolt, and the locals have to settle it themselves. Our job is to make sure no one leaves the system, and no one enters, except on an Imperial warship. Period. When a government emerges that has total local control, we leave."

"That why the captain sealed off the moons?"

"She didn't have much choice, especially once the Christers blew the *Saladin*. Not enough ships to cover the system, and it would take too long to get back and forth between the outer and inner planets."

"But what happens if they fight forever?"

"Has happened before," mumbled the major as she finished another huge mouthful. "Will happen again. But local problems have to stay local, and local killings have to stay localized. If the people of a system can't get along together, then why should we let them spread the disagreements?"

"What about refugees? People unjustly oppressed?"

"Two problems. First, half the so-called refugees are people who don't get along in the system and don't have the guts to change it. Either that or they lost out because they couldn't change and they want to run out with their creds and try somewhere else. The other half are various bad apples."

"What about real victims?"

The major snorted. "Victims? Real victims don't have access to a jumpship or to the money to pay passage out-system. They get hurt no matter what happens. But if you force a system to deal with its problems, over time, in most cases, the average person gets hurt less. Not always true, but you don't make policy on exceptions."

Gerswin took a bite from the rubbery yellow fruit. It tasted better than ripe yucca, but not much. He chewed slowly.

The major stood and headed for the serving table and seconds. Gerswin studied the food before him, mostly still uneaten. She made it sound so simple, as if the hellburners were just another tool, as if the ten thousand people trapped under the molten rock and airless surface of Gyros and Janus had personally created the rebellion.

Had they?

He shook his head. So much he needed to learn. So much.

He tried a bite of the bland meat as the major plowed back to the table with another full tray.

 XVI

M. C. Gerswin, Cadet 1/C
Section Beta Two
The Academy
Kystra, Alphane

This is printing off the main engineering screens, devilkid, because I was never much for the fancy cubes you talk and put your smiling face to.

Still black-jumps me to see you as a namesake of sorts. That's why the initials, but congratulations. We all got the invitation, and you deserve it. You earned it. Can't say I thought you'd make it, not because you lacked brains or talent, but it takes a lot of patience to put up with it all. You've surprised us more civilized types more than once, and probably will a few times more.

Hard to picture you as a fresh-scrubbed I.S.S. officer, but I'll get used to that. Marso—she cubed me—can't get over it either. She's gone straight line, the exec on the *Martel*, scheduled for promotion to commander in the next circular.

Guess I ought to offer some advice. It's free and worth that, but even an old engineer who's a broken-down commander has something worth passing along. People—they're important. I know it, but I could never put it into practice. That's the single most important thing. Don't you forget it.

Second thing is machines. You've studied the histories by now, how Old Earth went down despite its machines and how the colonies barely survived. That's history. But we didn't learn enough from it. I know, why should an old machine wrestler like me worry about machines? I do. Machines are tools. Every time you use a machine, you make a decision. When you build a new machine, you decide that machine and the resources it takes are more important than something else. That's fine if you know what you want.

A machine can cut a tree and turn it into lumber. A machine can pull ore from an asteroid and turn it into hull plates. The machine didn't make the asteroid, and it can't grow like a tree. All Old Earth's machinery didn't save it from the collapse. The Federation learned something, and the Empire learned from the Federation. We're careful about what machines we use, and more careful about where we build them and use them. We try to put them in deep space or on unusable planets or moons. We manufacture the dangerous stuff away from the planets we live on. But we manufacture, and we build ships.

We still deal with the Devil; we got better terms. That's something to remember. What it means, I don't pretend to know. Call it all the ramblings of a has-been engineer.

Anyway . . . congratulations again, and good luck, lieutenant!

> MacGregor Corson
> Commander, I.S.S.
> COMM/ENG STAFF
> Vladstok, MANQCH

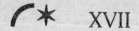 XVII

The black and silver of the I.S.S. officer's uniform merged with the long shadows and the lingering twilight of New Colora, even on the lower terrace of the Officers' Club.

A single officer sat at a small table in the walled corner farthest from the circular stone staircase that led to the upper level, a table that seemed to draw the shadows around it like a blanket.

Gerswin leaned back in the padded plasteel chair and let his shoulders rest against the stone wall behind him, let his eyes range out over the sloping lawn beyond the waist-high sitting wall on the far side of the circular table for two.

Now that his flitter and shuttle training was over, all he had to do was wait for the *Churchill*, due in less than two standard weeks.

He began to whistle, creating another tune as the double notes whispered out onto the vacant terrace and drifted downhill toward the training fields out beyond the manicured greenery of the club grounds.

The club was nearly empty, as it had been for the last half month, when the previous training cycle had been completed. Since half of the flitter pilots were techs, and weren't commissioned, and the latest officer class had yet to arrive, and the assault squadron normally based on New Colora, the Fifteenth, had just left for deployment with the Third Fleet, only a handful of officers were left to rattle around the club.

Within days, the Twelfth would be arriving for refresher training and regrouping. The next Academy class's pilot trainees would soon follow.

For now the club was empty, except for the cadre, the high-ranking staff officers, and a few transients, and special assignees, like Gerswin.

Gerswin broke off his soft whistling as the waiter approached.

"Another, ser?" The orderly's neutral tone nonetheless expressed concern about Gerswin's less than formal position, but he did not lean forward.

"No. Thank you. Not now."

He stared across the non-reflecting polished surface of the table, out over the stone sitting wall, and toward the low purple of the distant hills. In full daylight they were red-purple, not surprisingly, since most of the native growth had at least a trace of red in it. Only the mutated home grass had green or blue in it.

Gerswin laughed, a short bark, soft for all its harshness.

His home had been the original source of the blue green grass, but Old Earth looked more like New Colora than it did like the hist-tapes showed or than New Augusta, supposedly the most Old Earth-like of the colonized planets that had become, first, the Federated Worlds, and then, the Empire.

"That will change. Right? You're going to make it change. Right, Gerswin? Right, devilkid going home?"

He stared at the empty beaker and set it precisely in the center of the table.

Once more, he leaned back in the chair, aware how his posture irritated the always proper orderlies of the club. He began another song, with the off-multitoned whistle that no one else had ever seemed able to imitate.

This one—he'd composed the basic melody years ago, not long after he'd been picked up by the *Torquina*. While he'd elaborated it over the years, the sense of loss, the lack of identity, were more refined, a shade understated, but still the same basic theme. His theme, and it always would be.

Waiting to go home, he wondered if he ever could, as the notes spilled from his lips and whispered their clear wistfulness into the darkening twilight.

As he finished, he leaned forward and let the front legs of his chair touch the smoothed stone of the terrace. By now, the drier cool of the true evening was arriving on the hill breeze, with the scent of raisha. The long shadows had merged with the forerunner of night.

"Beautiful," a soft voice said.

He started, and looked to his left.

Sitting on the stone wall, her skirted legs hanging over the outside edge and over the grass a meter beneath her feet, the woman was half-turned and looking at him.

With an athletic motion she lifted her legs and turned so that she was still sitting on the wall, but facing him directly.

"You must be Lieutenant Gerswin."

With the terrace lights not on, and the last glimmer of twilight fading behind her, it took a moment for Gerswin to focus on the dimness of her face.

He stood.

"Would you care to join me?" He gestured to the empty chair, but did not move.

"I'm comfortable right here, and that might be best."

Her voice was young, but husky, and he judged from her profile, as she turned her head toward the staircase that led to the upper terrace, that she was little more than a girl.

In his loneliness, he had hoped for a woman. But she had heard the melody.

"As you wish," he answered, inhaling slightly as he reseated himself, not moving toward her. Her scent indicated she was a woman, but, as he had guessed from her profile, young. Obviously, the daughter of an officer, a very senior one. Few officers pulled accompanied tours anywhere.

"Would you please do another?"

Gerswin surveyed the terrace. Even the orderlies were gone. The girl had a pleasant voice, and the request was neither patronizing nor wheedling.

"Anything special?"

"Whatever pleases you."

He began to whistle softly, so low that no one more than a few meters away could have heard him, a greatly amended version of an old ballad he had learned at the prep school.

He recalled some of the words, and they flitted through his mind, though he could not, nor did he wish, to sing them.

. . . and I met my love, and I learned her worth,
on a faraway planet, a faraway planet called earth . . .

When he halted at the end, there was silence. For an instant, he thought she had gone.

"Are your songs always so sad?"

"No. Feeling down tonight. I just whistle what I feel. Not

sophisticated enough to lie in my songs." He frowned. "How did you know who I was?"

"You whistle, and you're from Old Earth. There's only one pilot with that combination, isn't there?"

Gerswin laughed, a bark again, but softer yet, and forgiving. He had his night-sight now that the twilight was gone and the terrace lights remained out. He studied the girl.

Short dark hair, cut just below her ears, large eyes, broad forehead, small ears, and a jaw that stopped just short of being square. Smallish, more handsome than pretty, but she smelled good and had a lovely voice, Gerswin decided, both qualities as important, to him, as mere looks.

Too bad she was the young dependent of some flight commander or marshal. Touch her, and he'd end up on some isolated station, or suicide assignment, if not planted under a shambletown.

"Your name?"

"Oh . . . I'm . . . Caroljoy."

"Carol Joy."

"No . . . Caroljoy." She firmly made the name one word.

"Sorry."

He looked away from her and into the western darkness.

"Lieutenant? Are you really from Old Home?"

Gerswin did not look away from the silhouette of the distant hills, where no light marred the blackness.

"I suppose so. That's what they tell me."

She let the silence be, and waited.

At last, he spoke.

"I am from Old Earth. That is what those who picked me up have told me. The place I knew does not resemble the Terra of the old tapes and stories. You cannot see into the sky beyond the clouds. The grass is purpled, what grass there is, and the trees are few, and only in the sheltered hills. There are some ruins, but most have been leveled. The people . . . some still remain, mostly in the shambletowns. And the others, the devilkids, hold the high plains, and, in turn, are hunted by the shambletowners. When I was not dodging the landspouts, or the ice rains, or the rivers of death, I was dodging the shambletowners and their slings.

"Sometimes that is a dream, only a dream, and sometimes this is."

From the stillness, her voice came back, husky soft now. "Do you want to go back?"

"Sometimes . . . but there I have to go, first, to become what I am. . . . To do what must be done. . . ."

"To remain a dreamer after all you have seen . . ." Her voice trailed off.

He laughed, a chuckle that was not.

"You sound older when you laugh."

"Perhaps I am."

"I must be going."

"Good night, Caroljoy."

"Good night, Lieutenant."

Gerswin watched her slip off the stone wall and onto the grass. His eyes followed her as she circled the pines and took the sheltered path that would lead her back to the side entrance to the club.

He knew the ladies' lounge was off that entrance, and wondered if her father or mother, whoever the senior officer she belonged to was, had suspected where she was.

Caroljoy—a pretty name. He had enjoyed her presence, and her voice.

He glanced down at the empty beaker once again. Should he wait for the orderly? Should he go back to the main bar for a refill? Was he really that thirsty?

There were sure to be the few regulars there, and all would fall silent once he walked in, except for a few conversations in secluded booths. Not one of the handful of junior officers would ever meet his eyes. Few enough had even through the Academy years.

He shook his head and eased himself out of the chair, leaving the beaker on the table.

As he did, as if the slight scraping of his movements had been a signal, the terrace lights went on, destroying the welcome shadow of the night.

Gerswin had to blink hard, squinting his eyes tightly against what seemed glaring floodlights, although he knew that the lighting would have been regarded as dim by most. His eyes were still unaccustomed to abrupt shifts in light intensity.

He held himself erect, refusing to stagger and admit any weakness, as his eyes adjusted and as he continued across the terrace toward the walk away from the club and toward his temporary quarters. He had already tabbed the drinks, the simple juices he had drunk.

For the time, and until he embarked on the *Churchill*, he was billeted in the farthest of the transient officers' quarters from the club, and he was the only one in his entire wing. While he enjoyed the isolation, he doubted that his room assignment was for his personal convenience.

The stone walks were dimly and indirectly lit, for which his eyes were grateful, and he saw no one as he walked the two hundred meters plus toward his billet. On his left were empty rooms, windows blanked and reflecting the glow of the walk lights, and on his right, sloping downhill, was the Terran grass that was no longer native to Old Earth.

From his own quarters a small glow lamp beckoned, and the old style door creaked as he opened it.

The room was empty, as always.

After slipping out of the still-unfamiliar officer's uniform, he stood in the small fresher unit to wash up. Then he pulled a robe around himself and turned to the standard planetside officer's bed. Back came the uniform coverlet, and he piled up two pillows before turning off the lights and stretching out in the darkness.

He had rearranged the furniture in order to be able to view the greens of the valley below from the bed, since the two straight-backed chairs were less than comfortable for any extended period.

Downslope, as his eyes adjusted, he could pick out the faintly luminescent shapes of the glowbirds as they began to dive for the emerging nightworms.

Every so often he could hear the hum of an electrobike making its way up or down the gentle slope that led up to the officers' quarters from the skitter fields and the training areas. The trainee barracks were shielded by an artificial berm, but he could pick out the glow above the darkness of the manmade hills that concealed them.

New Colora was a quiet planet, not that Gerswin minded that, but the stillness grated on some. There was always background music in the Club, sometimes loud enough to be heard from his room.

Gerswin's eyes narrowed. Something, someone, had slipped across the corner of his vision. He sat up and put his feet on the floor, more puzzled than alarmed, as he checked the time. Almost local midnight.

He hadn't realized so much time had passed since he'd gotten back to his small billet.

Tap. Tap.

Gerswin sniffed the air automatically and stood, his bare feet welcoming the chill of the floor tiles.

Tap. Tap.

He had seen someone, and that someone was at his door. The tap was gentle, almost delicate, but he did not know any women, not since Marcella had left with the rest of the Fifteenth. And she'd been a friend, not a lover.

He stood beside the door, ready for anything, he hoped, and opened it.

His mouth dropped.

"Not a word, Lieutenant."

She slipped past him and into the darkened room. When he did not move, she turned, took the edge of the door from his hand and closed it quietly.

A rustling sound followed, and he found her hands unloosening his robe, circling him, and drawing him to her.

"Why . . . ?"

"Don't ask . . . my choice. . . ." And her mouth left no room for words.

He stood, locked against her, returning the warmth of the kiss she had given, his ears pricked for the sound of footsteps, for an outraged parent, a marshal's duty officer. But only silence filled the air outside, silence and the distant murmuring of the birds hunting nightworms.

As that lingering kiss ended, as the outward silence stretched out and outward, he bent and gently, oh, so gently laid her upon the narrow bed, and folded himself into her scent, her warmth, and the huskiness of her murmurings.

He could not have spoken, had he wished to do so, nor would the woman have let him, for while her hands were gentle they were insistent, in the timelessness that is forever between two souls.

Later, much later, when she had gone as silently as she had come, Gerswin stared into the darkness, listening, unable to sleep, unable to dream.

Caroljoy Kerwin. The marshal's daughter. An innocent, he was sure, innocent no longer.

Why him? Why now? Why such intensity?

He was awake as the gray grass turned blue-green with the dawn, his questions still unanswered.

 XVIII

That key from the tower of time? Yes, that one, the one whose pages can unlock the mysteries of the myths? Could any words be that immortal in spanning the gulf between the days of chaos and the quiet order prevailing on Old Earth today?

Not words . . . not exactly, for the key is a small volume of coded entries, the order book of the operations center of Imperial Reclamation Corps base one [Old Earth].

What does it say? The words might be dry, but the stories told between their lines must be grander than the myths that surround them, if we could but decipher those order codes and sterile words.

> *The Myth of the Rebuilding*
> Alarde D'Lorina
> New Augusta, 4539 N.E.C.

⟨* XIX

"Five right," suggested the voice from the console.

Gerswin eased the stick right.

"Ten right," insisted the distant voice.

Gerswin ignored the latest suggestion as he felt the flitter rock, automatically leveling it while studying the vortex that loomed off the nose and above the ground fog that shrouded the prairie.

"Tall mother . . ." he muttered, not caring whether the relay was open.

"Scan indicated probable effective height of twenty kilometers."

"Spread?"

"Less than a kay at the spout, maximum before altitude dispersion is eighty kays."

"Range?"

"Twenty kays."

Gerswin wanted to wipe his forehead with the back of his gloved right hand, but did not. Both hands stayed in position, the left on the stick and the right on the thrusters.

Beep!

He glanced at the trim warning and bled enough from the starboard fan to correct the incipient yaw.

"What's the closure?"

"Half kilo a minute."

The pilot shook his head. He was headed east at damned near two hundred kays. The spout was tearing across the high prairie south and westward at more than one fifty.

"We got the data in the cube?"

"Need another five on this heading, Lieutenant." That comment was from the Ops duty officer at Prime Base, although Prime was the only base so far.

"That's cutting it close."

"Your choice. If we don't get another five, then we'll have to scrub and rerun tomorrow."

"What's Met say about tomorrow?"

"Could be worse than today. The jetstream's dropping and dipping south, and the ground level temperature will be higher."

"Hades! We'll do it!"

Beep! Beep!

Gerswin used both the fan bleed and the hydraulic boosted rudders to straighten the yaw while leveling the flitter again.

The purple black of the landspout now filled nearly half of the flitter's windscreen.

"Grit intake at ten percent," announced the console's warning system.

Gerswin could feel the dampness on his forehead.

"Three minutes to go, Lieutenant. Sure you can hold it?" The voice belonged to Major Sofaer, coming in from Prime.

"Fourth time on the same flamed line. No landspout . . . going to back me out."

"Port thruster in the yellow. Running time three point five."

THUD! THUD!

"Impact on rear port stub. Impact on forward port stub."

"Flame!"

Ding! Ding! Ding!

"Starboard thruster in the yellow. Running time three point five. Port thruster in the yellow. Running time three point zero. Closed system reserve two point four."

THUD! THUD! THUD!

The flitter slewed left, the nose jerking up, then from left to right.

"Multiple impacts, main fuselage."

Twisting full turns into both thrusters, Gerswin stamped nearly full right rudder and leveled the nose again. Then he dropped the power back to eighty percent.

"Prime outrider. Prime outrider. Data's in the cube. In the cube."

"Stet. In the cube. Flaming clear. Flaming clear."

THUD!

Ding! Ding! Ding!

"Starboard thruster in the yellow. Running time two point five. Port thruster in the yellow. Running time two point zero."

Gerswin blinked, blinked again, from the sting of the salty sweat running into the corners of his eyes, even as he completed the left hand bank away from the towering purple vortex of the landspout.

THUD!

Beep! Beep! Beep!

"Grit level at fifteen percent. Five percent power loss on port thruster."

THUD!

"Unidentified impact on forward port stub."

"Flame. Flame. Flame," grunted the pilot.

Gerswin eased the flitter back level and twisted up the power on both thrusters with a half turn more to the left. The sweat kept dripping into the corners of his eyes, but he left both hands in place, gave his head a quick downward snap to drop the helmet's impact visor.

The purple of the spout dominated almost the entire armaglass windscreen.

Gerswin flicked his eyes to the lower right corner of the bubble toward a spot where the ground fog had thinned momentarily.

Had he seen some sort of structure?

He caught himself before he shook his head, resuming his normal scan of the instruments.

THUD!

Beep! Beep!

"Impact on upper starboard stub."

"Grit level approaching twenty percent."

"You've got one minute, Lieutenant. Just one."

"Stet, Prime. Stet."

Ding! Ding! Ding!

"Impact on the rear port stub."

"Grit level at fifteen percent and dropping."

"Prime outrider. Wind sheer at ten kilos, two nine five and closing."

Gerswin glanced at the homer. Fifty-six kays to Prime.

"Interrogative closure rate."

"Three point five per minute."

"Interrogative course line of the sheer front. Interrogative sheer angle."

"Sheer angle unknown. Course line estimated at one zero five."

"Stet. One zero five."

The pilot edged his own course to two eight five, lifted the flitter's nose, and twisted in full turns.

"Grit level at twelve percent and dropping."

With the flitter stable for a moment, Gerswin snapped his head to retract the helmet's impact visor, and with his left hand wiped the sweat away from his eyes and off his forehead.

That done, he snapped the clear impact visor back in place.

"Should have opted for arcdozers," he muttered.

"Where would the glory be, Lieutenant?"

"Thanks, York. Thanks, loads."

"Grit level at ten percent and stable. Permanent power loss at ten percent."

Gerswin frowned. The fans in both thrusters would have to be repolished and retuned. Either that, or replaced with another set, if there was one to be had.

"Prime outrider. Less than one minute to sheer impact."

The pilot's eyes flickered from the thrust indicators to the balance lines, to the speed readouts, to the radalt, and down to the VSI, which still indicated a constant rate of climb.

He took a deep breath, exhaled slowly, and squared himself in the padded shell seat.

"Stand by for impact."

Even as he glanced through the armaglass of the canopy at the indistinctness of the western hills, blurred as they were from the clouds and the fog, the flitter lurched, throwing him against the broad harness straps.

Not only his stomach, but the instrument balance lines showed the flitter nearly ninety degrees nose down. The VSI pegged momentarily, then dropped back to a descent rate of two hundred fifty meters per second.

Gerswin twisted the thruster throttles around the detente into overload while bringing the stick back into his lap.

"Ground impact in fifteen seconds!" screeched the console.

A thousand kilos piled onto Gerswin's muscles and slender frame, and his vision blurred around the edges.

"Ground impact in thirty seconds!" screeched the console mindlessly.

Whhheeeeeeee!

"Prime outrider. Interrogative status. Interrogative status!"

"Stuff your status," he grunted without keying his transmitter. Instead, he eased the stick forward and to the left to bring the flitter level and back on course for Prime Base. Next came the down-throttling of the thrusters.

"Prime outrider. Interrogative status. Interrogative status."

Gerswin sighed.

"Status summary. Flying strike. Flying strike. Fusilage overstressed. Fans set for repolishing. Assorted external damage. Flitter down. I say again. Flitter down."

"Interrogative ETA."

"Estimate arrival in fifteen plus."

"Understand fifteen plus. Interrogative special procedures."

"Prime Base, that is negative this time."

Gerswin sighed again and checked the homer. Forty kays to go, and the screens showed clear skies between him and the foothills base.

Clear skies between him and base, but not overhead, where the high clouds still brooded. Clear sky, except for the ground fog.

He readjusted the thrusters and returned to his normal scanning pattern.

Another few minutes and he would begin the landing check list.

 XX

Gerswin took another step toward the Maze.

Did he want to go through the twisting and turning tunnels, where anything might wait in the upper reaches? Or where rats the size of Imperial cats lurked in the darkness for their next chance at dinner?

He laughed. There was no reason to face the Maze, not while wearing an Imperial uniform and stunner, but the old instincts died hard.

Overhead, the clouds rolled eastward in banks of darkened gray, but the air was dry and cold.

He circled more to the north, along the outcroppings that felt like rock, but were, instead, massed metal and bricks and compressed purple-red clay. Between the upthrust chunks grew an occasional patch of the purple grass or a small grubush, with its thin branches and straggly leaves.

Eventually he had worked his way north and west far enough to get around the pile of rubble from which the Maze rose southward and stood in the cleared area beneath the northern wall of the shambletown. He stood looking southward and uphill to the roughly four meter height of the shambletown wall, running as it did slightly more than a half a kay from the eastern end of the Maze to the western corner.

The shambletowners kept the area immediately downslope of the wall clear of debris, grubushes, and skinned carcasses. The debris and bushes offered too much concealment for both rats and coyotes, while carcasses, those too poisonous to eat, would have attracted the rats.

His nose twitched. In the confines of the more fastidious Imperial society, the odors were muted. Machine oil and deodorants, while strong, were blandly dulling as well. The mix of unwashed shambletowners, excrement, assorted garbage, and the underlying bitter stench of omnipresent rat all reached him, although he was well outside the walls and a good three hundred meters east of the gate.

The lone wall sentry had marked the Imperial uniform and passed the word, so well that by the time he had reached the gate, several others awaited him.

One—older by years than the last time they had crossed paths—he recognized immediately. Fynian, still squat and hulking, stood behind the conslor. Gerswin had not met the conslor, not this one or any of his predecessors, and he was amused by the indrawn breath as the man looked into his eyes.

While the conslor said nothing, Gerswin could hear Fynian's muttered "devulkid."

"Lieutenant Gerswin, Imperial Service," he announced.

"Conslor Weddin. What you want?" answered the other in clipped shambletalk.

"Want see shamble," Gerswin replied in kind, even getting the lilts in the right places.

"Devulkid," repeated Fynian under his breath, loudly enough for Gerswin to hear clearly.

"All right, stand? No kill, stand? No woman, stand?"

Loosely translated, you're welcome, but keep your hands off everyone, and don't try to make off with anyone's woman or all bets are off.

"No kill. No woman, stand," repeated the pilot. "You no kill, no fun, stand?"

Conslor Weddin frowned. That a visitor should place reciprocal conditions on a shambletowner was unheard of.

As the conslor debated, Gerswin discarded the idea of displaying the stunner and its powers. Using it would only induce some idiot to try to take it. He wished he had developed a few other weapons skills besides stunners, lasers, and hand-to-hand. None were exactly suited to his situation. The Imperial policy stated clearly that advanced and lethal weapons were prohibited for use against any civilians. And hand-to-hand combat was chancy merely as a display of force.

At last the conslor, presumably after meditating on the flitters and skitters that crossed the cloud-covered skies, nodded.

"Stand."

Gerswin bared his teeth in response, and to signify his agreement.

Weddin and his party stood aside, but Gerswin motioned for them to precede him, which, after a moment's delay, they did.

Inside the gate, a cobbled-together mass of twisted metal and woven grubush that screeched as it was dragged back into place, the stench was as high as Gerswin had remembered. He swallowed hard to keep the contents of his stomach in place and thanked himself for his foresight in eating only a light meal before setting out.

The one, two, and occasional three story clay brick buildings were crammed together, with narrow streets, narrower alleyways. Unlike the plains clay, the building clay was reddish-brown, without the purple tint that usually signified some degree of landpoison.

The pilot nodded. He had seen the outside clayworks often enough, had even stolen a food basket or two from the clayworkers as they turned the clay into a slurry and let it settle, then repeated the process time after time.

The "finished" clay was lightly fired in grubush-fueled ovens. Once the bricks were mortared in place, the walls were covered with a sandpaint mixture that hardened the bricks further and gave both interior and exterior walls a dingy white appearance. The few times the sun did shine, the walls sparkled, and that sparkle gave the shambletown a glitter totally unwarranted by its interior occupants, human and otherwise.

All the houses in the upper shamble, the newer section, had porches, not for people, but for the continual plant flats, designed to allow in light but not the continual rain or ice rain. The precipitation was collected off the inclined roofs and funneled to either the clay collecting barrels or the main settling ponds.

Outside of the stink of unwashed bodies, the people appeared relatively healthy, though uniformly thin. The men all had beards, usually straggly. An occasional limp or twisted arm showed a broken bone that had not set properly.

From the open space inside the gate, Gerswin strolled down the narrow street toward the square, watching to see if Conslor Weddin continued to keep an eye upon him.

The square, an oblong paved with rough stone fragments and measuring no more than forty by sixty meters, contained only a single platform, used for a variety of purposes, surmised Gerswin. It was vacant except for a few passers-by, and for

Gerswin and Fynian, who had apparently been instructed to follow the Imperial officer.

The muted sounds of children drew Gerswin to a freestanding porch off the southwest corner of the square, where were gathered close to a dozen toddlers. Gerswin stood by the brick wall enclosing the space under the roof and watched.

Two children, dressed solely in rough stained leather tunics, used miniature clay bricks to build a wall. Behind them, an even smaller child sat on the smooth brick flooring and sucked on the end of a wooden rattle. None of the children's hair appeared more than roughly cut, nor did any wear more than a loin cloth and sleeveless, patched-together leather over-tunics, despite the brisk breeze. The chill from the morning's frost had yet to leave the air.

A somewhat older child sat on the bricks at the feet of a shriveled and gray-haired woman and used a battered wooden pipe to produce a series of shrill squeaks, some of which resembled musical notes.

A toddler barely able to walk caught sight of the gray Imperial tunic and the touches of silver-embroidered insignia on his collars and pointed at the clean-shaven pilot.

"Ummm! Ummm!"

Gerswin looked at the wide gray eyes, and finally grinned.

She frowned and closed her mouth. Finally, she repeated the phrase again. "Ummmm!"

The wind shifted, and a new stench wrenched at Gerswin's gut, an acidic odor burning into his nostrils from the lower section of the shambletown.

He took a last look at the toddler, waved, and turned toward the half dozen steps that stretched the three meter width of the street that led southward to the older part of the shambles.

"Ummmm! Ummmm!" Was there a plaintive ring to those words?

Gerswin nearly stumbled on the first step, but caught himself and continued downward.

The street remained level for another fifty meters, flanked on both sides by the relatively newer and larger dwellings of the upper section, before narrowing at the top of another set of steps.

The officer could hear the uneven sound of Fynian's dragging limp as they continued downward.

Beyond the second set of steps, the narrow grid pattern of the upper shambletown dissolved into the twisting lanes of the lower town. The houses were no longer uniformly sand-painted, since in places the old facade had crumbled or been washed away.

More plant flats appeared in sheltered and glassless windows or on rooftops under patched old leather tenting, rather than in the relatively ordered porticos of the upper town. But the relative silence prevailed—a few whispers, a word here and there among the handful of people passing in the lanes, and few shambletowners at all.

Gerswin nodded. The old patterns had not changed, not yet, and perhaps never.

He turned down a lane he thought he remembered, glancing over his shoulder to see if Fynian still followed. The old guard trailed ten meters back, mumbling under his breath.

From a crossing lane appeared a woman, carrying an empty pottery crock half as tall as she was.

Gerswin stepped back barely in time to avoid colliding with her, intent as he had been on watching Fynian and trying to recall the path he had taken the single other time he had traversed the shambletown.

Like the others, the woman wore the sleeveless patchwork tunic that reached halfway between waist and knee, with a braided leather neckring to signify she had a mate.

She stumbled as well, and her eyes involuntarily made a momentary contact with Gerswin's.

As she recovered her jar and her balance, she froze, as if afraid to move either toward or away from Gerswin.

Gerswin stepped back another pace, until his back brushed the wall behind him, then walked around her, and continued on his way as if nothing had happened.

"Devulkid," explained Fynian in a rasping whisper, as he in turn passed her in his shadow trail of the Imperial pilot.

In the quiet broken only by murmurs and whispers, her indrawn breath whistled in the still morning air.

Gerswin shook his head and followed the lane through another series of turns, glancing upward at a familiar window only in passing, as he moved into totally unfamiliar regions of the lower area. He glimpsed a gray head through one window and a shadowy figure through another, but did not stop or increase his pace.

In the dimness of the lower shamble his breath formed a thin white cloud, like his own personal ground fog.

At the next turn, the reek of the leatherworks jarred him to a halt with the solidity of a wall.

He smiled, ruefully, and turned to the left. The last thing he needed was an in-depth look at or smell of the facility that converted rat and coyote and other skins into the leather that was one of the few materials resistant to the acidity of the rain.

The eastern end of the lower shamble ended abruptly in a three meter wide cleared space, followed by a two meter high wall. Beyond and above the wall, he could see the twisted beams and heaped bricks, stone, and clay where the Maze towered.

The single eastern gate, barred and manned by a single sentry, was to his right. He did not approach it, but turned back toward the upper town, seeking another route to avoid retracing a path close to the tannery.

Fynian followed, still mumbling and muttering, every third word some pejorative elaboration on "devulkid."

Three twists later, Gerswin halted at the small open area surrounding the covered settling ponds that ran like steps from the upper side of the shambletown into the lower section.

The woman he had upset earlier was at the lowest pond, along with a boy and an old woman. All three had brought large crockery vessels and were skimming water from the open section of the pond and pouring it into their own crocks.

Without retracing his steps or passing the three, he did not see any way to return to the upper square and the northern gate. So he waited in the gloom, his breath still a thin fog in the chill that seldom left the narrow lanes until late in the summer afternoons.

The older woman was the first to leave, staggering under the burden of the water.

The boy, who bore a smaller crock, was next.

Finally, the brown-haired woman finished dipping into the pond and stepped away, gracefully, Gerswin noted. She tugged and eased the heavy pottery vessel into a harness. Despite the lack of light, he could see the cleanness of her profile clearly.

For reasons he would not try to understand, for an instant he was reminded of another moment in darkness, another silence in time, another woman in another place barely familiar to him.

He shook his head to clear the image.

Caroljoy? To see her again? Not likely. Not at all likely, and even less likely that he would be successful if he made such an attempt.

A cough, and the whispered "devulkid," distracted Gerswin, called him back to the present, all at once. He glanced over his shoulder to see Fynian, still four meters behind him, like a tracking coyote, eyes bright.

When Gerswin looked back at the settling pools, the woman was gone. He shrugged and started for the steps that rose beside them to the level of the upper shambletown.

Behind him the shuffle of uneven steps reminded him that Fynian followed, stalking the devilkid through the shambletown.

Gerswin regained the square, this time from the northeastern corner and glanced over at the covered portico where the children had earlier played. They still played, from the sounds and motions, but he started for the northern gate from the far side of the square, avoiding the children, and the toddler who had cried out, "Ummm!"

The walls and the narrow streets felt more like a prison with each passing step, and he wanted out.

Forcing himself to maintain an ambling walk, he continued toward the gate, ears alert for any change in Fynian's conduct or pace.

The gate was closed, but the two guards leaped to push open the massive patchwork as if they were all too ready for the Imperial stranger to depart.

Gerswin could hear from the sounds behind him that Fynian was moving closer, but he was surprised that the older man followed him outside the shambletown and onto the flat beneath the wall.

Gerswin faced the shambletowner and watched Fynian pull a stone from his pouch as the gate squealed shut.

"No kill, stand?" Gerswin snapped sarcastically, as Fynian straightened the sling straps.

"Devulkid out shamble."

Gerswin pulled the stunner.

Thrummmm!

The sling and stone dropped on the hard clay, followed by the inert form of the shambletowner.

Both guards peered over the wall from their posts beside the gate.

"Guard. No kill, stand? Fynian try kill. Dreamtime, stand?"

Gerswin kept the stunner in full view until he was certain both guards understood that the shambletowner was only stunned. He retreated downhill, pace by pace, facing the wall as the gate squealed ajar and a single guard ventured out and began to drag the unconscious Fynian within, by his foot.

Gerswin glanced toward the discarded sling and stone, then at the closed gate and blank wall. Blank, as it had always been.

He turned and walked down the long slope through the scattered bushes and to the north.

XXI

The pilot peered into the work area.

"Still down?"

"Yes. It's still down," answered the gray-clad technician. "Some of the fans looked like fuel strainers, and we have one gilder/polisher. That was meant for touch-up work, not for rebuilding an entire fan structure. That's just the beginning.

"There's the frame. Not a single millimeter that doesn't need restressing. Got to be more than a half-million creds of damage."

Gerswin frowned, then let his face clear.

"How long?"

The tech put down her analyzer probe and turned to face the pilot.

"Lieutenant Gerswin, we do our very best. So do you, in your own way. But our ancestors, Istvenn take their souls, left a forsaken mess. No one ever designed atmospheric craft to fly through stone rains and acid winds, not and come out intact." She looked down at the already stained permatile flooring.

"Is it our home, anymore? If they didn't tell us so, I'd never have guessed. Purple-shaded grass, where it grows, and ground fog that can eat your lungs." Her eyes came up to meet his. "How you ever got this back, I couldn't guess. And how long it will take to rebuild it would be a bigger guess."

"Thanks," Gerswin said softly, before turning away from the tech and the battered flitter. "Thanks."

He could feel her dark eyes on his back as he walked from the temporary hangar-bunker that served more as a mechanical infirmary than as a maintenance facility.

"Four flitters, and not a one fit to fly."

His steps echoed as he entered the underground tunnel back to the administrative building, buried, like all the others, in the clay and native stone.

Even though the portal to the ecological laboratory was open, he rapped on the wall, as if he were knocking at another officer's private quarters.

No answer. He rapped the metal bulkhead harder.

Finally, he stepped inside.

As often happened, he found the two consoles humming, but unattended, and the swivels all empty. He scanned the telltales on the airlock control chambers, but the indicators on five were amber. Number three blinked both green and amber.

That was where Mahmood had to be.

He slumped into one of the swivels opposite a busily humming console to wait, tapping his fingers lightly on the console and whistling a slow dirge.

Gerswin ignored the cycling of the lock and kept whistling without looking up, even as the ecologist finished unsuiting and racking his labsuit in one of the dozen wall lockers.

"That's cheerful . . . about as uplifting as the subsonics on a hellburner." Mahmood Dalgati clicked the locker shut and straightened his impeccable whites before settling himself in the armless swivel behind the farther console, tapping out a series of inquiries on the screen.

"That's the way I feel."

"I take it that the flitters are all down?"

"Right. You know that. They've been down for days."

Senior Lieutenant Dalgati did not immediately reply, but pursed his lips as an entry scripted itself upon his screen.

Gerswin resumed his dirgelike whistling.

"Greg."

Gerswin stopped the whistling.

"You and your whistling can depress anyone. I'd suggest another theme, but whatever it was, it would probably get on my nerves. I take it you want to talk."

"No."

"Oh . . . you want to fly, to feel productive."

Gerswin shrugged.

"You can't. Not unless you can figure out how to repair the flitters better and faster than the techs. So why don't you put that overtrained, but undereducated and underused mind of yours to work instead of haunting the poor techs?"

Gerswin did not resume his whistling, but kept tapping his fingers on the edge of the console.

"Now you're feeling sorry for yourself, that you're just a poor barbarian from Old Earth, that no one understands you."

"Mahmood. . . ."

The ecologist laughed, gently. "Please don't bother with your dangerous voice. I'm well aware that, as a relatively untrained Service officer, your reflexes make you about twice as deadly as the average Corpus Corps officer."

"You exaggerate, Mahmood." Gerswin returned the laugh, his initial bark subsiding to a chuckle, although he did not sound amused. "Are you suggesting something?"

"I suggest nothing, my underactive friend. All things come to those who wait, particularly if they understand what they're waiting for."

"Ridiculous."

"No. Realistic. One's expectations color the surrounding world, and yours more than most. You have yet to learn what to expect, or what you want to expect.

"Have you ever studied the tapes of the Old Earth master painters? Or read the old Anglish poets in the original? Studied the old and outdated terrain maps? Tried to understand the ecology before it collapsed?

"Do you want your planet restored? Or do you want to badger the techs?"

Gerswin straightened up in the swivel.

"So I have to know what I want, is that it? What difference does it make?"

"I wouldn't put it quite that way. Permit me to digress momentarily, my friend."

"You always do." Gerswin leaned forward in the swivel, then tilted himself farther backward.

Mahmood pursed his lips and looked down at his screen. He touched the keyboard in several places until he was satisfied. Finally, he stood. Circling to his left, he looked at Gerswin, halting behind his console. The effect was undeniably that of a professor behind his podium.

"Right now, Greg, you're little more than a step above those barbarians you call shambletowners."

Another short bark issued from the pilot. "That's probably more than some would grant me."

"You are marvelously trained in techniques, and better trained than that in some weapons, but your mind has never considered the reasons for such training."

"Mahmood, spare me the rationalizations and the philosophy. If a flitter is up, it's up. If it's down, it's down. If it can be fixed, then you fix it."

"And if it can't be fixed, you give up?"

"You don't fly."

"Do you need to fly? Isn't there more than one route to a destination? Do you always have to rely on the biggest or the fastest or the latest piece of machinery?"

"Don't ask such stupid questions. You're humoring me, and I'm not in the mood for being humored." Gerswin was out of his seat, circling the other side of the office. "I'm flying through trash because no one else seems to be able to get even one damned data run. Because no one can program the dozers without terrain data. Because we're going to run out of time . . ."

The blond man with the eyes of a hawk turned on the professor and jabbed a finger. "You can sit and lecture. Or stand and lecture. Puzzle the riddles of the universe. Take forever to find the perfect solution. Right now, good old Terra is a curiosity. Oh, yes, the wonderful Empire will fix her up good. Now. What about tomorrow? Is it going to last? How long? How many flitters? How many dozers? How many young techs and pilots will they let good old Mother Earth murder before the great, grand, and glorious Empire gives up?

"There's nothing of worth left. No cheap metals. No radioactives. Nothing grows."

Gerswin picked up a swivel one-handed, holding it at arm's length.

"Look, Mahmood! Look! Now, how long can I hold this thing? Twice, three times as long as you can? Ten times? Some time I have to put it down. So . . . old Terra has an emotional hold on the Empire. For now. But what happens when the next Emperor has to let go? What happens if they put us down before the ecology is fixed?"

His voice softened to a whisper as he replaced the swivel on the tiles.

"Nobody thinks I think, just that I react."

He stared across the office at the ecologist, who had involuntarily retreated until his back had touched the row of wall lockers.

"Maybe I will read some of the old poets . . . and look at the old master painters. Maybe I will . . . and maybe I'll learn more weapons and the philosophy behind them. It just might make me angrier. But I'll take your advice, Mahmood, until everything is trained. And I'll read everything I haven't read. And then we'll see."

His voice sounded more like the call of the hawk he resembled as he concluded, "Then we'll see."

The ecologist wiped his damp forehead in the silence of the laboratory where he stood alone.

 XXII

Gerswin touched the inner portal stud and stepped through the endura steel arch as the door irised open. The inner and outer portal arrangement that led outside reminded him of an airlock.

He laughed once, aware of the sharp echo from the composite blue walls of the small chamber, and touched the second stud.

As the exterior portal opened, he marched through the center, out into the chill of the twilight, the wind ripping through his uncovered hair, the fine dust gritting against his skin like a continual abrasive.

Once outside, he kept walking eastward over the hard and uncovered clay, the reddish purple like solidified blood in the dim light that signified the sun's descent behind the shadows of the mountains to the west.

He stumbled as his right boot caught in a depression concealed by the heavier dust that took nearly a landspout to lift. He lurched, but regained his balance without slowing his pace.

Each meter forward took him that much farther away from the sheltering bulk of the artificial ridge under which the administration complex was housed.

Looking to the south, he could see the general outlines of the next artificial ridge, the one that contained the hangar bunkers.

When the ground dipped toward a dust-filled ravine, he stopped. No telling how deep the gully was under the heavy dust.

With the adjustment of his eyes to the darkness and his hearing to relative stillness, Gerswin turned back to face northeast, where remained the shambletown, the Maze, and what was left of the ruins. The Denv ruins were one of the few clusters left on the Noram continent, protected from the worst of the landspouts by the natural depression in which the old city had been built, and by the closeness of the foothills and the mountains behind.

His breath left a trail. The freezing temperature would have chilled most Imperials, but Gerswin was more than comfortable in his light jacket and flightsuit, free of the continual pressure of people and walls.

Strange how he never noticed the crowding until he took the time to step away from it.

He began to walk north, lengthening his strides until the ground seemed to melt away under the quick steps, until the bulk of the artificial hills dwindled away behind him and he was exposed to the full bite of the wind cutting in from the plains.

A rustle in the bushes to his right signaled a rat scurrying away, dropping into a hole leading beneath the surface and into what Gerswin imagined was an intertwining of rubble, animal tunnels, and undamaged foundations long since covered and forgotten beneath the hilly terrain above.

A low series of isolated bulges appeared to his left. Gerswin slowed, then stopped, and studied the evenness of the spacing.

He stepped toward the uprisings, each waist-high, each circular and perhaps a meter across. Bending down, he squinted, then ran his fingers over the powdered smoothness. The pressure caused more of the white powder to flake off.

Gerswin studied the low pillars. The sides toward the mountains were relatively straight, but the eastern sides sloped outward as they neared the ground, the weathering clearly directional in nature.

He began to walk westward, then turned north again, his eyes piercing the dark and running over each pillar he passed. After completing a quick circuit of the area, Gerswin pursed his lips. The thick pillars covered an area nearly a half a kilometer square.

He didn't know whether to be more impressed by the size of the structure they had supported, or by the fact that nothing but what appeared to be the foundation remained.

Shaking his head, he turned his steps back to the north and the ridge ahead, from which, if he remembered correctly, he could survey the territory he had once foraged.

Under his light steps, as the temperature dropped, the

ground began to squeak. The wind's whisper rose to a thin whine to match the cutting edge it turned upon the rolling hills and the man who walked them toward a ridge top.

Gerswin ignored the sound of his footsteps and the familiar song of the night wind as he trotted up the increasing incline toward the lookout, toward the ledge he remembered, where, in the darkness, a careful devilkid could watch the coyotes slink out of the hills toward the edges of the shambletown in their efforts to drag down an unsuspecting towner, or watch the movements of the ratpacks from the hidden tunnels that were all that had remained of the city that had stretched for kays along the front of the hills.

He patted the pair of stunners tucked inside his jacket. While neither should be necessary, to be prepared for the unnecessary was how he had survived outside the walls of the shambletown for so long, away from the guards, the walls, and the fires, and away from the scrawny plants that grew in carefully purified soil beds.

A two-toned whistle added a mournful air to the song of the wind, to the darkness of the starless night, as the man who had been a devilkid slipped up the trail to a view of his past.

⟨* XXIII

"Red three! Red three! Lieutenant Gerswin to the Ops center. Lieutenant Gerswin to the Ops center. Red three!"

Gerswin yanked on his boots and palmed the exit panel stud, ignoring the chimes from his own console. He could learn more once he was in Operations.

Moving through the portal at double time, he twisted and flipped himself to the side to avoid the other man in the corridor.

"Excuse me, Commander." The pilot snapped off a quick salute.

"Don't mind me, Mr. Gerswin. Just get to Ops."

"Yes, ser," Gerswin said over his shoulder.

He could see Commander Lancolnia's reflection in the metallic joints between the building sections. The commander was still shaking his head as Gerswin turned the corner toward the tunnel from his quarters to the Ops center.

While Operations was protected by a double portal, only a single guard was stationed at the entry console, not surprisingly, since the entire complex was secured, built to take the worst the weather and the locals—what few ventured from the shambletown—could dish out.

"Lieutenant Gerswin."

He offered his pass and slammed his palm onto the console screen.

"Captain Matsuko said for you to meet him at G.C., ser."

"Thank you."

"Yes, ser."

Gerswin went through the portals on a double bounce, feet scarcely touching the tiles.

Ground control was fifty meters down the operations corridor, directly beneath the low control tower that crouched over the bunker. The tower monitored both the flitter approaches, as well as the infrequent shuttles from the few I.S.S. ships to visit Old Earth.

Captain Matsuko was waiting, standing behind the three consoles monitoring the flitters and the field traffic.

"Interrogative power status, Outrider three. Interrogative power status."

"Port thruster in the yellow. Point seven zero. Starboard in the red. Point five zero and falling."

Matsuko drew Gerswin aside.

"Zeigler took three out, with Frantz as copilot. Topographic profiles, shot at an angle, for the ecologists. Zeigler hit a sheer line wrong, forgot to lock his harness, hit the overhead. Out cold."

"You need me to get her back? Talk her in?"

"Stet."

Gerswin pulled a seat up to the center console and scanned the screens, trying to assimilate the position of the disabled flitter and the meteorological data.

Without thinking, his head was shaking.

"Outrider three, Gerswin here. Interrogative full power on starboard thruster."

"Point five at the detente."

"Interrogative altitude and airspeed."

"Altitude is one thousand minus. Airspeed is one fifty. Rate of descent is one hundred per minute on full power. Estimated time on starboard thruster is two to five minutes."

Gerswin looked at Matsuko, blanking the comm link.

"She's over the rock piles. Take her more than six minutes to clear."

His eyes took in the displays, measuring, trying to calculate a vector to the flatlands or even the plains hills that would not force her to cross the sheer line again.

The line that had crippled the pilot and the flitter was nearly stationary, due east of Outrider three.

"Turn one six five."

"Turning one six five. Power on starboard thruster is point four and falling. Power on port is point six. Altitude above ground nine hundred minus."

Gerswin watched as the blip representing the flitter edged more southward toward the flattest terrain possible.

"Outrider three. Lag factor on that radalt is fifty meters. Lag factor is fifty meters."

"Stet. Lag factor is fifty."

"Interrogative status on tail compensator. Status on compensator."

"Tail compensator—what . . . ?"

"Status of tail compensator." Gerswin's fingers curled around the console keyboard's edge, digging in, but his voice remained level.

"Compensator has no reading. Crew visual indicates no compensator."

"Stet. No compensator. Begin blade deployment sequence. I say again. Begin blade deployment sequence."

"Stet. Beginning blade deployment sequence."

"Outrider three. When the blades lock, hit the power disconnect. As soon as the blades lock, hit the power disconnect, and dump the thrusters. Do you understand?"

"Blades locked, hit the disconnect . . . dump thrusters."

"That's affirmative. No power descent. Pick out the levelest spot you can dead ahead. Keep your nose down. Radalt hits one fifty, you flare. Flare at one fifty. At one hundred, pull full blade angle. One hundred, full blade angle."

"Stet. No power flare at one fifty, full blade angle at one hundred."

"That's affirmative."

Matsuko's hand blanked the comm link.

"What are you doing?"

Gerswin did not take his eyes off the console.

"No power for a turn, not without hitting the sheer line. Not enough power or time to cross the rock ridge ahead. No compensator for a powered blade descent. Flat rock auto is the best I can do."

He brushed Matsuko's hands from the console.

"Interrogative altitude, airspeed."

"Passing four hundred at one hundred." The woman's voice was low, but clear and steady.

"Nose up. Nose up, three. Airspeed at sixty to seventy as you pass two hundred."

"Stet. Nose up. Passing two fifty, airspeed, eighty."

"Nose down a shade."

"Stet. Nose down. Speed seventy."

"Flare at one fifty. Flare at one fifty."

"Flaring—"

The transmission ended as if cut by a knife.

Gerswin stood so abruptly the swivel slammed and clattered into the console behind.

"Was that a transmission loss?" asked a new voice.

Gerswin shook his head, slowly, forcing himself to unclench his tightened fists. He looked at the two console screens, then at the floor.

Matsuko looked at Gerswin's face, then snapped. "Is two ready to lift?"

"Yes, ser."

"Launch and vector to three's last position. Medic on board?"

"That's affirmative, ser."

"Launch."

"Two. Outrider two, this is Opswatch. Cleared to lift. Vector to target is three four five. Three four five."

"Opswatch, Outrider two, lifting. Will be turning three four five."

Gerswin looked at the met screen, then at Matsuko.

"Captain, that vector's wrong. They'll cross the sheer line."

The tech on the end console began computing.

"He's right."

"Outrider two. Course correction. Course correction. Sheer line at three five zero. Turn two seven zero. Two seven zero."

"Thanks, Opswatch. Turning two seven zero. How long this course?"

"Outrider two. Estimate five minutes, then a vector of zero zero five."

"Stet. Turning two seven zero. Climbing to one thousand. Climbing to one thousand."

"Understand climbing to one thousand."

Gerswin took his eyes away from the screens and stepped farther back, still shaking his head slowly, as if unable to believe that the flitter had crashed into the rocky flats northwest of the Imperial base.

". . . killer planet . . . Istvenn take it. . . ."

". . . the lieutenant couldn't . . . no one could have . . ."

Gerswin's steps took him to the backless couch outside Matsuko's office, and he sat down, staring at nothing, trying not to think about how Miri Frantz must have felt as the flitter mashed into the rocky upthrusts with both forward speed and a descent rate approaching a thousand meters a minute.

But what else could he have suggested? Leaving her on thrusters would have plowed her into solid rock at nearly two hundred kays. If only he'd tried to get a better reading on the actual terrain slope. . . . But there had been so little time.

If he'd been there. . . . But he wouldn't have flown through a sheer line unprepared.

". . . have the target in sight . . ."

Gerswin's ears caught the transmission from Outrider two, and he jerked himself erect, walking back to the control area, standing quietly behind the swivel where Captain Matsuko sat.

"Understand you have the target in sight?"

"That's affirmative. Deploying blades now."

"Stet. Understand blade deployment."

The console was silent, with only a single amber blip, motionless, as the flitter began its descent.

"Interrogative target status."

"Opswatch. Target has sustained maximum structural damage. Maximum structural damage."

Matsuko winced. Gerswin and the other pilots understood the implications of the shorthand expression.

Maximum structural damage to the flitter meant maximum structural damage to the crew.

A hush dropped over the operations area, as the surrounding techs and officers waited.

"Opswatch. Hovering over target. Lowering medic. Preliminary indication is that target crew totally immobile. Totally immobile. Will report later."

"Stet, three. Standing by for later report."

Gerswin took a last glance at the screens and moved away until he was in the silent and open corridor between the comm consoles and the now-vacant administrative section of Operations.

He knew the results, but hoped against hope that someone, somehow, had survived the crash, even though flitters did not carry the same crash capsules as shuttles.

The muted sound of murmurs in the control section died away enough that Gerswin could hear the last of Outrider two's transmission.

". . . say again, no survivors . . ."

The I.S.S. lieutenant took a deep breath, squared his shoulders, and started toward the exit portal. He needed to be alone.

Ignoring the sound of steps behind him, he reached the portal before Matsuko touched his arm.

Gerswin stopped.

Matsuko gestured, as if to pull him aside, and the lieutenant followed.

"Greg. You did the best you could, the best anyone could have."

Gerswin swallowed.

"I made a mistake. Wouldn't have if I'd been in the cockpit, but so hard to do through comm link."

"Mistake?"

"Radalt has vertical and horizontal lag. Makes a difference in rugged terrain. She wasn't experienced enough to look beyond the heads-up to gauge terrain. Can't do that over remote."

He shook his head again.

Matsuko shook his head slowly in reply. "I liked Zeigler, and . . . Miri . . . you know . . . but, you . . . Can't you not . . ."

Gerswin looked at the polished tiles of the floor, knowing Matsuko had broken off his response and was studying his face.

"Look, Greg. Nobody else could have given her half a chance."

"Half wasn't enough."

"No. But unless you can find another dozen like you, it's better than she would have gotten otherwise. Zeigler bent orbit, not you. You even had enough sense to keep the recovery bird from doing the same thing. Don't forget that."

Gerswin said nothing.

Matsuko patted him on the shoulder.

"You try too hard to be perfect. Do the best you can, but don't expect perfection on everything, all the time, even when lives are at stake. That's a bigger trap. Think about it."

Matsuko stepped back to let Gerswin leave.

Gerswin could feel the deputy ops boss's eyes on his back long after the portal had closed between them, long after he had retreated to his quarters.

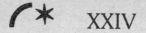 XXIV

"Tell me, Greg. Does the flitter do what you want? Or do you make it do what you want?"

Mahmood scarcely looked up from his console as he asked the question.

"What does that mean? Another theoretical question?" snapped Gerswin, still wearing his flight gear.

"Not so theoretical as you think. Presumably, you have a goal in mind. You seem to assume that the goal is independent of the means."

"No. Even a dumb devilkid knows that the means will influence the end." The pilot took four steps away from the console, turned, and paced back toward the biologist.

"Then why don't you apply that knowledge to your flight techniques? Without looking at the maintenance records, I'd be willing to bet that while you have the best record of accomplishment, you also have the record of most damage to equipment."

"Mahmood, have you ever tried to fly gently through the fringes of a landspout? Or to gather data through stone rains and acid winds?"

"Have you?"

"I've flown through everything."

"Gently?"

"You don't understand."

"Greg. I'm not fighting you. You are fighting yourself."

"Fighting myself?" Gerswin paced toward the blank inner wall, and turned before reaching it, pacing back toward the man and the console.

"There are at least two ways to do anything. Usually, the best way requires both the most understanding and the most direct application of that understanding. Very few people are capable of that. Mostly frustrated athletes."

Gerswin frowned. Again, the philosophical biologist refused

102

to get to the point. He didn't know why he ended up coming back to listen all the time. Except . . . he brushed the thought aside.

"Frustrated athletes? Would you stoop to explain that?"

"No. Not unless you will consider stooping to listen, and begin by stopping that continuous pacing. Sit down."

Gerswin sighed. Loudly, and partly for effect. He let himself thud into the low couch, turned and let one leg dangle over the arm as he faced the other.

The biologist straightened behind the console, and, for the first time, concentrated directly on the pilot.

"Greg, think about it this way. Our military culture tends to separate people into those who can build or repair things and those who use them. You are a pilot and an officer, trained to understand enough about technology and people to use both. Your techs understand how to repair things, but not really enough about their missions for you to be able to use their products to the fullest degree possible."

Mahmood waited.

Finally, Gerswin answered.

"So you think I'm just a user? That it's bad to be just a user?"

"I never said that. Nor did I say that you were. I merely made an observation on the training imparted by our system. Would you say that what you do with a flitter requires as much as you can get from the machine?"

"Sometimes more."

"Have you really ever studied the flitter? From each single composite plate up? From a series of stress vectors? Have you ever tried to rebuild one with the technicians?"

"Of course not. I'm not a tech."

Again, Mahmood waited.

"Where are you going? What are you asking? You telling me that I ought to be a tech?"

"Not exactly. Let me ask the question more directly. How can you get the most out of your flitter if you have no feel beyond the superficial?" Mahmood waved aside the objection the pilot was beginning to voice. "Yes, I know. You have your spec charts, and your performance envelopes, or whatever all the facts are that you learn. You are taught all the maneuvers that a flitter will take, and the associated stresses. But who designed those maneuvers? Who set those limits? And how? By trial and error? Or did someone really dig into what a flitter is and what a pilot can do and put the two together?"

"Test pilot."

"Are you a test pilot?"

"No."

"Do you want to be one? Or better than one?"

"Of course."

"Then how do you propose doing it? By going out and doing the same thing day after day? Destroying flitter after flitter, and maybe youself in the process, by going beyond the established numbers without understanding the machine?"

"You make it sound so simple. Just go out and be a tech. Learn the flitter. Be an instant expert!"

"No. I never said that. You said that. I never said it would be easy. I never said it wouldn't take time. I only said that it was the best way, and the hardest."

Gerswin bounced to his feet.

"I don't know why I listen to you."

Mahmood did not respond, just let his dark eyes meet the hawk-yellow glare of the young pilot's.

Finally, the hawk-eyed one looked away.

"Thanks, Mahmood. I think."

And he was gone, quick steps echoing in the long corridor outside.

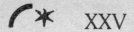 XXV

Fluorescent lines on the clay marked the landing area.

Gerswin lined up the cargo skitter, sluggish with the weight of the technical team stuffed into the passenger section and with the effect of the higher altitude, on the rough square between the hills and below the target mountain.

As the nose came up, he began twisting more and more power to the thrusters, bleeding off airspeed as the skitter wallowed downward. Theoretically, the skitter had more than enough power, but the currents swirling around the hills to the north and south of the landing site had left him the choice of an approach into the wind—with the mountain blocking any wave-off—or with a downwind approach with a steeper descent angle, but room for error. Gerswin had chosen the downwind approach. At least that way he could break it off without plowing into the mountains.

He didn't expect any ground cushion, and there wasn't any as the skitter mushed down and thumped onto the ever-present purpled clay well within the landing box that had been outlined by the advance team.

"Perdry!" he called. "Too much gusting here. Make them sit tight until I fold the blades and shut down."

The pilot knew the major would complain, at least to himself, but the last thing Gerswin wanted was some eager beaver tech, running out after the greatest find of the old technology, getting himself bisected by a rotor caught in the uneven gusts.

His fingers moved through the retraction sequence quickly but evenly.

"Blade retraction complete," he announced. "Clear to disembark."

As Perdry let down the ramp, Gerswin methodically continued through the shutdown checklist, matching his actions against the lightlist on the console.

By the time he had secured the cockpit, the entire technical team had disappeared over the rise, and he and Perdry were left with the skitter. The cargo, except for a few light cases, also remained, untouched.

Gerswin frowned. Was there any reason why he couldn't see what all the enthusiasm was about?

"Perdry?"

"Yes, Lieutenant?"

"I'm going to walk up there and take a look. When I come back, you can. Think one of us ought to stay with the bird."

"Fine with me, Lieutenant. They're going to be here a while. A long while. Besides, I saw it."

"Why do you think they'll be here a while?"

"They left all their gear just to take a look. And what they're looking at isn't an easy orbit break."

Gerswin inclined his head quizzically.

"Big doors, like huge portals into the mountainside. They're carving away the lock with the lasers, but so far nothing touches the metal. Never will, I'll bet."

Gerswin closed the canopy, swung himself down from the high steps in the fusilage, and jumped the last meter to the hard clay.

"See you later, Lieutenant," called Perdry. His long legs dangled from the side of the ramp where he sat staring up at the few patches of grass between the rocks, mostly on the higher parts of the hillside that was mainly red sandstone.

Gerswin took the pathway toward the ridgetop nearly at a trot, absently noting the lack of grubushes and the signs of coyotes or rats, and wondering why. Grubushes and rats existed in the worst of areas. But he did not smell a high level of landpoisons.

At the top of the ridge, he stopped and looked. Scarcely fifty meters below, the technical team was gathered around a portable screen. Fifty meters beyond them—

Massive! That was the first word for the metal portals that hulked above the chunks of fused stone that had already been carved away from the black metal. With the darkness of the metal that reflected no light, they could have been the proverbial Gates to Hades, looming as they did out of the mountainside that rose another thousand meters above them.

As he began down the gentle slope, a number of incongruities stood out.

For one, the stone chunks that had been carved away by the Imperial tech team's lasers were the same glassy texture all the way through. Second, the last thirty meters before the gates was not clay, but the same blackish and glossy stone that had been carved from the area surrounding the gates. Third, the gates were sealed, not merely closed. Two half-meter wide black metal beams, seamless, crossed the entire front of the gates, including the thin line that marked the break between the two.

Gerswin moved silently downward until he could hear the discussion, but not so closely that he seemed to be eavesdropping. Only the first set of Imperial physicians had noted, right after his initial capture, his exceptional hearing and actual reflex speed, and he had done his best since to insure that both were overlooked. Recent examinations indicated only very good physical abilities.

". . . some sort of nuclear bonding. Anything that could break the bond would probably destroy most of this mountain range."

"Why not bring in an accelerator?"

"Darden, do you happen to have one stashed in orbit? Or do you have the fifty million creds it would take to get one here and assemble it?"

"So a frontal approach can't work."

"Why don't we bore parallel until there isn't any shielding and come in from the side?"

"Do you have any guarantee that they didn't surround the entire complex with that black metal shielding?"

"Look at it. It had to be added later. Along with the beams. It's just plated over everything, even over the joint between the two doors. There's no break at all. Besides, if they could have shielded the whole thing with a nuclear bond, why build it under a mountain?"

"Any other ideas?"

The conversation lapsed for a moment, except for a few mumbles Gerswin could not hear clearly enough to understand.

"Then we'll try Peelsley's idea. Take the number one laser bore and probe the sides. Take the most promising, and see if we can find a weak spot."

Gerswin watched as the cart was wheeled up to the rock next to the right hand door and connected to the pulse accumulators, which were, in turn, connected to the portable generator.

The pilot shrugged and walked back to the skitter.

Perdry was still propped against the frame of the open ramp door, legs dangling down. He was eating from a ration pack.

"Got another pack here, Lieutenant. Want some?"

"Wouldn't mind at all. Techs have their own."

The crewman leaned back to reach behind himself and brought forward the square pack. Field issue, cold but edible, and about half protein, half carbohydrate.

Gerswin found himself wolfing the ration, metallic overtaste and all.

"Lieutenant?"

"Ummmm." Gerswin had to swallow before he could answer.

"What are those things?"

"Don't know. Look like the Gates to Hades. Expect there's a lot hidden here on Old Earth, if you knew where to look."

"Is it true that they could do things that the Empire still hasn't figured out?"

"Could be," the pilot mumbled while gulping down the last of the cakebread. "There's a sphere in the weapons museum at the Academy that hasn't been broken with any weapon or tool short of a tachead.

"Maybe not that. Nobody's tried. Say it was pre-Federation, Old Earth make, just before the Collapse. About the size of a ball." He sketched a circle in the air with his right hand. "Weighs nearly as much as a corvette. Mass? Who knows? Doesn't seem to follow the laws we know. Takes special supports."

"Old Earth built it?"

"Who knows?" Gerswin shrugged. "It was found on an Old Earth installation, somewhere . . ."

Perdry tucked his legs up and braced them on the ramp edge.

"Could we build doors like those in the mountain?"

"Doors wouldn't be a problem," he answered deliberately, recalling the conversation he had overheard, "but the black metal they sealed them with . . . I don't think so."

"If they could do that, why did they let everything fall apart?"

Good question, thought Gerswin the devilkid. "Have to feed people, and something went wrong. Not enough food, not enough power, not enough time. Riots, fighting, starvation . . ."

"So we really don't know?"

"Not really."

Gerswin crumpled the recyclable container and put it into the bin built into the cargo door. Ducking back out, he stepped onto the ramp and stretched.

"Think I'll go back and see how they're doing. Unless you want to."

"No thanks, Lieutenant. Those big portals freeze me cold. Take your time."

Gerswin dropped off the cargo ramp and began the trek back up the hillside.

By the time Gerswin reached the technical team, the laser had disappeared into the deepening bore. Still visible were the two techs in self-contained suits.

A light rain of vaporized rock was dropping onto the clay/rock apron outside the tunnel, while the other techs and officers clustered around the portable screen.

Gerswin caught a motion out of the corner of his eye and drop-turned, but recovered when he realized it was one of the three sentries on the surrounding ridgetops.

A single tech, hands on hips, stood several paces away from the group that monopolized the planning screen. Gerswin forced himself to amble up slowly.

"How does it look?"

"It may take a while longer, Lieutenant. They slapped that black stuff and the beams over the whole thing. Then they covered it with rock and fused the rock solid. It looks like they did it to guard a tunnel into the mountain. They had to have done it in a hurry. The laser should get past the shielding before long. I'll bet it's less than five meters back."

Gerswin nodded, then asked, "Have you ever seen anything like this before?"

"No. I don't think anyone else has, either, if you can believe how excited the commander was. He sent off a message torp as soon as we got a good cube of the exterior. I'll bet he shows up as soon as we can get inside."

The pilot shook his head slowly, hoping the commander and commandant did not arrive with another complete entourage.

"You're right, Lieutenant. You're right."

While Gerswin wasn't exactly sure what he was right about, he decided to stay close to the tech, since the commander, assuming that distinguished officer did arrive, might not question anyone presumed with the technical party, but might well instruct Gerswin to stay with the skitter if he went back to the landing area.

The tech shivered in the rising chill of the afternoon wind, drawing his jacket tighter as the light dimmed.

Overhead the swirling gray clouds seemed a shade darker than usual, but Gerswin had already checked the meteorological situation. There were no landspouts in the area. Even had there been, few if any went beyond the first line of hills, and the gates were well beyond the first foothills.

The area seemed strangely quiet, and Gerswin and the tech looked up. The rain of recongealed stone had stopped, as had the hissing of the laser.

The pilot and the technician watched as the laser and the accumulator cart slowly backed from the tunnel bore, guided by the two suited techs.

The shorter suited figure, whose gray shiny suit did nothing to conceal her physical endowments, raised a clenched fist overhead and shook it.

"I guess the commander will miss the opening of the show, Lieutenant. Why don't you come along?"

The man grinned.

Gerswin repressed his own grin.

"I'd like to, thank you."

"It will be a bit, until the tunnel cools and we're sure there's decent air inside. They'll have to check for background radiation inside as well."

"Background radiation?"

"You couldn't prove it by me, but the only way I know to get the front of a mountain turned into solid glass is with a nuclear device."

"But there's no radiation outside, is there?"

"No. That just means they used a clean burst."

Gerswin took the time surveying the hillside, the clouds, and the massive gates themselves, still standing there in unshining black, as if Old Earth's ancients had been led to Hades and the gates barred behind them.

The gray of the clouds lightened and the wind dropped to a mere breeze.

Another equipment cart was trundled into the laser bore, where it remained for a time before being withdrawn. Another data bloc was taken from the cart and inserted into the portable screen console.

Whatever the results, they appeared satisfactory, from what Gerswin could see from all the heads nodding.

Major Hylton, the tall officer directing the operation, led the first group into the laser bore, less than two meters high.

The technician nodded at Gerswin, and the two trooped with the second group, just a few meters behind the major. Nearly half the party had to stoop.

After roughly eight meters, the tunnel veered to the left and broke into a dimly lit space. One by one, the officers and technicians, and, finally, the former devilkid, stepped through the ragged opening into a larger passage ten meters wide and more than five meters high.

Twin strips of glowing panels built flush into the ceiling lit the unadorned passage, unless the light blue, fist-sized, square tiles which walled the sides of the corridor could be considered decoration.

Looking to the left, Gerswin could see only a set of three meter high doors, black metal finished and also apparently welded shut. There was no indication of the giant gates which stood on the far side.

He turned back and looked at the corridor before the party.

The passage sloped downward gradually for another fifty meters to end in still another set of doors. The massive endurasteel doors, each three meters high and two meters wide, hung open, sitting intact on twin hinges each longer than Gerswin's arm.

The pilot sniffed. The air had but the slightest tinge of age to it, and Gerswin could feel the hint of a breeze coming from the open doors.

"Why didn't they lock those as well?" asked Major Hylton.

"Maybe they figured anyone who could break the exterior bonds could break these as well."

"No time," muttered Gerswin, but the corridor was so silent

that his low words carried to the major, who turned to identify the speaker.

"That might be, Lieutenant. That might be."

The major glanced back at the sealed doors behind them and at the ragged breach through the tiled wall.

"Darden, you and N'Bolgia stay here. Just in case," ordered the major.

In case of what, wondered Gerswin. Two people won't be able to stop those doors if they're powered.

Despite his misgivings, he followed the major and the others through the openings and into a square hallway, from which branched three other corridors.

The major took the right hand one, the one which had a red arrow pointing again downward. That corridor ended abruptly less than a hundred meters farther when it expanded into an archway which led to a semicircular hall. The hall was filled with low, wide consoles arranged in arcs facing the circular section of wall. On the wall stretched a map of the Earth, continent by continent.

Gerswin frowned at the arbitrary markings within the continents, then relaxed as he realized they represented not only the topography, but some sort of political boundaries.

He searched and found the Noram boundaries and tried to compare them mentally with what his current charts showed. The wall display was different. To what degree he was uncertain, although some of the differences were obvious. While the coastal areas seemed the same, off the western Noram coasts, where the display showed ocean, there were also a series of lines enclosing "political" boundaries, as if to indicate that the continent had extended farther once than it now did.

Several moments passed as the group surveyed the room.

"Look!"

Gerswin studied the map again, trying to figure out what he was to look for, when he saw the blinking red dot slowly traversing from the lower left toward the upper right.

He pulled at his chin. Something else about the wall map bothered him, not just the moving dot, although he wondered about it as well.

His mouth dropped as it hit him all at once, and he wanted to pound his own head for his slowness in understanding. The display was neither painted nor embossed, not a static display, but a composite projection.

The display showed the actual terrain as it existed right at the moment. The lines represented some sort of governmental or political boundaries dating back to the time the projection had been developed. That was why the lines on the western Noram coast were projected out over the ocean.

But what were the occasional lights on the map? Some seemed stationary while others moved. Gerswin could see three red ones, two pale blue ones, and a green.

One of the red ones—stationary—seemed to match the position of orbit control.

"That's it!" he whispered, but his voice carried in the quiet.

"That's what, Lieutenant?" asked Major Hylton.

"Just a guess, Major. Red lights represent strange orbiting bodies. Blue and green are known, probably what remains of their network."

"Are you suggesting that this equipment is operational?"

"Has to be. One red light moves."

"After more than a thousand years, Lieutenant?"

Gerswin shrugged, wished he had kept his exclamation to himself. "Check it out. One red light should have orbit control position. Others may be captured satellites, hulks, objects in orbit. Wouldn't be surprised if the green or blue lights are satellites in orbit, maybe beaming information here . . . somewhere, somehow."

"That center light is about right for orbit control," offered one of the techs.

"If you're right, Lieutenant, this could be the find of the century. Think of it. Actual operating pre-Federation equipment."

Gerswin refrained from shaking his head. While they would have discovered what he had speculated, sooner or later, the discovery only left a sour taste in his mouth. Why, he could not have described, but the bitterness was hard to swallow.

He edged back toward the archway while the technicians' speculations continued.

"What sort of power . . ."

"Can you believe the clarity of that display? Must have a resolution . . ."

"Consoles sealed shut . . ."

Quietly, he ducked out and headed back up the passageway

to where the three corridors had branched. Since the two guards were on the outside of the portals, chatting to each other, where neither could see the junction, he was able to follow the green arrow without being challenged.

Despite the passage of who knew how many years, there was no dust on the smooth and seamless floor.

Gerswin shook his head. Could the Empire build something to last more than a dozen centuries, without any outside direction, and still have it function? He doubted it, and that bothered him as well.

What else lay under the scoured rolling hills and the rock of the mountains?

The green arrow led him to a series of five doors, plain ordinary hinged doors, doors that stood open.

Gerswin peered inside the first door.

Another narrow corridor beckoned, lined with doors at three meter intervals. The pilot walked down the passageway to the first door and stuck his head within.

His suspicions were correct. The small rooms were quarters, each with an alcove for a bunk, though none remained; a built-in desk with an oblong console, now covered with a flat metal plate; and two built-in lockers. Besides the gray metal of the built-ins and the console, nothing had been left.

A quick survey of the next few rooms showed only a similar pattern.

Gerswin retreated to the larger corridor and checked the second of the five doors. Same pattern. That was true of the third and fourth doors as well.

The fifth door led him down a wider corridor to a set of double doors, closed, but not locked. He glanced back the thirty meters to the open door before opening the double doors and stepping through. A vacant room, roughly thirty meters on a side, greeted him. On the far side, two sets of double doors, spaced equidistantly along the wall, stood closed.

Gerswin suspected he would find another room behind them, empty except for plated-over spots in the wall and flooring, but he crossed the room he would have described as a dining hall in quick steps and pushed back one of the swinging doors. It moved silently at his touch, and he looked into a narrower room with plated-over spots on walls and floors that had once been a kitchen. A sealed archway was the only other sign of an exit.

Gerswin nodded as he recrossed the ancient dining hall and retraced his steps back to the original junction. The two guards did not hear him as they discussed the merits of freefall dancing.

He slipped past the open portals and began to follow the black arrow. As he turned the first corner and walked toward another set of open portals, similar in size and construction to the pair he had just passed, he could hear the murmur of voices behind him.

Once he was through the still-shining portals, he stood at the top of a sharply descending ramp that made a right angle turn roughly every twenty meters. He started down.

The overhead lighting was still furnished by the twin panel strips built in flush with the overhead, still with the same constant intensity.

After what Gerswin judged to have been a descent of nearly fifty meters and four complete circuits, the corridor ended abruptly. Facing the pilot was a wall-to-wall, floor-to-ceiling sheet of the black metal that had sealed the main exterior gates. Unlike the outside, this time the metal was featureless, merely a smooth finish across the corridor.

In the middle, at eye-level, were a series of symbols. One was a red hand held up in the human halt signal. The second was comprised of three luminescent green triangles within a shining yellow circle. A single word was beneath, which Gerswin could not read. The third symbol was a skull and crossbones.

Gerswin smiled grimly in spite of himself. The message was clear.

After a last look to make sure the way was completely sealed, he turned and trudged back up the ramp.

He slowed as he heard the sound of approaching footsteps.

"Gerswin here!" he called.

"Lieutenant?"

"The same."

He waited as one of the techs peered around the corner, laser in hand.

"It's him, ser."

"What are you doing here? Why didn't you wait?" Leading the crew was Major Hylton.

"Just wanted to take a look around, ser. Didn't want to get in your way."

"Lieutenant, in the future, please refrain from exploring on your own. We could have failed to recognize you, and we do need some transportation back to Prime Base."

Gerswin smiled.

"Sorry, ser. I'll be more careful."

"What's down below?"

"Hades only knows. Sealed with that black metal about two turns down."

"Sealed?"

"Yes, ser. Three clear danger signals posted."

"Should see that . . ." muttered one of the techs standing next to the major.

"Yes, we should see that," repeated the senior officer.

Gerswin stepped to one side. "Probably more your orbit than mine, Major."

"Well . . . We should have at least an overall idea of what's here for our report."

Gerswin stood next to the wall as the dozen technicians followed the major on his downward travels.

Then he turned and climbed back up to the portals and the two guards, who were still swapping stories.

"Gerswin here," he announced. "I'm returning to the skitter to get ready for the return trip."

"Fine, Lieutenant."

"Hey, what's down there?"

"Something they'll wish they hadn't found. My guess, anyway."

At the inquisitive, nearly hurt look on Darden's face, Gerswin expanded his cryptic remark. "A current geographic projection still operating from satellite transmitters, a bunch of empty quarters, and a sealed tunnel they'll never open, marked with universal danger symbols. The projection seems to be updated moment by moment."

"Still operational?"

"Absolutely. The major doesn't know whether to be in ecstasy or worried as Hades."

"Worried is what he ought to be," opined N'Bolgia.

"You serious about that projection, Lieutenant?"

"Dead serious. Shows the mountains, the oceans. Think it even shows I.S.S. orbit control."

"Anything else?"

"That's enough. Sealed consoles, empty rooms. Place was closed down permanently for a reason. Don't understand why the projection was left operational."

"Doesn't make much sense."

"No. Not now." Gerswin shook his head. "Anyway, that's all."

"That's enough," offered N'Bolgia.

"Might be," returned Gerswin as he turned away from the two and headed back up the corridor toward the exit tunnel and the skitter.

Outside the clouds had lightened, and another group was making its way down the hillside from the ridge.

In the middle of the group, mostly officers, Gerswin could make out the slightly rounded figure of the commandant, Senior Commander Mestaffa.

Gerswin sighed and waited, standing beside the laser-bored tunnel until the others reached it.

"Lieutenant, have you seen Major Hylton?"

"Yes, ser. He is checking out the installation."

"Installation?"

"Yes, ser. I am sure the major will be able to brief you. It begins about eight meters back into this tunnel. That's the entrance to the old structure. Fully lit."

Gerswin did not smile at the thought of acting more like a tour guide than a pilot.

"Thank you, Lieutenant."

"Yes, ser."

Gerswin started to head back toward his skitter when Captain Carfoos snapped, "Where are you going?"

"Back to my skitter, Captain. Make sure it's ready for the return. Can't leave it here overnight. So I either take it back empty or full. Need to get it preflighted and ready."

"All right, Lieutenant." Carfoos tapped a Marine near the rear of those waiting in line to follow the commandant. "Kyler, you take the lieutenant's position here."

"Yes, ser."

Gerswin snapped a salute at the captain and took a long first stride toward the skitter. Trust some career types to post a guard long after the real need had passed.

The wind swept through his hair as he reached the ridgetop and looked down. Four skitters were lined up across the flat space below.

He started down.

Perdry was checking the tail section when Gerswin reached the cargo ramp. The tech dropped to the clay and took several steps toward the pilot.

"Interesting, Lieutenant?"

"One way of describing it."

In short sentences, Gerswin recounted his tour of the ancient installation, concluding with his encounter with the commandant and his entourage.

"Sounds like them," observed Perdry, pointing in the general direction of the other three skitters. "Took three to bring in what we brought with one."

Gerswin nodded slightly.

"Lieutenant? That place bad news?"

"I think so, Perdry. Think so. But not for the reasons they think. Has secrets they won't be able to understand. Drive them crazy with worry. Wonder what else is hidden here."

"Bad news," affirmed the tech. "Definite bad news." But he returned to his checks.

Gerswin started on the other side of the skitter, letting the mystery of the gates drop into his subconscious, for the moment.

Not that he could do anything at all. Not now, perhaps not ever.

(* XXVI

"Put on your gloves first, Lieutenant," suggested Markin.

"Gloves?"

"The plasthins. You can still feel what you're working with."

Gerswin frowned. "Why the gloves?"

"The turbine blades are polished as smooth as we can get them. The tolerances are in thousandths of millimeters. You touch that blade edge with your fingertip—there's a touch of dampness and acid there. Also, it's sharp enough to cut your finger. Then we have to worry about blood and water and acid. Sooner or later, that could unbalance the blade or weaken it." Markin laughed.

Gerswin did not bother to hide his puzzled expression.

"That's the official line. But most times, especially here, one of you hotshots will beat the blades to frags before they have a chance to weaken."

Gerswin finished pulling on the ultrathin tech gloves.

"So why the gloves?"

"A couple of reasons. It gets the techs in the habit of being careful around delicate machinery. Also keeps you from carrying in contaminants that really could scratch things up."

Markin stood by the thruster access panel.

"Move over here, Lieutenant."

Gerswin stood to the left, but as close as he could to see what Markin was doing.

"Here's the standard access, the one you use for a preflight. Now . . . See here? Through the tech access panels? Don't open this in the open hangar bays or out in the field except in an emergency. It will change the temperature too quickly and let in contaminants at the ring level."

Gerswin edged forward.

Markin pointed.

"This is what I wanted to show you. You can see the joint here, the whole series."

The tech touched the base of one of the individual blades with his gloved fingertips and gently worked it free. The entire curved blade was soon in his hand, nearly half a meter long and perhaps ten centimeters wide, the curve so slight as to be forgotten, so smooth it was mirrorlike in finish despite the darkness of the alloy.

"See how easy it comes out?"

Gerswin nodded.

"Don't you wonder why it stays in when you're flying?"

"Never thought about it."

"All right. You saw how I took it out. You try another one."

Gingerly, gingerly, the lieutenant touched a blade. He could feel the wobble, though he could not see the motion, as he eased it out of the mounting ring.

"Now put it back in."

Gerswin did, with the same exaggerated care, oblivious to whatever Markin was doing.

"Now take mine and replace it."

Gerswin took the proferred blade. It felt faintly warm to the touch even through the plasthin gloves, which were supposed to be thermally insulated.

He eased it into the slot, but for some reason, the blade jammed when it was halfway into place.

"Seems jammed."

"Leave it there. Don't push it. Don't force it. Just support it."

The pilot frowned, but did as he was told.

"Does it feel cooler now?"

"Yes."

"Try again. With just a tiny bit of pressure. Just a bit."

The blade eased most of the way in, but an edge remained, not visible, but Gerswin could tell.

"There's an edge stuck out."

"Is there?"

"I'm sure."

Markin lifted a scopelike instrument from the kit at his feet and stood beside Gerswin, who stepped back to let the tech look at the mounting ring.

"Where?"

"There."

"You're right." Markin put down the instrument. "We'll wait a moment, till it cools down enough to get out easily."

"Cool down? You mean the blades are that heat-sensitive?"

"I played a bit of a trick on you, Lieutenant. I gave you full therm thins there, for hot engine work. When you're done, I'd like them back."

Gerswin shook his head.

"Not sure I understand, Markin."

"Simple, ser. The thruster blades and the mounts are heat sensitive. Cold now . . . they are. That's why the blades are loose. If you shook the engine without the seal ring in place, every one would fall out.

"While you were taking out the second blade, I switched blades and used a lasetorch on the one I gave you to heat it up. That's what happens when you light off. As the thruster speed builds, the heat increases, blades tighten.

"Now, before we forget, would you pull the one you put in?"

Gerswin was tempted to pull the wrong one out of perversity, until he remembered he might be the one flying with the flawed blade. He handed the substitute, which had cooled enough to slide out easily, to Markin, who examined it with the scopelike instrument.

"Stet. Right one, or should I say wrong one," grunted the tech. "Here's the right one. Want to put it in?"

"If you don't mind."

"Go ahead. You're the pilot who'll fly it."

Gerswin tried to insure that the blade was seated correctly and identically to the others.

He felt relieved when Markin inspected his work with the instrument and rechecked the retaining seal. As he waited while Markin reclosed the tech access panel and then the preflight panel, he let his eyes run over the smooth finish of the flitter, admiring the way in which the techs had managed to return it to flying condition time after time.

"Lieutenant, the question is: Did you get the point?"

"Markin, I'm just a dumb pilot. Can see the reason for care. If something got inside the housing once the thruster heated up, you would get increased stress on both blade and housing. Enough to cause a fracture?"

"Lieutenant, I'll give you half. You might make a better tech than a pilot. That's the tech answer."

Gerswin shook his head. What was the pilot answer?

Markin smiled.

"Lieutenant, what happens if you're in a hurry and feed full power to that thruster before the blades have heated up?"

Gerswin almost pulled at his chin with the gloves still on his hands, then jerked his left hand away, realizing that his skin was damp and not wanting to contaminate the gloves.

"Oh . . . Sorry, Markin. Not thinking clearly. If the blades aren't tight, they'd vibrate. Could that vibration snap them at the base?"

"They're probably stronger than that," answered the tech, "but if you had some that had already been stressed by too many full power cold starts, you could throw at least one. And if it let loose at the wrong angle, you'd lose the whole thruster."

Gerswin shivered.

"Would it go through the housing?"

"Never seen that. The composite is tough. A loose blade could bounce back into the fuel line sprays."

This time Gerswin nodded slowly.

"Guess I've got a lot to learn, Markin."

"You're young, Lieutenant. You got time. Especially here, you have time."

Gerswin nodded again, slowly pulling the thin thermal gloves off from the wrist backward, careful not to touch the outside surfaces.

"See you tomorrow, Lieutenant."

"Tomorrow, Markin," agreed the pilot.

Tomorrow, and tomorrow.

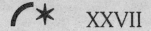 XXVII

Gerswin recognized Captain Carfoos. The last time he had seen the rail-thin officer with the limp brown hair had been outside the Gates of Hades, when both the commandant and Carfoos had assumed that Gerswin was a sentry.

At the recollection, Gerswin repressed a snort.

"Major Hylton is waiting. Go on in, Lieutenant."

Gerswin wondered at the tone of the captain's voice, which mirrored indifference or resignation. Gerswin seldom saw Carfoos, and could not tell what the flat inflections meant.

"Yes, ser."

The major was alone.

"Sit down, Lieutenant."

Gerswin took the armchair across the console from the major.

"We have a problem, Lieutenant. Not a major one, but one of which the commandant and I felt you should be apprised, since you were in at the beginning."

"Something to do with the black gates into the mountain?"

The major nodded. "The Gates to Hades, as they are popularly called around the base." He cleared his throat. "We had hoped to find some material, some artifacts, which might give us an insight into pre-Federation high technology, particularly into the composition of that nuclear bonding metal.

"We were successful, in a way. We did get an insight."

Major Hylton motioned to the junior officer.

"Come over here, Lieutenant, where you can see the screen."

The major moved his swivel to one side. Gerswin stood and moved around the console to the major's left.

"Watch. We found one operating console, but it was locked—except to provide the following message. After we copied the message—you'll see and hear it in a minute—we tried to analyze both the console and the message, but when we opened the console, which took a stepped-up cutting laser, it triggered some sort of destruct circuitry that none of our scans had even revealed. The whole thing melted down."

The major frowned and looked back at his screen. "So did everything else. The lighting, the screen wall projection are gone. So far, at least, the orbital controllers have had no luck in locating the feeder satellites."

Gerswin kept from shaking his head and waited.

Major Hylton touched a stud on the console.

A text was displayed on the screen, slowly scrolling upward, with the top line fading as it moved off the top as another replaced it at the bottom of the screen. Gerswin could pick out some of the words, but many were totally unfamiliar, and the thrust of the message eluded him.

This time, he did shake his head.

"I thought that with your background you might have a better understanding than any of us did the first time through."

"No, ser. Got some words, but that's it, and most of them are Imperial. Remember, there is really no written language left on Old Earth, especially for a devilkid."

"Devilkid?"

"Types like me. Running around outside the shambletowns."

"I see."

The major cleared his throat again. "In addition, there was an audio tape." He touched another stud.

Ding!

The single clear tone echoed through the office before the words began to roll from the console speakers.

This time Gerswin caught some of the phrases, recognizing that the intonation was closer to shambletown than Imperial. The ancient voice tolled like bells from the oldest cathedrals of New Colora, and Gerswin shivered at some of the phrases.

"What do you think, Lieutenant?"

"Warning, with the sound of a dirge."

"Did you understand what was said?"

"Not all of it, but enough to know that unless we understand a lot more than they did, we'd better not play with their tools."

Hylton frowned. "You understood more than I did, more than I still do when I hear it." He pointed vaguely toward the screen. "Here's the translation into modern Imperial, at least according to the scholar from New Avalon. Both text and verbal messages match, of course."

The written version was not as long as it had sounded. Gerswin watched the words march up the screen, each one pounding against him like a laser against his personal screens.

To our future, should there be one:

This was once a military installation before we put aside weapons based on our planet. Would that we had put aside the other dangers.

The outside gates were designed to bar anyone with less than advanced technology; the interior precautions are designed to stop all but the most enlightened.

The satellite map was left to show the product of a somewhat advanced technology and to provide a record should a great time have passed.

You may be beyond us, and our secrets may be both insignificant or incomprehensibly simplistic. In those cases, this message is irrelevant.

If you are puzzled by the black metal bonding and cannot conceive of any way to breach it, do not try. Beyond the metal lies only those radioactive wastes from the most hellish weapons and systems ever conceived by the mind of man. The wastes are buried in solid granite far beneath the installation, and surrounding the granite, itself enhanced in density, is a shield of impermite, the black metal.

Why do we leave such a heritage? It is possible that a future society may need those resources. While we cannot conceive of such a need, we have secured them. Even we could not reclaim them, had we the time. Anyone who has the ability to recover them should be aware of their legacy. A complete listing of the materials follows this message.

Today, our vaunted technology is beginning to take its revenge upon our planet.

The ocean levels are rising and the mean global temperature is increasing. The winds are steadily wreaking more destruction, and the earth can no longer sustain the billions who must eat.

We have reached the stars, but the stars cannot reach us. We have tried to rebuild our sister planets to sustain life, but cannot complete that effort, for those resources have been diverted to produce food now that our arable land is vanishing.

We had attained an uneasy global peace, based on sufficient food for all. But the food is no longer sufficient, and the riots have begun.

Nothing is certain, nor whether this message will survive. No monument upon the tortured face of the Earth is assured of survival, for already the winds throw boulders across the high plains. Nor will the warrens beneath the surface long survive, not when so many organic toxics permeate the very soils and rocks of the continents.

This is not the original message of this monument. The installation was converted once from its military purpose to a memorial for that peace which we felt would be permanent, and as a monument to the success of our technology. We have converted it once more.

Call it a mausoleum, and learn from what you see, and from what you do not.

Gerswin looked up.

The major said nothing, waiting for Gerswin's reaction.

"So that *was* what happened."

"You speak as if it were nothing new."

"Close enough to the shambletown legends."

"Shambletown?"

"That's where the people live now. The descendants of most of the survivors. In the shambletowns."

"Oh, that's what they're called."

Gerswin just nodded, puzzled at the major's apparent indifference to the scope of what he had just reviewed, even if the senior officer had seen it a dozen times.

"Anyway, Lieutenant, I wanted you to hear the cube and see the translation, since you were there. I wanted to make sure that you understand the situation."

Gerswin shifted his weight.

The major looked up at him, seemingly unaware that Gerswin had been standing the entire time, but said nothing.

"What comes next, ser?"

"We've referred it to High Command and resealed the tunnel for the time being. The scientists tell me that not even a tachead would dent that material. There's some low-level background radiation around the outside gates. It would seem that someone tried a hellburner, unsuccessfully, against them. A long time ago. All it did was melt rock over and around them."

This time Gerswin did not comment.

The major shrugged. "What else can I do? No equipment to do more is available. No one seems interested."

Gerswin repressed a nod.

"Could be discouraging if the knowledge became widespread," he volunteered.

"It could be," affirmed the major, "but it wouldn't change anything. I doubt that the Emperor would broadcast that Old Earth had a pre-Collapse technology which we still cannot match."

"I understand, ser."

"I believe you do, Lieutenant. I believe you do, but not for the same reasons." He sighed. "But that's not the issue." The major stood. "Do you have any more questions?"

"No, ser. Appreciate your sharing this."

"Just my duty, Lieutenant. Just my duty." He gestured toward the portal. "Have a good tour."

"Thank you, ser."

Outside in the staff office, Captain Carfoos glanced up and fixed a glare on Gerswin. "You done, Lieutenant?"

"Yes, ser."

"Then we'll see you at mess some time."

"Yes, ser."

Gerswin turned and walked out, not for the Officers' Mess, but for his own quarters.

He wished Mahmood were still on Old Earth, but the senior ecologist had left nearly a standard year earlier on the *Casimir*, which had carried in the new ratings and officers and carried out those going on to new and generally better opportunities.

Not that Mahmood had continued in the Service. The former ecological officer was doubtlessly now fully ensconced in his new position as the Chairman of Ecology at the University of Medina.

"But why?" Gerswin had asked. "Why?"

"My studies and recommendations here are complete, Greg. There isn't much more I can do. I'm a scholar, just a scholar. All I can do is to get people to think."

The memory of that statement still churned Gerswin's stomach if he thought too much about it.

So much knowledge . . . unused . . . lost . . . ignored . . . as if no one cared, as if no one remembered the tired planet that had destroyed itself to give men the stars.

He tightened his lips without breaking step.

(*   XXVIII

The lieutenant showed the sketch and specifications to the technician.

"Can it be done, Markin? With the balances like that?"

"Strange-looking knife, if you ask me, Lieutenant."

"Need weight, penetrating power."

"I don't see how it could be effective much beyond five, six meters."

"Computer says it will do what I want up to six meters all the time. Beyond that . . ." The lieutenant shrugged.

"The weight specifications make it heavy. I'd sure rely on a stunner. Could you even throw this thing?" The technician lifted the sheet as if to somehow better picture the weapon.

"Can't throw it until I have one in hand. Like at least three, but probably need five or six, if we could manage it."

"We?"

"I'd like to help. Want to understand how. They may have to last me a long time, and the next time you'll be in some other forsaken system."

Markin chuckled.

"Lieutenant, any time you want to use your hands is fine with me. We'll use one of the out-of-the-way bays, where the commander doesn't see one of his officers, Istvenn forbid, dirtying his hands and learning metalwork."

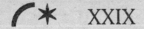

XXIX

Gerswin checked the time. 1752. Too early to enter the mess.

He passed the mess portal and entered the next one, the one to the junior officers' lounge. Lieutenant Hermer sat in the recliner nearest the door, her tall figure buried in her own thoughts, her hair as dark as the black finish of the chair in which she sat. The small room, less than six meters on a side, was otherwise empty.

Gerswin saw a faxtab, obviously a recent reproduction of one from the latest supply ship, which meant the news inside was three to four weeks old. He picked up the flimsy sheets and began to read as he circled the table, unwilling to sit down in either the other recliner next to Lieutenant Hermer or in the too-soft bench couch.

Usually he ignored the faxtabs for the technical publications which he took off the screen in his quarters at night. The Service kept its bases up-to-date on technical information through the torp network, but items such as soft news, the latest updates on the Emperor and his Court, came through personal torp messages or the straight news bulletins fed into the commnet.

Faxtabs were a mixture of everything. Gerswin noted that Newparra was still under quarantine, and the *Okelley* was listed as returning from there, mainly because the son of a prominent baron was on the commodore's staff. Gerswin knew the replacement ship was the *Sandhurst*, a fact ignored in the once-over of the faxtab.

Absently, he turned to the second flimsy page. A name caught his eye, and he stopped.

His mouth dropped open as he read the small item:

His Grace, Merrel, son of the Duke of Triandna, and Caroljoy Montgrave Kerwin, daughter of Honore Balza

Dirien Kerwin, Admiral of the Fleet and Marshall of the Marines, were married under the Old Rite ceremonies at the Triandna Estates recently. The ceremony and reception were private, but the Emperor is reported to have attended, according to informed sources. No comment was available from either the Imperial Court or His Grace the Duke.

Gerswin put the faxtab down on the table.

Could he have expected anything else?

Five years, and he had sent nothing, said nothing, written nothing. Nor had she. Not that he had not thought about her. But what could he have sent to someone he was not even supposed to know?

He glanced over at Lieutenant Hermer, who was still buried in the old-fashioned text, then at the table. He checked the time. 1755. Still too early, and right now, he didn't want to stand at the edge of the table waiting for Captain Matsuko, who would arrive promptly at 1801.

Gerswin looked back down at the faxtab and its slightly scattered pages, then away, as if it burned his eyes.

"Forget it!" he muttered, louder than he intended.

"Forget what?" Lieutenant Hermer's head popped up from her text like a turtle's from its shell.

"Nothing, Faith. Nothing. Forgot anyone was here."

He turned away, shaking his head.

Hard it was, sometimes, for him to remember that he was just a devilkid from Old Earth, and one lucky enough to have gotten an I.S.S. commission.

"Are you all right, Greg?"

Faith Hermer had not gone back to her book, but had marked her place and closed it. She was standing by her swivel.

"I'm fine. Surprised, that's all."

He refrained from glancing back at the faxtab, not wanting to call her attention to it, but wishing he had not left it folded to the page on which Caroljoy's marriage announcement appeared.

Marriage, of course. No mention of anything else, but the union announced as if it were a matter of state or of commerce. Probably it had been a bit of both, if the Emperor himself had attended.

"Are you sure you're all right?"

He jumped and turned at the sudden touch on his shoulder.

"Hades!" He bit off the exclamation as soon as he had said it. After sighing and taking a deep breath, he looked up into the woman's pale green eyes. He had to. Faith Hermer was nearly two meters high and stood taller than any other officer on Old Earth.

"Faith. Sorry I jumped. Surprised and thinking about it. You caught me off-guard."

She chuckled, deep-throated, and the sound relaxed him even before she spoke again. "You must have been surprised. No one has ever caught you off-guard. Not to my knowledge."

He nodded and checked the time. 1800.

"Late if we don't blast."

"All right. You don't want to talk about it now. I'll be around if you do." She smiled and pointed to the exit portal. "Blast, Greg. That is, unless you want to sit at the foot of the table opposite Matsuko."

He was already moving toward the mess before she finished the sentence.

Caroljoy—married, of course. So why did it surprise him?

 XXX

Gerswin hefted the double-ended knife, cradled it, and flipped it from hand to hand. Not at all like the jagged blade he had carried as a devilkid, or the sterile, straight survival knife in his flight boot sheath.

He looked up from the knife to the target—a plastic square set at man height on a hummock of clay five meters away. The plastic presented roughly the same resistance as an unarmored man.

"Here goes," he muttered to himself.

The first cast missed the square entirely.

The second knife wobbled, but hit the plastic and dropped onto the clay beneath the target.

The third hit the plastic square at an angle and skittered off.

Gerswin sighed and marched forward to reclaim the three knives, casting a sideways look at the clouds gathering over the plains. The afternoon's pale sunlight had been the first in days, and, as usual, had not lasted more than a few hours.

He leaned down to get the first knife.

From what he had studied of the meteorological data, the only places where there was more sunlight than cloud cover was over open ocean. No one could explain to him the reason for the phenomenon, at least not in terms simple enough to be sure it wasn't scientific doubletalk.

He put the first two knives in the hidden belt sheath and picked up the third.

The wind began to whine. Soon, if the darkness roaring in from the east were any sign, it would begin to whistle as the temperature again dropped toward freezing.

With the one knife in hand, he retreated to the one spot he had measured out and scratched in the bare clay.

Feel the knife; sense the balance; and . . . release!

And miss.

"Hades!"

Gerswin took the second knife and let it fly with full force.

The twinge in his left hand brought him up short. He realized he had gripped the double-edged blade far too tightly. A slash ran across the base of his thumb, scarcely more than skin deep, but blood welled out.

He squeezed the edge closed with the fingers of the same hand, then let the cut bleed as he threw the third knife with his right hand.

All three had struck the target, but none had stuck.

Gerswin studied the target before starting after the knives.

The gathering clouds choked off the last scattered beams from the sun, and the first gust of wind ruffled his tight-curled blond hair. Absently, he started to push the hair off his forehead before he realized that it was too short to get in the way, as it had been for nearly ten years.

He reclaimed the three knives once more and straightened the target with his right hand. He walked back to his mark, juggling the unsheathed knife in his right hand. He intended to be equally proficient with either hand.

"Right now, it's equally inaccurate," he mumbled.

His next cast bounced off the plastic, but the second did not. Gerswin tried to reclaim the feeling of the second with the third. He did, and two heavy knives remained solidly within the plastic as he walked up to reclaim all three.

Four steps to the target in the whine of the wind. Reclaim the blades and straighten the target. Four steps back to the mark.

Three more throws.

Reclaim the knives.

Throw again.

Reclaim.

Throw.

Reclaim.

Throw.

He kept up the pattern until it was automatic.

When he finally quit, not because of darkness, though most would have had to, two out of three casts were sticking within the target, either right or left-handed. He quit because the increasing wind gusts kept knocking over the target, not because the ice rain bothered him, light tunic or not, nor because of the nagging twinge in his thumb.

The bleeding had stopped, but streaks of rain-diluted blood

decorated his trousers as he headed first to stow the knives in his quarters and then to the medical section. He did not intend to wear the knives until he was one hundred percent accurate with them within their range.

With practice every day, within weeks he would have that skill. After that . . . another weapon. But, first, the knives, for they could be used anywhere.

Anywhere in the Empire and on Old Earth.

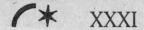 XXXI

The flitter dropped from the clouded sky toward the plateau and its grasses and grubushes. Gerswin watched the readouts in the heads-up display as he eased the flitter down into the clearing nearest the site he hoped was there.

From the topography maps, he had narrowed the search to six plateaus corresponding to his memories. This was the fifth he had actually investigated. His searches of the first four had failed to disclose any indication of the brick stairwell, the garden plots, and the hidden trail he remembered.

The computer and the maps had been better in some ways than his memories. The pilot smiled wryly at the thought. In two of the first four sites he had discovered evidence of recent habitation. In the future he would look into recruiting possibilities, assuming those whom his descent had frightened away were indeed devilkid types.

As the flitter settled, Gerswin let more and more weight drop onto the skids, leaving power on the rotors until he was certain that the flitter was solidly grounded on the mesa top. Next came the blade retraction and storage. Before shutting down the fans, he checked both the EDI and heat scanners. Both showed negative.

He shook his head. A devilkid could be waiting in a below-grade gully, or a buried and fully charged laser pack could have been sitting right in front of the flitter, and neither detector would have shown a thing. They weren't designed for terrain work.

Much of the Service's equipment wasn't designed for Old Earth usage.

After half-vaulting, half-climbing from the cockpit, he touched the closure plates and tapped in a lock combination. While it wouldn't stop a trooper with a laser, the flitter was secure against anything less, and Gerswin didn't expect to meet the equivalent of an Imperial Marine marching through the grubushes in the chill and steady wind of the gray fall morning.

He sighted against the hills to the west, checking his orientation. If he were right, then the hidden stairs he hoped to find were nearly a kay to the west, just above a sharp dropoff to the more sheltered valley beneath.

Light as his steps were, each one crisped slightly on the heavy sand that surrounded the flitter. His breath, slow and even, formed a trailing plume behind him as he slipped toward the shoulder-high grubushes a hundred meters westward.

He sniffed the air gently, trying to detect a scent that might have been there once, a faint odor part soap, part perfume. All he could smell was the bitter-clean odor of the grubushes, nearly uncontaminated this far above the plains and near the mountains. Only a single line of foothills remained between the mesa and the granite peaks that divided the continent.

The air was cold, and outside of the grubushes and the faintest scent of landpoison carried from the plains by the east wind, clean. No rat scent, nor the lingering odor of coyote or kill—the smell was right.

His right hand brushed his waistband, under which was the double-ended sheath with the twin throwing knives, and touched the butt of the stunner. While he had practiced with the knives to the point where his accuracy was nearly one hundred percent on stationary targets, targets were only targets, and the stunner might be more reliable. For now, anyway.

Glancing at the sky, he gauged from the thinning of the clouds whether there might be some sunlight later in the morning. He shook his head, although he could sense some warmth on his back. The thin jacket he wore over his flight clothes was enough to break the wind, and that was all he really needed. Imperial officers born on New Augusta or other warmer planets avoided the outside whenever possible, wearing the double-layered winter uniforms and parkas whenever they were exposed to the cutting winds of Old Earth.

As Gerswin neared the area he intended to search more closely he stopped to check the grubushes, looking at the waxy berries and branches for some sign of harvesting. He found none, not even any sign of the mountain mice that lived on little besides the berries, or so he recalled.

He straightened and surveyed the western end of the mesa

that lay before him, checking the hills to firm up his bearings. Turning more toward the north, he headed for the unseen dropoff he knew lay ahead.

Suddenly he stopped, cocked his head and looked at the all-too-even notch between the two hills to the west and at the dark wedge of gloom behind the notch. He compared that gray to the indistinct gray of the clouds and the line of gray leading to the notch.

"The road of the old ones . . ." he murmured, not sure where he had heard the phrase, but knowing that he had, somewhere, some time.

His eyes traveled the small open sand and clay space around him, checking the bushes, trying to find a pattern, any pattern at all. Finally, he settled on a slightly wider spacing between two grubushes. He eased through what seemed almost a lane toward the western edge of the mesa, a path that became increasingly rocky as his steps closed the gap between himself and the nothingness that waited as the surrounding bushes became shorter and less closely spaced.

Again, he stopped, not for a conscious reason, but because he felt he should, and studied the area around him.

To his right, his eyes settled on an irregular heap of stones, seemingly random, but too regular and too high to have been an accident of geology.

He took one step and paused, sniffed the air. He found nothing but the eastern plains odor of landpoison and the cleaner and nearer scent of grubush.

He took another step, another pause, another sniff.

Finally, he took a deep breath and a quick dozen steps until he stood before the tumbling wall fragment that failed to reach his waist.

It had been higher, he recalled, but, then, he had been shorter, and it had been years earlier. How many he never knew, for time had no meaning to a devilkid on the run, forced from the only home he knew by shambletowners with torches, running and hiding, burying himself beneath grubushes in the pouring rain that had hidden the killers' approach.

He bit his lower lip and studied the rough wall of hewn red rock. At last, he looked over the edge and down the steps—to find them half-covered with drifting sand.

The wooden cover he remembered was gone, and only the nitches in one line of stones supported that memory.

With a sigh, he stepped over the stones, tapped them to insure they were solid. None moved with the taps, nor even with a push, and he eased himself down into the dimness.

After twenty rock-hewn steps and a half-turn west, he was past the drifted sand and in the tunnel where he could stand, just barely. A faint hint of grubush oil tickled the edge of his senses. Memory, or a residue of what had been?

Another fifteen steps and another turn, this time to the south, took him into the main room.

The embrasured and now-uncovered window slits filled the space with more than enough light. Two piles of leather fragments and dust sat across from each other in the southwest corner, the dust spilling across the corner of the permanent clay brick table whose surface was covered with glazed tiles. Each handmade tile had a slightly different design, but all bore a sun/cloud motif.

Gerswin swallowed and turned to the other outside corner, where a second waist-high clay brick counter topped with the crude fired tiles stood. Beside it was what could only have been a ceramic oven, equipped with a chimney and handmade clay piping. One section of the pipe, where it entered the brick wall, had broken apart, and the fragments were scattered across the golden brown floor tiles.

Outside of the centimeters-thick dust and the two piles of leather fragments, nothing perishable remained in the room.

He looked up at the ceiling—a good half-meter above his head. Faint grease-smoke lines traced themselves across the smooth surface, smoke lines he did not remember.

His feet took him to the room that opened northward off the main room, but with one glance he turned away.

The drifted dust outlines of two skeletons on a thicker pallet of dust were all that inhabited the room.

He did not enter the small room next to his parents' room, but did dart a look at the dusty outline that had been his pallet.

The one remaining space was the south room, the one which had looked out over the canyon. Gerswin found himself standing there.

The single window gaped open, the hide covering long since gone, above the flat tile-topped brick expanse where his father had done so many strange things.

Gerswin nodded, more to reassure himself than anything else.

He turned his palms up, looked at his hands, a young man's hands, then at the dust on the floor, and finally at the alcove in the narrow corner behind the archway, the alcove that contained the air duct that a small boy had crawled up so many years earlier.

How many years earlier? How many?

For a time he studied his hands, then stared out the unglazed window at nothing.

He looked once more at the dust on the floor tiles, sniffed again the total emptiness, and turned back toward the tunnel to the mesa top. He did not need to take the other stairway, the one that had led down to the spring, the one through which the shambletowners had poured one distant night, slings and spears in hand, with their rat grease torches flaring.

As he entered the tunnel leading upward, he looked at his hands still yet again. He shook his head to clear his vision.

Later, at the top step, he paused, but turned away and did not look back, and stared instead at the clouds overhead, which reminded him of night, not morning.

The clouds were thicker than when he had brought the flitter down, as if they had decided against allowing the sunshine to break through. And the wind was stronger, the chill more pronounced, as the click of ice droplets began to pelt his jacket and burn his face.

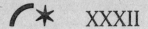 **XXXII**

Gerswin glanced up from the Operations oversight console. Captain Altura, the Imperial Auditor, was leaving Major Matsuko's office. She did not appear particularly pleased.

Her lips were set even more tightly than when Gerswin had met her at the hangar-bunker right after the shuttle had dropped her three days earlier. The captain's fists were half-clenched as she marched out toward the tunnel to the number one hangar-bunker.

"Opswatch, this is Outrider three. Interrogative permission to lift."

Ferinya, the duty controller, looked at Gerswin. His eyebrows raised questioningly. "Permission to lift?"

"Why not? Met status is clear now. Squall line coming in."

"Outrider three. Cleared to lift. Interrogative destination and fuel status."

"Artifact survey run. Plan on file. Estimate air time at two plus stans. Fuel status is plus four."

"Stet. Understand survey run for plus two. Fuel status four."

"Stet. Outrider three lifting."

Ferinya turned to Gerswin. "Do you know what that was all about, Lieutenant? She already had clearance."

Gerswin shrugged. "No. No passengers or cargo on the schedule."

"What was what all about?"

Lers Kardias stood by the console, his stubby fingers tapping on the hard console top.

"Lieutenant Starkadny requested clearance to lift twice. No explanation," explained Gerswin.

"Oh . . . That is funny." Junior Lieutenant Kardias shook his head. "You ready to be relieved, ser?"

"More than ready."

"You stand relieved."

"I stand relieved, and you have it."

Gerswin picked up the light pen from the console and slipped it into the arm pocket of his flight suit. "Good luck, Lers. There's a squall line coming in."

"Thanks."

"Which of you was responsible for sending that flitter off without me?" The chill voice of the Imperial auditor stopped Gerswin in his tracks.

He turned back to face both the console and Captain Altura. Lieutenant Kardias had swiveled in the chair, but had not stood.

"I was, Captain," answered Gerswin.

"Could you explain why?"

"First, no passengers listed. No cargo either. Second, pilot requested clearance. Third, no one notified Opswatch that you were to be included."

The sandy-haired captain said nothing, but clamped her lips together until they were nearly white.

Gerswin waited a moment, then asked, "Is there anything I could do, Captain?"

He caught the "now what have you said?" look from Lers Kardias as Captain Altura glared at him.

"Mister Senior Lieutenant, you have done quite enough for the moment. Anything else would only compound that."

Gerswin laughed—a single harsh bark.

"Ms. Captain, I followed the order book. I would have gladly delayed the flitter if anyone had asked me."

"I told the pilot."

"On every Imperial base, schedules and clearances are controlled by operations. Bases are not ships, Captain." He paused. "Would you like a tour of the maintenance facilities?"

"I've seen them. The conditions and status are better on Charon."

"Charon's an easier planet."

"Than Old Earth?"

Gerswin nodded. "I'll show you. Come on with me."

"Show me what?"

"Not what. Why."

"Why what?"

Gerswin had already turned away, as if to lead the captain, his quick steps heading toward the southwest base exit.

The captain looked at Lieutenant Kardias, then at Gerswin's back, before, with a shrug, she followed the senior lieutenant.

At the inner portal of the exit he turned to wait for her.

"Your home system?"

She clamped her lips shut tightly, then released them.

"New Augusta."

He nodded and stabbed the portal release. Once in the small room between the inner and outer portals, he walked over to the line of lockers. He checked one, then another, rummaging through several until he located a double-lined jacket with thermal gloves.

"You'll need this."

"It's summer."

"You'll need it. Ice rain."

"Hail, you mean?"

Gerswin shook his head in disagreement and offered the jacket to the captain, who donned it but stuffed the gloves into the side pockets and did not seal them.

As the outer portal opened and the two stepped through, a gust of wind from the east, sweeping along the edge of the berm, caught the captain unaware, knocking her into the lieutenant.

Gerswin steadied the woman with his left hand, submerged a grin, and continued toward the point where the ridgeline began to slope away toward the south.

"Watch the clouds."

Captain Altura said nothing, looked at the bare clay interspersed with grassy humps. Finally, she took his advice and raised her eyes to the roiling and speeding mass of varied gray that hurtled toward the mountains in the distance to her right.

Gerswin watched her, not the clouds, as the winds quickly turned her pale cheeks reddish with the cold, and fluttered her short and sandy hair with each gust above the steady chill breeze that whipped around them.

The darker cloud that presaged ice rain was nearly overhead before the droplets began to sound against their clothing and the hard clay.

Click! Click! Click, click, click!

The captain held one in her bare right hand. So cold was the droplet that it did not begin to melt for several moments.

"Why don't you put on the gloves?"

"I might, thank you."

As she struggled with the two gloves too large for her long-fingered but narrow hands, Gerswin glanced at the clouds. Not quite dark enough for a landspout, but the wind velocity would continue to rise and the temperature to drop.

As she finished donning the gloves and looked back at the darkening clouds, Gerswin whistled the first three notes of a tune, the one he thought of as a lament for Old Earth.

The melody had come to him after he'd seen the black Gates to Hades. With the auditor's impatience, the chill, and his own wondering what he was even doing trying to explain Old Earth to a number-cruncher, the first three notes had slipped out before he cut off the melody.

"What sort of instrument was that?"

"What?"

"That you were playing." Captain Altura was still adjusting the too-large gloves, trying to make them fit and to keep them from falling off her hands.

"No instrument. Sometimes I whistle." Gerswin gestured, as if to change the subject. "Warm day. Wind is still lighter than normal, only about twenty kays here."

"What's normal?"

"Here? Around thirty. Hundred's not uncommon. Had two hundred a couple of times. Once or twice we lost the measuring tubes. Spout threw a two-ton chunk of rock through the number four hangar-bunker door one time."

"I don't believe that."

Gerswin shrugged. Why bother? "Check the logs. About two years ago."

He gazed out to the southeast, still lighter than due east, then back to his left, toward the main body of the ice storm.

"Lieutenant?"

"Yes, Captain."

"Why is everyone so prickly here? I ask Matsuko to justify some costs, and he throws a databloc listing of logs and damage reports at me and tells me to search out anything that would contradict the official reports. He practically dared me to question him."

Gerswin frowned, glanced down at the damp clay, and said nothing.

"Lieutenant?"

Gerswin shrugged again. "What can I say? Doesn't sound like him. He's punctual, proper. Polite."

It was the captain's turn to look down at the clay underfoot, to scuff at a tuft of purpled grass.

"I overstated the case. He was proper, very proper. I questioned, and he politely referred me to the datablow containing every single listing that supported every single item."

Gerswin looked at her oval face and strong nose, at the scattered freckles that seemed blanched in the gloom, and raised his eyebrows.

"Don't you understand? He didn't explain. He didn't even take the time to show me an ice storm. In effect, he said, 'Waste your own time. Don't waste mine.'"

"He's like that."

"But everyone is like that here. At least, that's how it seems. Even when you want to explain, you don't. You just say 'Follow me' and head off into a storm. A few sentences about how cold it is, and you think that explains something."

Gerswin sighed, scuffed the clay with his right foot.

"I'll try to put it in perspective. Old Earth is something you experience. You don't explain it. How could you? People think that it's just like the histapes, except nothing will grow, and some fertilizer and a little technology sprinkled over the clay will do it.

"How can you explain landspouts that rip the tops off hills, that turn all-weather flitters into crushed metal in microseconds? You try, and someone says that it's just a tornado. But it's not. There were ten million people within three hundred kays of here right before the collapse. Maybe three hundred shambletowners and a couple dozen devilkids left. Not a single building or a ruin more than a meter high left standing. Place flattened by the spouts, except in one or two valleys.

"You try to tell someone, and they say that it was just the collapse. You stand here, and you don't believe me when I say it's summer. Winter here . . . You think it's cold on the poles of Charon? Winter ice rain will sand off three mills of metal from a flitter in a single flight on the exposed side, and that's just on ground or stationary time."

Gerswin looked over at the captain, who did not raise her eyes from the ground.

"Right now, more than twenty percent of the pilots sent here are casualties. Those who make it through become the best in the Service, and you can check their records if you doubt it. That's the young ones. Older pilots avoid flying around here. Better for them and us.

"Get a good dozen cases of toxic shock every year, just from the hot spots no one has found. But it's not glamorous, like scout duty or combat.

"The rain's so acid that outside uniforms don't last a tour, and you should know what replacement costs mean to a junior officer.

"But that's the story no one tells. How could anyone on New Augusta believe that Man's home planet is dangerous to Man's existence?"

Gerswin laughed once, and the bitterness echoed against the whistle of the rising wind.

"Why are you here?" Her voice was nearly lost in the wind, so softly had she spoken.

"Another question. Most people here believe there's something to save. Something that should be saved."

"I think that's what you believe. This is nowhere. Oh, yes, it's Old Earth, and the home of Man. But everyone here is either local, a problem child, or on a pre-retirement tour.

"Can't you see it, Lieutenant? The great crusade to save the home planet was over before it began."

"Is it? Just got three arcdozers on the ship that brought you. Decon teams have cleaned up most of the toxic hot spots around the headwaters of the two nearest rivers on this side of the continental divide. Starting on the big one now. Years before the results come in, but it's a start."

"Nobody on New Augusta really cares. The new Emperor . . ."

"Long as they keep funding, we'll keep plodding."

"You're just like Major Matsuko."

Gerswin shook his head, then noticed the whiteness at the tip of her ears.

"Time to go in. Frostbite."

"We haven't been out that long. And you only wore your uniform."

"That's me. Not you. Face a bit numb? Ears?"

"Yes, but—"

"Inside." He took her left arm and firmly guided her back to the portal.

Once inside, he helped her take off the heavy, ice-encrusted jacket and placed the jacket and gloves in the heated equipment locker.

The Imperial auditor half-shivered, half-shook herself. "Is there any place to sit down and relax, get a cup of cafe or liftea?"

"J.O.'s lounge, off the mess."

"That sounds fine. Is it warm?"

"Same as anywhere else."

He tapped the inner portal release, and they stepped through, Gerswin leading the way up the tunnel until it intersected the outer perimeter corridor. Gerswin turned right, quick steps clicking on the smooth floor.

Neither said a word until Gerswin stopped at the lounge portal and touched the access plate.

"After you, Captain."

"Dara, please."

Instead of replying, he inclined his head momentarily as if posing himself a question. He did not answer the unthought question, but followed her through.

He went straight to the sideboard.

"Cafe?"

"Liftea."

He poured two and set both mugs on the narrow table where Dara sat. He seated himself across from her.

"You're from where?"

"Here. Local. First, last, and only, so far. Except for some of the kids from the civilian techs on the farm."

"The farm?"

"That's what they call the research center south of here."

She put a forefinger to her chin, then dropped it as a furrow appeared momentarily in her forehead.

"Wasn't there a report—"

"—about the training and education of an Old Earth native. Yes. There was. I was. *Education Review*, New Augusta, Volume 87, number three, if you want to look it up. End of subject."

The auditor closed her mouth and studied his face. Gerswin looked at the sideboard and the two steaming pots—one for cafe, one for liftea.

"Oh . . . I think I understand. Do you talk about your impressions of the Empire?"

"Sometimes."

"What about Old Earth? Not what's happened in the Service, but your own feelings."

"Home. Like to see her restored. Don't know if it can be done. Like to see it."

The captain took another sip of the tea, holding the old-fashioned mess mug in two hands and letting the steam drift up and around her face, so near her chin was the mug.

Gerswin took a sip and placed his own mug back on the dark gray plastic of the table.

"How did you end up an I.S.S. officer?"

"Why not? Good reflexes and enough brains to scrape through the Academy. Besides, didn't know enough Imperial culture to do it any other way. Devilkids don't know all the graces. The Academy assumes nothing."

"Do you regret it?"

"The Academy? The Service? No."

"You paid a high price, Greg."

He stiffened fractionally at the use of his first name, but said nothing, and nodded for her to continue.

"You've been commissioned what, ten years, and you're a Senior Lieutenant? I was commissioned eight years ago, and not from the Academy."

"And you're a captain. You're an auditor."

"You're a pilot. Direct line. I'll bet most of your contemporaries are captains."

"You may be right."

He took another sip of the liftea before adding, "But it always takes longer in non-Fleet commands."

"I hope you're right." She pursed her lips, wet them with her tongue, and pursed them again. Then she looked at the sideboard, before glancing down at the table. Finally, she met his eyes. "How can you whistle like that, like you did outside?"

Gerswin wondered if he had made a mistake. Captain Altura was nice enough, outside of her role as Imperial nitpicker and auditor, and attractive in a stiffly friendly way. But she was no Caroljoy, nor even a Faith Hermer, who was always warm and friendly even when she disagreed violently on specific issues.

Gerswin looked at the tabletop.

"Can you whistle like that again?"

"Captain—"

"Dara, please."

"I don't often. Personal. Escaped me outside. Was watching the clouds and wasn't thinking."

She reached across the narrow table and laid her hand on his. Her fingers were cool.

"Would you whistle or sing, whatever you like, just one song?"

Gerswin wet his lips, half-closed his eyes, and began. The first notes were shaky, but he let them come, hoping that no one else would walk into the lounge while he did.

As he finished a shortened version of the lament, he realized that both her hands grasped his right hand.

"That was beautiful."

He tried to withdraw his hand, but her fingers tightened fractionally, and he did not want to seem as though he were yanking his hand loose.

"I'd like to change. I'm still cold. Would you come with me?" Dara Altura stood slowly, her grayish-green eyes fixed on his, as her fingers lingered on his hand before slowly sliding off as she rose.

Gerswin stood also, but let his hand slide away from hers.

"You're too kind, Dara. But I appreciate it."

Her eyes hardened slightly.

"Not you. Me. Long story, and I'd rather not go into it. Not for a while. I'll see you at the mess, if you like. And I enjoyed talking with you."

"You sure?"

Gerswin smiled, trying to convey the mixture of sadness and confusion he felt.

"Unfortunately."

"Friends, at least?"

"Friends."

She laughed, with a gentleness he had not heard before. "You're probably right." Then she shivered. "I am cold, and I will see you later."

Gerswin stood there watching the portal as she left, then shook his head after she had disappeared. The last thing he needed was getting entangled with someone who mistook his songs for him, or someone who thought they understood and didn't.

"Understand what?" he asked aloud, breaking off his conversation with himself as the portal opened again.

Faith Hermer marched in.

"See you're at it again, lover boy." While the words were sarcastic, her voice was soft.

"Don't understand," he said to her, not exactly caring if she understood, but knowing that she did.

"You understand. You just don't want to, Greg."

"Suppose you're right."

"Do you want someone to talk to?"

"No. Not now. Appreciate the thought, though." He looked into her clear gray eyes, ignoring her twenty centimeter height advantage. "Really do."

"I know."

He turned to go, since he felt grubby and wanted to clean up before 1800. Captain J'rome carried on the punctuality established for the Junior Officers' Mess by her predecessor, Major Matsuko.

His steps were a shade slower than normal as he marched up the corridor.

Why the blatant invitation by Dara Altura? Why had he turned her away? She was attractive, bright, not unsympathetic. He had no attachments, certainly not now.

Or did he?

It wasn't as though he were celibate.

He shook his head again, and it seemed like he was always shaking his head. He wondered about Faith's arrival, Faith Hermer, who had never pushed, but never pushed him away, though he had kept her at arm's length and then some.

He kept walking toward his functional quarters and the console with the texts on circuit design and security. Circuit design and security.

He kept walking.

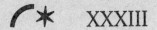 XXXIII

The blond-haired captain pulled the functional armless swivel up to the console. After bending over and touching the rear power stud, he sat down and squared his frame before the pale screen.

"Access code?" the machine scripted.

He looked around the dimly lit office. At the far right end of the Operations bay he could see the island of full light where the duty tech waited and watched.

"Access code?" The query blinked twice.

"BlindX, Beta-G." The letters did not show on the screen, and the officer hoped his finger placement had been accurate.

"Login at 14:18:33 N.A.E.M.T. VM/TSTAT NOT AVAIL. Request subset/matrix."

The captain frowned, then finally tapped in his request.

"Beta Jumpsched."

"**invalid entry**"

He gnawed at his upper lip, tried again.

"Beta sched jumpship."

"Please enter type of matrix and parameter dates."

"Array."

The single word blinked on the screen for a moment before the console scripted the system's reply.

Matrix arrays:
1. By inbound date
2. By j/s type
3. By dptg sys
4. By ult dest sys
5. By comb array; enter in pref ord.

The captain gnawed at his upper lip once more. Slowly, he touched the keyboard studs before him.

"Array 1/2// after 1/1/3025."

"35 data elements found. Do you wish all included?"

"Yes."

"Wait. Display follows."

The captain shook his head. Thirty-five jumpships. Just thirty-five since the rediscovery. He sat and waited for the matrix display to print out on the pale screen.

He leaned around the console to check the main Ops area, but the duty tech had not moved, nor had anyone else entered the bay.

As the matrix printed across the screen, he quickly scanned some of the names. The *Torquina* was there, not the first, but the second, and that made sense. The scout would have had to have been first. He just hadn't thought about it.

The *Churchill* was there as well, near the middle of the matrix. He ran over the totals—three scouts, two research ships, four corvettes, three destroyers, two cruisers, and twenty-one transports. Roughly two transports annually for the past five years, less than that before.

He tapped the reset.

"Subset."

"Gamma sched jumpship."

"Authorization codes."

The captain frowned again. There had been no request for the code for historical data. He shifted his weight in the armless swivel, worried his upper lip with his teeth, and finally tapped out a random-appearing mixture of numbers and letters. He lifted his fingers and waited.

"Request subset matrix."

He let his breath out slowly and lowered his fingers back to the keyboard.

"Array 1/2."

Only two ship names printed on the screen, the *Aacheron* and the *Khanne*, both transports, the first scheduled for Old Earth arrival in three months, the second in ten.

He tapped two more studs.

"Subset."

"Pers/file/Ops."

"**invalid entry**"

"File/Pers/Ops."

"**invalid entry**"

"Personnel/Operations/File Alpha."

"Authorization code."

He tapped in another set of numbers and letters.

"Operator not authorized. Do not repeat."

He frowned before hitting the reset.

"Subset."

"Personnel/Operations/File Alpha."

"Authorization code."

The captain tried another code he had picked up.

"Operator not authorized. This station not authorized. Do not repeat."

"Istvenn!" The exclamation was low and followed by a headshake, then by another keyboard entry.

"Subset."

"Clear."

"Sysoff."

The screen blanked.

The captain leaned forward and reached around the console to cut its power. Then he eased the swivel back and stood, stretching and looking toward the still-quiet duty section of the Operations bay.

"Need to know more before you try again," he said to himself, as he turned to leave the dimly lit row of consoles.

He shook his head once more, then squared his shoulders and was gone into the shadows of the off-duty hours.

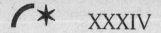

XXXIV

Gerswin shifted his weight slowly, soundlessly, as his eyes continued to adjust to the darkening night. He lay stretched behind a hummock topped by a single scraggly yucca.

The evening breeze, light for a change, carried the faint and chilled bitterness of grubush, reclaimed soil from the fields ten kays to the east, and the even fainter scent of landpoison. Here, in the lower foothills and under the scattered table mesas, the already faint smell of landpoison was lessening with each passing year.

Gerswin stiffened as his ears picked up the faintest hint of a padding step, a scraping sound of leather against bush. He thought he felt the faintest of vibrations in the packed clay under his elbow, but dismissed it as imaginary.

The breeze picked up, and with the moving air came the unmistakable musk/spice scent of a devilkid—male, young. With that scent came the more rancid odor of shambletown leathers.

The sounds, faint as they had been, dropped away as the devilkid froze to listen.

Gerswin smiled, but did not move a muscle otherwise. The wind favored him this time.

A faint scrape rustled through the night.

Gerswin brought up the starlighter camera, checking to see that the light intensifiers were operating. He waited, breathing lightly as the spice scent grew stronger.

He hoped he was far enough from the coyote track to the hidden spring, and that his own route to his stalking spot had been circuitous enough that no trace of his own scent would be carried to the approaching devilkid.

Brown hair, shining somehow with nothing but the darkness of black clouds overhead—that was what Gerswin caught sight of first. Brown hair bound with a single twist of thong and hacked off ten to fifteen centimeters below the leather.

The I.S.S. officer waited, unmoving, starlight camera focused, for a clear shot. One would be all he would get.

The devilkid slipped out from the opening between two grubushes five meters in front of Gerswin. He pressed the stud.

Click.

Swish! Thud!

Rolling to the left and cradling the camera, Gerswin came to his feet even as the sling stone buried itself in the clay where he had been lying.

The even, pad-pounding of quick feet indicated that the retreating devilkid had opted for speed rather than silence.

Gerswin grinned wryly. Noise was relative. He doubted that any Impies more than a few meters away would have heard any of the encounter except for the thud of the sling stone. He looked over at the gouge in the clay.

Had they been watching from where he had waited, they might have heard nothing. The gouged path showed the stone had passed through the spot where his head had been.

He scowled, then focused the starlighter lens on the gouge and the position where he had waited. He could use the lab equipment to add an outline once he was ready to present the pictures to Matsuko.

By themselves, the pictures might not be enough, but then again, they might be.

Hoping the first picture had turned out as clearly as he had seen the devilkid, Gerswin straightened and began to whistle as he trotted back toward the base. He had a ways to go, since Matsuko had forbidden him to take a flitter. Getting the Ops officer to allow the camera work had been hard enough, even with Mahmood's backing.

While Gerswin could have borrowed it without the Ops officer being the wiser, the problem was that he needed the pictures to make his case. Trying to explain how he had obtained them would have been sticky, to say the least.

He shrugged. The pictures were the first step, just the first of many.

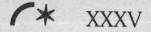 **XXXV**

Gerswin caught his breath, forcing himself to inhale and exhale slowly. He waited behind the crumbling, sheered-off pillars that no longer supported anything but air, each now a two meter high pedestal nearly a meter across.

He sniffed lightly, aware that he was still downwind of his quarry, hoping that the wind direction did not change before the devilkid arrived at the spring.

Pursing his lips, he studied the ground, the hill rising on the far side of the thin trickle of water that passed for a stream. What water there was soaked itself into the clay less than a kay down the valley—less than a kay from the clean spring to a poisoned sinkhole.

The deadness of the lower part of the hill valley was more evident than in the worst of the high plains locales, and the odor of the landpoisons stronger, and even more bitter. The flattened quagmires to the east, the flats running to the sea, contained little besides blackened and poisoned water seeping seaward.

The shambletown to the north was smaller than Denv, and poorer, and the lack of any healthy flora or fauna besides rats, a scraggly variety of ground oak, scattered coyotes, and an occasional grubush underscored the reasons why the Imperial ecologists, Mahmood and his predecessors, had chosen to begin with the high plains and work seaward.

So far the dozers and the techs and the farmers had managed to push the habitable line a hundred kays east of the main base and roughly fifty kays north and south.

At that rate, Gerswin estimated as he waited, it would take nearly ten centuries just to reclaim a sizable chunk of the eastern side of the Noram continent. The techs claimed the work was getting easier as they developed their techniques, but how much better could it get?

He shrugged and gave up the mental estimation process as

he concentrated on listening for the sounds he knew had to come.

Shhhhhpppppp.

His devilkid quarry was easing along the far side of the small valley, dancing from one concealed position to another, still well beyond the range of the stunner Gerswin carried.

From his prone position Gerswin did not strain to see the other, but watched, relaxed, as the other moved closer.

The wind began to die. The I.S.S. captain checked the swirl of clouds overhead to see if the wind patterns were about to change, if they might leave him upwind with a sudden shift.

He frowned, easing his head back to focus on the devilkid, who had slowed unexpectedly as he sensed something was not quite right.

A pebble buried in the clay on which Gerswin rested chose that moment to begin digging through his camouflage suit and jabbing at his thigh muscles. Knowing the devilkid was studying the approach to the spring, the part where the water was nearly pure, Gerswin ignored the sharp ache, and waited unmoving.

Finally, the devilkid darted from behind a low heap of blackened stone and across ten meters of open ground before ducking behind one of the truncated pillars that matched the one sheltering Gerswin.

Gerswin gauged the distance. It was still too far for a clear or a clean shot. He let his eyes ease toward the clouds overhead, which seemed motionless in the gray stillness, to recheck the possible wind patterns.

The eastern hills were warmer than the high plains. This showed in subtle ways—the more rounded terrain, the damper nature of the clay, and the lack of organic rubble of any sort.

The devilkid moved again, and Gerswin refocused on the quarry as the other slipped from pillar to pillar until he was directly opposite Gerswin, less than twenty meters away across the thin ribbon of water.

Once the devilkid moved, Gerswin would have a clear shot. He waited, putting aside the growing discomfort from the clay and the imbedded pebbles that dug into his legs and thighs.

The wind ruffled his hair from behind.

From behind?

Gerswin uncoiled like an attacking coyote, legs driving him

straight across the soggy clay banks of the stream, lifting him over the thin trickle with one long bound.

The devilkid had begun to streak back toward cover nearly as quickly as Gerswin had moved, weaving between the pillar stumps, back toward a narrow crevice in the valley wall from which Gerswin suspected he had come.

Thrummm!

The running devilkid dodged to the right.

Thrumm!

Crack!

A nut-sized stone struck the pillar Gerswin was passing, but he plowed on.

Thrumm!

Crack!

Thrummm!

Crump.

The devilkid collapsed as his last stone rebounded off a pillar into Gerswin's ribs. Gerswin ignored the bruised feeling and approached the limp body carefully. While he could tell the youth was unconscious, he had to wonder if there were another devilkid nearby.

The boy could have easily beaten Gerswin to the nearly hidden split in the rocks at the edge of the valley had he not changed directions.

Gerswin threw himself sideways.

Crack!

The second devilkid also had a sling, and knew how to use it. The stone had passed through the spot where Gerswin had been standing instants before, and only a faint whir had tipped him off, a sound so soft he doubted that anyone but a devilkid could have heard it.

Crack!

Gerswin dropped behind a pillar.

Nodding to himself, he calculated the newest devilkid's position, right behind a stone heap beside the split in the twenty meter high stone wall from which both had come.

He uncoiled himself across the distance to another and shorter pillar, skidding behind it as his boots nearly lost all purchase on the clay-covered pavement underfoot. The next pillar stood five meters uphill, a distance he would have to cover mostly in the open, but that position would give him the altitude to get a shot behind the stones.

Glancing back, he could see the first devilkid still lying unconscious and face down on the dark clay between the truncated pillars.

Gerswin knelt and pried loose a rock, or rather what looked to be a section of an antique brick of some sort. He hefted it in his right hand, still holding the stunner in his left. Lofting it toward the stone pile shielding the devilkid, he timed his departure for the next pillar as the stone clattered down.

Skidding behind the pillar, Gerswin watched as the devilkid ran downhill toward the stream, well out of range before Gerswin could bring the stunner to bear.

The I.S.S. officer bounded back downhill, sprinting full speed for a moment, then settling into a ground-covering lope.

Gerswin's smile was fixed on his face, grimly fixed. There was no cover below the pillared area where the spring rose for at least two kays, just scoured and smooth clay, which meant that the devilkid had every expectation of being able to outrun him.

Gerswin stepped up his pace slightly, and immediately saw he was beginning to close on the tattered tunic of the other. The devilkid had cleverly maneuvered him into a position where he couldn't use the stunner until the devilkid was well on the run.

By now the ground was flatter, and the edges of the valley were beginning to melt into the rolling terrain of the lower plains. Gerswin kept his legs moving evenly and his stride in rhythm, even as the devilkid tried to increase the pace.

Gerswin did not break stride as he watched the other gain ten meters. Slowly, his longer and more even stride began to narrow the distance between them once again.

Still, by the time he was within thirty meters, he could feel his own heart thudding, and he slowly brought the stunner into position.

Thrumm!

The devilkid's right leg spasmed. He tumbled into a heap, but still tried to crawl before fumbling with a set of leather straps.

Thrumm!

Thrumm!

It took Gerswin two shots to get the devilkid, in his haste to avoid taking another hit from the deadly sling.

As he closed on the stunned devilkid, he noted the red hair, the too-thin face, the concealed curves, and realized that his second quarry had been a girl.

He bent to scoop up the sling, suppressing the wince he would have liked to express as his ribs protested. While he doubted that the rebounding stone had cracked them, the muscles were certainly bruised.

He shook his head, gingerly. The computer analyses had given him more than enough locations to check out, and he still had another ten of the most likely to do, with less than two weeks remaining on his leave.

Matsuko had been firm. Firm, but fair. If Gerswin spent his own time corraling devilkids, and if they could be reindoctrinated with some basics, and if they could pass the intelligence and aptitude tests, then, and only then, would he recommend training.

Gerswin shouldered the girl's limp and all-too-light body and began the uphill march back to the first devilkid, trying to make his steps as quick as possible.

He disliked leaving anyone unconscious in such terrain, but neither the rats nor the coyotes liked daytime, and there had been no shambletowners near when he had taken off after the girl.

He broke into a trot, slipped another power cell into the stunner, awkwardly, since he was moving and balancing the girl. Then, as he holstered the stunner, he picked up the pace.

As he passed the blackened sinkhole where the stream disappeared into the clay, the hint of a familiar and rancid odor drifted to him on the wind.

He sighed, and tried to step up his trot, hoping he could get back to the pillar area before the shambletowners took out their frustrations and long-time hates on the unconscious devilkid.

Scrpppp.

The sound had come from the rocks on the left side of the valley, and the scent of shambletowners strengthened.

Gerswin glanced over at the rocky area in time to see a figure diving for cover.

He was on the right side of the stream, exposed to view, but too far from any of the sheltered spots on the left for a sling stone to have too damaging an impact, if indeed any of the shambletowners had the nerve to try.

Except for a quick survey of the area, there had been little contact with the Birmha shambletown, and no reason to maintain such contact when the Base resources were already spread so thinly and when the shambletowners themselves seemed to resent any intrusion.

Plick! Plick!

Large, isolated rain drops began to fall from the darkening clouds as Gerswin topped the last rise where the ground leveled out onto the narrow valley floor.

A slinking figure darted toward the clearing where the devil-kid presumably still lay.

Thrumm!

Plick! Plick, plick.

The stunner bolt passed over the pillar behind which the shambletowner had dived. The scene was silent, except for the rain and the pad-pound of Gerswin's feet.

He slid to a stop at the edge of the clearing, nearly losing his hold on the girl. The boy was still crumpled where Gerswin had dropped him. Gerswin lowered the girl next to a pillar and crossed to the boy, studying the surrounding area and listening.

Whrrrr!

Crack!

Gerswin rolled forward, wincing as his bruised muscles protested the sudden movement.

The two shambletowners were neither as sure nor as quick as the devilkids had been. He located them instantly, still not in cover.

Thrummm!

One pitched forward. The other ran.

Thrumm!

The second shambletowner dropped in mid-stride.

The Imperial officer waited, studying the valley, breathing deeply, and listening.

After the silence had continued and when he had restored his own oxygen balance, he bent and checked the condition of the dark-haired boy.

The youngster had moved slightly, and his breathing was returning to a pattern more like a deep sleep. Gerswin shook his head. Either the Impies or the shambletowners would have been under full stun for at least another hour.

Slowly, he shouldered the boy's form, nearly as light as the girl's, then walked the several meters to recover her.

With the double load, and with the fine drops of rain pelting on his head, his face and shoulders, he concentrated on putting one foot in front of the other as he headed down the valley to his pick-up spot. His feet left deep marks in the clay, marks that were being erased by the light rain within minutes of his passing.

He never looked back at the unmoving forms of the shambletowners. The coyotes might get them, and so might the rats. And they might not.

His even steps brought him back down toward the rolling plain that eventually, kilometers eastward, would turn into a black quagmire, back toward the pick-up spot where his equipment was sealed into a stun-protected pack, and from where he would signal for a flitter.

He sighed.

A grim smile then flitted across his damp face, as the rain-wind swirled about him and plastered down the tight blond curls of his hair.

The two he had picked up would make it, Matsuko be damned. He suspected the others would as well, if he could keep them from destroying each other and the Impies who would have to guard them at first.

If . . . If . . . If . . .

He sighed again, but did not slow as he slogged downward through the wind and the rain.

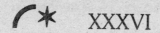 XXXVI

Gerswin scanned the screen, studying the eight figures, all stretched on the flextile flooring. The cots were empty.

Five young men, three women—the results of six months of preparation and two weeks of leave—waited like the caged animals they resembled.

"Eight, Captain? Just eight who meet the minimums?"

"That's an estimate, Harl. Just an estimate."

Eight, thought Gerswin. Were eight all there were, or all he and Imperial technology could find and drag from the ruins of the planet?

He took a deep breath.

"Hold these, Harl."

He handed the weapons belt to the technician and palmed the portal release.

"Ser! Clerris and N'gere are still recovering."

"I know. That's why this is my job."

He eased inside the portal, waiting until it was securely closed behind him before moving farther into the converted dormitory.

Quiet as he had been, the two figures closest to the portal rolled out of sleep and into a crouch.

The first one to his feet was dark-eyed, with the shining depth of cat-eyes, dark-haired, and wore the tattered, raw, and uneven leathers and fur of the plains coyote. He was bareheaded and barefoot.

The second slid to her feet with more grace, but just as swiftly. Instead of leathers, she wore the discarded sack trousers and jacket of a shambletowner. Green eyes burned under the short-hacked thatch of black hair.

Gerswin stood there, barehanded, balanced, waiting for the attack he knew would come.

The boy launched himself—a dark streak half invisible in the darkened room.

With even greater speed, Gerswin stepped aside, letting his arms strike so swiftly that they never seemed to have moved from their half-raised position in front of him.

Thud.

The fall of the crumpled figure that had been Gerswin's attacker shook the flextile floor.

The girl pretended to look down and turn away, scuffed one bare foot on the smooth surface underfoot, then the other. A third scuff, and a fourth, followed, each one narrowing the distance between her and the I.S.S. officer, each one alerting the six others in the dormitory.

Gerswin smiled, flicked his eyes to the still-slumped figure in the corner and back to the girl.

"You lose, devilkid," he observed.

"No!"

Again . . . Gerswin faced a dark streak, so quick that the men watching through the screens could not see what happened, only that the results were the same.

Two figures lay beside each other in the corner to Gerswin's left, both breathing, both stunned.

The six others attacked—roughly together. Seven bodies merged and blurred, the motions so fast that the Service observers and outside sentries did not move, uncertain what to do next.

Before they could decide, the chaos sorted itself out, with bodies falling and being thrown aside, until a single figure stood alone.

Gerswin shuddered, took a deep breath, and wiped the blood off his forehead with the back of his right hand. His ribs ached again, and criss-crossing his forearms were a net of gouges. The blood continued to ooze from his forehead.

He took three steps to his left and yanked the boy, his first attacker, into the air.

The youngster's eyes blazed, but he did not strike.

"Devilkid you. Devilkid me." Gerswin pinned the boy with his eyes as he spoke, although his attention was also on the seven others. "I talk. You follow. Stand? Stand clear?"

He set the boy on his feet and turned away, toward the girl, listening for the possible signs of another attack.

The whisper of a foot was enough.

Like lightning, Gerswin whirled and struck, ducking under

the streak of the other, planting a stiffened palm under the youth's sternum, followed by an elbow across the jaw, and a sweep kick to leave an even more crumpled heap of devilkid.

"Devilkids you. All devilkids. Head devilkid—me! I talk. You follow. Stand? Stand clear?"

He grabbed the girl who had attacked second.

"You stand?"

"Stand."

Less than five standard minutes later, he stood in front of the eight—all eight—his back again to the portal, the blood still dripping from his forehead.

"Teach you talk good. Teach you clean good. Teach you learn good. Stand?"

"Teach us fight good?"

"Learn good first. Then fight. Stand?"

"Stand?"

Gerswin went down the line, repeating the process with each one, forcing a commitment and a personal loyalty, which was all that could bind them now.

"Be back. You wait. No fight."

Not one moved as he turned his back and walked out through the portal. Once he was gone, the eight approached each other warily.

Outside, the two techs, the two sentries, and the sergeant of the guard stepped back as Gerswin moved away from the portal.

"Long flight ahead, Harl." There was a twist to his lips as he said it. "Long flight."

"Yes, ser."

"I'll be at the flight surgeon's, then over with Major Matsuko and the commander."

"Yes, ser."

"Don't go in there. Not one of you. You wouldn't last a minute."

"Yes, ser."

His quick steps echoed on the tile, then faded as he entered the tunnel.

Finally, Harl cleared his throat.

"Eight of them . . . like him?"

"He's better."

"Fine. Eight of them half as good as him?"

The guard sergeant shook his head slowly. "They kept saying he was as good as a Corpus killer. They were wrong. He's better, lots better. Lots better."

Harl looked at the corridor down which the captain had disappeared. "Who would believe it?"

"That's a weapon, too."

Harl screwed up his face as he wrestled with another question.

"Why does he want them?"

"Why did the commander let him round them up?"

Harl frowned, then relaxed.

"He has a reason for everything. He always does."

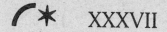

About that tower of time on Old Earth where no towers exist? A metaphor, no doubt, but D'Lorina never makes that clear.

A tower in the traditional sense would rear to the skies, but in the days of her mythical captain, for whom she presents a rather convincing case, by the way, nothing reared into the skies of Old Earth, and even the mountain tops were scoured lower by the stone rains and the landspouts.

The only tower that she could refer to is the single building dating from that period, and it is less than a tower—far less. That building, and I use the term loosely, is the administration and operations bunker of the original Imperial Interstellar Survey Service. It is now preserved as a monument. A fortress of time would have been a far better metaphor, but precision in imagery was not the principal purpose of D'Lorina's scholarship.

She makes a convincing case that *a* captain, more likely a series of strong captains, existed, but it is doubtful that such a case could ever be completely verified or disproved, or that anyone living today could ever understand the darkness of that period, or unravel the darker secrets, or, if sane, would want to do so.

> *Critiques of the Mythmakers*
> Ereth A'Kirod
> New Avalon, 4541 N.E.C.

⟨* XXXVIII

The flitter touched down on the flat expanse of sand protruding from the purple-gray waters. The whine of the thrusters faded and was followed by a *click* as the canopy slid back.

Two figures in coveralls emerged and dropped to the grayish sand, their knees and black flight boots vanishing in the mist that drifted above the waters and over the sandspit.

With the dampness and the chill, with the gray mist and purpled water rippling solely from the tidal pressures beyond the delta, came the odor of death. Not the hot odor of death in the arena, nor the odor of hot metal and oiled death, nor the decay of swamps, nor even the moldiness of an ill-tended graveyard, but the metallic residue of death so long embalmed that only the inorganic heavy metals remain, those and the faintest whiff of past life.

Gerswin turned to his left, toward a black shimmering stump with a single limb that rose three meters from the purple waters.

"Maps say this was a heavily forested delta two thousand years back. Another century and it will be gone."

"Just kill-water," answered the other. "Why show me? Kill-water is kill-water."

Gerswin shook his head, jabbed his left hand at the stump.

"Didn't have to be. Doesn't have to be. We can change it. You can change it."

"Kill-water is kill-water."

The pilot snapped his head up in a single fluid motion to let both visors retract into the helmet housing. His hawk-yellow eyes caught the youth, slightly built like Gerswin himself, but with a fringe of dark hair showing beneath the back of his helmet.

"I'm the captain, Lerwin. Captain. Life-water is what we need, and you're going to New Augusta, and Alphane, and

New Colora. You're going, and you're coming back. Life-water. That's the reason. You forget, and I'll chase you to the corners of the universe. Stand?"

"Stand."

Gerswin did not contest the sullenness of the response, instead motioned to the flitter.

The two figures climbed the recessed hand and toeholds of the military craft and settled back into the cockpit. Within moments, the whine of the thrusters broke the stillness of mist and silent water, and the *click* of the closing canopy was lost in the power of the engines.

The gray mist swirled away in the small tornado of lifeless sand and hot air that spurted behind the lifting flitter. No sooner had it lifted into the overlying haze than the gray mist oozed back over the sandspit, concealing it from all but the most careful, or well-instrumented, observer.

In the flitter itself, Gerswin touched the course plate, let the course line and map come up on the screen in front of the other.

"You heard of Washton, Lerwin? Washton, stand?"

"Stand."

"Watch."

Gerswin triggered the recorded sequence, the tapes and visions he had screened from the Archives, from the old records, scanning the course read-outs as he did.

"Opswatch, Prime Outrider. Interrogative met status. Interrogative met status."

"Prime Outrider, landspout at three four five, thirty kays. Negative on sheer lines. Interrogative fuel status."

"Ten plus. Ten plus."

"Understand ten plus. Your course is green."

"Stet. Prime on course line."

Lerwin did not comment on the transmission, engrossed as he was in the visions of sweeping green velvet lawns, white structures, and antique vehicles traversing pavements of black and white. And everywhere was sunlight, the glittering golden sunlight no devilkid on Old Earth saw.

Gerswin glanced from the instruments at Lerwin, then back at the course line and through the armaglass of the canopy at the ground fog and the swamp beneath it.

Lerwin did not look up from the glitter and the brilliance of the old records until his small screen blanked.

"Real? Here? People?"

"Not here. Where we're headed. Washton."

"Prime Outrider," the commnet interrupted, "Opswatch. Landspout at three four five. Twenty kays and closing."

Gerswin switched his attention back to the long view screen, then nodded.

"Opswatch. Interrogative course change."

"That's affirmative. Affirmative. Suggest change to zero eight zero for point five. Say again zero eight zero for point five."

"Changing to zero eight zero for point five."

"Understand course of zero eight zero for point five."

"Stet, Opswatch."

Gerswin leveled the flitter on the more eastern course and checked the projected fuel consumption of the new course line and timing. The change would cost him fuel, but the extra consumption was well within the reserve.

He hoped that convincing Lerwin would do the job. Since Lerwin was the most stubborn of the bunch, if Lerwin could be persuaded to understand the problem, he could reinforce the urgency Gerswin was attempting to instill in the remainder of the devilkids.

Gerswin sighed, and his shoulders slumped momentarily as his eyes flicked across the board before him.

The studied simplicity of the controls and indicators reflected all too well the Imperial design and expenditure, an expenditure level that could and would not be continued once the uniqueness of the great home planet clean-up campaign gave way to some other quixotic quest, once the Imperial Court decided that Old Earth would take forever to fix up.

The contrast between the devilkids and the Imperials . . . The devilkids were brighter and already had the potential to be far better officers and pilots than all but the very best of the I.S.S. Not that ability meant much in any large organization, but it would take ability to solve the environmental problems of Old Earth, not politics.

Despite the landspouts and sheerwinds, most of the first-stage land mapping of Noram was completed. In real terms, the handful of reclamation dozers had just begun the sifting of soil, gram by gram, to remove and destroy the landpoisons, and the reclamation crops had been harvested twice. Ten thousand square kays so far—it sounded so impressive and was so small.

The task was big, so big, sometimes he wondered about the possibility of anyone ever completing it.

"Dark glooms got you?" asked Lerwin.

"Hell of a contrast," responded Gerswin, ignoring the thrust of Lerwin's question. "Old Washton and landdead here. No!"

"Different," grunted Lerwin. "Old Washton like that? Real like that?"

"Real. Outplanets like that now. You'll see. Old Earth was greener than all. What we need. What we'll get."

Even though he hadn't looked at the screening Lerwin had just seen since he had canned it weeks earlier, Gerswin could still remember the emerald grass, and the sun, the golden sun that had shone down on everything, on the white marble buildings, the towers, the water that had seemed so blue.

He'd managed to compare some of the vistas in the tapes to the rubble, enough to convince himself that the ruins identified on the maps were indeed the sites on the ancient tapes. For the others, after Lerwin had a chance to spread the word, he had planned a set of comparison tapes, side by sides of the ancient tapes and the present ruins.

"Prime Outrider, this is Opswatch. Cleared to resume direct approach to target."

"Opswatch, Prime Outrider, steering zero five zero."

"Understand zero five zero. Zero five zero is green. ETA point eight."

"ETA at point eight on zero five zero."

"What did you say?" Lerwin asked after listening to the transmissions and cocking his head in puzzlement.

"You'll learn. Like a new language. Takes time. Takes practice. Just practice."

If Lerwin were anything like he'd been, speech was so much slower than thought, particularly when the devilkids had so little use for anything beyond the rudimentary trade talk.

Gerswin kept up his continual scan of the board before him, the screens, and the gray vistas spread out toward the unseen horizon. Gray was the color of the clouds above, the intermittent ground fog beneath, and darker gray the barren hills themselves, with occasional patches of purpled grass, bushes, and an infrequent bent tree.

Contrasting with these omnipresent grays were the bare brown shades of short rocky hilltops or small mountains.

"Deadland," observed Lerwin.

"Deader here than on the high plains. Landpoison collects on the lower grounds."

A green dart lit on the homing panel.

Gerswin edged the stick and the flitter leftward and locked in the course change, centered on the beacon he had placed on his surveillance runs.

"Clear look, Lerwin. Clear look. Stand?"

The younger man shifted his weight in the copilot's seat.

"Clear look, stand," he agreed, but the tone of his response and his restlessness indicated what Gerswin was afraid might be a lack of comprehension.

The gray-brown hills beneath became less pronounced, but even with the gentler terrain, the deadland grass remained sparse and harder to pick out as the ground fog patches became more frequent.

Every so often, the flitter passed over a darker and shinier gray, with mist rising above it, that denoted water—a slow-flowing river, a dead lake.

"Prime Outrider, this is Opswatch. Interrogative status."

"Opswatch, Prime Outrider. Status green. Locked on target locator."

"Understand locked on locator."

"Affirmative. Affirmative. Will report arrival."

The pilot shifted his attention from the communications back to the terrain. The first visible signs of what once had been a capitol city were becoming more evident—the white line of cracked and fragmented shards that had been a highway, the all-too-regular mounded humps, and, here and there, the actual stump of brick and steel that remained after the twisting and grinding power of the centuries of landspouts.

The green beacon dart began to pulse on the console.

Gerswin noted the dark steel gray band below the eastern visual horizon. That was the river, and the speckled dark gray and white beyond was the swamp that had been a capitol.

"All those humps—houses. Places to live. Stand?" Gerswin gestured with his right hand briefly, before dropping it back to the thruster controls.

Lerwin followed the motion with his eyes.

"People, all?"

"Millions."

"Deadland now," concluded Lerwin.

Gerswin gave a small nod of agreement and recentered the course line for the beacon and the white stump of stone where he had placed it. He began to throttle back on the thrusters before deploying the rotors for the slow overflight circles he had planned.

As soon as the airspeed dropped below 200 kays, he began the deployment sequence. Shortly, the high-pitched whine of the thrusters dropped into a lower key and was supplemented by the *thwop-thwop* of the blades as the flitter began a slow circle of one island in the swamp.

"Opswatch, this is Prime Outrider. On target. Status green. Estimate time on station at point five. Point five on station."

"Prime Outrider, understand arrival on station. Time on station point five. Request you report departure. Report departure."

"Stet. Will report departure."

To the west was the flat, near-glassy expanse of the river, and to the east, a series of islands of varying sizes, each surmounted with white marble block, some conveying structure, others merely a jumble. Gerswin continued to circle the island closest to the point where the swamp merged with the river, letting Lerwin see it clearly.

From the center of the island the flitter circled rose the square stump of white marble perhaps sixty meters. At the sixty meter point the former spire ended, not with a clean cut, but along jagged edges, as if a giant had broken off the top with a single blow. To the northwest, midway between the island and the higher ground that led out of the swamp, was a line of shattered marble, lying barely exposed above the swamp water like a stone quarrel pointing the way to an unknown destination.

Gerswin tapped a stud on the panel.

"Lerwin. Watch the screen. Check the island, then the screen. Stand?"

"What?"

"Watch the screen. Watch outside."

A scene from the ancient tapes flashed onto the screen in front of the co-pilot's seat. On the screen stood a marble obelisk, stretching from emerald grass and stone walks into a clear blue and cloudless sky. The view changed to show the spire from the air, as well as the lower marble buildings at the edge of the rectangular expanse of grass that surrounded the marble spire.

Lerwin's eyes flitted from the stone stump on the island to the screen and back to the island, and back to the screen.

"No. No . . . Yes?"

Gerswin banked the flitter out of the circle and headed slowly eastward to the hilltop less than two kays from the ancient monument.

Again, he put the flitter into a circle. The building or buildings beneath had also been white marble. All that remained were white stones streaked with rust and coated with a grayish film. Under the stone jumble, this time Gerswin thought he could detect a squarish pattern of sorts, although when he had first surveyed Washton, he had found it difficult to match the tapes with the devastation that time and the landspouts had wrought.

He tapped the screen controls again, this time to bring another view of the ancient capitol before Lerwin.

"Washton, Lerwin. What was. Now what is. Stand?"

"Was . . . is? All landdead, swampdead. This was that?"

Gerswin nodded enough for the motion to be clear, still concentrating on trying to keep the flitter close enough to the right angle and altitude for the comparisons to be clear to Lerwin, and to take his own shots of the ruins with the small tapecubes mounted on the port forward stub. The views he had taken this time and the time before would have to do for the others, since trying to convince the commander and Matsuko to allow him such a cross-country jaunt for each of the devilkids wasn't even an off-nova possibility. Two flights—the recon run and this one—had been justified for research purposes this year. And he couldn't wait another year.

As he circled, while the devilkid Lerwin looked from screen to ruins to screen, Gerswin scanned from board to horizon to screen to Lerwin to board, trying to gauge the impact on Lerwin.

Lerwin said nothing.

Finally, Gerswin broke off the circle and headed for the religious shrine on the top of one of the higher hills.

There, again, he repeated the process, and through the screen shots and the comparisons, Lerwin said nothing.

"Prime Outrider, this is Opswatch. Recommend departure no later than point two. No later than point two."

"Opswatch, this is Prime Outrider. Understand departure in point two. Interrogative met status."

"That's affirmative. Landspout line developing to the northeast."

"Interrogative closure."

"Projected at one five zero kays. One five zero."

"Stet, Opswatch. Will notify of departure."

Gerswin scanned his own small weather screen, saw nothing, and switched his attention back to Lerwin.

"Time for one more, Lerwin, before we sprint back home."

The flitter eased out of the bank and toward the scrubby hills to the southeast of the pile of darkened stones that the map had indicated was once a cathedral.

"Another shrine."

Gerswin jabbed the screen tapes control to bring up the second shrine. While it had not been so impressive to begin with, the destruction was more clear-cut. The landspouts had scoured everything clean except the foundation outlines and dumped the stone and iron into a twisted heap at the eastern end of the unnaturally flattened hilltop.

Lerwin shook his head through the entire three circuits by the flitter.

"Could show you more, but most places are gone, covered with swamp. Some I couldn't identify. Sides, don't want to end up scrapped by the landspouts," observed the pilot as he began the rotor retraction sequence.

"Opswatch, this is Prime Outrider. Departing target this time. Course two seven five. Two seven five."

"Prime Outrider, understand two seven five."

"That's affirmative."

The moments in the cockpit dragged on as the whine of the thrusters built along with the airspeed.

Gerswin wondered why he was depressed. He had apparently succeeded in getting his point across to Lerwin. He had been able to get some solid shots of the ruins, which would please Matsuko.

"Prime Outrider, this is Opswatch. Suggest two eight five. Suggest two eight five."

"Two eight five. Coming to two eight five. Steady on two eight five."

The flitter rocked, and Gerswin checked the thrusters. Steady and in the green. Course two eight five and five standard hours to go before touchdown.

Another standard hour passed before Lerwin spoke.

"Why?"

Gerswin didn't answer immediately. What could he say?

How could a people reach the stars, how could they build systems that could still map continents, shelter them under a mountain, and have them operate fifteen to twenty centuries later? How could they build materials that Imperial technology could not understand or duplicate and not stop the devastation of their own planet? How could they forge materials impervious to hellburners and indecipherable to Imperial engineers and have been so unable to stop the collapse?

"Why?" asked Lerwin again.

"Don't know." What else could he say? What could anyone have said?

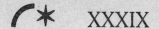 XXXIX

Kiedra studied her reflection in the mirror one last time before glancing down at the single packed kit bag by the bunk. She still wasn't used to a bunk. Even with the hard panel of composite she'd found to put under the mattress, the Imperial bedding felt too soft.

The plain gray tunic was adequate, certainly better than patched leathers stolen from shambletowners, and although the cloth was soft, it resisted everything but the rain. Nothing resisted the rain. Best were the boots, supple enough to run, but hard enough to shield feet from the shards . . .

She frowned. Hard to forget that there wouldn't be any shards where she was headed. No shards, no landpoisons, no king rats or she coyotes—just machines and people.

Gerswin had emphasized the people, and the piling of scent upon scent, all muted, as if the people were locked behind windows.

She looked back into the mirror, green cat-eyes facing green cat-eyes, tight-curled black hair facing tight-curled black hair. Gerswin had told her, when she had asked, that she was attractive. But he'd never raised a hand to her, and the other devilkids—the males—were more interested in the Imperial women. The Imperial men . . . The techs eyed her appreciatively, that she could tell from their breathing and the conversations they thought she had not overheard, but they shied away from her.

The officers were another matter. All were taller than she was, but while they were polite and would help her learn anything, not one ventured even a casual touch.

"Devil-woman . . ." Kiedra had heard that enough.

She bit her lip. Just because she had objected to being pawed that one time.

Gerswin had not been exactly kind to her when he had arrived on the scene after that incident, although he had certainly been cool enough to Lieutenant Kardias and not at all sympathetic about his broken arm. But then Gerswin had glared at her when no one was looking.

She shivered. There was the real devilkid, with the cold fire in his soul and the weight of the night on his heart.

She sighed, squared her shoulders, and left the kit bag by the bunk. She had more than a standard hour before she had to be at the hangar-bunker for the shuttle to the *Churchill.*

As she marched toward the captain's quarters, her quick strides made up for any shortness of leg she might have had.

While the faint trace in the fainter dust outside his portal indicated he had gone, she buzzed anyway. Waited. Buzzed again. And again.

Then she checked the time. Still enough for her to look outside and make it to the shuttle.

Her steps took her to the south lock portals, and she went through the inner and outer ports as quickly as she could. The whistling wind flapped the lower edges of her tunic and tugged at the flat waistband, but the absence of machine oil and musty human stink was a relief. She took a deep breath of the ice cold air, exhaled slowly, and turned her head to search the ridgeline and hillside, while her ears strained.

Crack!

The sound of a slingstone hitting something came from the left, and Kiedra hurried toward the sound, unconsciously adopting the quick sliding run of a devilkid on the hunt, hugging the side of the earth-covered administration building until she crossed the highest point of the ridge.

On the other side, as she had hoped, was Gerswin, practicing with a shambletown sling.

She stopped and watched as he effortlessly fired off three stones in a row.

Crack! Crack! Crack!

The last split a head-sized rock, placed above the man-shaped target, in two.

Gerswin walked over to the target, reclaimed the stones, replaced the "head" with another rock, and stalked back to another position, with a different angle and distance.

Thwick!

Kiedra blinked. She had not seen the blade, but there it was, buried so deep in the target that only a sliver of metal showed.

Gerswin turned and started to walk farther from the target, then turned and dropped, letting go with a single sling cast, all in one fluid motion.

Crack!

The stone bounced off the "chest" of the battered plastic target.

The captain looked uphill, and even at that distance, she felt the yellow of his eyes chilling her. He motioned her toward him with a single curt gesture.

Within moments, it seemed, she had covered the distance between them.

"Should be on your way to the shuttle."

"Should. Will be. Came . . . to say good-bye."

"You'll be back. Not too long."

"Too long." She shook her head, violently. "Why aren't you there to see us go?"

"Don't like good-byes."

"We do?"

He looked at the clay.

Slowly, as if she were moving it a great distance against heavy grav, she extended her left hand until her fingers wrapped around his. She squeezed gently.

"Kiedra. You'll be fine. Learn everything you can."

She said nothing. Their eyes met, hers drinking in the cold, brown-flecked yellow of his, and the darkness behind the yellow and the chill they radiated.

"Late for the shuttle," he reminded her.

"I'll make it." She did not let go of his hand, squeezed his fingers more tightly.

Finally, he smiled faintly, and leaned forward to brush her cheek with his lips.

A fatherly kiss, she felt, though she had never known one.

"Do what you want and what you must, but come back, Kiedra. We need you. All of us."

She withdrew her hand and stepped back, wanting to dash away, to run for cover, any cover. Instead, she inclined her head.

"I will be back, Captain. We all will."

She sensed Gerswin did not move as she turned and marched back toward the portal, back toward her single kit bag and the shuttle to the Empire, and the training that awaited her and seven others.

She let the single tear on her cheek dry untouched as she hurried through the portals toward her bag and the shuttle:

"At ease, Captain."

Gerswin relaxed slightly, but his position scarcely changed, not that it had been Marine-straight to begin with.

"Sit down. I know it's not in your nature, Greg, but sit down anyway." The major gestured to the chair across the blank table from him. Matsuko was one of the few officers on Old Earth Base who ignored consoles and the access to the central data banks they represented.

Gerswin sat.

"I have orders, orders to New Augusta."

Gerswin did not look directly at the olive-dark face of the Operations officer, nor down at the shining surface of the table from behind which Matsuko presided. Rather, his glance appeared disinterested. If he looked too intently at anyone, the automatic intensity of his gaze made the subject of his observation uncomfortable.

"Congratulations, Major. Know it's what you wanted. Hope the duty assignment is also what you requested."

"I'm being assigned to the War Plans Staff—Admiral Ligerto—after three months home leave.

"That's not why I asked you here, however." Matsuko held up a set of fax flimsies. "I recommended you as my successor and your promotion to major, since Captain J'rome has also been transferred, as you know."

Gerswin did not breathe a sigh of relief at Captain J'rome's transfer, but most of the techs would.

Matsuko laughed, but the sound was forced. "I suppose one and two halves out of four isn't bad."

Gerswin frowned. "One and two halves."

"You know the one. The remaining two halves out of three? You get a temporary promotion to major, contingent on continued performance, and permanent no later than five years

181

if not remanded or made permanent before, and you are assigned as Deputy Operations Officer.''

"That's what I've been doing, in fact."

"But not in name, and this makes it official."

"The new Operations Officer?"

Matsuko nodded. "Reiner D'Gere Vlerio."

Gerswin raised his eyebrows. The impressive-sounding name meant exactly nothing to him.

"You might be one of the few who doesn't know him, or his family, I should say. He's the youngest son of one of the more powerful Barons of Commerce in the Empire, Baron Fredrich Reiner Vlerio. His house controls the databloc licenses."

Gerswin nodded in response. He could understand the money and power involved there.

"You don't seem impressed, Major."

Gerswin appreciated the immediate promotion, but shrugged. What could he say?

"Some skepticism might be healthy. Major Vlerio was the lead scout pilot on the Analex Reconnaissance, and he was the only pilot from his section to return. We'll leave it at that. That's what is in the official records. Since then he has been attached to assignments at headquarters."

Gerswin was seeing a picture he didn't appreciate.

Matsuko laughed the short laugh that was not a laugh.

"He brought his orders with him, as well as yours and mine. Your promotion is effective today, but you do not take over as Deputy Ops boss until tomorrow, when Reiner takes charge."

Gerswin understood. How he understood. Major Reiner Vlerio needed a good fleet or out-systems tour, and the fleet wouldn't have him after the Analex screw-up. No one trusted him not to foul up. Gerswin was appointed official custodian. If one Major Gerswin failed, there was no great loss to the Service, and if he succeeded, his status and promotion were assured, although only a few would know the special circumstances.

"I see."

"I think you do. I think you do, but not as much as you need."

"Would you care to explain, ser?"

"Major Vlerio is wasting no time. He has already requested a flitter to survey a landspout and tasked Lieutenant Deran as his co-pilot. While I could overrule him, since he doesn't take over until tomorrow, I won't."

"I understand, Major." And he did. Vlerio had had assignments at headquarters and certainly had friends left. Or acquaintances who would bow to the family's power.

"I'll take care of it. When does he lift off?"

"One stan."

"Then you'll excuse me."

"Good luck, Greg."

Gerswin merely nodded. He left the office and headed for Jeri Deran's quarters, hoping she was still there.

She was.

Petite, black-haired, black-eyed, dark-skinned, and with a hard and brassy voice that had more than once stunned male officers expecting a softspoken lady.

"To what do I owe this visit, Captain?" Jeri Deran had not stood up, but had remained seated on the edge of her bunk, pulling on her second flight boot.

"Your health, Lieutenant."

"My health. Healthy as a damned scampig! What's this health crap?"

"What do you know about Major Vlerio?"

"That he's Matsuko's successor. That he'll make the officer evaluations, and that he's the only ticket out of here. That's all I need to know right now."

"Wrong, Jeri. Need to know that most officers who fly with him don't survive. Also need to know that Matsuko is still Ops boss, and that I'm now Deputy Ops boss."

"Crap, Captain! Sheer unadulterated crap! You're trying to blow the one chance I've got to get out of here."

She had yanked on her second boot and stood, glaring at Gerswin.

"You run around like a tin god, and all the techs bow as you pass. So do half the pilots, and damned if I can see why. So . . . No one else can make a flitter do what you can? So what? You can do your own repairs? So what? You've been here ever since you got out of training, what, fifteen years ago? You're still a captain—"

"Major, now," Gerswin corrected quietly. A faint smile played around the corner of his lips.

"Pardon me, Major. So you're a major, so recently you

don't even have the insignia. After fifteen years you finally made it, and you'll have to spend another five here to pay it off, until you're so specialized you'll never get off this stinking ball of poisoned mud. I beg your pardon, you are from here. I forgot. If you wanted to, you could never leave our revered ancestral home. But I want out, and not after fifteen or twenty years of 'Yes, ser, anything you please, ser.'"

"Going through a landspout will get you out quicker, and in a silver urn." Gerswin's eyes flared, and even Jeri Duran took two steps back away from him, though he had not moved, until her back was against the bulkhead. "You want to fly with Vlerio?" he pressed. "Fine. I'll see that you do, until you're sick of it and sick of him. But not today. For other reasons, I've got to see that the . . . major . . . survives in spite of his . . . impetuosity."

"You talk a good line . . . Major . . . but no orbit break."

"Do you want the next long-distance spout study? Solo?" Gerswin looked at the lieutenant, whose glance dropped.

"Do you want to be permanent shuttle liaison?"

He waited.

Only the hiss of the ventilators broke the silence of the small quarters.

"What do you want, Major?"

"Call in sick in about fifteen minutes. Call me. I'll be there. That's all."

"All right . . . Major. But if you—"

"Understood, Jeri, understood. I don't break my promises." Gerswin started to leave, then turned back. "Understand this, too. You say a word, one single word, and the whole base will know how you want to use Vlerio, both on and off duty! That I can insure."

"You are without a doubt the meanest bastard left on this mudball, and I hope you end up the last."

"Do you understand?"

"Yes, I understand. Now would you please get the Hades out of here so that I can get sick, recently promoted Major Gerswin, not that you haven't given me every possible incentive?"

Gerswin left, at a walk approaching double-time, for the Operations center to rearrange the schedule, and to insure that Markin was the tech on the flight.

He'd already made sure that the equipment crew would take as much time as possible in issuing Vlerio his gear.

He shook his head. A flight to see a landspout, for Hades' sake. There were much easier ways to commit suicide, but the last thing he needed was Vlerio's death under any circumstances, much less under those that could be construed as suspicious.

Gerswin stepped up the pace. Vlerio might not be pleased, but the major wouldn't complain publicly—not until he took over as Operations officer.

In the meantime, all Gerswin had to do was to get him through the flight in one piece, if he could.

Getting Vlerio to the flight line would be the easy part. Getting him through the flight and getting him to accept what he needed to know would be the hard part.

Gerswin sighed as he turned into the Operations center, only half-aware of the way the other officers and techs backed away from him. He had a lot of arranging to do before he and Vlerio took off. A lot.

He gnawed at his lower lip as he dropped in front of the console. The flight time would be pressing before he knew it.

Three faxcalls and fifteen minutes later he was heading for the tunnel toward the hangar-bunker, hoping Markin had already gotten there.

He could see as he approached the flitter that Vlerio had already arrived, and that the major had brought his own gear, tailor-made from a shiny black fabric.

Gerswin refrained from shaking his head. The material would be worse than useless if Vlerio were ever forced down away from Base.

"Captain! I had requested Lieutenant Deran for this flight."

"Sorry, ser. She called in sick. Nausea. Might be toxic shock. No one else was ready, and I thought you wanted to leave on schedule."

Vlerio looked as if he had not decided whether to frown or glare.

"All right, Captain. We'll do the best we can."

He slapped the fusilage of the flitter next to the thruster intakes.

Thud.

"Disgraceful, Captain. This hull is a patchwork, absolute patchwork. Hope the thrusters aren't in the same sorry condition."

The major moved toward the inspection panel, but Gerswin was there first, easing the fitting and holding the panel open for the major's inspection.

"They've had some care, at least." Vlerio frowned as he checked the seal dates. "Why such a short time between overhauls? So many frequent rebuildings are expensive, Captain, extremely expensive. Hard to justify on a budget these days, you know."

"Yes, ser. Airborne debris level is much higher than standard here. Requires replating sooner."

"Ah, yes. The Service had that problem on New Colora part of the year. Stormy seasons, you recall. But we solved that one with the installation of particle screens. You should have looked into that, Captain."

"We did, Major. The density altitude and power requirements would have required the installation of HG 50s, and it's cheaper to replate than to re-engine and re-engine."

"When we get back and when I'm settled in, I'd like to review that data, Captain. We might be able to find a way around that particular problem."

"Yes, ser." Gerswin closed the access panel and trailed the major as Vlerio checked the skids and completed the rest of the preflight with non-committal grunts.

Vlerio took the left hand seat, the pilot's position, as Gerswin strapped himself into the right hand seat.

"Checklist?"

"Up and ready," answered Gerswin.

"Aux power?"

"Green."

Vlerio continued through the checklist and through the start-up competently enough.

"Ready to lift."

"Opswatch, Outrider two, ready to lift, request met status and bunker clearance."

"Bunker clearance?" asked Vlerio without putting the question on the commnet.

"Sometimes the wind sheers outside the hangar-bunker can hit eighty kays. Need a reading before we lift and clear the doors."

"Eighty kays?"

Gerswin ignored the question to listen to the clearance.

"Outrider two. Met status is green. Winds less than twenty kays. Cleared to lift and depart. Interrogative fuel status."

"Opswatch, fuel status is four point five."

"Understand four point five."

"Stet."

Gerswin nodded at Vlerio, who was gripping both stick and thrusters too tightly.

He waited a moment before clearing his throat. "Major, we're cleared to lift. The wind will gust from the right as you clear the bunker."

"Oh . . . Stand by, Captain."

"Outrider two, lifting."

"Stet, two. Have a good flight. Watch those purple beauties for us."

"That was an unauthorized transmission, Captain."

"Yes, ser."

"Find out who made it."

"Yes, ser. I'll check the log when we get back. The wind is from the starboard."

The flitter lurched forward on ground cushion and through the hangar bay portals.

Gerswin kept his hands near the controls, afraid that Vlerio would fail to compensate for the loss of ground cushion if an unexpected gust swept the flitter, or that he wouldn't get the aircraft pointed into the wind quickly enough.

While the flitter rocked and the skids nearly scraped the tarmac outside, Vlerio slowly maneuvered it into the wind and tilted it forward into a liftoff run, quickly feeding turns to the thrusters.

Once airborne, as the major studied the heads-up display, Gerswin surreptitiously wiped his forehead with the back of his sleeve, then dropped the helmet's impact visor back in place. His mirthless smile, as he watched Markin do the same from the corner of his eye, was hidden behind the tinted impact visor.

"What's the vector to that storm, Captain?"

"Zero four five, Major. Approximate range is six five kays."

"Estimated time to closure?"

"On thrusters or with blades deployed?"

"Thrusters," answered Vlerio as he began the blade retraction sequence.

"Ten standard minutes, give or take two."

"Stet. Blade retraction complete."

"Outrider two, this is Opswatch. Suggest course change to zero seven zero. Probable wind sheer one zero kays before the leading edge of the landspout."

"Understand recommended course change to zero seven zero," answered Gerswin, since Vlerio showed no inclination to handle the communications with Base.

"Negative course change," said Vlerio on the intercom.

"Opswatch, this is Outrider two. Negative on course change. Maintaining zero four five this time."

"Outrider two. Understand maintaining zero four five. Advise that probable wind sheer differential is plus one five zero. Plus one five zero kays. Running three three zero slash one five zero. Strongly recommend course change."

Gerswin studied the horizon and the purpled mass rising above the gray of the lower-lying clouds that obscured the ground.

"Opswatch, this is Outrider two," answered Gerswin. "Understand recommendation for course change. Interrogative met status behind sheer line."

"Outrider two. Met status behind sheer line estimated at plus seven."

"Understand plus seven."

Gerswin cut in the intercom.

"Recommend immediate course change, Major. You have two minutes to sheer line impact."

"Captain, the air is clear for another seven kays, and we're at three thousand, no tac-running."

"Major, I recommend a course change to zero nine zero."

Gerswin watched the faint line as it appeared on his met screen, so close that it was about to kiss the screen point that represented the flitter, and put his hands on the controls, waiting for what he knew would happen, sensing Markin tightening his harness behind him.

"Captain, I've been through—"

Thud! Thud!

"EMERGENCY!!"
BRRIINNNGGG!!!

"Ground impact in less than two minutes!"

The scream of the emergency warnings rang through the intercom as the flitter pitched nearly ninety degrees nose down and to the left.

Gerswin glanced at the EGTs running into the red, and at the airspeed, which was climbing back from a reading of next to nothing. He overrode the major's frantic attempts to yank the stick back into his lap, only letting the nose ride up slightly.

"HELL!! Damned nose won't come up!" grunted the major.

Gerswin felt the perspiration pop out on his forehead as he watched the instruments and fought the major's actions, waiting before pulling out. He kept the nose down.

"Ground impact in thirty seconds! Impact in thirty seconds!"

Thud!

The flitter shuddered at the impact on the port side, and Gerswin again leveled it, his strength overriding the major's easily.

Lurching to the right as the left thruster dropped to half power, the flitter continued to fall as the airspeed climbed back across the two hundred kay mark.

Just as the speed reached two hundred, Gerswin smoothly brought the stick back into his lap.

"Ground impact in thirty seconds!"

"Ground impact in sixty seconds!"

As the airspeed bled off in the climb, Gerswin began to lower the nose, keeping the thrusters at full power, studying the EGTs and the vertical speed indicator.

Slowly, he eased off the power on the right thruster, aware that the major had finally released his hold on the controls. Gerswin did not look at Vlerio as he began a turn to starboard.

"Outrider two, this is Opswatch. Interrogative status. Interrogative status."

"Opswatch, status is green. Port thruster is amber. Say again. Port thruster is amber. Overall status green this time. Course is one zero zero. Altitude is point eight, climbing to three."

"Recommend course of zero eight five."

"Changing to zero eight five."

With the purpled mass of the landspout to the west blocking the direct rays of the afternoon sun, the light level in the cockpit was scarcely greater than on the ground below the clouds.

Gerswin could see that while Vlerio had clenched both fists, they were unclenching slowly as he watched the purple fury passing the flitter kays to the west.

Clunk! Clunk! Clunk!

The flitter rocked slightly at the three rapid-fire impacts.

"Ice, Captain?" asked Markin.

"Think so. Could get hit with a few more."

Gerswin eased the stick more to the right to get a greater separation from the trailing and more diffused end of the spout.

The EGT on the port thruster refused to drop from the amber to the green, and the power loss was approaching fifty-five percent.

"Major, we're going to have to cut this short. We've got about twenty minutes max left on the port thruster."

As he spoke, Gerswin began a climbing right turn designed to gain altitude for a return to base behind the landspout. The altitude would be helpful in case the thruster quit altogether.

"Go straight back in, Captain."

Gerswin sighed.

"We can't, Major. Wouldn't have enough time to set down, much less clear the hangar-bunker before the spout hit, and we'd have to use a high power approach."

"You have it, Captain. Do what you think best." Vlerio's words sounded like they had come from between clenched teeth.

"Stet, Major."

"Opswatch, this is Outrider two. On a return curve for touchdown behind the spout."

"Outrider two, understand returning to base."

"That's affirmative. Returning to base. Turning three three five for ten."

"Outrider two, recommend three five zero for twelve, then one nine five for approach."

"Stet. Turning three five zero, and leveling off at four point zero."

The cockpit flared with the return of the sun as the flitter cleared the shadow of the landspout. Gerswin squinted until he tossed his head to drop the dark helmet visor in place. The brightness of direct sunlight still bothered his eyes.

Backing off power to both thrusters, Gerswin reduced the right to fifty percent and the left to thirty. But the EGT on the left continued to inch through the yellow toward the red.

"Outrider two, this is Opswatch. Landspout shifting to course of one seven zero. Spout will pass east and south of main base. Estimate CPA in one minute. If necessary, you can commence approach on heading one nine zero."

"Stet. Heading one nine zero."

"Landing checklist . . . up and green."

Gerswin did the checklist himself, rather than ask Vlerio to do so, forcing himself to go through each item methodically.

"Outrider two, cleared for approach and touchdown."

"Stet. Interrogative met status and damage."

"Damage estimate not available. No reports of structural failure. Strips clear. Grids clear. Standing wave antenna down. Landspout now three kays at one six five."

Gerswin nodded. The spout was following the normal pattern of steering back to the southeast once it neared the foothills. Most didn't make it to the base itself.

"Opswatch, Outrider two commencing descent."

"Understand commencing descent. Interrogative power status."

"Port thruster is in the red. Three zero percent power. Will use low power, high angle descent to full touchdown."

"Interrogative emergency status."

"That's negative. Will require ground tow. Will require ground tow."

Gerswin eased the nose up as he triggered the blade extension sequence.

Once the rotors were fully operational, he eased back the power on the left thruster, with most of the power to the blades coming from the right engine.

Thwop, thwop, thwop, thwop. . . .

The sound of the rotors always reassured Gerswin. If necessary, he could always bring the flitter down on blades alone, with no thrusters, but he'd rather not have to do an autorotation with Major Vlerio sitting in the pilot's seat.

"Opswatch, this is Outrider two. Have base in sight. Commencing final."

"Stet, Outrider two. Tow crew standing by."

"Have crew in sight. On line to grids."

"Harnesses tight?" he asked over the intercom.

To the left, even across Vlerio's immaculate flight suit, he could see the half kilo wide swath of raw clay where the landspout had plowed through a hilltop east of the base.

"Little damage over to the left, Major," Gerswin remarked as he brought the nose up another increment before the final flare to the spot on the grid outside the bunker.

He thought he heard a cough from Vlerio, but he was concentrating on the EGTs, the power, and the touchdown itself.

He smiled behind the tinted visors as he got the flitter on the grid without even a jar.

"Commencing blade retraction, Markin."

"Stet, ser."

Markin had the crew door open, watching the retraction and folding sequence.

"Opswatch, Outrider two on the deck. On the deck and shutting down."

"Stet, Outrider two, Interrogative damage status?"

"Port thruster down. Probable replacement. Fusilage impacts."

"Stet, two. Cleared to shut down."

"Blade retraction complete," Gerswin announced, and Markin vaulted from the crew door to the tarmac to take charge of the tow hook-up.

Gerswin began the shutdown sequence, starting with the exterior lights and the fusilage heating.

"Ah . . . humm," coughed Major Vlerio.

"Yes, Major?"

Gerswin turned in the seat to face the senior officer.

"All right, Captain. I am neither stupid, nor unnecessarily vindictive. But I do not like being treated like an idiot, and before we leave this flitter, I think we need to get some things straight."

"I understand, Major."

As he spoke, Gerswin completed the thruster shutdown. He could finish the rest once the flitter was towed, if necessary.

"Starting tomorrow, I am the Ops boss. Period. You are my

deputy. Deputy, not puppet master, not the power behind the Ops boss, but deputy. Do you understand?"

"Major, I understand completely. You are the Ops boss, and you can't afford to make mistakes. If you don't succeed, then neither do I."

Vlerio snapped his head, and both sun and impact visors retracted. His forehead was damp.

"Then why did you go out of your way to make a fool out of me in front of the senior tech?"

Gerswin snapped his own visors up and let his hawk-yellow eyes bore into the major's. "Because you insisted on this damned flight. Major Matsuko wouldn't tell you no, and no one else could."

Gerswin jabbed his hand at the raw clay gouge on the hillside nearly a kay behind the major. "No one who hasn't spent some time here ever seems to understand how dangerous the spouts are. I could have let you go out and kill yourself. I didn't have to step in. You would have. Lost a flitter and crew. For what?"

The major was beginning to tremble, with what Gerswin feared was out-and-out rage.

"Markin wants to go home. He's got half a tour left before he can retire. He'll say nothing. Nor will I. Everyone knows you saw a spout up close, and maybe it was a damnfool thing to do, but you did it and you're back. No problem. May be an asset because the pilots will all know you've been through it. I take the responsibility for the damage, and you become Ops boss."

"You're clever, Captain. Too clever."

Gerswin sighed, grabbed the edge of the seat. The flitter rocked as the crew turned it for the tow back into the bunker.

"Major, think about it. Did I do anything against your interests? Anything? If I had wanted you out of the way, I could have stayed in the Ops center and vectored you right into the sheer line. With Jeri Deran as copilot, we wouldn't have found as much as a kilo of scrap metal."

Gerswin waited, wondering if the apparently hot-headed major would stop to understand.

"I guess you're right, Captain. At least, I see what you tried to do. But I still don't like being treated like an idiot."

"Major, I'm sure there was a better way to handle it. But I

didn't have much time. You have a great deal more managing experience. That's why you're the Ops boss. I understand all the local problems. That's why you need me as deputy. I'll tell you the problems, and you make the decisions, and if we do it in private, you get all the credit."

"And the blame?"

"Major," and Gerswin forced a laugh, "Headquarters will *always* blame the boss. That's why you need all the credit you can get."

Vlerio nodded, slowly.

"All right, Captain . . . or Major, I should say. We'll try it. But don't ever, *EVER*, pull a stunt like this one again!"

"Yes, ser."

Gerswin waited until the flitter came to a halt inside the hangar-bunker. Then he finished the last three items on the shut-down checklist.

By the time he looked up from his work, Vlerio was gone.

⌒＊ XLI

The tap on the portal was gentle, yet a dull and hollow sound rang through the metal—so much metal for a planet which had so little that had not been oxidized, fragmented, or scattered in dozens of differing and unique ways.

Although he had been sleeping, his bare feet touched the cool tiles before the first echo from the tap had died away.

"Yes?"

"Greg?"

He touched the entry stud, and the panel irised open.

Faith Hermer stepped through the half-open portal, not waiting until it was fully open, her head a scant few centimeters under the top of the frame.

She touched the closure and locking studs in quick succession, and sat down on the foot of his bunk, automatically ducking her head to avoid the non-existent upper bunk.

Gerswin remained standing, leaning against the wall next to the built-in console. He could sense all the conflicting emotions she radiated—impatience, excitement, fear, and . . .

He shook his head.

"It might be that bad," she said lightly, "but you'll survive. You always will."

He frowned. "Not what I meant."

Amazingly, she returned his gruffness with her shy smile. After all the years he had watched her, he had come to appreciate that shyness, the gentle warmth it conveyed without invading or demanding anything.

His frown easing, he asked, "You're in a hurry?"

"In some ways. The shuttle brought my orders, mine and Lieutenant Glyner's. They're on a tight turn-around. After they unload, they'll take us to the *Andromeda*."

"Orders?"

"I told you. I asked for reassignment to a combat position."

195

He had asked the same, and he nodded slowly. For all her size, Faith had quicker reflexes than all of the other Impies, and a better sense of judgment.

"The Dismorph thing?"

She nodded in return.

"What about me?"

"The only orders I know about were mine and Glyner's." Her eyes met the hawk-yellow of his. Then she looked at the smooth and faded gray of the Service quilt on which she sat. "Greg, they'll never let you go. Once Vlerio is retired, they'll just send another. You've given them enough native-borns to begin running this place in a few years—but only if you're here to control them. They'll never release you, even if you are the best combat pilot in the Service. Once Vlerio is retired . . . Don't you see?"

"See? See what?"

"You're all that holds this place together."

"Me, and an Ops officer, an exec, a commandant, and another two hundred assorted military and civilian types."

"Greg." Her voice was low, in the quiet, no-nonsense tone he had come to recognize.

"Appreciate the flattery, Faith, but it's hard to believe."

She sighed, and the slight wash of air carried her scent toward him, the odor of excitement muted, and the sense of sadness deeper now.

Shifting his weight slightly, he wiggled his toes against the cool tiles, abstractly glad that he did not have to pull on his boots just yet.

"I could have said it better. What I meant was that you will be the only one who can hold things together in the future, when things really get tough."

He barked a two note laugh.

"When they really strip us for combat support? Aren't we where they put people to keep them out of trouble? To keep them from fouling up the great and glorious combat arm?"

She did not answer his questions, her eyes dropping.

Her hand strayed toward the top fastening on her tunic, but tugged at her shoulder, straightening the fabric where it did not need straightening.

She patted the bunk.

"Please sit down, Greg."

He slid onto the quilt next to her, but she did not look at him, instead letting her hand touch the top fastening of her tunic, then dropping it.

She turned to him, and he could see the liquidness of her wide eyes. At the same time, he was more aware than ever of how she towered over him and wondered if that was why he had always avoided getting involved with her, despite the attraction she held.

"Greg?"

"Yes?"

"I don't have much time. Not here, perhaps not ever, and . . . and . . ."

"Sssshhh."

He touched her lips with his forefinger, understanding finally, with a cold certainty, that she did not want to ask, had never wanted to ask, and had waited year after year for him, while he had waited for her.

This time, his fingers touched the top fastening on her tunic, and the second, his eyes widening as he realized that she had worn nothing under either tunic or trousers. He closed his eyes as his lips touched hers, and her hands found him.

Despite the heat building between them, between skin and skin, the sense of time dropping forever through an hourglass that would never be turned, each touch tingled, and lasted, lasted and tingled, as they moved together, clothes falling apart, as if in slow motion and freefall.

When the last shudders had died away and her hands traced his body as if to store him within her memory, within her fingertips, he traced her cheekbones with the forefinger of his left hand.

She sighed, regretfully, once, twice.

"It's better this way."

"Better?"

"You're still afraid of women, you know. Yet your whole body breathes desire. Half the women in this base would give anything to have what I've just had. And you don't see it. Maybe you can't, or won't."

"Better?" He repeated his question.

"I'm not sure I could have left if this had become a habit. You're addictive, you know." She laughed lightly, but with an emptiness behind the teasing tone.

"Why not? Most of the men here feel that way about you. Give them a chance—"

"Greg."

The quiet stretched between them, as he ran his forefinger along the line of her collarbone and downward across her satin skin.

"Not—" But she broke off the protest, and drew him to her, her fingers digging into his shoulders as her lips covered his.

Some time later, as they lay side by side, shoulder to shoulder and thigh to thigh on the narrow bunk, she repeated her earlier statement.

"It's better this way." But the sadness was stronger.

This time, he waited.

"You belong to no one, not even yourself. Or maybe you belong to Old Earth. You can give without giving everything, and that's not enough for me. Not in a lifetime. But I'd stay, hoping that you would, and you wouldn't. You couldn't."

Again he said nothing, but held her closer and stopped her words, and let her tears bathe them both.

Presently, she leaned away and took a deep breath.

"Time to go. I nearly waited too long to come. The shuttle lifts in less than two hours."

He wondered how he would have felt if she had not come, but only watched as she stood, slipping her uniform back on with quick gestures.

"One last thing. Greg?"

"Yes?"

He met her eyes, but she did not flinch from his level hawk gaze.

"Don't see me off."

He dropped his glance, not that he had to, but because he understood, though he wanted not to understand, and because all he could do was look as she walked away.

As she tightened the waist bands on her trousers, he stood and slipped over to her, aware and not caring how much taller she was.

He lifted his head, and she bent hers, but only their lips touched, sharing salt and sadness.

"Good-bye, Greg."

"Good-bye."

He watched as the portal closed, then slowly began to pull on his uniform, single piece by single piece.

The boots came last, always last.

$\bigcap *$ XLII

Commander Byykr leaned back in the swivel. With his considerable additional bulk on the joints, it creaked.

Gerswin stood at attention.

"Sit down, Major. Or stand, whatever you want, whatever's comfortable. I know you're not the sitting type. Strange officer you are, young man and old man, patient and impatient."

The green eyes that peered from the rounded face of the base executive officer were the man's sole sharp feature, the only hint of intensity.

His soft voice continued, as Gerswin relaxed slightly and settled into the straight-backed chair opposite the corner of the commander's console.

"This is the second year in a row you've requested assignment to a combat position, and I'm going to recommend that your request be denied. Before I do, I'm going to tell you why, and I hope you will understand. My decision, of course, is not final, but the commanding officer usually takes my recommendation, and the recommendations of commanding officers are rarely overturned."

Gerswin nodded without speaking.

"Do you have anything to say at this point?"

"No, ser. Like to hear your reasons."

"You don't seem terribly surprised, and I'm not surprised that you aren't. I wouldn't even be surprised if you had put in this request merely for the purposes of declaring your loyalty. I won't put that to the test, nor will I attempt to find out if your request is a bluff. For your sake, I almost hope it is, because the stakes are far higher than I suspect you understand. You belong here, not in combat, unlike Captain Hermer, who is now a major, by the way, and who was kept here far longer than she should have been."

Gerswin shifted his weight slightly, but did not turn his eyes from the commander.

199

Byykr coughed twice and leaned forward in the swivel, which creaked as he moved, and turned in his seat to look at the mural to his left, and to Gerswin's right. The often reproduced holoview was that of the Academy Spire, mirrored in Crystal Lake.

Byykr's sharp green eyes came back to rest on the younger major.

"In some ways, Major, you would have been better as a chief tech, but you're too aggressive and quick for that. I'm not being critical, but you have the kind of understanding and technical competence that is usually provided to the Service by its technicians. I'm told by those who should know that you can probably rebuild a flitter from the deck up, and that you know biologics better than all but the best of the ecologists.

"I wouldn't know how much farther your abilities go, but I do know they go farther than any other officer on this base today. That kind of knowledge in a line officer will make you invaluable as someone's executive officer some day, but, combined with your skill as a pilot, it makes you extraordinarily dangerous to the standard political-type officer. And outside of the field bases, like Old Earth here, most commanding officers are usually political types. Why do you think the mortality is so high in combat? No—don't try to answer that. It wasn't meant for an answer."

Byykr cleared his throat and continued. "I hope you can understand the point I'm making."

"It would seem that my career is at a dead end. The more I learn, the more dangerous I become, and the less likely I am to ever leave."

"That's possible. But it doesn't mean that your career is ended. You'll doubtless become the operations officer, probably as soon as Vlerio leaves next year, both of which I've already recommended. After a tour or a little more in that slot, if you don't retire, and I'd certainly recommend against that for you, you'll become the base executive officer, and probably, by that time, the odds-on favorite for base commandant."

"But I'll never leave Old Earth on a Service tour, is that it? Why not?"

"Simple. You know too much, and you're far too good a pilot, and a good leader, even if you are a loner. You get assigned to combat, and with your record, any combat coordinator would give at least his right arm to have you as a heavy corvette or destroyer commander. The problem is that you'd get assigned the suicide missions. You're good enough to survive most of them.

"That means they'd start dumping you with missions they'd like to have done, but couldn't delude themselves into believing anyone could pull off. From the point of view of the Service, that would be a disaster."

"Disaster?"

"Absolutely." Byykr coughed once. "Every young hot-blood would be trying to beat your record, and all of them would die, along with a lot of innocent crews. If you survived yourself, the Service might never recover from your example, and even if you didn't, they'd have to award you the Emperor's Cross posthumously, which would inspire too many others to emulate you.

"So any good, experienced, political officer would immediately assign you a dirty quiet job guaranteed to kill you and your ship. Without any gain to the Empire and without any publicity. That's too much of a waste of talent, even for an old cynic like me.

"Besides, you're doing a good job here. Things get done. People are happy, for the most part, when by all rights they ought to be miserable. We old goats can complete a tour here and retire with a pat on the back. So you stay."

Gerswin smiled a wry smile. "You aren't totally encouraging."

"That comes later. What I'm trying to make clear is that the combat service represents a form of suicide for you, at least in a conflict environment like the present."

"And it doesn't for Major Hermer?"

"Not as much. For reasons embedded in the psychology of the race, most commanders don't regard women as a personal and physical threat, unless the commander is female. Then, there are still few enough top women commanders that they need to nurture every possible ally for their own future.

"My hopes for the major are that by the time she's recognized for her abilities either this war is over, and that should be soon from the spacio-political outlines I've seen, or she will have been promoted or otherwise protected by a political officer type with enough brains to see what an asset she can be.

"You, on the other hand, are not a team player, even though you build better teams than any officer I've ever had the privilege of supervising. You are goal-oriented, and nothing seems to stop you, except death, and one gets the feeling you've already bought him off."

The commander swiveled to look at Gerswin directly. He cleared his throat and coughed, louder this time, blocking the cough with his clenched and pudgy fist.

"I know, Major, you've got nearly twenty-five years in service, but these days careers of fifty aren't uncommon, and there's no mandatory retirement age. All you have to do is pass the stress physical every year. I won't, according to my private med source. But you, you've got plenty of time, and who knows? I could be wrong. Maybe you can convince my successor, if you want.

"By then, in any case, this Dismorph thing will be over, and at least it will be harder for a political type to use you as an expendable."

Gerswin nodded for what seemed the tenth time in the largely one-sided conversation.

"Understand your points, Commander."

"Now," continued the executive officer, "you can appeal, which will leave a record in the files, or you can wait until next year, and re-submit without prejudice in the annual career plan order request submissions."

"I'll have to think about next year when the time comes. No appeal now."

"Do you have any other questions, Major?"

"None you haven't already answered, ser."

The swivel creaked as the hulking, white-haired officer eased himself to his feet and offered his hand to Gerswin.

Gerswin snapped to his own feet and took the proferred handshake.

"It's been a pleasure to watch what you can do, Major, and I hope to be able to continue watching for a while."

"Thank you, Commander. Based on your advice and observations, I expect I'll be doing the same type job for a time to come."

"I hope so, Major. I hope so."

Gerswin stiffened into full attention.

"That's all, Major."

As Gerswin left, behind him he heard the creak of the overtaxed swivel as the commander replaced himself in it.

 XLIII

H.M.S. *Black Prince*

MacGregor C. Gerswin, Major, I.S.S.
Old Earth Base
I.S.D.C. 1212
New Augusta, Sector III

Dear Greg,

I thought about sending you a cube, but this is quicker and more certain. In my vanity, I thought you might have heard about the difficulties we had to surmount here last week. If not, you should get the whole story some time, but not, for the reasons of official censorship, from me.

Enough to say that we came through all right, although a measure of that is that I was among the more junior COs (that's right, commanding officer of my very own Imperial corvette) of the squadron, and now am the senior commander of a rather less impressive squadron, led by the *Black Prince*. What you taught me helped a lot, and so did the skipper of the *Graystone*. (Rumor has it that he was the only Academy graduate not from Old Earth ever to come close to your record in piloting at New Colora.) His family will probably receive the Imperial Cross. Never have I seen such incredible coverage from such a small ship. They say it was a corvette, but looked more like an armed scout to me.

I wish I could tell you what's likely to happen next, but now that everyone understands the situation, I expect our operations will become more measured and deal from our strength. In a way, I feel sorry for the Dismorphs, but not sorry enough. Without the *Graystone*, and, I admit to some degree, the little we were able to accomplish, we might not be here to talk about the next offensive.

Enough said about it. We could have used you, but had you been where you really could have been used, none of this might have happened. I know that's cryptic, but let's leave it at that.

Surprisingly, I miss Old Earth. Not just you, although I can't delude myself into believing that isn't a big factor, but the planet itself, for all the grayness, the winds, the ice rains, and the cold, cold, and cold. It was home to our ancestors for a long, long time. Out here, or should I say, in here, where the stars spray together like clouds in the night skies, Earth seems so far away, and yet important that it should be reclaimed for what it was. I once thought that it ought to remain as it stands as a memorial to human stupidity, but that will always be with us. . . .

The console is blinking red in three points, and I'll close because who knows when I'll be able to steal another few minutes, and I do want to get this off to you. I regret nothing, except that I didn't have the nerve to come to you earlier, but you have made a light where there was none, and the path ahead is brighter for it.

My love,
Faith

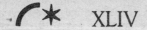

XLIV

The major glanced toward the open doorway, then stood, brushing back the swivel, and leaving the torp fax flimsy on the flat working surface of the console.

Thud!

The old-fashioned door shuddered in its frame with the force he had imparted.

The flimsy fluttered off the console in a back-and-forth sideways flight before diving to the floor behind the swivel.

The major retrieved the message before it had finally settled, holding it firmly in his left hand.

He read it again, knowing he had not overlooked anything, centering his attention on the last paragraph.

". . . In addition to next-of-kin, Major Hermer's Form DN-12 requested you be notified under clause 3(b), principal-at-interest . . ."

His eyes skipped upward toward the beginning.

". . . in the most honorable tradition of the Empire . . . Major Faith X. Hermer . . . awarded the Emperor's Star (posthumously) . . . action beyond the call of duty . . ."

The words spilled through his mind like the spring run-off of the Great West River, roaring past him without meaning. He placed the single flimsy back on the console.

His feet carried him in a tight circle in front of the console. Two, three circuits, and he reversed direction automatically, feet moving him back around the circle, though he could hear the whispers from outside the closed door.

Twenty minutes ago, he had been reviewing a recon pattern for the southeast basin when a junior tech had tiptoed in and placed the flimsy on his console, bowing and scraping the whole three meters from door to console and the whole three meters back from console to door.

The major stopped his circling and took a single deep breath, then another, clenching and unclenching his fists, tightening the muscles in his forearms, loosening them. The inside of his left forearm brushed his waistband and the hardness behind it.

Without volition, the throwing knife was in his left hand.

Thunk!

Heavy and impenetrable as the plastic of the door was, it could not resist the knife buried there to half its depth.

He walked to the door, slowly eased out the heavy blade and replaced it in the waist sheath.

He opened the door deliberately, not looking back at the flimsy on the console and stepped outside his small office into the general Operations area.

Two of the techs at the end of the nearest row of consoles failed to look away quickly enough, but the major ignored them as he marched toward the duty console.

Frylar, Technician First Class, said nothing, waiting.

"Tell Vlerio . . . be back later. Sick leave . . . if necessary. Need air. Be outside."

He stepped away, conscious of the faint click of his boots in the envelope of silence that seemed to surround him as he hurried toward the southwest lock doors.

Mechanically, his hands touched the correct studs, and he passed through the inner door, and, in turn, through the outer portal, and into the rain.

Rain sleeted from the low clouds, not cold enough to fall in ice droplets, instantaneously soaking the thin gray indoor tunic.

The man ignored the chill, and the cold passed from his awareness as if it had never been. His long strides carried him toward the practice yard.

He held throwing knives in each hand, advancing on the rain-swept targets as if they were the enemy.

Thunk!

Thunk!

He recovered his weapons and stepped back, three steps, four, five, six, turning, hefting them as if to drive them through the plastic coated foam of the target heads.

Thunk!

Thunk!

The thin wail of the wind inched toward a shriek as the storm center neared the Imperial bunkers crouched under their cover of stone and heavy clay.

Thunk!
Thunk!

The rain sheets became waterfalls pouring from gray oceans overhead.

Thunk!
Thunk!

The wind shrieked like a corvette with its screens wrenched apart, and the waterfalls became solid walls of water from which the major emerged, still hefting the knives that seemed to cut through the storm itself, ignoring the calf-high torrents that pulled at him.

Thunk!
Thunk!

⟨* XLV

"You've been avoiding me."

The I.S.S. lieutenant had green hawk-eyes and tight curled black hair. Her eyes were level with the major who stood by the battered console.

Outside of the panoramic pictures of the western peaks spread on the wall behind the console, the small office was bare of decoration. The flat top surface of the console and the working surface to the right of the screen were also bare, except for the small pile of hard copy reports in the left-hand corner, and for the thin and tattered publication lying next to the console screen.

The lieutenant's eyes darted to the publication and drank in the title—*Program Key Locks—Patterns and Uses*—before returning her eyes to the hawk-yellow stare of the major.

"Have I?"

"Yes," she answered.

Each waited a moment, then another.

At last, the major's lips quirked slightly. "Guess I have." He shrugged.

"I said I'd be back. I know you didn't promise anything. But you're cold. Like the ice rain. And you're not."

Inclining his head, he returned her statement with a puzzled frown.

"Cold like the ice rain, but I'm not?"

"You know what I mean. Under your ice . . ." She broke off her own statement with a half-shrug, half-headshake.

"Suppose so." He cleared his throat, looked down at the smooth flooring, then back at her. "Didn't mean to hurt you. Or to string you along. Hoped you'd understand."

He looked away from the directness in her eyes.

"Techs say you lost the woman you loved. That you won't let yourself care again. That you throw your knives like hate."

209

She glanced over his shoulder at the halfholo view on the far right, the needle spire of Centerpeak.

He did not look up.

"Lost . . . one way of putting it. Lost both." His head came up abruptly, and his eyes locked hers, both unwavering. He said nothing.

This time she looked away, her eyes seeking the thin volume on the console, noting the irregular print of the title, the yellowed tinge to the pages. *Program Key Locks* had all the hallmarks of an underground datapick manual. She wondered where the major, the devilkid dedicated to the Service and to the reclamation of Old Earth, had discovered it, and why.

Realizing that she was letting her thoughts avoid dwelling on his isolation, she forced herself to raise her eyes back to his.

"You make it hard to talk," she said.

"True. Hard for all of us devilkids. Harder for me, I suspect. Maybe not."

He took a half-step away from the console toward her.

"Kiedra . . . not the one for you."

She did not move, standing perfectly still as if encased in solid ice rain.

He took another step, lifting each of her hands into his. Gently.

"Not now. Not ever."

He could see the glistening sheen building in her eyes, refused to let himself be moved, refused to let the ice that surrounded him crack, and stood, hands holding hers.

"Not ever?" She tilted her head fractionally to the side and back, moistened her lips.

Gerswin resisted the urge to brush her lips with his, instead leaned forward and let them brush her forehead. He stepped back, but did not release her hands.

Kiedra blinked twice, though no tears fell from the corners of her eyes, and swallowed.

"Still not easy," her voice husked, almost dry.

The major shook his head gently, squinting once as if the soft light in the small office were more like the glare above the clouds or on the peaks represented behind him on the wall.

"No. It's not."

"Can you tell me why?"

"Not now. When I can, you won't need me to."

"Should I understand?"

Gerswin shrugged.

"Depends on what you remember. Depends on what you value, and on what I value. Right now, we have to value different things."

He released her hands. His own tingled from the contact with the strong coolness of her fingers.

"Greg . . ."

She did not finish the statement she began, but looked down, to the console, to the floor, then back to the yellow hardness of piercing hawk-eyes.

Finally, she began again. "Can't be Greg, can it? Has to be Captain. Or Major. Or Commander. You have too much to do, too much to let yourself go right now."

He did not answer, but met her eyes. Again, she looked away.

"So strong . . . and so hurt . . ." She lifted her head, her chin, and gave a little shake. "So few will look past the hawk."

His lips quirked once more.

"Hawk? I think not."

"Hawk," she affirmed. "A hawk with a heart too big for hunting, and a purpose too vast not to."

He shrugged. "Hawk or not, poetic words or not, some have stood by you . . . and will when I cannot. Will be for you alone, when I cannot."

"There is that."

"Then do not disregard it."

"I do as I please."

"Do as you please, Kiedra. Do as you please."

"Do I sound that awful?"

Gerswin had to grin at the mock-plaintive note in her question.

"Not quite."

The lieutenant studied his grin and the forced twinkle in his eyes. After a moment, she returned his expression with a smile.

"Should I laugh or cry?"

"Should I?"

"Both!"

The lieutenant followed her exclamation by throwing both

arms around the major, kissed him hard upon the lips, and dropped away as quickly as she had struck.

"That's for what you've missed, and for treating me fairly. Not sure I wanted to be treated fairly, and I reserve the right to reopen the question."

With that, she turned.

The major did not move as he watched her cross the last few meters and leave the office, an office that felt barer than before.

He swallowed, then took a deep breath. His chest felt strangely tight, and he inhaled deeply again, shaking his shoulders and trying to relax. His eyes felt hot, not quite burning, but he blinked back the feeling, finally looking down at *Program Key Locks*.

"Hope Lerwin appreciates her . . ."

His words sounded empty in the office, echoed coldly against the flat walls.

He sat and stared for a long time at the console screen.

Long after the echoes had died, long after the lieutenant had vanished, long after, the index finger of his left hand touched the console keyboard.

He sighed once more, then resumed the work he had started what seemed ages ago, before an early spring had come and gone in the space of a few afternoon moments.

XLVI

The red-headed lieutenant waved.

"Come on, Captain."

Gerswin smiled. The devilkids, as they trickled back to Old Earth, uniformly referred to him as "Captain," for all that he wore the single gold triangle of an I.S.S. major on his tunic collars or his flight suits.

The lieutenant waved again from the open hatchway of the dozer's armored cockpit. "Come on."

Gerswin broke into a quickstep for the remaining fifty meters across the tarmac.

"Getting slower there, Captain."

Gerswin shook his head to dispute the fact, but grinned and said nothing as he swung into the cockpit and closed the hatch behind him.

Lieutenant Glynnis MacCorson closed her own hatch and strapped in.

"Damned cargo run," she grumped.

"You still like it."

"You're right. Since they didn't want any more flitter pilots, had to find something else to run. Didn't matter if it was big and ugly."

She turned to the controls before her, controls more like a spacecraft than a flitter.

"Everyone's aboard, Lieutenant." The tech peered into the cockpit through the hatchway from the small passenger/cargo/living section of the arcdozer.

"Stet, Nylan. Commencing power-up."

Gerswin watched, unspeaking, as she ran through the checklist which centered on the fusactor powering the behemoth that could have swallowed an I.S.S. corvette for breakfast and converted it into constituent elements.

"GroundOps, Dragon Two, departing for town. Estimate time en route one point one."

"Understand time en route one point one. Cleared for departure."

"Stet, Dragon Two on the run."

Gerswin shook his head. Speed the dozers weren't made for. The new town, as yet unnamed by the transplanted shambletowners, the few retired techs, the married Service techs, and the handful of immigrants, was less than ten kays away, down a wide and hard-packed causeway with no turns. What would have taken a minute or three by flitter was a major undertaking by dozer. But then, dozers weren't normally used for transport, except on their way to and from major refits at the base.

Before too long, Gerswin reflected, it might be worth the expense to set up a forward maintenance facility, particularly as the dozer operations moved eastward.

Dragon Two was carrying the back-up fusactor for the town. While it could have been airlifted in sections by flitter, assembly was easier at the base, and the arcdozer's slow and even speed made the transport practical.

Once the power source was deposited on its foundation, the structure and distribution system would be completed around it.

Glynnis smiled happily as she checked the monitors, and as the dozer tracs rumbled across the hard packed clay, compacting it still further.

Gerswin shifted his weight in the seat normally used by the senior tech and let his eyes slide over the blanked out bank of controls that would normally monitor intake, processing, and treatment of the tons of dirt, clay, and organic matter that a dozer processed hour by hour, day after day.

A movement caught his eye, and he glanced up.

At the top of a low embankment ahead of the dozer and to the right of the causeway stood a group of shambletowners, old shambletowners dressed in tattered coyote leathers. They stood, blank-faced, and watched as the dozer rumbled toward them.

Their eyes were slits, their faces hard in the bright light of a morning that was only partly cloudy, with a few traces of a cold blue sky above the mottled white and gray clouds.

"Not exactly friendly," observed Glynnis.

"No. We've changed a few things."

"And they don't care for the changes. Can't say I have much sympathy. Did so well under the old way, didn't we?"

Gerswin saw the leathers of the sling and repressed the urge to jump as the missile hurled toward the dozer.

Crack!

The stone slapped against the cockpit armaglass, leaving only a streak of dust.

A figure on the end of the line of shambletowners was reloading his sling with another smooth stone.

Fynian, Gerswin thought, although the man was looking down and not directly at the major.

Crack!

Glynnis shook her head.

"Really are out after us."

"Devilkids and Impies one and the same to them."

"We know different, Captain."

Gerswin smiled faintly. "For them, it's all the same." He looked back over his right shoulder at the shambletowners, still standing in a line on the embankment. "If we succeed, Glynnis, won't be the same for us, either."

"Take longer than I've got, Captain."

Gerswin nodded slowly and settled back to watch the lieutenant as the causeway rolled slowly by. He drank in the tall plains grasses that were beginning to fill in the spots where nothing had grown, and glanced from checkerboard field to checkerboard field where the organic sponge grains grew and would be harvested again and again until the soil was ready for grasses or food crops for people or livestock—not that there would be much livestock for a long time to come if he and the ecologists had much to say about it.

How long before the land was ready? He shrugged. Mahmood's prediction had been ten years after the first sponge grains and outcropping. So far, for the few lands that had completed the process, Mahmood had been right.

He missed the idealistic ecologist, but who could blame him for retiring to take the ecology chair at the college on Medina?

Time passed people by, slowly, ponderously, just as the dozer had passed the shambletowners, but with the same kind of unstoppable force.

"You know your records still stand, Captain?"

Glynnis' words broke his reverie.

"Records?"

"The ones you set for the Academy Ironman. Lerwin came within five minutes. No one else has come within twenty, and they never will."

"Someday, someone will. Time passes."

The cockpit lit as the clouds let the sun break through, and Gerswin absorbed the warmth momentarily before tapping the vent to bring in more cool air from outside. Too much light and heat still bothered him.

"They say ice water runs in your veins."

"Anti-ice, maybe."

Gerswin knew he was being distant, but he hoped she would understand.

Whether Glynnis did or not, the lieutenant said nothing else as the dozer rumbled over the highest point on the trip and began the equally gentle descent toward the town.

Gerswin relaxed as much as he could, and tried to enjoy the slow pace of the trip, away from the base, from the constant flow of communications that cluttered the Ops screens, all of which had to be monitored and evaluated before Vlerio had a chance to see it, much less act on it. With Vlerio off with the base commander for the three days ahead, Gerswin could leave Lerwin to watch the screens and the day-to-day activities.

Anything really serious and Lerwin could reach him in seconds.

Gerswin watched as the town wall appeared ahead on the right. Before he knew it the dozer was slowing, gradually, heavily, but certainly.

"GroundOps, Dragon Two at destination. Beginning cargo drop this time."

"Stet. Understand cargo drop. Report when drop complete and proceeding to station."

"Stet. Will report when proceeding to station."

Gerswin eased himself out of the operator's seat. He stood in the space behind the two front seats as Glynnis and Nylen began to maneuver the dozer around to place the materials drop section, where the fusactor sat, as close as possible to the reinforced ferroplast slab.

"Twenty reverse on the right rear."

"Twenty right rear."

"Bring up the left a touch."

"Stet."

"Stress load on the ramp is point nine five and steady."

"Lieutenant, we've got it on the downslope and clear of the joints. Hold the tracs."

"Locked and holding . . ."

". . . three more on the left . . ."

". . . right corner sticking . . . liquid slick it . . ."

". . . clearing top section . . ."

". . . load factor on the ramp at point eight three and dropping . . ."

". . . clear of the ramp, and in position."

"Understand clear of the ramp."

"That's affirmative, Lieutenant. You're clear to move forward."

Gerswin watched as Glynnis wiped her forehead with the back of her jumpsuit sleeve.

"On the roll."

Hands flicking across the console, Glynnis eased the dozer away from the uncompleted section of town wall and back down the incline onto the causeway, bringing the dozer to a stop.

"That's done, Captain."

"Nicely," he commented with a smile.

"No . . . But we got it done. Sloppy on the trac balancing."

She pushed several stray red hairs off her forehead and squared herself in the seat.

"You leaving now?"

"Don't want to go out on station while you plow up my favorite purple clay and change it into old-fashioned dirt. Not now, anyway."

"Sure about that?"

"I'm sure."

"Have it your way, Captain." She flashed a smile. "See you in a week or so."

He nodded, then ducked down the passageway and out through the crew exit.

The other tech, Krysten, snapped a salute at him as he slipped outside and landed lightly on the packed red clay.

After returning the salute, he walked back toward the uncompleted section of the wall, paralleling the half-meter deep prints the dozer had left in the work ramp.

As he reached the spot where the fused clay wall had been left untouched, he waved again at the dozer. Glynnis had already begun to inch Dragon Two forward and toward the golden plains beyond, toward a destination out beyond the golden green of the sponge grains, out over the horizon where the line of dozers methodically extended the borders of arable land.

Even seventy meters away, Dragon Two still towered over the wall and Gerswin, seemingly taller than either as it crept eastward.

In time, Gerswin turned and walked through the opening in the wall and past the ferroplast foundation where techs were already beginning to erect the remainder of the back-up power station around the fusactor. His feet took him toward the central square of the town that had no name.

At first glance, the new town could have passed for an updated and cleaner version of the old shambletown, with white glazed finishes over thick walls of fired bricks. But the streets, rather than narrow canyons, opened to the sky, boulevards radiating from the square. The houses, neither individual nor wall-to-wall, clustered in groups, standing in the midst of more open space than any shambletowner would have ever dreamed, although none were taller than two stories, and all possessed the thick walls. Instead of hide covers the windows had double-paned armaglass for their still small apertures.

The streets were paved with gray stone slabs cut with lasers, and stone flower boxes appeared at irregular intervals, filled with blue ice flowers and a yellow flower Gerswin did not recognize.

He passed an expanse of green turf, a park with several skeletal structures on which two children clambered. The grassy space was surrounded on three sides by clustered housing, and by the boulevard on the fourth.

One child wore a jumpsuit, the other a leather tunic over cloth trousers.

The major nodded at the mix of shambletown and Empire, but kept walking toward the central square.

The sunlight dimmed as the clouds above darkened and cut off the direct rays, and as the wind rose again. So much for the hint of a real summer.

He sniffed the air, drawing in the hint of the rain which would likely fall, rain since it was mid-summer. Only in the warmest of the supposed summer months was there little or no chance of ice rain, not that the ice rain bothered him much.

"Good morning, Major."

"Good morning."

Gerswin returned the greeting although he did not recognize the man who had passed him. From his dress, the man was a retired tech, one of the few who had elected to remain once their obligations had expired, despite the landspouts and the cold.

Like the shambletown, at mid-morning the central square was mostly deserted, except for the handful of older men of Imperial origin, and three younger women, all noticeably pregnant.

Gerswin surveyed the buildings, all white glazed brick except for the community hall, which boasted a stone columned front and a short belltower that reached roughly fifteen meters above the square.

The square itself consisted of a boulevard running in a rectangle around a central park two hundred meters on a side. Despite the grass, the bushes, a few flowers, and the pathways, something was missing.

He looked again.

Trees! Only a handful of dwarf trees were scattered amid the statues, the pathways, and the hedge maze on the right side where two boys and three girls shrieked as they tore down the dead-end and hidden corridors.

He nodded in understanding. With the high winds, the town couldn't afford the damage of a substantial tree thrown into a building.

After sniffing at the air and discovering nothing but the smells of newness—new brick, new stone, new plastics—he glanced around the square again before beginning his walk to the right and toward the street that would lead to the landing field at the western side of the town.

His steps slowed as he passed two women who sat at opposite ends of a stone bench rising out of the too-green grass imported from New Colora, grass originally from Old Earth.

". . . that's him . . . one they call the Captain . . ."

Gerswin ignored the whispers and kept walking.

"Captain of what? He's a major."

"Some say he's the devil's Captain . . . Was a devil-kid. . . ."

". . . good-looking in his own way. . . ."

Gerswin kept walking and let the voices fade into the background as his steps brought him opposite the community hall.

His eyes passed over the closed endurasteel doors. Automatic portals would have taken too much energy—particularly for civilians, the Service had noted. Gerswin had agreed with the decision, but not for that reason.

He turned right, down toward the main gate and the short landing strip beyond.

A patch of green before the wall and the gate appeared as he approached—another park. The tops of the mountains behind the foothills were barely visible under the whitish gray of the higher than normal clouds. The lower stratus layers that raced westward above the town had not reached the foothills yet, nor had the rain begun to fall, although it would.

Gerswin caught the glint of a flitter, the one coming to pick him up and increased his already quick steps.

While the town represented the future, he felt ill-at-ease on the wide streets between the low buildings. He understood why the older shambletowners had not taken the offer to move from their crowded lanes, even though the confinement of the shambletown was not for him and never had been.

Would he always feel uncomfortable in the future he was helping to build? Would the reclaimed lands seem strange after the desolate high plains of purple clay, purpled grasses, coyotes, and ice rain?

He paced onward, his face set in an expression showing neither joy nor sadness.

XLVII

Gerswin juggled the heavy, double-ended and double-bladed knife in his left hand, then balanced it on his fingertip, finally flipping it end over end into the air, where he snatched it right-handed at its mid-point.

He glanced at the targets, ignoring the figure who waited behind the wall at his back, the wall that surrounded the make-shift practice range. The last glimpse he had caught indicated that Major Vlerio was still waiting, although it had only been minutes since he arrived.

Vlerio's approach had been diffident, almost hesitant. When Gerswin had stopped to walk over, the other had motioned him back, saying, "Finish up. However long it takes. I'll wait."

Gerswin raised his eyebrows in puzzlement, but turned from the target and began to walk away.

Abruptly, he dived to the left, twisted in mid-air, releasing the knife, and tucked. He came out of the roll on the balls of his feet, the second knife in his left hand momentarily—before it too sped toward the target.

Dusting his hands on the legs of the old flight suit, he trotted forward to retrieve the knives. As he covered the nearly ten meters between him and the target he had chosen, he checked his accuracy.

Both knives would have penetrated the heart, had the target been a man, although the first had not gone through the plastic-shielded and stiffened foam as much as he would have liked.

He frowned as he stepped up to the target, listening, but there was no sound of movement from Vlerio. He eased the first knife from the target and replaced it in the waistband sheath. The second followed.

Glancing upward at the clouds, he could see the light gray darkening in the north, a sign that the ice rain would be returning.

He sniffed, but the air remained dry, with little hint of moisture.

Reiner Vlerio still sat quietly on the far side of the back stone wall, waiting patiently, although Gerswin knew he was ready to leave Old Earth for his promotion to commander and his transfer back to New Augusta in whatever obscure screen-shoving assignments detail his orders had brought.

Gerswin took a deep breath and walked to the far left end of the unofficial practice yard. Once, he had been the only one who used it, but most of the other devilkids had taken up his example and practiced with their own versions of unpowered weapons. The sling was one of the few that they all used. As if by unspoken custom, none practiced together, and anyone who might be using the range left whenever Gerswin appeared.

Improvements had appeared from time to time. While Gerswin had built the wall behind the targets and the target stands, Lerwin had added the side walls and the swinging target. Lostwin had added the rear wall and the stone bench, the one on which Vlerio waited. Glynnis had provided the sandy pit and the high target.

Gerswin smiled and broke into a sprint for the right side of the yard.

Crack! Crack!

As he fired the second stone, he dove into a roll, discarding the sling and coming up with the knife, right-handed this time.

Thunk!

He surveyed the three targets. Had they been human, two would have been dead. One he had only struck in the "shoulder." That had been the second sling stone.

Retrieving the two sling stones, the sling leathers and the knife, he replaced all three in their hidden sheaths and trotted to the rear stone wall, only meters from Vlerio, whom he ignored by failing to acknowledge the other's presence.

He turned to face the targets, his back nearly touching the stone wall, then began a zig-zag sprint toward the swinging target to the left of the three "standing" targets.

Crack! Crack!

He flung himself into a dive that would land him in the sand pit, bringing out the knife with his left hand and releasing it before he plowed into the heavy sand.

Thud!

After picking himself out of the sand and dusting off the cold and damply clinging grains, he shook his head.

The sling shots had been on target, but the first had merely been to get the target moving. The knife had not been accurate; it had bounced off the middle standing target.

He retrieved the sling stones, the sling, and the knife. This time, when he picked up the second stone and pressed his fingers against the rounded smoothness, the stone split, as stones often did after hard and repeated use.

He tossed the fragments over the wall behind the targets, ignoring the twin *clicks* as they struck the rocky clay of the slope.

Vlerio was still sitting on the stone bench.

Gerswin pursed his lips, exhaled deeply, and replaced the weapons. The major wasn't known for his patience.

Rather than vault the chest-high irregular wall, Gerswin walked around it.

Vlerio looked up as he approached.

"Rather impressive, Gerswin."

"Like to keep in shape."

"It must help your coordination, although I doubt you need much help there. Such primitive weapons might not be much good in combat, not against lasers or stunners, but you'd probably be safe in any back alley in the Empire."

"Possibly," Gerswin answered non-committally. He smiled as he seated himself on a section of the wall where he generally faced Vlerio, who, in turn, twisted toward Gerswin.

"Not primitive," added the junior major. "Unpowered. Difference there. Knife and sling are much better in-close weapons than lasers."

"I didn't come to debate weapons, but I would be interested in a less cryptic explanation of why you think so."

Gerswin shrugged.

"Close in, lasers aren't that selective. Hit innocents as well as targets. If you intend to destroy whole companies of troops, why bother with hand weapons at all? Use tacheads or particle beams and boil off the whole area. Hand weapons are designed for individuals. Otherwise, just dangerous toys to make people feel good. You can run out of charges for a laser or a stunner. Damned difficult to run out of stones, and you can use a knife over and over."

"What if you want to occupy territory or seize a specific objective?"

"You can't take it with unpowered weapons, have to question why you want to take it at all. A laser or beam fire-fight won't leave much behind. So why bother with losing troops? Vaporize it with a beam or tachead. Costs less in money and personnel."

This time Vlerio was the one to shake his head.

"You're still a barbarian, Gerswin. Dangerously direct."

"Never said I wasn't. Just don't believe in wars unless it's for survival. Or freedom. Anything else is an excuse." Gerswin paused. "But you didn't come to talk about philosophies of conflict."

"No. I'm leaving tomorrow, and I wanted to talk to you before I left. Alone."

Gerswin automatically scanned the slope before nodding. Not certain what he could say, he waited for Vlerio to go on.

"I don't like you. Not that I dislike you, because I don't. Not that I don't admire you, because I do. But I don't like you. You can be as direct as a knife, and as sharp. One way or another, if you want it done, it gets done."

Vlerio gestured toward the practice yard. "Like your training. I've watched the Corpus Corps practice. You want more perfection than they do. You don't know all the techniques, but if I had to bet on the outcome of a contest between you and any one of them, I'd bet on you. When you and Lerwin practice on the mats, people watch, and they swallow. Like watching carnacats."

"You're a modern barbarian warlord, Gerswin. One who knows all the technology, but who's kept touch with the need for personal example and the inspiration of personal combat.

"I don't like you, but my success as Operations officer is because of you. Because of you, I'm going to get a promotion I thought I'd lost when I was assigned here. You know that, and I know that, and Commander Manders knows that. Now, my last tour will still be a nothing, but it's a nothing with the diamonds on the collars, and that's important to me."

Vlerio stood, and Gerswin slipped off the wall.

"I didn't like you when I came, Major, and that hasn't changed. But whether you're a barbarian or not, whether I like you or not, you do a damned good job, too good to be wasted.

So you're my successor, and I'm told that your promotion to major has been made permanent."

The older officer smiled a tight smile. "I wish I could be more positive personally, Gerswin, but that's the way it is."

Gerswin met the other's eyes, trying not to be too direct in his glance. "Appreciate your honesty, ser."

"Don't worry about that. Just prove I was right." Vlerio nodded curtly, and turned, his heavy steps carrying him eastward toward the portals back into the base complex.

Gerswin swallowed, knowing that what Vlerio had said had cost the man. Maybe he'd been too harsh in his private judgments of the major.

He looked down at the hard-packed clay, then at the empty bench.

Click! Click! Click!

The ice rain splattered against the stones of the walls and against the slabs of the bench as the wind picked up, and as the whispers of the air built into a thin wail that announced the on-coming storm.

XLVIII

Crunch. Crunch. Crunch.

Each step echoed, ringing off the dingy white walls between which the man walked. His deliberate steps left a track in the centimeters of ice crystals that formed a layer of pavement above the stone and clay that served as the foundation of both streets and alleys.

He crossed the main street, scarcely wider than the back way he tracked. Both were empty in the late winter afternoon.

A quick glance to his left, up toward the old square, revealed no one, nor any tracks down toward the older section of the shambletown where his steps had taken him, as they always did on his infrequent visits to the past.

So cold were the ice flakes that his feet scarcely slipped as he completed crossing the larger lane. Once past the crossing and back between two walls of the narrowing lane, he stopped, listening.

. . . crunch . . .

The single step stopped.

He nodded, waiting, but his distant shadow moved not at all.

Click! Click! Click, click, click!

The ice crystals continued their faint clatter as they struck both the walls and the smoothness of the Imperial all-weather jacket.

His eyes flickered up toward the nearest window, vacant, with only a small remnant of thonging wrapped around the lashing post to show where the vanished hide covering had once been secured.

Most of the crowded-together structures on the old lane were vacant, for they had been the ones given to the younger couples, or those without status in the shambletown—those who had been the first to move to the new town.

He took another step, silently until his boot touched the crystals, and the *crunch* reverberated back up the lane behind him. The echoing step-*crunch* from his unseen shadow whispered back down the slanted lane to him.

. . . *crunch* . . .

A tight smile creased the slender man's face, framed loosely by the jacket's unlined hood, as he resumed his journey down the crystalline lane and away from the larger cross street. With his gray trousers and the silver gray of the jacket and his light steps, had there been no sound of ice, his presence would have been silent. Then the one who followed could truly have believed that a graying ghost again stalked the old shambletown.

Whhhrrr.

The man in silver and gray sprinted the three steps around the curve.

Crack!

Powdered white wall plaster puffed out from the impact of the sling stone and drifted downward to join the white crystals that had already covered the clay and stone of the shambletown pavement.

Crunch. Crunch. Crunch.

This time, the man in silver timed his steps to match those of his hidden pursuer as the two seemed to float through the ice fall toward the wall of the abandoned tannery where the lane dead-ended into an even narrower cross lane.

Whhhrrrr.

Crack!

Another stone powdered the flaking white and time-dimmed wall plaster, striking less than a meter from the hooded man and breaking off enough of the plaster to show a brown circle of crumbling brick beneath.

The silvered man dropped his deliberate stride and sprinted the last few meters down the remaining and steepest section of the lane, darting around the corner to the left.

Crack!

Crunch. Crunch, crunch, crunch.

The shadowy figure of the follower edged down the lane, a bent figure, dark in tattered tunic and leathers, with a gnarled right hand on which there were white hairs above the scars, twirling the sling with a killer stone within the straps. His head turned slowly from side to side, as if he listened for the faintest of sounds.

He neared the dead-end corner and paused.

. . . *crunch* . . .

The sound was light, but not immediately on the far side of the blind corner.

The dark and bent man studied the crystals and the widely-spaced footprints held therein. The distance between prints stated that the man in silver had continued his head-long flight around the corner, possibly into the distance toward the wall and the Maze beyond.

The bent man lifted his head slightly, as if sniffing at the steady wind that brought the ice crystals down in their steady beat against walls, leathers, and faces, and piled those icy fragments on flat roofs, empty clay, and stones.

Finally, he eased around the corner, still bent, then straightened as he whipped the sling up and around toward the slim man in silver who stood ten meters away twirling his own sling.

Crump!

Crack!

The bent and gnarled man swayed, then bent farther over, as, at first, his fingers let slip the leathers of the sling, and as his heavy legs refused to hold him erect any longer.

The man in silver folded his leathers into a flat package, returning them to their hidden pouch, and strode forward into the crystal rain toward the fallen figure.

At last, he stood over the man in leathers and pushed the thin silver hood back off his short and curled blond hair.

His yellow hawk eyes glittered in the gloom of the approaching dusk as he saw that the fallen one still continued to breathe, though he lay face down in the heaped ice droplets.

Gently, as if the older man were a friend, the silver and blond man turned the wounded man over until he rested on his back.

"Devulkid . . . yaaa . . . devul . . ."

His eyes opened wide as he gasped the last word, but no longer did they see.

The man in the all-weather silver shook his head, then stooped and lifted the body in his arms, ignoring the sour odor, the grease, and the blood from the old man's caved-in temple.

Surprisingly, the body was light, and the more-than-once pursued man in gray and silver carried it lightly as he retraced his steps back toward the upper town and the bare stone slab where he would leave the few remaining shambletowners another legacy from their past.

Click. Click. Click.

The ice rain continued to fall on the all-weather finish of the Imperial jacket.

Crunch. Crunch. Crunch.

Each step, each sound, carried the survivor farther into the past and the future simultaneously, aging and rejuvenating him at the same instants, until he found it increasingly difficult to focus on the narrow lane before him.

A deep breath, then another, and he resumed his journey with a body that weighed heavier with each step upward.

With steps more and more deliberate on the slippery footing, he at last entered the square. A single line of footprints, nearly obscured by the ice rain that had fallen, appeared at right angles to his path. He wondered who else had stalked the old ghosts of the shambletown, before realizing that the other prints were also his.

He placed the already-stiffening figure on the white stone of the single upright bench and turned, plodding out toward the gate that was frozen ajar only slightly wider than a body width.

This time, he did not turn back. In time, had there been anyone out in the ice storm, they would have seen a silver-gray ghost with glittering yellow eyes and hair like yellow flame vanishing into the storm from whence he had come. But no one was abroad, and he vanished as silently as he arrived.

Click. Click. Click.

XLIX

Gerswin slammed the console stud.

A single flitter and the spares for one dozer. *One* dozer. Period.

He shook his head and called up the justification that had arrived with the inadequate spare parts.

"Req. 1(b) three(3) class delta flitters, mod. B(4).

"Sup. One(1) class delta flitter, modB(3), per ConsComp Reg. D-11(b), as modified Alstats 11-yr."

While as Operations officer Gerswin did not know the exact content of the Alstats message referenced, he had a good idea of how it had been applied to Old Earth, and the fact that all Old Earth Base requisitions had been cut by two thirds did not surprise him. Virtually everything but trace element foodstuffs had been cut back over the last three years, and from what he could tell from the few supply ships, all the out-bases were being shorted, some worse than Old Earth.

Right now, though, the base needed equipment. There wasn't any metal, nor any native power source to speak of, except the wind, and maybe, near the coasts, some sort of tidal power. The sun shone a fraction more, according to the records, than it had thirty years earlier, the first time detailed records had been entered, but until the ecology could be returned to its pre-collapse state or some approximation thereof, and the particulate-based cloud cover reduced, solar power was out as any sort of reliable alternative.

Gerswin sighed. Everything wound together in a web.

He needed more dozers to reclaim the land and re-establish a usable ground cover and a solid agriculture base. Each dozer required support equipment, personnel, spare parts, and the power to maintain them. Imperial deployed technology was based on fusactors, handy unitized fusion reactors easily produced by any technologically advanced system and impossible to produce anywhere else. Most important, fusactors were expensive to transport. Since an arcdozer was essentially a moving fusactor, the Empire disliked shipping them to distant points. Finally, since fusactors were unitized, once assembled, they were almost impossible to repair and were designed to melt into an impermeable bloc within their own shielding in cases of malfunction.

Without dozers, he couldn't reclaim. Without reclamation, the base couldn't support itself, except slightly above subsistence level, because Imperial technology was all geared to either fusion power or high-energy synthetics.

Without local metals, which no longer existed except in deep deposits or in system asteroids unreachable without high energy technology, the locals had no way to develop substitutes with which to rebuild their planet and their society.

Gerswin didn't have enough dozers to continue full-scale reclamation more than a tour or so into the future, and that was assuming rather optimistic projections. And so far, the base had just begun to make a dent in reverting the ecology.

"So you worry . . ."

He hadn't realized he had spoken aloud until he heard the echo of his words in the small office.

He frowned.

The Empire wouldn't close down Old Earth Base yet, but with the resource commitment it required, he could see the supply lines getting tighter and tighter, year after year.

"What can you do? Order more equipment they won't send you? Exaggerate the requirements along with everyone else? Then they'll cut everyone back farther."

He flicked off the screen and stood, stretching, looking at the lighter gray square where Vlerio's holoview of his wife's estate house had covered half the wall opposite the console.

His steps circled the console.

The old exec, Byykr, had understood some of the problem. But Byykr was gone, and Commander LeTrille was merely going through the motions. Commander Manders understood, but was too tired to start a fight with the Imperial bureaucracy, although, Gerswin admitted to himself, Manders usually took his recommendations.

What good was a recommendation when you couldn't get what you needed and didn't know what else to recommend?

What did Old Earth need?

Metal, power, and arable land.

The arable land might be possible before too long. Acreage had increased to the point where at subsistence level it would support most of the scattered Noram population, assuming the produce could even be distributed. But the land still required a sponge grain scavenge crop every third year.

The power was barely adequate and completely dependent upon the Empire. One possibility existed—coming up with an oilseed plant that could be refined to approximate synthetic fuels—but that required more land, reduced food crop yields, and demanded a refining technology which would require metals and power.

He shook his head.

"Face it, Gerswin. You don't know enough. You can't figure your way out of this one."

As for the metal—unless they could literally mine something . . .

His eyes glinted, and he sat down at the console, flicking it back on and beginning to punch in the numbers, the requests for data.

Finally, when all the requests had been routed, he sat back in the swivel.

Then he laughed.

"It works, or it doesn't."

With that, he stood and walked over to the small wall locker, from which he removed his set of practice knives and sling, plus the quarterstaff.

He whistled three double notes, then stopped before touching the exit stud and stepping out.

"Marliss, I'm going to get some exercise. Should be back in less than an hour."

"Yes, ser."

The major refrained from frowning. The man, a former shambletown youth, was fresh from recruit training and nearly cowered every time Gerswin looked at him.

The idea just might appeal to someone, and the scale was modest enough. A mere two fusactors to power a river reclamation plant.

He remembered what Mahmood had said about drainage. If all those metals were still being leached into the waters, then they'd have to end up in the major drainage rivers.

Now . . . If the ecologists and the engineers could figure out how to make it work and package it, and if Manders bought the idea . . .

He shrugged. If not, he'd try something else.

He straightened the leathers of the sling and whirled it experimentally as he touched the southeast interior exit portal, easing himself and the staff through. He needed more work with the quarterstaff, but Zyleria was on leave, and she was the only one with real training in handling it as a weapon.

He stepped through the outer portal and into the chill outside air.

Plick. Plick. Plick.

The scattered rain droplets hit his flight suit, the last from the passing dark shower under the overclouds, and were gone with a gust of wind.

Gerswin turned west, toward the area he used for his practice with what both Vlerio and Matsuko had called "primitive" weapons.

The key was hope. If he could convince the Empire that certain investments would reduce the long-term costs, and that the improvements would begin fairly soon, he had a chance. No Emperor really wanted to be the one to abandon Old Earth, but it would be harder and harder to get more than a token commitment in the years ahead.

He glanced at the lower hills to the west where the first generation pines had been planted. Trees—they would help. Then some oilseeds; a source of metals—not much, but enough to keep things going for a while, and time.

Crack!

The first stone smacked into the center target head.

Crack!

Crack!

 L

Gerswin blinked and studied the figures on the console again.

Old Earth Base was getting shorted again. Transport costs were attributed by the mass cube ratio multiplied by the energy cost. The farther a destination drop, the higher the imputed cost. Although the out-base runs were supposed to be rotated so that every base was assigned the first, second, third, or fourth drop in roughly equivalent numbers, Gerswin could find no record of Old Earth ever having been assigned first or second drop order. The effect was to increase the energy costs. Yet Old Earth was not listed on the "hardship" destination drop port list, which would have allowed a greater cost ratio.

While the I.S.S. picked up all the costs from its overall transport budget, and not from each base's budget, the political implications bothered Gerswin. If it had only been the mass-cube energy cost assignments, he would not have been so concerned, but the same sort of calculations had been employed in determining costs for foodstuff supplies, personnel transfers, spare and replacement parts, and even for dietary trace elements. The composite gave a picture of Old Earth Base as either inefficient or exceedingly expensive to operate, or both.

Gerswin pursed his lips.

Added to that were the actual personnel assignment policies, which tended to order either low performers or trouble-makers to Old Earth. Although he doubted that anyone was trying to close down the base, or that someone was benefitting from the current allocation practices, there was no doubt in his mind that no one in the I.S.S. hierarchy was able or willing to stand up for Old Earth, even to suggest simple fairness in an allocation system that failed to account for any of the special problems the reclamation effort faced.

Cling!

"Gerswin."

"Major, five minutes before your meeting with the commandant."

"Thanks."

Gerswin tapped the console and stood, straightening his tunic, shrugging his shoulders to relieve the tightness caused by too many hours in front of the screen. With a last shrug, he left his own space and covered the short length of corridor that separated him from the commandant's slightly more elaborate office.

Manders was standing beside his console, which was switched off, as Gerswin swept in.

"Good afternoon, Greg."

"Afternoon, ser."

"What landspout did you tangle with now? You have that look, the one that spells trouble."

"That obvious?"

"With you? Yes." The senior commander sighed, then gestured toward the swivel across the console from him. The older man sank into his own chair.

"Now . . . Can I do anything about your problem?"

"Don't know. Thought I'd ask." Gerswin frowned. "Just finished an analysis of the outship cost-formulas. Do you know why we're always last drop, or next to last drop, but why they don't classify us as hardship or special circumstance?"

"Commander Byykr brought that up once, shortly before he retired. I do not recall the reasons, but I do know that he looked into it rather thoroughly. I'll have it checked on and get back to you. No sense in your doing anything more until you see what, if anything, he did."

Manders cleared his throat. "Not sure it makes any difference in any case, since the shipping costs aren't tabbed against our account."

"Not in the budgetary sense, Commander. Presents a one-sided holo. Shows Old Earth as a conventional base with twice the operating/transport costs of other comparable bases."

"Are you suggesting that is deliberate, Greg?"

"No, ser. More likely that there's no champion at headquarters. It's not that anything's *wrong*. More that Old Earth deserves a special category and hasn't gotten it."

Manders looked over at the wall holo of the Academy Spire, mirrored in Crystal Lake.

Gerswin did not follow his glance. He knew the holo well enough. If it were not a duplicate of the one which had hung on Commander Byykr's wall, it was close enough that the differences were insignificant.

"I've had some of this conversation before, Greg, with Commander Byykr, and there's a bit more to this than meets the eye. I just can't remember why at the moment." He turned back toward Gerswin. "Now. There's something rather more personally important you should know."

"Something I should know?"

The senior commander turned in his swivel. "I'm sure you've heard the rumors." He paused. "About the *Hildebard*?"

"Know she didn't arrive as scheduled," responded the major, still standing.

"Sit down."

Gerswin eased into the swivel.

"Do you know the implications?" The base commander leaned back in the padded swivel. His office was the only one in the entire base with comfortable chairs for visitors.

"Equipment shortages . . . especially turbine fans. Hardest to get around. Morale problems for Imperials due for transfer . . . general feeling of being abandoned."

"There are a few other difficulties, Greg." The commander paused theatrically.

Gerswin frowned. Commander Manders had used his first name twice in minutes. The familiarity was unusual. It was also a message, and the ramifications were even more unexpected.

"The new executive officer?"

Old Earth Base had already gone without an official and permanent executive officer for more than six months, and not a few of the duties had fallen in Gerswin's lap, in addition to his own responsibilities as Operations officer.

"That's the second most important."

Forcing himself to avoid frowning, Gerswin tried to figure out what Manders was hinting at. Usually, the commander was direct, sometimes sarcastically so in private, and the guessing game implied that it was important for Gerswin to come up with the answer.

"All right," began the major. "Assuming the *Hildebard* is a casualty, another three months is the minimum before we get another transport. If High Command can juggle the schedules. Nine months is double the time for critical replacements. Means a rush courier, breaking regulations, or promotion from base cadre."

He shook his head as the implication hit. "Only one officer here meets minimum standards, ser."

The commander nodded in return. "That's right. The message torp that arrived today confirmed that. There's more, Commander."

Gerswin swallowed at the cavalier announcement of his promotion. Promotions to commander were nearly impossible for non-Imperials to get these days, with the cutbacks in ships, and the reliance on smaller and smaller craft and their lower operating costs.

"More?" He knew the statement sounded stupid as he said it and tried to follow on. "That sounds like it means unpleasant news of some sort."

Manders snorted. "And for what are executive officers being groomed, Commander? Think a bit, Greg."

The combination of sarcasm and the gentler use of his name momentarily stopped Gerswin from saying anything.

"Base commander. They need you somewhere else?"

"I wish that were true. My stress profile is edging up into the red. That's the real problem."

Gerswin nodded. If Manders was being pushed off the edge, with his generally low key approach, his willingness to delegate, the pressures must be more than Gerswin realized. Either that, or the senior officer pool was thinner than the Empire let on.

"You're nodding. Would you care to share your thoughts?"

"Just a guess, really. Both XO and CO are high stress positions here. Require tech knowledge, quick decisions. Weather makes it combat environment without combat. Project is long term. Requires engineering no one has ever tried, and no quick way to verify results. Material failures are high. Few officers interested or qualified."

This time, the base commander nodded.

"You're right. The new exec was one of only two out-base commanders or majors within the qual envelope." Manders grinned wrily. "That leaves one major, or should I say, commander, Greg, who fits."

"In the entire Service?"

Manders shook his head.

"Not necessarily, but among those who can be reassigned. What good does it do to move a qualified officer from one spot to another if the replacement officer needs the same qualifications?"

"I see. There were others, but you'd have to replace them."

"Right. You could be transferred to Bolduc, losing the advantage of your local experience, and the exec there promoted to exec here, and the Service would lose two experienced people . . . not to mention the transfer costs, and the ships . . ."

Gerswin pursed his lips. It made a certain sad sense, especially if the Empire really didn't want to plow too much into Old Earth.

"What about you?"

Manders laughed a laugh that was half-sardonic, half-chuckle. "In simple terms, they told me to dump everything I could on you in the next year, and to keep my stress levels down. In other words: Manders, survive until your executive officer knows enough to take over, because there isn't anyone else, and we don't have the ships and people to pull you out."

The new commander looked down at the tiles and the worn carpet.

"Stupid to project ahead, but doesn't that imply that every base commander will have to be either Old Earth born or trained here? Or someplace equally tough?"

"Not stupid. Unfortunately true, as far as I can see. My own records indicate there may be as many as five or six who could succeed you."

"The devilkids?"

Manders nodded. "And perhaps the two pilots from The Hebrides."

"Understand their home environment's as rough as anything around here, and just as cold."

The base commandant stood and turned to the console. He picked up a hard-copy flimsy and handed it to Gerswin.

"That's the text."

Gerswin scanned it, observing that he was indeed promoted to commander, permanently, and effective immediately, in order to take over duties as executive officer, Old Earth Base. Evaluations on his performance would be submitted via torp quarterly, vice-annually. The expected transfer/retirement date of the current base commander was hereby extended six months.

"Get your stuff up here immediately."

"Ops?"

"Have to detail Hassedie for the next six months. Next Ops boss will be incompetent, or worse, but Lerwin's too junior, even in our circumstances, and no one else has a prayer."

"Rule of thumb is no incompetents above the Ops boss level?"

"Usually, Greg. Usually. But don't count on it."

Gerswin quirked his lips. "Understood."

"And . . . ?"

"And?"

"I've got some spare insignia. You'll need them for your swearing-in tomorrow."

⟨* LI

What was, was. The past defines itself. Historians refuse to accept that definition and instead superimpose their analysis of the past through the eyes of the present. Thus, history becomes a pale reflection of the present, while the true past is lost behind the reflected image presented by historians who would have us see what they believe, rather than what was.

> *Politics in the Age of Power*
> Exton Land
> Old Earth, 2031 O.E.C.

The commander frowned as he read the report again.

"In black and white, no less . . ."

Commander Byykr had been thorough, exceedingly thorough, exploring avenues Gerswin would not have considered, but the avenues made no difference in the conclusion.

"The ideal world is described as 'earth-type prime,' or ETP, based on the original biosphere of Old Earth. Those worlds classified as unique or with special hardships are measured in terms of their deviation from ETP parameters. . . .

". . . any attempt to classify Old Earth as a hardship station or as severely deviant from existing standards would (1) cast doubt upon those standards; (2) cast doubt upon the original standards-setting process, which could lead to pressure for reconsideration for a number of bases and systems; (3) require an unpleasant explanation of the circumstances leading to the collapse of Old Earth, which, in turn, would cast some doubt upon the Empire and its traditions; (4) would require a recomputation of all mass-cube ratios and other costs for all out-systems . . .

". . . under such conditions, the ETP model could then be attacked as a mere statistical standard, and one with no basis in reality . . ."

There was more, phrased in a scholarly manner, but what was left unsaid by the scholarly phrases of the former executive officer was even more interesting.

While Gerswin did not have Byykr's or Manders' background in Service politics, he understood enough. The politics of the situation meant that any attempt to change Old Earth's status would undermine the tacit consent on which all Imperial hardship and transport formulas were based.

Hidden more deeply in the report was that the cost-ratios and transport formulas were skewed to make a profit for suppliers of energy systems, particularly for those who had backed the

Old Earth reclamation effort. While Gerswin couldn't be absolutely certain, Byykr's report seemed to point clearly in those directions.

The commander shook his head. If he attempted to improve the cost ratios, then Old Earth would lose supporters immediately if he succeeded. If he did not, over the long run current Service support would erode, as more and more members of the headquarters staff saw what they regarded as a disproportionate amount of funding going into a planet with no military significance, funding that could go for ships and equipment in short supply.

Gerswin reread the entire report again, looking for other possibilities. Then he stored a copy in his own personal files.

Manders had been right. There wasn't much that could be done—not now, at least.

With a sigh, he flicked his console from the Byykr report to the day's stacked messages, and to the long vertical row of amber lights on the right side of the screen.

⌒* LIII

Gerswin looked at the empty office, the walls freshly cleaned and resealed, the old furniture recoated with yet another layer of flexcoating, enough to erase all but the deepest scratches.

"Commander?"

He turned in the portal to face his orderly/gatekeeper, Senior Technician Nitiri.

"Captain Geron needs to speak with you, ser."

Gerswin shook his head. Manders had barely lifted planet-clear and the calls were already coming.

He fingered the linked diamonds on the dress grays. Senior commander yet, if only because they couldn't find anyone else remotely qualified that wasn't more urgently needed elsewhere. Or was it because, if they had to scuttle the base, they could blame it on a native-born?

Wondering how long he really had, Gerswin sat down before the antique but perfectly functional console.

"Gerswin."

"Yes, Commander. Captain Geron at the river separation plant. We have a difficulty here."

Gerswin frowned. "Thought you were only a pilot stage."

"We are, but we still have a problem."

The new base commander nodded at the image in the screen to continue.

"Do you remember the initial bioassays, which showed a small fish population with high heavy metal and toxic concentrations in their tissues?"

"Recall the problem, but not the specifics. Go ahead."

"Apparently, that shows more than bioaccumulation. It may signify actual biological adaptation."

Gerswin winced, realizing as he did that commanding officers were supposed to be impassive in the face of the unexpected.

"It looks like you understand before I finish the explanation."

"Let me guess. Those fish that swim through the cleaner water you discharge are showing signs of distress. Is that it? One species, or across the board?"

"It's preliminary. Only one species so far, but it could be some sort of benchmark."

"How much of the total flow are you diverting and processing?"

"Istvenn, this is only a pilot. Less than twenty percent at the lowest possible flow levels. Have to estimate as little as two percent at flood stage flows."

"Dilute it."

"What?"

"Dilute it," repeated Gerswin. "Pump some of the untouched river flow and mix the two streams before discharge back into the river.

"Dilution isn't a solution."

"I know. But it will give both us and the fish time to adapt. Hate to think we stopped trying to figure out ways to clean up the water because cleaner water proved toxic to one kind of fish. If they adapted one way, there's always the chance they can revert to the original stand, or that we'll end up with two varieties—one that likes arsenic or lead or whatever, and one that doesn't."

"Commander, that assumption is not fully grounded in any science."

"Probably not. But we need cleaner river water for the other organisms we'll have to reseed, and we need the metals as well. What's the iron concentration?"

"Low. Lower than the estimates so far. Lead is higher. So is cadmium. Arsenic is about as we suspected. Organics are higher, but they're relatively easy to shunt and reduce."

"How much iron are you getting?"

"Peak is less than a half kilo an hour in present operations."

"All right. Go ahead and figure out a dilution mechanism to use until you have a chance to figure out a better solution."

"Yes, ser."

The captain's cool tone told Gerswin that the scientist was not pleased. Neither was Gerswin. Some forms of carp could, and had, adapted to anything. That didn't mean the water should stay dirty. Besides, the pilot operation was just the first step. If the mechanism worked, Gerswin intended to duplicate what could be duplicated and see if he could wrangle the spares necessary to open another station, the second one powered by natural sources, like the tidal bore in the Scotia area.

If all the remaining metals on Old Earth were dissolved, then they'd have to be undissolved.

At least *that* problem could be defined and resolved.

 LIV

After viewing the remnants of Old Earth a century following the ecollapse, the theologian Mardian was moved to say, "There are no saints in Hell, nor dawn on Earth. For neither Hell nor Earth permits hope or light."

While this view of the ecological condition of Old Earth may have been exaggerated, there are enough accounts of the damage verified by Federation records, and later by Imperial records, that it would be difficult to ignore the extent of the devastation.

Yet all of recent history within this sector of the galaxy has been affected at least indirectly by the scars of the fall of mankind's first home, and by the later struggles to reclaim that once-shining symbol. . . .

The Empire—The Later Years
Pietra D'Kerwin J'rome
New Avalon, 5133 N.E.C.

LV

Gerswin studied the text on the console, frowning as he did so. The ambiguities troubled him, but any good regulation should have some just to allow for local flexibility.

Still . . . B.P.R. 20012(b) was specific. ". . . all officers and technicians, as well as any detailed or civilian personnel under contract, shall be housed within the base perimeter in all but Class II(b) installations . . ."

Old Earth Base was not a Class II(b) installation. Period.

Gerswin leaned back in the swivel he had inherited from Manders and pursed his lips.

Sitting forward after a period of reflection, he tapped another inquiry into the console.

As the response began to appear, he smiled.

"Had to be there, somewhere . . ."

The intercom buzzed.

"Gerswin."

"Commander, the executive officer is here."

"I'll be ready in a minute."

"Yes, ser."

He scanned the lines on the console, picking out the key phrases.

". . . as defined by either (a) the Standing Order of that Base's establishment . . . or (b) a current survey of the boundaries as entered in the Base Operating Procedures and as maintained by the Service . . ."

Gerswin put the regulation on hold, blanked the screen, stood up, and headed for the portal.

"Come in." He nodded at Commander Glyncho, who wore dress grays, as he usually did.

Gerswin had on a new flight suit, the only concession to rank being the linked diamonds of a senior commander on his collar. He turned, knowing Glyncho would follow him back into the office.

Gerswin motioned to the swivel at the corner of the console. "Seat?"

"Thank you. I do appreciate your courtesy in seeing me, especially given your busy schedule, and the heavy demands on your time."

Gerswin inclined his head and raised his eyebrows in inquiry.

"I have been thinking about this a while. As you know, my family has remained on New Augusta, what with the close family ties that exist there. I'm sure you understand. While I was hoping that I could make a unique contribution to the reclamation of Old Earth, sometimes things seen from New Augusta take on a different perspective when experienced in person. I'm sure you also appreciate that."

Gerswin nodded. "New Augusta does have a unique perspective."

"My talents, as you have pointed out, are mainly administrative in nature. Frankly, on a base which has become more and more involved in actual hands-on reclamation, my special expertise just isn't fully applicable and can't be utilized to the degree I had originally hoped for when I was assigned here as executive officer."

Gerswin nodded again. "Afraid this has become a highly tech operation, not at all a normal Service base, Glyn."

"That's just it. The mission is important, but it's not the typical I.S.S. mission. And I don't have the specialized technical knowledge to be much more than a supervisor of the clerical staff and a high-powered screen monitor."

Glyncho swallowed. "Now—"

BUZZZ!

"Excuse me, Glyn."

Gerswin turned and jabbed the stud.

"Gerswin here."

Captain Lerwin's face filled the screen.

"Captain, emergency report from the Scotia station. Class I spout caught their research sampler on the water."

"Damage?"

"The sampler's fusactor cracked. They shut it down, abandoned it, and it's sunk in twenty meters of water."

"That in the tidal bore?"

"No. Offshore."

"Stet. If you can reclaim it, lift the team out there and do it. If you can't, send the techs with that silicon fusing gel and encapsulate it. Then we can lift it out safely."

"Cost?"

"Blast the cost. Need the fusactor if we can save it. If not, we'll let the mass cool and reclaim what we can later." Gerswin paused. "Lerwin?"

"Yes, Captain?"

"Find out why that sampler wasn't secured with a Class I spout incoming."

"Yes, ser."

Gerswin broke the connection and turned back to Glyncho.

"You were saying, Glyn?"

"Nothing, really."

"Take it you're thinking about transfer, or retirement?"

"You saw the response to my transfer request."

Gerswin nodded.

"That doesn't leave me much choice. I can either stay and route screens, or retire. Since my family can't come here—"

Gerswin did not bother to correct Glyncho. Any family that wanted to could come, provided the sponsor opted for a double tour. What the executive officer was saying was that his wife was not about to leave New Augusta for more than ten years on Old Earth.

". . . you would rather retire and spend some time with them," Gerswin finished the sentence.

"That's right."

Gerswin smiled his official pleasant and warm smile.

"I can't say I blame you under the circumstances, and if you want, I'll be happy to endorse your request with an observation that I recommend speedy approval in view of your past service, and for humanitarian reasons."

"That would be most appreciated."

"No problem. Look right to it."

Gerswin stood.

"Like to talk further, but you heard the problem that just surfaced."

Glyncho stood in turn.

"I understand. I just wish I'd been able to take more of the load off you."

"I know. I know."

Even before the portal had fully closed behind Glyncho, Gerswin was back at the console, checking the status of the fusactors assigned to the base, to see if there were any spares left.

No spares remained in inventory. The virtual freeze on high tech shipments to all but the highest priority bases was beginning to tell in more ways than one.

The old dozers were getting harder and harder to repair, and simpler and simpler to operate as Glynnis and her technicians eliminated and cannibalized to keep them running. While the town was starting to sprout some local technology, there was neither the technical nor the personnel background for sufficiency, and there wouldn't be for years to come.

Besides that, there was the bigger resource problem. The Empire's military and its machines were equipped with metallic support systems or those based on complicated and high tech synthetics. Old Earth had no metal deposits left, not to speak of anywhere near the surface. That meant no local metal to replace plates worn by years of struggling against unyielding clay and the corrosiveness of the landpoisons. No metal with which to convey power beyond the single new town outside the base. No metal for trinkets such as jewelry. No metal—except through the Empire, or from Imperial mining of the system's few remaining metallic asteroids. Both sources were expensive.

The only local source were the few kilograms produced from the Scotia and river reclamation works. While those small stocks were insignificant, over the years they could help.

But even the reclamation metals required energy. And the cost of either transport or reclamation energy was dear, Gerswin knew, so dear that every piece of equipment sent to Old Earth cost as much, if not more, to ship than to build, and required the commensurate paperwork and elaborate justifications.

He bit his lip. For a time, he had hoped that Glyncho could have helped in circumventing the Imperial bureaucracy, but the man had simply no real understanding of technology, or ecology. Without either he had been unable to comprehend the needs, the rationales, or the sheer magnitude of the task.

More than rock-bottom basic sufficiency in non-recycled food and wood replacement for synthetics was a decade away.

"Decade?" he muttered as his fingers closed out the arc-dozer inventory check.

Glyncho, he reflected, unable to dismiss the commander from his mind, had been nice enough, just incapable of dealing with the situation.

Gerswin sighed. Who knew what sort of replacement the Service would throw at him?

Already, the base had far too much deadwood. Lerwin ran Ops, rather than Major Trelinn, who was no improvement on Major Limirio, who had resigned after one year of her tour. Trelinn still had three years left on a tour that unfortunately might well be extended.

Major Hassedie, who was nominally in charge of Administration and Facilities, was smart enough to give most of the real work to either Glynnis or Kiedra. But the native personnel gap was still a problem. The devilkids were one generation, but there weren't any more coming along, not more than two or three since Gerswin had drafted the first batch. Devilkids were good, but scarce, and the oldest of the children from the new town were a good ten years away from an Imperial education, those that could qualify. That was assuming the Empire would even continue the policy of educating the brightest of the outworld youngsters with the continuing cutbacks.

Personnel, metals, energy—his head pounded with the concepts and numbers he juggled.

The amber light on the console reminded him of the housing question, the one he had laid aside earlier, before the Scotia problem and Commander Glyncho.

Lerwin—Lerwin and Kiedra—if they wanted to live in the town, as opposed to the cramped base quarters, that was all to the good if he could find a way to do it, and a way that represented an advantage to Old Earth, the Service, and the base. A cursory look at the regulations only exempted agricultural and research personnel, and they were certainly neither.

Buzz!

"Gerswin."

Lerwin's face appeared on the screen.

"The exec gave the number one and three research techs on the sampler R&R back at base. Number two broke her arm when a sampler sling snapped. She was flitted back here for regeneration therapy. Number four was left with two warm bodies and asked for replacements, but the exec never got around to handling it."

Gerswin sighed again.

"Glyn has requested retirement, and I have concurred. Need me to work on the techs?"

"No need. No sampler. Have to encapsulate."

For a moment, the two exchanged looks through the screen.

Finally, Gerswin laughed. "Still think this is a better place than your hills, devilkid?"

Lerwin snorted.

"Better you than me there, Captain. Encapsulation team on the way. No spouts expected for another forty hours in Scotia. Should be enough." The captain and former devilkid paused, then licked his lips. "About our request, Captain?"

"Think I may have a way to do what the regs say I can't. Let you know."

"Thanks."

Gerswin tapped the stud, stared at the blank screen, then touched the intercom stud.

"Yes, Commander?"

"Would you tell Major Hassedie that I need to talk to him about a base survey, in order to update the Base Operating Procedures? Later this afternoon, if possible."

"You're scheduled clear at 1445."

"That would be fine."

As the screen returned to dark gray, Gerswin looked at the line of blinking lights on the console and shook his head.

First things first, like resurveying the base perimeter to include the new town. He might even get more equipment that way. If not, at least the native borns wouldn't have to stay cooped up in the burrows of the old base, and that would help morale.

He touched the first light on the console.

LVI

"Commander, this is most irregular."

Gerswin raised his eyebrows at the image of the dapper major.

"Most irregular. Captain Lerwin is not the most senior of the captains in Operations. As a matter of fact, he is near the middle in seniority, yet the records show he has been the deputy operations officer since he was a temporary captain, over the heads of a number of officers senior to him."

"Linn," Gerswin sighed, "you've known that for two years. Why are you bringing it up now?"

"Because of this." Trelinn raised a white square of paper. "How can you justify recommending him for major? There are men and women here who have spent a decade more in the Service than Captain Lerwin."

"Are you questioning Captain Lerwin's ability? Are you ready to put any complaint in fax?"

"Commander, Captain Lerwin is a most capable officer. That I do not dispute, but his range of experience is rather limited."

"I happen to prefer excellence in a limited area than mediocrity in many. Commander Manders was satisfied with his performance when he made Lerwin the deputy. I have been satisfied, and you have given him good solid ratings."

"But what about the impact on morale of passing over more senior captains?"

"Haven't noticed a problem. Everyone knows that the people who work for me are judged on ability, not seniority. Sometimes seniority and ability go together. More often, they don't."

"I see," answered Trelinn slowly.

"No, you don't, Linn. You use that phrase whenever you disagree and don't want to say so."

Trelinn's mouth opened to protest, but he stopped short of

saying anything as he saw how Gerswin watched him, the intensity obvious even through the antique console screen.

"Linn," continued Gerswin implacably, "four kinds of personnel end up here—troublemakers, incompetents, deadenders, and natives. The incompetents are almost always senior to everyone else. This is not a forgiving planet. Check the record, in case you've forgotten. Ability is what's needed, not seniority. Ability is what I reward. What I encourage."

He cleared his throat for emphasis before continuing. "And what I expect you to encourage."

LVII

Pad, pad, pad, pad . . .

His breath coming easily, Gerswin continued to put one foot in front of the other, step after step, as he narrowed the distance between the base administration/operations complex and the new town.

Lerwin had taken a fresh uniform and underwear for Gerswin when the junior officer had left earlier. He had only smiled when Gerswin told him he wanted to make the trip on foot.

Gerswin hadn't bothered to point out that he ran at least five or six kays every day. The new town was only about seven, certainly not any more difficult for him along the clear expanse of the causeway than his normal forays through the hills, the young trees, and the old grubushes.

Pad, pad, pad . . .

He kept his breath patterns even, step after step, as he reached the top of the low rise that marked the rough midpoint between the two complexes.

Ahead, against the overhead clouds that darkened the twilight, he could see the glow of the town, as well as the nearer light beams of the official base shuttle as it headed back from the town to the base center.

His steps were heavier than they often were, not because of weight, but because he ran with military issue boots rather than barefoot. At least twice a week, to keep his feet tough, he ran barefoot. Only once in all the years since he had returned to Old Earth had he cut his feet, and that had been near the base itself.

His barefoot runs usually carried him through the more deserted country, away from the park used by the non-native Impie personnel, and away from the bunkers and landing grids.

Pad, pad, pad . . .

The ground shuttle was less than a kilometer away. Gerswin could hear the whine of the electrics as it neared him.

Realizing he was beginning to shorten his steps, he consciously made the effort to stretch each stride slightly, still keeping his rhythm as even as possible.

The lights of the shuttle swept over him as the squat bus eased over a rise and the whining let up. The driver raised a hand, and, without breaking stride, Gerswin returned the gesture. He resisted the urge to grin as well. How often did the driver and his passengers see the base commander running down the causeway, complete with frayed flight suit and boots?

He suspected the whole base knew of his obsession with exercise and hand weapons, but to know and to see the boss trotting down the causeway were two separate matters.

Thinking about the weapons, his hand dropped to his belt to insure that knives and sling leathers and stones were still there. While there were fewer predators around the base, both the coyotes and the shambletowners continued to roam the area, and neither were terribly friendly.

Gerswin smiled wryly, a substitute for a shrug as he kept his legs moving.

As he came through the last hillside cut, the new town and its few scattered lights blinked into place, and he began the gentle descent toward the northern gates, still open in the gathering dusk.

The former devilkid doubted that the gates would ever need to be closed again, but had left that decision with the elected town council.

With the leveling of the causeway tarmac for the last half kilometer, Gerswin stretched out his stride and picked up the pace. He slowed only when he reached the gates.

Once inside and past the single guard who had saluted in surprise, he began to walk to cool down before reaching Lerwin and Kiedra's new quarters—home, he mentally corrected himself.

Inside the town walls and directly behind the guard post was the shuttle station, used by both the military shuttle, which had passed him on his run, and the town's shuttle, which stood waiting and empty except for the driver.

Gerswin nodded approvingly as he passed the town shuttle, which used an alcohol-powered external combustion engine system. The brains, talent, and initiative for rebuilding were beginning to appear—just not the raw materials, at least not yet. That was his job.

Beyond the station was a small park, two hundred meters on a side, with low trees, supposedly Old Earth stock, and cold-resistant grass. On one side stood a brick and earthen composite, partly pyramid, partly tunnels, and partly labyrinth walks.

Gerswin could hear the shrieks and murmurings of children at play, but paused, since he could not see any. To his right, out of a grass hummock, popped a curly blond head, which disappeared so quickly Gerswin might have doubted he had seen it in the deepening dusk.

The base commander smiled and resumed his walk along the boulevard toward the central dwelling section.

Shortly, he turned left onto a stone walk. A hundred meters later, he stopped.

The Commander checked the dwelling, a single-story, white-walled structure with two doors, one for each of the two families. All of the quarters buildings in the new town were multi-family, ranging from the relatively smaller ones such as the one before which he stood to larger structures that accommodated three to five family groups.

Even the smallest were more spacious, and certainly more comfortable, than the old shambletown dwellings or the stark base quarters and their bunkered recirculated air.

Lerwin and Kiedra's new home was like all the others, with an old-fashioned hinged door. The door itself was a synthe-plast, and the only distinguishing touch on the exterior was a square plaque set into the whitened exterior plaster on the right side of the sheltered entryway. Gerswin studied the design on the plaque and chuckled.

A single slender pine tree appeared above a pair of crossed weapons, the weapons being a double-ended throwing knife and a standard issue hand laser.

Just before he stepped up to the door, it swung inward. Lerwin stood there, grinning.

"Sooner than I thought, Captain, but not much." He stepped back. "Welcome to our home."

"Glad to be here, Lerwin. Glad to be here." He forced himself to keep from mumbling the words, wondering why he suddenly felt so tongue-tied when he had known them both for so long.

Lerwin wore a pair of rough-woven brown trousers and a shinier Imperial-made tunic. While Gerswin could hear footsteps farther inside, he did not see Kiedra.

"The curtain to the right is the guest quarters, for now, at least," announced Lerwin. "Your clothes are there. If you want to, there's an old-fashioned shower down the hall, and the water is . . . well . . . warm."

Gerswin nodded and stepped into the small room—bare except for a single bed, a red-and-black woven rug, and a small table next to the head of the bed. All the furniture appeared handmade.

His undress grays, without insignia, his dress black boots, and a set of clean underwear were neatly laid out on the bed.

A curtain covered what he presumed was a closet. He walked over to the curtain and pulled it back. The clothes shelves were empty, as were the hooks and hangers. The inside of the closet and the walls were all plastered in a light tan finish. The floor was a silver-shot synthetic black stone, made locally with some Service help, Gerswin recalled.

Gerswin noted the towel beside his clothes, scooped it up, and peered out into the empty hall before he walked to the room that contained the shower, a built-in bath, and sink. Toilet facilities were connected, but behind another wall. The only doors in the house appeared to be the front door and the door to bath and toilet, not unexpectedly, since doors required either Imperial synthetics, imported substitutes, or high-energy local products.

Within another ten years, some locally grown timber would start to become available, but the major timber supplies were closer to twenty years away. The real problem would be to keep down demand and native cutting until the newly replanted and re-established forests had succeeded in stabilizing the ecology.

Gerswin shook his head as he undressed. One complication always led to another.

A clink and a clatter from the kitchen area reminded him to hurry, and he finished stripping off his damp flightsuit.

The shower was an enclosed tile stall, curtainless and doorless, but with a baffle-staggered wall design to minimize spray. The tiles were reddish glazed squares set in mortar.

Lerwin had been right. The water was warm. Not hot, not cold, but warm. His shower was quick.

After shutting off the water—there was a single, long-handled faucet lever—he toweled himself dry, rubbing his hair with the thin towel which resembled worn-out Imperial issue.

A glance out the door showed an empty hallway, and, towel wrapped around his waist, he carried his exercise clothes back to the guest room where he dressed. Once presentable, he folded the exercise clothes and put them on the table, then straightened the bed, and headed for the front room.

The living room, a boxy space roughly four meters on a side, was vacant, although the small table at one end was set for three. Closer to him, and to the entryway where he stood, with the front door to his left and the sleeping rooms behind him, were a low couch and two tables, one low and square, the other to the right of the couch, and two fabric sling seats. The dimness of the room was only partly lifted by the single lamp on the table to the right of the couch.

"Now you look the part, Captain." Lerwin marched through the archway by the dinner table with a covered bowl, which he set down there.

"Part of what?"

"Visiting dignitary."

"Visiting, yes. Dignitary, no."

Lerwin grinned. "Ha! Almost got you to act like an Impie."

Gerswin couldn't resist giving him a grin in return. "Almost. Not that far gone. Yet."

"Sit down, Captain. Ki says dinner won't be ready for a while. Deputy Ops boss's requests kept her working too late."

"You didn't?"

"Afraid I did."

Gerswin eased himself into the left-hand sling chair. Lerwin took the right.

"Where did you get these?"

"Lostwin makes them."

"Makes them?"

"Scrap. Whatever he can get."

Gerswin frowned. Supposedly, the Imperial scrap went to the converters, both for power purposes and for security reasons.

"Just the common things. Broken seats, furniture, panels. He has to replace it with equal mass conversions. Perfectly legal."

Gerswin ran his hand along the frame of the chair in which he sat, recognizing it was a section of flitter bracing that had been cut and molded into its new function.

"Nice work. What about the shambletowners?"

Lerwin understood the question. "Not much into furniture yet. Lostwin can make about enough for those who are interested. Has a waiting list already."

The base commander nodded. He needed to push up the schedule for tree planting. Resource needs were growing faster than food requirements. Without Imperial synthetics, and without wood, the incipient recovery would turn into a sickening crash.

"Need more trees."

Lerwin nodded.

Gerswin stood as Kiedra walked in.

"How do you like it, Captain?"

"Much nicer than quarters. Much . . . warmer."

"You made it possible—everything possible."

"Just helped. Just helped." Gerswin gestured toward the couch, a movement as much a question as an invitation.

"Dinner won't be ready for a few minutes." Kiedra sat on the low couch, tucking one bare foot under her as she settled down.

The quiet stretched out.

"Haven't seen anything like the couch. Lostwin's work?"

Kiedra laughed, three soft musical notes in a row. "Not exactly. He made the frame. Ler, here, made the cushions."

Lerwin looked at the black synthetic stone floor.

Gerswin shook his head in an exaggerated motion. "The talents I never found out about."

Kiedra bolted upright. "I forgot the liftea!"

Returning moments later with three mugs on a tray, she offered the first to Gerswin. He took the mug, but waited until she had reseated herself.

"To you, and to your home, and future happiness."

"To your own success, Captain."

"To your future, Captain."

The three sipped the hot tea with the orange spice aftertaste.

Gerswin cupped the smooth pottery mug in his hands, letting the steam from the tea drift into his nostrils, and studied the dark and slender black-haired woman opposite him.

Happy enough, she seemed. More than happy—more alive than he ever recalled.

She and Lerwin were good for each other, he decided, while repressing a sigh at the memory of a devilkid who had not wanted to leave him, though he had never touched her. His lips quirked momentarily.

Better the way it had turned out, much better for everyone. They had been the ones who had pushed for the changes that had let Imperials, devilkids and all, live in either the town or base quarters. They would provide the nucleus for rebuilding—if he could keep enough Imperial support coming.

"You look rather serious, Captain."

"Reflective."

"You're always reflective."

Gerswin laughed, a single bark. "Point. Point." He took another sip of the hot tea, letting the heat relax him as the liquid warmed his throat.

"Long time from Birmha to here, that what you thought?" asked Lerwin.

"Something like that," admitted Gerswin.

"And that you've got a long way to go?" added Kiedra.

"Ki!"

"He does. A lot farther than we do. A lot farther."

Gerswin's eyebrows went up. "What do you mean?"

"You were a captain when you gathered us together. Now you're base commander. Have you looked at your official holos? Or your physicals and stress tests?"

"Of course."

"Notice any changes?"

Gerswin frowned, not wanting to follow the conversation in the direction it was heading. "Not really. A few lines, perhaps."

"Not even that. In more than ten years, you haven't aged. We may look a bit older, but haven't you seen that devilkids don't age as rapidly as the Impies? The Impies notice. I can tell you that. And they sure notice about you."

"That's absurd."

"Is it, Captain?" Lerwin's voice was low, but gentle. "Is it really? I remember more than I should, that is, if I'm only as old as the medics tell me I am. Hard to say, when day follows day in the hills with the coyotes and the king rats."

"Time will tell." Gerswin shrugged, and forced a soft laugh. "Time will tell."

He wanted to ignore the quick look between Lerwin and Kiedra, the look of resignation and agreement, but decided against it.

"You two. You think I know something special. Or am something different. I could die tomorrow, and I suppose I could live a long time. I don't know, and all I can do is keep trying to do my best."

Kiedra lifted her mug.

"To your best, Captain. To your best for a long, long time." She sipped the tea before putting the mug down and standing. "If you will excuse me, it's time to see if dinner worked out. Next time, Ler can do it."

Lerwin shifted his weight and turned toward Gerswin. "You think we're crazy?"

"No. Don't like to think about it. Too much to do, and too little time even if you do have five score years. And if you have more . . . have to ask how human you are, especially . . ."

"Especially if you're a devilkid," finished Lerwin.

Gerswin nodded.

The two officers sat in the sling chairs, silently, watching as the deputy administrative officer placed two low serving dishes on the narrow dining table.

"That's it, for what it is," she announced.

The scent was spicy, but clean, and carried a strong scent of vegetables, but fresh vegetables, not the few dehydrated types carried in on the supply ships or the standardized varieties grown in the base tanks.

The two stood, and Gerswin pulled the straight-backed chair from the corner to the place indicated by Lerwin.

"Smells good."

"Should. All fresh."

"Fresh?"

"Local gardens beginning to produce," explained Lerwin.

Gerswin took a mouthful. The taste was vaguely familiar, although he could not remember ever tasting anything like the dish. The meat was chicken, easily enough explained by the embryos he had ordered and received right after he'd become base commander. But the meat was wrapped in a thin coarse flour shell and covered with a reddish hot sauce.

"Tastes good."

"Recipe from the archives, from that cache of old books they dug up and stored in the library. Had to modify it some because we didn't have everything, but the second or third time it turned out pretty well."

"Second or third time?" Gerswin swallowed, suddenly realizing another facet of common town life he'd overlooked—food preparation.

As a devilkid, he'd eaten whatever he could get, fresh, raw, or occasionally cooked over open coals. As a career unmarried officer, he'd eaten aboard ship or station, or rarely, in private homes.

Now, Lerwin and Kiedra had to figure in food preparation, at least for off-duty periods, and who knew what other additional things, into their routine.

He shook his head.

"Something wrong?"

"No," he mumbled after swallowing. "Just a few things I hadn't fully considered." He took another mouthful, savoring the taste and trying to recall where he had tasted it before.

. . . on a clay plate . . . flickering lamp . . .

The already dim lighting of the room seemed to dim more, and Gerswin stared at the table, at two tables—one smooth and plastfinished and narrow, the other heavy, covered with dark tiles. One with matched crockery, the other with cruder and darker pottery.

Gerswin blinked, squeezed his eyes, uncertain whether he was trying to call up the image or push it away. His eyes burned.

"Are you all right, Captain?"

Lerwin's voice sounded ages and kilometers away.

"Captain!"

Gerswin opened his eyes and took a deep breath. The box-like room swam back into focus.

"What happened? You all right?"

"Was it the 'dinner?"

He shook his head, strongly, then wiped the dampness from his cheeks. "Just realized where . . . why the food was familiar . . . that's all."

Lerwin's frown was half-puzzled, half-concerned.

Kiedra's mouth dropped open. She shut it, then asked, "Serious?"

Gerswin shrugged. "Don't know why I'd remember something so far back. Don't know if it really happened. Couldn't have been very old. Table seemed so big."

"Do you remember your parents?"

"Just glimpses. Think my mother had the blond hair. Father was heavier. Maybe not. All men look big to children."

Gerswin reached for the heavy tumbler—local manufacture—and took a long swig of the water, still a trace metallic, but far better than the best once available.

"Speaking of children, Captain," Lerwin asked softly, "what do you think?"

"Think about what?" Again, Gerswin caught the shared warmth between the two, and felt himself on the outside looking in at something he could not share.

"It's like this . . ." added Kiedra.

"Ki . . . we agreed . . ."

Gerswin swiveled his head from one to the other. Children? Children. Children!

Lerwin's increasing protectiveness toward Kiedra, their pushing for their own quarters, the room for guests, for now, as Lerwin had put it—all of the indicators were there.

"Congratulations," Gerswin said softly, catching Kiedra's eyes and holding them. He turned to face Lerwin. "Won't be easy, but I wish you the best."

"You don't object?"

"To what? You love each other."

"But . . ."

Gerswin barked a laugh. "Look. Why are we reclaiming our planet? To make it into a pastoral museum? Has to be for people. People and their children."

Gerswin could sense the relief in Kiedra, feel her tension ebb. But Lerwin still sat on the edge of his chair.

"You mean that?" asked the other man.

Gerswin did.

"Yes." He did not explain, but the absolute assurance in his voice seemed to satisfy Lerwin.

"Obviously," added the commander, "I made the wrong toast, but time enough to rectify that." He looked back at Kiedra. "When?"

"Seven months, if all goes well."

Gerswin shook his head and laughed quietly. "You'll make an old man out of me yet."

"Never!"

"Never."

Kiedra's affirmation of his relative youth held a note of sadness, almost pity, that Gerswin pushed away with another mouthful of the dinner.

Lerwin followed suit, but Kiedra stood.

"I'm full. Be back in a minute."

Gerswin frowned. He'd never seen a devilkid full. Not hungry, but never full.

"Pregnancy," Lerwin answered the unspoken question. "Medics say that's normal."

Neither said anything while finishing what remained.

Lerwin stood and took both his plate and Gerswin's.

"No. Be right back. Kitchen's too small for everyone."

True to his word, Lerwin reappeared with three steaming mugs, disappeared again, only to return with three tiny squat glasses.

"Not brandy and cafe, but liqueur and liftea."

Behind him followed Kiedra, her face a shade paler. Lerwin helped her into her seat, and she immediately took a small sip of the liftea, and smiled faintly.

"Some aspects of motherhood I can do without. They'll pass, I am told." She took another sip, and Gerswin could see the color begin to return to her face.

Lerwin eased his chair up to the table, and inhaled from the glass without drinking.

Gerswin followed his example, trying to place the scent, half bitter grubush, half spice. "Another local product?"

Lerwin nodded.

Gerswin sipped carefully, expecting the liqueur to burn. He was not disappointed.

Kiedra left the liqueur alone, but continued to sip from the liftea, saying nothing.

"How much leave do you intend to take?"

"Do I have to decide now?"

"No. Just wondered who I'd get to do the job, and for how long." He grimaced. "Shouldn't get into shop talk, but too many Imperials are just putting in their time."

Gerswin took a swallow of the liftea to clear away the residual flame from the grubush liqueur, then stood.

"Enjoyed the dinner. Enjoyed the company, and especially your news. Won't mention it. That's your joy to spread."

"You aren't going? So soon?"

The base commander forced a grin at Kiedra. "Duty calls. Lucky my locator didn't already summon me." He raised his right arm and let the sleeve slide back to reveal the wrist circlet. "Besides, you need the rest, and don't tell me otherwise."

He stepped back from the table. "You've done a lot here, more than I could have expected. I appreciate your including me. Means a great deal."

Lerwin did not move to stop the commander, but eased toward the front entryway.

Gerswin smiled at Kiedra. "Take care. See you."

He reclaimed his exercise clothes and boots before making his way to the front door.

"Goodnight, Lerwin. Wish you both the best. You deserve it."

"We owe it all to you, Captain."

Gerswin shook his head. "No. A bit perhaps, but we all owe a bit to someone."

Lerwin stood at the open door, waiting.

Gerswin gave him a last smile and went down the walk in quick steps. A hundred meters down the walk, he glanced back over his shoulder. Lerwin still was outlined in the entryway. Gerswin did not look back again as he headed for the shuttle station.

He looked up, instead, and toward the north. He could see a scattering of stars through a break in the clouds which closed even as he watched.

His boot steps echo-whispered in the stillness, matched only by the faint swish of the southerly wind.

His lips tightened as he thought of Lerwin, Kiedra, the two of them. Lerwin, with his arms around her, despite the whipcord steel that underlay her being.

The single barked laugh that exploded from him cracked across the sleeping new town like thunder from a departing storm.

He speeded up his steps toward the waiting shuttle, feeling

one step ahead of the ice rain, and two ahead of the landspouts.

The linked diamonds he had not worn to dinner weighed on his empty collars and on his thoughts.

"Some day . . . some day . . ."

The words sounded empty, and he could see the shuttle and the driver waiting, waiting, waiting to take the base commander back to command central.

⌒✶ LVIII

Thwop, thwop, thwop. Thwop, thwop, thwop . . .

Gerswin ignored the regular sound of the flitter's deployed rotors as he surveyed the irregular patch of felled pines and the scattering figures of the shambletowners.

"Not just a tree or two," he observed, a wry smile invisible beneath the helmet's impact visor.

"Lower, Captain?" asked Lostwin from the pilot's seat.

"Barbarians," a third voice murmured.

Gerswin glanced up to see Glynnis leaning forward between the pilot's and co-pilot's positions, trying to get a better view of the damage to the trees, trees that she and her crew, or other crews, had laboriously tanked from seeds, then planted in the hillsides they had treated earlier.

"Anything else to see?"

"Not for me," answered Gerswin. "Glynnis, anything you need?"

"No. Not here. Need mulchweed, and we'll have to do it by hand. Slope's too steep to leave uncovered, but we'd do too much damage with heavy equipment. Need the weed until the trees we replant take, and that's another couple of years."

"Back to base?"

"Back to base," Gerswin affirmed, taking a last look over his shoulder as the flitter banked southward into a nearly one hundred eighty degree turn.

As he suspected, even as the flitter turned, the industrious shambletowners were creeping back from cover with their ax-knives to worry down another batch of trees.

"They're at it again!" protested Glynnis.

"Lostwin can't run cover for the trees forever, Glynnis. Whenever we leave, they'll be back. The wood, young as it is, is better than grubush or scrub. They'll use it, now they have the habit."

"Just let me get my hands on them."

"My sympathies," offered Gerswin sardonically.

"Don't you care?"

Gerswin ignored the question. He cared, but his options were limited.

Lostwin said nothing, leveling the flitter on a direct descent toward the base landing grids.

Click, click, click.

A swirl of ice rain slapped at the fusilage, ceasing as suddenly as it had pelted from the dark gray clouds overhead.

"Been a cold year," reflected Gerswin, leaning back in the co-pilot's seat. "Not as much grubush since we reforested."

"We left a five kay patch around the shambletown. How many of them are left there, anyway?"

"Enough to need more fuel. May be saving their grubush and using our pine."

"Are you defending them?"

"No. Speculating."

"Do you know what you're going to do to stop them, Captain?"

"Not yet. Some things to consider."

"Opswatch, Outrider Two turning final. Commencing descent."

"Outrider Two, Opswatch. Field is clear. Ground crew waiting."

"Stet."

Gerswin checked his harness and straightened himself in his seat. Automatically scanning the gauges and finding no fault, he watched Lostwin as the younger man's sure touch brought the flitter to a hover outside the number two hangar-bunker.

As soon as the flitter was down inside the hangar, blades folded and shut down, Gerswin vaulted out, helmet under his arm, to head for his office.

Glynnis was right, in one respect. The problem wasn't about to go away.

His quick steps covered the distance across the hangar, through the tunnels and to his outer office.

Nitiri looked up as Gerswin marched through.

"Anything major?" the base commander asked the senior technician.

"No, Commander. Two buzzes and a fax of some sort from Major Trelinn. Major Geron left word that he's got most of the equipment he needs for the Scotia refining plant, all except one part. It's all on your console."

"Thanks, Nitiri. Hold anything except an emergency."

"The tree thing?"

Gerswin nodded. "More ways to botch it than to solve it."

He locked the portal behind him and set the helmet in the small locker.

While he could have consulted the files through the console for exact citations, he did not. He knew the Imperial law that applied and that governed, since Old Earth had neither laws nor governing bodies larger than the individual shambletowns.

Imperial law was simple. If the locals did not injure Imperials, the most that any base commander could do was to remove the locals from the area to avoid damage to Imperial property and citizenry—provided that did not conflict with existing treaties, local laws, or special provisions. None of the latter existed.

The minute he issued a relocation order, Trelinn and who knew who else would be protesting, both on general principles and because they would have an issue with which to assault the commander. On the other hand, if he didn't, the devilkids, the civilian Imperials, and the people of the new town would be upset at his failure to protect the forest.

Gerswin glanced at the I.S.S. banner on the wall, smiled a hawkish smile, and touched the console keyboard.

"Get Major Trelinn and have him up here as soon as possible."

"Yes, ser."

Trelinn arrived as if he had been on call.

"Commander, I'm so glad you've found time in your crowded schedule. I was hoping we could discuss a number of things which have come up."

"Sit down, Linn. First thing is the tree problem."

"The tree problem?" Trelinn frowned. "The tree problem? You mean that bit of vandalism by the locals. Shocking, but minor. What else could you expect? No, I was hoping we could review your review of the annual performance standards—"

"Linn. Performance standards can wait. The tree problem is more urgent. Now why did you say it was expected?"

"There's been no attempt at education, no ethnocultural field work, merely a strong-arm attempt to recreate a vanished ecology, rather than a thought-out and studied effort to build on the existent flora and fauna.''

"How would you define a studied attempt?"

Trelinn paused, giving Gerswin a long look, before continuing. "I would think that the first step should have been a study by a well-respected expert, backed by a full team data-gathering effort, plus, at a bare minimum, the in-depth study and analysis of at least one member of the culture.''

"Would the ecology chair at a major Empire university qualify as such an expert? Say, from Medina, Saskan, New Augusta, or Hecate?"

"What are you leading to, Commander?"

Gerswin smiled. "Just trying to see where you stand, Linn. Now, would someone like that fit your definition?"

The dapper major shrugged. "How could they not?"

"The name Mahmood Dagati chime?"

"The one who wrote *Principles of Planetary Ecology*?"

"The ecology chair at the University of Medina?"

"He's the one," confirmed Trelinn.

"Is indeed, Linn. Conducted the field studies here. Took him nearly seven years. Give you the console keys to his work.''

"That does not mean his recommendations were followed.''

"After we're through, I'd suggest you read them yourself and make that determination. Fair enough?"

Trelinn nodded cautiously. "I would say that would be a fair procedure, so fair that I'll probably do little more than skim them, because your willingness to share them indicates to me that the Service has followed Dagati's recommendations." He paused. "What about the evaluation of the culture?"

"Cultures," corrected Gerswin quietly. "Or perhaps survivors and culture.''

"Rather a curious description, Commander.''

"As you suggested, Linn, the studies were done. Give you those keys as well. Have to access them through a security console.''

"What?"

"Rule 5, Section 3, of I.S.S. Procedures—'data prejudicial or containing a judgment prejudicial to a native culture . . . shall not be disclosed to that culture . . . nor made available in any form where it can be disseminated.' The so-called prejudice rule."

"Would you summarize what you recall of the cultural reports?"

Gerswin shrugged. "Simple enough. Two cultures, if you can call them that. Shambletowners and devilkids. Term devilkid coined by the shambletowners. Shambletowners exhibit strains of a genetic predilection toward cultural and personal paranoia in the extreme, manifest high degree of xenophobia, rigid customs, low level of innovation, low birth rate. In this climate, traits that maximize group survival."

"And the devilkids?"

"Survivors. Adaptable, intelligent, quick reflexes, open-minded to the point of amorality. Egocentric, loners, avoid society. Largest social unit the family. Might tend toward a clan structure if numerous enough."

Major Trelinn shook his head for the first time. "Neither sounds terribly appetizing. One cooperates without intelligence; the other has intelligence without cooperation."

"Shows why field work or preaching won't work. The shambletowners won't trust a word you say. The devilkids are impossible to find, and respect only force, or their own conclusions. We don't have the resources to deal with either, except on a few case-by-case instances."

"But there are some shambletowners in the new town?"

"A few. Mainly because they had no hope in the old town. Too far down the social ladder, or too ambitious. Probably lose some of their children, or the children will adopt the new town as the basis for their paranoia. Culture's insane, but so are some of the individuals, in or outside that culture."

"So what are you going to do about the tree problem?" asked the major.

Gerswin repressed a sigh, glad that Trelinn had finally gotten around to asking the question.

"What would you do if you were in my position?" countered the commander.

Trelinn pulled at his chin. "The shambletowners won't believe you, and you can't force them to leave the trees alone. What about some sort of barrier?"

"Possibly the best ideal solution, but we don't have the

power or the equipment to cover all the area they can and will damage."

The dapper major frowned. "How much damage can they really do?"

"If they could, they would heat with wood all the time. They need it for their pottery, tiles, and cooking. One reason we got some younger shambletowners was that they were cold.

"Shambletowners could take out a whole watershed in the next two years. Trees are too young and the undersoil isn't stabilized yet."

"That much damage from so few?"

"Linn, those are only five- to ten-year-old trees. There's not much undergrowth yet, either. Another twenty years and there'd be no real problem. But not now. Check what deforestation did to Old Earth to begin with."

Gerswin kept from shaking his head and waited.

"You only have two choices, don't you? You can accept the damage, or you can relocate them. Is there anywhere they can go?"

Gerswin nodded, as much in relief as in agreement.

"That's one reason for the whole reclamation effort. Only a few of the shambletowns had stable or positive population projections. Some few areas they can go to until the land here will support them in higher standard."

"But not so desirable?"

"Very little difference for the next century. After that, shouldn't matter."

"I don't know." Trelinn pulled at his chin again. "Difficult procedural problem you face, Commander."

Gerswin stood. He'd gotten the best that he could.

"Well, I appreciate having your thoughts, Linn. Think about it, and if you have any other ideas, let me know. Here are the access keys I promised, if you still want to check them."

The commander handed a small square of paper to the major, on which he had noted the pertinent key words and numbers.

"There were a few other matters . . ."

Gerswin managed to repress yet another sigh.

"I understand. Until I get this resolved, afraid I can't focus on other things as clearly as I would like."

The commander moved toward the portal, toward Trelinn.

The major took the hint and stood, inclining his head.

"I appreciate your involving me in this, Commander, and look forward to continuing our discussions later."

Gerswin said nothing, but inclined his own head in return.

The major left, not a hair on his head out of place, his uniform still creased and immaculate, and without a sound.

Once the portal had closed behind Trelinn, Gerswin permitted himself the luxury of a deep breath. The man was so obsessed with procedure that thinking came last, if at all.

He reseated himself at the console and drafted the order he wanted. Then he buzzed Nitiri.

"Look this over. Fix it, if you think it needs fixing, and then fax it to Admin Legal. About half an hour after it hits the legal console, expect a buzz from Trelinn and whoever else is on the side of the benighted shambletowners."

"Yes, ser."

Gerswin stood, stretched, and paced around the office. Finally, he sat back down to address the blinking lights on the console.

⟨* LIX

The flash of the double red lights at the edge of the console caught Gerswin's attention before the sharpness of the sound.

Buzzz! Buzzz!

"Gerswin."

The image on the other end was Lerwin's.

"Problem, Captain. Lostwin was bringing in the fourth load of those Denv shambletowners, landing them outside Birmha."

Gerswin nodded.

"Finished off-loading, and one of the Birmha types unloads a sling on the Denv group."

"And it went downhill from there?"

"Worse. Trelinn orders them to stop. They didn't. He scrambled out of the cockpit and starts using his stunner. The Denv types know better, but not the Birmha types."

"How badly was he hurt?"

"Cracked ribs, medics think. Gash across the face. Still enroute back to base."

"That the last flitter load for now?"

"Yes."

"Tell the medical staff. I'll take care of the rest."

Lerwin nodded, and Gerswin jabbed at the console, waiting for Nitiri's face to show.

"Yes, Commander?"

"Anyone out there?"

"Haskil."

"Come on in, then."

Gerswin turned and walked toward the portal. He did not feel much like sitting in any case, and the office seemed smaller and more enclosed than ever.

"Yes, ser?" repeated Nitiri as the portal closed behind him.

"Need to convene a Board of Inquiry on Major Trelinn's actions this afternoon. As soon as possible, and within the next few days. Done strictly. Make sure the board is totally impartial. Rather have officers sympathetic to Trelinn than openly hostile."

Nitiri's head moved fractionally, as if in disapproval.

"You disapprove, Nitiri?"

"No, ser."

"I do, but that's not the question. Imperial law is rather strict about firing on civilians except in self-defense."

Gerswin glanced at the blank wall across from his console, the spot where he had never hung any holos or honors, unlike Manders and his predecessors.

"Is that all, ser?"

"That's all, Nitiri. That's all."

⟨* LX

The dapper man with the pencil-thin mustache stepped through the portal, followed by two armed technicians. He wore a plain gray tunic and matching trousers.

"You can go." The commandant motioned the techs back through the portal.

"But . . . ser . . ."

"Where can he go?"

"Yes, ser."

They left, and the portal closed behind them.

"Have a seat, Linn."

"No, thank you, Commander. What I have to say will not take long. While I appreciate your kindness in seeing me before I leave, and while you know I am less than perfectly happy with the way in which the Service has considered my years of devotion, those are not the reasons for my request."

The commander nodded, remained standing.

The dapper man, stockier but no taller than the commander, coughed, then cleared his throat and looked from one side of the office to the other.

"I suppose it doesn't matter," he continued, "but as a matter of principle alone I wanted you to know that I understand exactly what you are doing and why. Although I can applaud the technical skill with which you have managed to accomplish your goals well within the laws of the Empire and the regulations of the Service, I find your ultimate objective of eliminating the shambletowners nothing less than genocidal."

The stockier man paused, as if waiting for a reaction.

"Linn, unlike you, I did not attempt to stun down an entire population."

"That misses the point, as you well know!" The dark-haired former major's voice began to rise, in both pitch and volume.

"Who knows you are a former devilkid? Who knows the

shambletowners killed your parents? Who knows your drive for reclamation is merely a tool to destroy the shambletowners and their culture?''

"Linn." The hawk-yellow eyes of the commander caught the other, who fell silent, stepping back a pace in the face of the glance.

"First," responded Gerswin, "the I.S.S. and everyone else knows I'm a devilkid. Never hid it. Second, parents' deaths are a matter of record for everyone. You found it. Third, shambletowners are doomed whether I do anything or not. Mahmood Dagati proved that. Fourth, you are incompetent and refuse to face it. Fifth, you'd rather have a dead Earth than abandon your precious belief in procedures or do anything remotely resembling work."

The commander stopped as he watched the other's bright eyes and realized that Trelinn was not listening, but merely waiting to finish his statements.

"You still want to destroy the shambletowners, and they know it. They fear you like the devil. They cringe when you appear. They frighten their children with stories about you."

The commandant took a step forward. Trelinn backed away.

"Fear. You project terror and fear. You use it to cow everyone. But I'm not afraid of you, and I know what you are."

Gerswin shook his head.

"Sorry you feel that way, Linn. Won't be easy for you. Anything else?"

"No, Commander. Just remember that *I* know what you are, and I'm not totally without friends on New Augusta."

"Suppose you're not." Gerswin smiled as he finished the observation, and the former major stiffened as if repressing a shiver.

"Is there anything you want to confess?" asked the officer who had resigned.

"Confess? Hardly!" laughed the commander, with a single hard bark. "Stand by what I've done, and what has to be done. Still a job to be done here, a real job. Will be a lot to do long after you're dust, Linn. Has nothing to do with shambletowners." He paused before concluding, "Have a good trip home."

The commander leaned back and tapped the intercom. The portal opened, and the two techs came bursting through.

"Mister Trelinn says he's through."

The ex-major said nothing as he was escorted from the commander's office.

 **LXI**

EXECUTIVE SUMMARY

WRIT OF APPEAL
IN RE
Gillis Marjinn Trelinn
Major
Interstellar Survey Service

Charge: Use of deadly weapon against non-Imperial
       citizens (I.J.C. 40(b))
Finding: Guilty, with mitigating circumstances

Charge: Endangering I.S.S. Personnel through violation
       of Imperial Judicial Codes (I.S.S. Regula-
       tion, Part C.3)
Finding: Guilty, with mitigating circumstances

Summary of Defense:

(1) The defendant claimed that a standard issue stunner was not
a deadly weapon within the meaning of the Code; that the
conduct of the non-Imperial citizenry constituted a threat
to I.S.S. personnel; that the local commandant's decision
to relocate a portion of that citizenry incited the non-
Imperial citizenry against which the weapon was used;
and that the use of non-lethal force was solely to protect
Imperial citizenry.

(2) Defense further contended that the non-Imperial citizenry
was incited by the local commandant's relocation decision; that the defendant's use of force was necessary to
prevent injury to Imperial personnel; and that since the
stunner could not inflict lethal injuries the defendant did

not violate the Imperial Judicial Code for the reason that his actions did not constitute the use of a deadly weapon and were designed to protect rather than endanger Imperial personnel.

Court of Inquiry Findings of Fact:

(1) Historical, practical, and legal considerations all define a military issue stunner as a deadly weapon.
(2) No actual violence nor injury occurred to Imperial personnel until after the defendant attacked non-Imperial citizenry with the stunner.
(3) The defendant and three other Imperial personnel suffered injuries of various degrees requiring extended medical treatment.
(4) In the outbreak of violence that followed the discharge of the stunner by the defendant, between five and fifteen non-Imperial citizens were injured.

Summary of Appeal of Verdict:

With regard to both counts, the defendant claimed that procedures were irregular in Court of Inquiry findings of fact; that procedures were irregular in the assignment of personnel to the Court Martial; that the disregard of seniority in base assignments and duties deprived the defendant of due process; that the standard definition of a deadly weapon should not be applied to unique and primitive circumstances; and that the behavioral pattern of the particular non-Imperial citizenry is uniquely prone to violence, thereby requiring an earlier reaction than in the case of normal self-defense tests.

Summary of Appeal Tribunal Findings:

(1) The verdict on both counts is upheld; the appeals are denied.
(2) The local commandant acted within the scope of both the Imperial Judicial Code and the Regulations of the Interstellar Survey Service.

(3) The finding of mitigation and suspension of sentence upon receipt of the defendant's resignation from the I.S.S. is within the scope of the code and the service regulations.

(4) No further appeals need be heard.

 **LXII**

The greenish-blue tint of the wall imparted a restfulness to the small room with the empty console and the two standard padded chairs. Three tattered faxtab flimsies lay upon the single table. The flextile floors were the standard dark gray of Imperial outposts everywhere. The portal to the main corridor was open, but the interior archway to the rooms behind was closed.

Three lights on the console blinked, then shifted from green to amber as the messages were recorded and stacked for replay.

After a time, a thin-faced technician wearing a pale blue coverall and the insignia of the Medical Corps walked through the open portal from the corridor and took the small swivel chair behind the console. She shook her hands as if to relieve the stiffness in her fingers and forearms and pulled herself up before the twin screens.

Carelessly pushing a wisp of short black hair back over her right ear, she touched the studs on the keyboard and began to scan the incoming messages that had been held for review.

She did not look up at the hum of voices that approached as the archway opened from the consulting rooms in the rear.

Through the archway stepped a short and stocky, though not heavy, woman with strawberry blond hair, blue eyes, and a peaches and cream freckled complexion. Her coverall was the dark brown of the reclamation technical support staff. On her shoulder patch were the twisted spears of fire and water, above the twin linked spheres of barren wasteland and green forests— the insignia of the landbuilders, whose dozers systematically scoured the poisons from the land and prepared the way for the replantings and reforestings.

The second woman, of medium height with natural silver hair marking her as from Scandia, wore not only the coverall of the Medical Corps, but the linked gold bars of an officer on one collar and the twined serpents and staff on the other.

"You're sure?" asked the blonde in a tone that indicated she was repeating a question in hopes of getting another answer.

"That's what all the tests show."

The blond woman, her eyes still bright with tears unshed, looked down at the dark gray of the floor tiles, then at the blank wall to her right. "I don't know. I just don't know."

"Decanting wouldn't hurt you, not at all," pressed the doctor.

"Can I let you know tomorrow? I need to think."

"Take as much time as you need. Don't push it. If you're sure tomorrow, that's fine. Another few days wouldn't matter one way or another. But make sure you think it through." The doctor's voice dropped a note as she saw the technician at the screens.

"Thank you." The support tech squared her shoulders, turned, and walked out through the still-open portal.

The medical tech at the console looked up at the doctor to catch her eye. Then she waited until the footsteps had faded down the corridor outside.

"Another one, Captain Lysendra?"

"Oh . . . Madrigel, I'm sorry. What did you ask?"

"Another one?"

"Yes. Another one. I just don't understand it. They don't want to carry the children, and yet somehow none of them can remember taking the contraceptive antidotes."

"And the problem?"

"They don't want to carry the children, but they want them to live."

"I wondered why you mentioned decanting. Can we actually do that here on base?"

"If it doesn't turn into an epidemic. Of course, the children will have to be fostered or sent to the Academy home. Under the regs, if they chose a Service career, they'll owe two tours here."

"Will she," and the technician gestured at the open portal, "opt for decanting?"

"So far, four have. One decided to carry the child to term."

"Five? Out of how many?"

"Five."

"That's a lot for this base."

"Or not enough, depending on your viewpoint," mused the

doctor, as she turned and headed back to her small private cubicle to think.

"Not enough?" wondered the technician.

Her fingers traversed the keyboard. A series of items appeared on the left-hand screen.

With a coding she was not supposed to know, the woman entered an authentication and another inquiry. The response to that second inquiry replaced the other material on the screen.

Her mouth formed a slight "O," and her eyes widened as she read the lines as they formed on the screen. So the would-be fathers were from the captain's reclamation finds, the devilkid pilots and dozer drivers that tackled the hotspots and fought the landspouts.

"I wonder . . ."

She tried another inquiry, but the screen only printed:

"Unauthorized information. Restricted by regulation R/C 230(b) and standing order I.S.S. 435."

Two lights on the incoming lines blinked green, and the technician erased the left hand screen, while taking the first call on the right.

"Medical Services, Technician Hru-Sien. May I help you?"

Standing Order 435? There was no Standing Order 435.

She could not shake her head, not while routing the call, but smiled instead, mechanically, and she directed the call to Dr. Lysendra.

Standing Order 435 indeed.

LXIII

The commander glanced down at the plastone tiles of the corridor flooring, absently noting the swirled smoothness of the surface. One way to tell the older or more heavily traveled sections of the Administration bunker was by the flooring. The clear sections were new or total replacements. The swirled sections were those that had been remelted and refinished, the colors washed together in abstract but regular patterns.

His boots clicked faintly on the opaque swirls as he approached the open Operations portal.

The corridor lights were at half-intensity, their normal off-duty setting, but the lack of full interior light was artificial dimness, not the honest gloom of twilight or dawn.

Without thinking, he adjusted the linked diamonds on his right collar before stepping through the portal.

"Who's . . . oh, Commander . . . Anything I can do for you, ser?" The duty tech stiffened behind the console as he recognized the base commander.

"No, thank you, Derla. Just checking. Carry on."

He walked to the left, around the console toward the small cubicles that served as offices for the senior ops tech, the deputy ops boss, and the Operations officer. The last office was the one he had used, after Vlerio, and the one Trelinn had used before he'd been replaced by Lerwin.

From behind him, the lights of the duty section cast his shadow, a hazy outline, over the plastone floor blocks before him. The shadow was clearer near his feet and grew increasingly indistinct as it stretched away toward the unlighted sections of Operations in front of him. To his right, the two rows of consoles hunched in the darkness, vague outlines at the edge of reality.

He stopped at the first cubicle on his left, that of the senior tech, and looked through the old-fashioned open doorway. Not even the Operations officer himself rated a full portal. The technician's cubicle was dark, though Gerswin could easily make out the console, the two straight chairs that faced it, and the swivel that was neatly drawn up before the blank screen.

The neatness of the arrangement reflected the organized mind-set of Versario, the current Operations senior technician. Gerswin nodded before continuing to the next doorway.

The second darkened room also contained a console, a swivel and straight chairs, but none were aligned neatly, but almost randomly, with the swivel pushed back from the console, as if Captain Harwits had shoved it back on his way out of the office. On the wall facing the console was the holo view favored by most Imperial-born graduates of the Academy, the Academy Spire. This one outlined the tower against the setting sun, rather than showing the reflection in Crystal Lake. A pair of solideo cubes rested on the console, glowing faintly, though brightly enough for Gerswin to see that they represented two different young women.

The corners of his lips twisted upward momentarily, and he nodded before resuming his tour.

The office in the left rear corner of the Operations section belonged to the Operations officer. On this night, as on every other night when the Ops boss was not on duty, merely on call, the door was open, but the lighting off.

Gerswin stepped into the office, the faint click of his boots dying out as he crossed onto the thin local carpet that Lerwin had brought in. Other than the carpet, three solideo cubes, and a wall-hanging of an intricate corded design that screamed the name of its creator to Gerswin, the office was as bleakly Imperial as it had been ten, fifteen, twenty, or fifty years earlier, the personalities of the men and women who had inhabited it erased by the sheer functionality of the standard equipment and layout.

The commander turned to face the diamond-shaped wall hanging, the starkness of the black and white cording a symbol in itself, studying the straight lines that seemed to curve, and the knots linking black and white, black and white. Kiedra's work, and impressive, he thought, although he had never considered himself as any judge of art.

After a time he backed away and stepped toward the console and the three solideo cubes. The one on the left corner was the closest. He leaned over to study the image of mother and son.

He judged that the image was less than a year old from the fact that Corwin's chubbiness of cheek had nearly disappeared. The boy sat on his mother's knee, held gently with her right arm and hand, and the cleanness of the devilkid profile was already emerging from the chubbiness of infancy.

The commander stared at the cube. Last week, he'd watched as the boy had walked in with Kiedra to meet his father as both parents went off-duty. The steps had been fiercely independent.

Would Corwin have the strength of his parents?

The cube offered no answer, and the commander shifted his concentration to the second solideo, the one of Kiedra standing alone in the doorway of their home, in full dress uniform and with captain's bars glinting. Shortly, Gerswin knew, her promotion to major would come through to match Lerwin's, but her decision to go into facilities planning, while a great help to Gerswin, had put her on a slower advancement track.

The third cube showed all three—father, mother, and son—standing in the sunlight that was still infrequent, in the square of Denv Newtown.

The commander's eyes locked onto the image of the child again, scarcely more than knee-high to his parents, but with his jaw squared as if to declare to the world that he was ready to stand on his own.

"Wonder what it would be like . . ."

The inadvertent words escaping startled him, and he broke off the vocalized musings with a shake of his head.

With what he was, and with what he had to do, better Kiedra and Lerwin than he.

A child . . . What would he do with a son? Or a daughter?

Had Faith survived . . . or had Caroljoy . . . he pushed his past out of his mind. Those had been different days, and, besides, he was what he was, and the job was not done. As if it ever would be, the thought crept back into his mind. He pushed that away as well.

Resisting the urge to look back at the cubes and the wall-hanging, he walked toward the door, heels clicking softly as he crossed from the patterned weave of the rug to the milky refinished swirls of the floor tiles.

Once outside Lerwin's office he paused, but did not turn, before continuing back toward the duty tech.

"Everything in order, Commander?"

"Everything . . . as it should be, Derla. As it should be."

"Good night, Commander."

"Good night, Derla."

His boots echoed more sharply as he picked up his steps on the return trip to his quarters, and sleep. Sleep that would be dreamless, he hoped.

He fingered the linked diamonds on his collar absently, then dropped his hand as he turned into the proper radial for the commander's quarters.

LXIV

"Take her straight up," stated the commander calmly. "Ten thousand meters above the base."

"Straight up?"

"Circle if the power consumption worries you."

The flitter's lift-off was shaky. Adequate, but shaky, as the lieutenant twisted power into the thrusters, and as the flitter, older than the pilot by far, shuddered out of ground effect and into flight.

"Opswatch, Outrider Five. Departing prime base at zero nine four zero. Estimated return at one one zero zero."

"Outrider Five. Understand return at one one zero zero. Interrogative fuel status."

"Fuel status is two plus five. Two plus five."

"Understand two point five," corrected the voice from the console. "Cleared to depart."

The commander stared straight ahead from the co-pilot's seat through the armaglass canopy while the pilot completed departure procedures, and the flitter circled into the morning sky.

Inside the cockpit, the faint odor of machine oil and ozone dissipated with the slow but steady influx of colder air as the flitter circled upward.

"Do you know why you were assigned here, Lieutenant?"

"That was the requirement of my contract, ser."

The commander could have added the unspoken sentences and resentments to the technically correct answer, but chose to ignore them. Instead he asked another question.

"I take it that you would rather have had a first assignment with the fleet, then?"

"I'm grateful for the education and training that the Empire provided, Commander—"

"But you question the value of I.S.S. officers being assigned to Old Earth when they didn't chose their parentage."

The commander's thin smile was hidden behind his impact visor.

The young officer said nothing.

"What would you do, Lieutenant, if you lost all power—like this."

As he spoke, the commander twisted all power off both thrusters and yanked the stick back into his lap.

Whheeeee!

Pitching up and to the right, the flitter bucked once again, and the port stub wing dropped sharply.

The pilot pushed the stick forward, leveled the flitter and dropped the nose, at the same time swinging the port thruster throttle back around the detente and manually feeding fuel to the engine.

Two coughs and the flitter was back under power.

Without hesitating the lieutenant completed the airstart on the starboard thruster and matched both thrusters at the three quarter power level, leaving them there until the exhaust temperatures dropped into the green and until the flitter was re-established in a gentle climb.

"Just now, Lieutenant, your actions answered one question."

The pilot refused to look toward his senior officer, instead kept his attention on the controls and indicators, still scanning the exterior view as well.

"Would you explain, ser?"

"An airstart is difficult in one of these old birds. Most Service pilots come close to crashing or bring them in with cold rotors. Blood will tell, Lieutenant, like it or not."

The commander cleared his throat and continued. "Take her back up, and I'll show you what's been done before we put it in context."

The flitter leveled off at ten thousand meters, with the slight hiss on the background which indicated the efforts of the pressurization system to keep up with the inevitable leaks.

"Keep heading zero nine zero."

"Yes, ser."

To the east, near the horizon, was a patchwork of gray-brown and purple-gray. Closer to the nose of the flitter, at roughly a thirty degree angle below the horizon, an irregular swath of darkish brown marked the division between the wastelands and the green and gold that stretched from beneath the flitter out toward the purples and browns. The commander gestured.

"See that line? What we've reclaimed. Basically three hundred kays from the mountains, runs five-six hundred kays north-south."

"Yes, ser."

The commander turned in his seat to study the lieutenant. The junior officer shifted his weight, but kept his eyes running through the continual scan patterns embedded by his training.

Only the hiss of the pressurization system and the whine of the thrusters murmured through the cockpit.

"Remember the landspouts? Or were you too young when you left?"

"I remember one. It killed my mother, Commander."

"Now that we've reclaimed this sector this far out, we've reduced the annual numbers at the base and the new town to less than ten anywhere nearby. Climatologists tell me we'll never eliminate them, but we will be able to reduce their intensity to normal tornadoes." He paused. "There were a hundred my first year. They still have a hundred or so on the Scotia coast. One reason why our latest push is there."

The flitter crossed the demarcation line between the reclaimed land and the ecological wilderness to the east, bucking several times to the hiss of the pressurizers.

Farther to the east began to appear dark gray clouds, thicker and more threatening than the scattered gray and white puffs above the flitter.

"Bring her about to two seven five, then due north along the border line."

"Yes, ser. Coming to two seven five."

"To bring back a planet's a big job, Lieutenant, and I need the best people possible, no matter how I have to get them."

The commander scanned the board himself, but refrained from pointing out the slight imbalance between the port and starboard thrusters.

"You wonder if I mean that. Whether it's just words. But I do. Just how much you'll find out."

The tightening of the pilot's muscles was apparent to the commander, who shrugged. That was the first reaction they all had, all of them who came home from the comforts of the Empire and the excitement of the Academy and the advanced training.

"Turn north, and steady on zero zero five."

"Yes, ser."

"Wild outside the northern perimeter, and you need to see it all before you understand."

"Yes, ser."

The commander smiled again behind his impact visor, and the flitter, pressurizers hissing in the background, steadied on zero zero five.

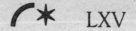 LXV

BALLAD OF THE CAPTAIN

I flew home one night, as skagged as I could be,
and found an Eye Corps Impie
a-waiting there for me.
I asked the Ops boss, and my dear O.D.,
what's this Impie doing,
a-waiting here for me?

The Ops boss, my dear O.D.,
here's what he said to me.
You devilkid, you dumb kid,
can't you plainly see,
it's nothing but a rubbish dump
that Eye Corps sent to me.

Oh . . . I've cleaned this wide world,
a million kays or more,
but a rubbish dump in uniform
I hain't never seen before.

I flew home the next night, as skagged as I could be,
and found an Eye Corps cruiser
a-blasting out at me.
I asked the Ops boss, and my dear O.D.,
what's this Impie doing,
a-blasting out at me?

The Ops boss, my dear O.D.,
here's what he said to me.
You devilkid, you dumb kid,
can't you plainly see,
it's nothing but a landspout,
a-heading out to sea.

Oh . . . I've cleaned this wide world,
a million kays or more,
but a landspout with a laser
I hain't never seen before.

I flew home the last night, as skagged as I could be,
and found an Eye Corps fleet,
a-boiling up the sea.
I asked the Ops boss, and my dear O.D.,
what's this Impie doing,
a-boiling up the sea?

The Ops boss, my dear O.D.,
here's what he said to me.
You devilkid, you dumb kid,
can't you plainly see,
it's nothing but your captain
a-coming home for tea.

Now . . . I've cleaned this wide world,
a million kays or more,
but the captain drinking tea,
I hain't never seen before.
But the captain drinking tea,
I hain't never seen before.

                    Anonymous Ballad
                    Reclamation Period
                    Old Earth

"What's the bare minimum?" asked the hawk-eyed officer. His gray flight suit bore the worn embroidered silver diamonds of an I.S.S. commander.

The woman behind the console looked up from her screen. "A full cohort?"

"That many?"

"Commander . . . you asking that about the most ambitious project anyone ever tried?"

"But one hundred plus arc-dozers? Are there that many in the entire Empire? We've got thirty—not much better than scrap. Each year, there's less in the way of supplies."

"You've been here a long time, Commander. It's sometimes easy to forget the size of the Empire." She paused, as if amazed that she had dared to correct him, then completed in an even softer tone. "Think of it this way. If each system only needed ten, the total number in the Empire would still exceed 5,000. New Glascow probably builds or refits close to a thousand annually."

The commander nodded. "You're right. Too parochial. Problem isn't the total resources of the Empire, but the diminishing surplus available for out-bases and lower priority activities."

The gray-suited commander pursed his lips tightly, frowned. Only after the silence had dragged out for several minutes did he smile. As he smiled, the commander could see the technician trying not to shiver at his expression, and, not certain why, he barked a laugh, either at her or to distract her, or both.

"Since there are so many, then we'll just request them." His smile faded, and he stepped back from the console. "Put in a request for two full cohorts, to be delivered six standard months from now. Code it priority red."

"But . . . Commander. No one here has the authority for a priority red."

"Fine. Code it as a 'recommended priority red.' I can certainly recommend, can't I?"

"The form doesn't allow it."

"Put in priority red where the level code is. Note that it's a recommendation in the remarks section."

"Yes, Commander."

He could smell the scent of fear, could almost feel the questioning in the mind of the black-haired petite technician.

"Wondering whether the old man has gone jump-struck? Thinking I'm sealing my fate? Could be. But only fifteen of thirty dozers are operable, and half of those are cripples. There's a freeze on parts and fusactors, and the only things with enough power to do the job are dozers. So we need them, and we'll get them."

The technician glanced back at her screen, but did not move her hands from her lap.

"Go ahead, Evyn. Recommended priority red, with copies to everyone you can think of."

"Copies?"

He nodded.

"That way, they won't be surprised when the Emperor gives them to us."

Her eyes widened farther, if possible.

For no reason that Gerswin could fathom, the look in her eyes reminded the commander of the look in Lerwin's eyes, the look when the medical diagnosis on little Jurrell had come in. How many years ago had that been? How many years? Corwin had been four then, and Jurrell had barely been walking, a little over a year old. Gerswin could still recall, could still sometimes see, the darkness behind Kiedra's eyes, although Ellia's birth had helped.

Gerswin kept from shaking his head.

"Not crazy, Evyn," he temporized. "Just planning."

He smiled a hard smile again, in spite of himself. This time he saw her shiver.

Still, she lifted her hands and began to code in his request.

The request was the first step, the sole easy part. Getting the dozers would be harder. But with all the cutbacks in the fleet ships, not impossible. No, not impossible.

He smiled again, and turned, heading back toward his own office.

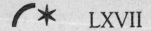 LXVII

For the fifth time in as many minutes, the man in the undress black uniform of a senior commander in the Imperial Interstellar Survey Service glanced over at the blank screen of the single room's faxset. Then he stared out the narrow window.

Not that the view was wonderful. On any other planet besides New Augusta, a visiting commander would have rated at least a small suite in senior officers' quarters. On New Augusta, it was rumored there were more admirals than battlecruisers in the I.S.S.

The rumors were true, particularly if they included the Imperial "retired reserves," those members of the Imperial and high court families who had served a single tour of active duty and then been "retired" to the Emperor's Reserve Corps. The I.R.C. had a small squadron of its own, permanently based in Gamma sector, in which the titled and untitled members of New Augustan society served their reserve time.

Gerswin laughed out loud, thinking about a corvette captained by a reserve fleet admiral, with a full admiral as an exec, and where senior commanders served as seconds in comm or drive billets.

With the laugh, he looked again at the blank screen, then at the narrow window, and stood, stretching, in his blacks.

He eased toward the thin pane of armaglass through which he could view the courtyard. While the window did not open, he could almost imagine the scents from the garden that ran down the center of the quadrangle. From his second floor vista, he could estimate what the view of the rows and rows of silverflowers spilling out over green leaves might be from the higher floors, particularly from the suites with the balcony terraces.

His room was dim, partly because he had damped the polarization to cut the glare from the mid-afternoon sun, and partly because, with the interior lights off and a single window not much wider than a man, there wasn't that much light to begin with. Add to that a color scheme based on dark green, highlighted with thin silver slivers, said to be the favorite of His Highness J'riordan D'Brien N'Gaio, and the room made Gerswin think of evening, even at dawn.

"Will you, someday, go forth in green evenings, Commander?" he asked himself sardonically, before turning from the garden view back toward the screen.

Three days he'd been waiting so far, just for her to return. While he had quietly inquired about her schedule when he had left Old Earth, she had been scheduled to be on New Augusta. Now the days mounted up, and it would be harder and harder to justify additional days in a duty status, as opposed to leave. More important was the return jump-ship schedule. Three days, that was how long she had overstayed her planned return date, and no one could say when she would be returning.

Cling!

The screen chimed but once before the commander had crossed the room and punched the acknowledgment stud. Hawk-yellow eyes peered at Nitiri's image on the screen.

"Yes? No?"

"Too easy," returned the senior rating, who wore the technicians' counterpart of the I.S.S. undress blacks. "Her social secretary deferred. I insisted she ask the Duchess herself. The Duchess took the call personally."

"And . . . ?"

"Senior Commander Gerswin? From Old Earth, I presume? I would be more than happy to receive the commander personally late this afternoon. At six, Mr. Nitiri."

Gerswin frowned.

"That's what she said?"

"Word for word."

Gerswin pursed his lips.

"I've arranged for a flitter to the estate. At the officers' gate, 1725. Satisfactory, Commander?"

"Yes. More than satisfactory. Thank you. See you then."

"No, ser. Protocol."

"Alone?"

"She said personally. Means you." Nitiri looked levelly through the screen at his commanding officer.

"All right." Gerswin paused. "Thanks . . . again."

"My pleasure, Commander. And good luck, ser."

"Need it, I think . . ." Gerswin mumbled as he concluded the transmission and edged toward the window once more.

For some time he surveyed the green and silver garden, motionless at the armaglass.

At last, he turned and sat down on the couch that doubled as a bed. After easing off his boots, he stretched out on the cushions, narrow as the space was configured as a sofa.

Three hours to go. What would she say? What could he say?

He regarded the ceiling, blinking occasionally, letting his eyes traverse the smooth translucency that gave the impression of ivory depths.

For a time he regarded nothing, letting his thoughts drift.

For an even shorter time, he dozed.

Finally, he sat up and began to strip off his clean uniform to shower and to don an immaculate set of blacks.

At 1720, senior Commander Gerswin arrived at the visiting officers' transportation gate.

"Commander Gerswin?"

"Yes?"

"Ser, I hope you don't mind . . ."

"But?" asked Gerswin.

"The Duke of Triandna has sent his own personal flitter for your transportation, and I took the liberty of rescheduling the Service flitter you had requested."

"Fine."

"It's the lavender one, straight ahead."

The flitter the technician pointed out shimmered in a cream and lavender finish that could only have been obtained with lustral plating.

Rather than the military steps into a cockpit, or handholds to a canopy, the passenger flitter offered a side portal opening into a small salon, furnished with a settee and two chairs, lavender hangings and a low table. Behind the hangings, Gerswin glimpsed a single pilot, uniformed, unsurprisingly, in lavender and cream.

"Commander," announced the pilot, standing and stepping around the hangings, "please make yourself at home. I know you'd be more comfortable up here, but in the interest of space, this was configured without a copilot's station."

"Appreciate the thought," answered Gerswin, as he settled into the chair that gave him the best view of the small cockpit.

The pilot resumed his position.

Shortly the aircraft lifted smoothly, without a shudder, but, reflected the passenger, a trace heavily.

At 1755, the flitter touched down, and the passenger portal swung open.

"End of the line, Commander. I'll be waiting whenever you're ready to return."

"Appreciate that. You have any military background? Nice handling there."

"A bit. I did a tour with Blewtinkir. That left me mustered out, fit just for domestic transport, but it's not a bad job. Duke and Duchess are better than most here on New Augusta." There was a faint pause. "See you later."

Gerswin took the hint and exited.

At the far side of the landing stage stood another functionary, female, young, black-haired, and nearly as tall as he was, also garbed in the apparent ducal colors of lavender and cream.

"Senior Commander Gerswin?" Her voice held a tone of uncertainty.

"The same. Were you expecting someone else?"

"No, but . . ."

"I suppose I don't look my age."

"The Duchess is expecting you, ser. If you would follow me." She turned as if she expected he would fall in line.

Gerswin smiled, but said nothing further to the woman, who either had a far different picture of what to expect of Commander Gerswin, or who did not believe he was himself.

The exterior gray glowstone walk led to a gentle ramp of what appeared to be glowstone tiles, but the ramp, which ended at an open and arched doorway, seemed to grab at his boots and legs.

"There's a restrainer field here. The faster you try to move, the more it slows you. If you came through the portal running, it would be like hitting a bulkhead."

Gerswin nodded but said nothing, noting the military phrasing of her veiled warning.

Inside the portal, the gray glowstones continued as the floor of an open-walled corridor running through the center of the villa, room after room opening away from the cream columns of the hallway. Gerswin dropped his eyes momentarily, wondering how the glowstones could be so gray and yet add illumination.

His eyes came up in time to stop him in front of a painting done in some sort of old-fashioned oils. The canvas was a good three meters wide and taller than he was.

He ignored the incongruity of an oil painting depicting a space battle and, instead, read the golden plate at the bottom of the severe but gilded frame.

"Death of H.M.S. *Graystone*, Battle of Firien's Star, Dismorph Conflict, 3121 N.E.C."

Gerswin stepped back a pace and studied the painting again, ignoring his guide.

The style was as restrained as the medium. At first glance it merely showed an I.S.S. scout in space, several energy beams focused on her screens, with a starry background. One star, with a distinctly green tinge, was brighter than the others without seeming larger. The scout's screens glimmered with the unhealthy orange tint that preceded total screen collapse.

Gerswin noted another oddity. The canvas was unsigned, and though he was no expert, the obvious quality of artistry of the work evoked an intense sense of impending doom. At least, it did to him.

He shook his head.

"Well, you are an I.S.S. officer, it seems."

Gerswin frowned at his escort, who stood waiting.

"Every one of you, the good ones, sees the picture and stops. Some of them sigh. Others, like you did, shake their heads sort of sadly."

Gerswin looked at the oil again.

That battle had taken place nearly fifty years earlier, about twenty-five years after he'd finished his training on New Colora and gone to Old Earth. Firien had been one of the few Dismorph successes, before they'd been ground down by the sheer might of the Empire. He'd read the analyses and couldn't fault the Dismorph tactics. The Imperial tactics could be and had been faulted by virtually every independent military analyst within and without the Empire. That particular battle had cost a number of senior admirals their careers, not to mention the loss of lives and ships. Follow-ups had not been without losses, either, Gerswin recalled . . . one very personal . . . He pushed the thoughts of Faith back, but his eyes remained on the canvas, though unfocused, for a time.

Gerswin brought himself back to the present and regarded his guide.

"The picture is a mystery to everyone now in service here, except the Duchess, and, of course, one presumes, His Grace. She commissioned it, but from whom and for what reason no one else knows." The guide looked down the corridor before continuing. "She hoped you would see it." Again, the guide glanced around, before continuing even more softly, "And it's said that the only open argument between Her and His Grace was over the placement of the canvas. That was before my time."

Gerswin took a third long look at the scene.

The junior lieutenant who had commanded the scout had received the Emperor's Cross, he recalled—posthumously.

The senior commander resisted the urge to shiver, although the corridor was not at all cool.

"Her receiving chambers are to the right."

"You're not coming?"

"No. You're expected alone. Her Grace can summon anyone instantly, of course."

Gerswin nodded. He would have expected no less.

"Thank you."

He turned and walked toward the indicated portal, the open one framed in cream hangings.

The room inside was not the immense chamber he had anticipated from viewing the rooms through which he had already passed. Rather it was more like a rustic summer study, with white plaster-swirled walls, dark wooden floors covered with rich wine-patterned carpet. The wall farthest from the portal was entirely of armaglass and overlooked the sweeping west lawn and the shadows of the late, late afternoon.

The lady stood behind a carved but simple bleached wooden desk with flowing lines.

Her hair was white, but her face was unlined, and her figure as slender as it had been the one night he had known her nearly eighty standard years earlier.

Gerswin inclined his head, willingly, as he had done to no one from the day he had left the Academy.

"My lady."

"Caroljoy, Commander. Caroljoy."

"You know I did not know. Not then."

"I didn't want you to. Nor do I regret it now."

She moved around the desk, gently, gracefully, but with the deliberate grace of an older woman who understood her fragility, and settled herself on the loveseat.

"Sit down, please." Her eyes were still clear. Still bright.

Gerswin sat, shifting his weight on the firm cream silk cushions to face her.

"Your face is a little sharper, I think, and there's a bit more muscle to your upper body, but you haven't changed much at all."

"Nor have you."

"Spare me the polite necessities, Commander dear. For all the capabilities of Imperial medical technology, I know what I am. And that's an old woman. Perhaps a lovely old woman, but an old one."

Gerswin opened his mouth, and she held up her hand.

"Oh, I know. I'll be around for years yet. I'm not in the grave. Not even close, but I'm old. You—you're still young, and you may be for centuries yet to come, from the look of you.

"I don't know which is worse, dear Commander, but now I'm content."

He did not attempt to answer, or to question, but sat, waiting in the deep afternoon light filtered by the tinted armaglass, watching, and studying the still-fine features he had only seen before etched in the darkness, etched in his memories as if it had been yesterday.

His vision blurred momentarily, and he blinked, shook his head.

"You do remember. I'm not surprised. Not surprised, but gratified." She paused.

Gerswin swallowed, and waited for her to go on.

"What did you think of the painting?"

Gerswin could feel the chill in his spine.

"Impressive . . . sad . . . Almost a memorial, I would think."

"That's important, particularly for you. Though you wouldn't know why."

Gerswin shook his head again. So much was unsaid, so much implied.

"I've sent for some tea, and I would appreciate it if you would join me."

"Pleased to."

"You're still the quiet one. Can you still whistle that odd and two-toned singing?"

He nodded, feeling as shy as he had so many years earlier.

"Don't give it up."

"I don't whistle much now, not in company."

"Would you mind terribly?"

The commander smiled, a tentative smile, a smile as if more than eighty years had been wiped away for a moment. He cleared his throat, made two gentle sounds, and began the melody she had been the first to hear, the only one to hear completely.

He wondered if she had dimmed the light to the study, as, for a moment, the light-strewn study dimmed to call up an evening parsecs and generations away. He did not look up, but concentrated on the intertwining of the two themes, the strength of a weary Old Earth and the fire of love won and lost.

As he let the last paired notes trail off, his eyes came to rest on the Duchess. Her cheeks were wet, and the dampness showed him that after all the years, she still needed no cosmetics for that perfect pale complexion.

Gerswin swallowed again, hard, and looked away. Looked out into the afternoon that was shading into twilight, looked for the shadows he felt gathering in the back of his mind. Looked and waited.

After watching the sun touch the distant trees, he turned back to Caroljoy, who met his eyes.

Without smiling, he extended his right hand and took her left, squeezing it gently.

She returned the pressure, holding his hand as he held hers. After a time, she lifted her long fingers from his.

"I believe the tea is ready."

Her Grace, the Duchess of Triandna, nee Caroljoy Montgrave D'Lir Kerwin, touched the inset controls on the arm of the loveseat. A younger woman entered instantly, also wearing the Duke's colors, and guided a slide table toward them.

On the table were two lustral teapots and a pair of Djring cups in their saucers, the porcelain already glowing as the light level in the study dropped.

A faint clink echoed through the silent room. Gerswin glanced at the woman serving the tea, catching sight for the first time of the pallor beneath her already pale face, and the tightness of the muscles in her arms which had nearly snagged the table on the chair across from the loveseat.

The younger woman had also wiped tears from her cheeks, as Gerswin could see from the smear beneath her left eye. Unlike Caroljoy, she relied on cosmetics.

"Almost," said the Duchess. "Almost I could reach back."

There was another clink as the server placed the porcelain cup and saucer on the elbow height table that had appeared beside Gerswin. A second clink followed as another cup was placed next to Her Grace.

"That will be all, Drewnique."

Gerswin took a sip of the liftea.

"Liftea is both simple and complex, and has a clean taste," she said quietly. "Martin didn't like flavor mixtures, and I assumed that preference came from you. But he did like liftea, and I thought you might."

Gerswin frowned. Martin? From him?

The sense of chill returned to his bones.

He looked into the Duchess's eyes, Caroljoy's eyes. This time, he dropped his glance, feeling a hint of tears that never came.

"Martin?" he asked, his voice barely above a whisper.

"Martin MacGregor D'Gerswin Kerwin."

"Why didn't you let me know?"

"Because I wasn't brave enough to leave New Augusta. Because I did not want to continue bouncing from Service planet to Service planet. Because I came to love Merrel and because it was important to my father that we marry."

She stopped and took a sip from the Djring cup.

Gerswin stared out through the armaglass at the shadowed lawn and took a breath deeper than normal, mentally cataloguing the scents in the room as he tried to gather himself together.

Caroljoy . . . the spice of her was richer, fuller, but had not quite peaked to the cloying of age.

The liftea . . . the pungency similar to cinnamon, but without the dustiness and with the orangeness and mint.

Trilia . . . the background fragrance that hinted of flowers that were not present.

"He didn't object?"

"How could he?" The statement was simple, the implications of strength profound.

Gerswin did not pursue. He darted a look at the glowstones before taking another sip of the liftea from the Djring cup that weighed less than a trilia blossom in his fingers.

"Martin . . . looked much like you, with the hawk-eyes, except his were green, and with the fantastic reflexes. Of course, he became a pilot, after he graduated with honors, and then went from the corvette to commander of his own scout. He was so proud, and even Merrel was proud of him."

Weight, with the inexorable chill and mass of a glacier, settled on and around Gerswin.

"Firien's Star?"

"He could have escaped, but he covered the *Sinta Mare* . . . and the others. The Emperor's Cross . . . upstairs with my jewels." She shrugged, as if trying to lift a burden off her shoulders and not quite succeeding. "Now, once in a while, I can look at it."

Again, silence cupped the room in its unseen hands.

What could he say? He caught himself before he started to shake his head.

"Lieutenant . . . I mean, Commander, we all have our chains to the past. I am not asking you to share mine, nor would I trade anything that has been, and that includes you. At times, I have wondered, but I would not. Martin's childhood was one of the most wonderful times of my life, but that time had passed already when he died, and I had not understood that. All parents die a little when their children become real."

She smiled, and while the smile was faint, the warmth brought a benediction to Gerswin.

"Young Jane made up for it, later, some, but neither Analise nor Jerzey were comfortable here. Jane liked to visit, and who could deny her? She had Martin's eyes, and saw everything. She still cubes me, but they come in batches, now that she's on the Rim expedition."

Gerswin felt more lost at each word, and concentrated on trying not to shake his head at all the implications that tumbled from her words. If Analise had been Martin's wife or the woman who had his child, who was Jerzey?

"Jane? Jerzey?"

"Jerzey was Analise's husband. I've lived with it all for so long it's really quite clear. Lieutenant . . . pardon me, but, you know, dear Commander, I still think of you as that dashing young lieutenant." She cleared her throat, softly, and took another sip of the liftea. "Like his father, Martin fascinated the ladies, but he never even knew he had a daughter. Neither did we. I found that was a possibility several years later, well after Firien, from his friend Torvye, who brought it up to console me."

She held up her hand. "No need for details, but Analise was adopted out, and by the time I found her, had married Jerzey, a decent sort, if a rather mundane barrister on Herkimer. Jane found it too mundane as well."

"So she joined the Service?"

"A familial weakness, I would guess," suggested Her Grace, her mouth upturned slightly at the corners. "She also took her grandfather's name, but, enough of the history. You do well to humor an aging lady."

"Not humoring," he protested. "Not at all."

Martin a grandfather? What did that make him? Or Carol-joy?

"You've been most kind," he began hesitatingly, "particularly in view . . . of everything . . ." This time, he did shake his head. There were no words to express the conflicting feelings ricocheting back and forth under the black undress armor he wore.

"No," she answered with a smile best described as sad, "I am not kind. I had always wondered, but never had the will to search you out, to learn whether you had survived the deserts of Old Earth and intricacies of the I.S.S. I'm the type who always wants to know how the story ends, even my own story, but not at too great a cost. . . . You should understand . . . those of us who are weak, dear Commander."

Weak? While he could understand, weak was not a word he would have applied to the woman beside whom he sat. He touched her hand again, grasped it gently.

He could not ask the favor for which he had come, not for Old Earth, but, most of all, not for himself.

Instead, he glanced at the glowstone floor tiles once more, then around the study, finally settling his eyes on the small flower bed visible straight through the armaglass and centered in the lawn ten meters out from where the two of them sat.

"You hold your keepsakes in your thoughts, don't you?" he asked.

Gerswin suspected that from the villa itself, from a hundred little signs, from the lack of solideo cubes on display, from the simplistic lack of ornateness that surrounded him. Only the oil painting in the main hall that would someday be acclaimed a masterpiece was an exception to that pattern, and even the deep feelings behind the painting were cloaked in simplicity.

What else could he say? Except his good-byes, and he was not ready for those. Not quite yet, not when he had just discovered he had lost two precious things he had never known he had had.

Instead, he picked up the Djring cup and sipped the single cold drop of liftea left in the bottom. That single drop was no more pungent than the first, but held a hint of bitterness that he welcomed.

"That is where they mean the most. Most keepsakes, I have found, are displayed for the impact on others. For memorials, that is suitable, but not for one's self."

"The painting?"

"Martin deserved that, and more. Every spacer who sees it will never forget it, and what else is a memorial for? The sorrow is mine, and, now, perhaps a small bit of it will be yours."

The senior commander nodded to the Duchess, Her Grace, as if to acknowledge a pleasantry, and put his hand to his cup. He did not drink, belatedly remembering he had finished the last bitter droplet already. He centered the cup and saucer on the table by his elbow.

"Getting late," he observed, his eyes flickering toward the western panorama. His right hand covered hers gently.

"Yes. It is. Night falls sooner for some."

He shifted his weight, edging slightly closer to her, but without turning to look at her. A faint breeze brushed his cheek, as if the conditioners had come on, but noiselessly.

Gerswin worried his upper lip with his teeth, then decided.

The senior commander eased his hand from hers and stood, bowing to Her Grace.

"Again . . . you've been most kind."

"Commander dear, is that all you have to say?"

Gerswin felt the sigh go through him, stiffened his shoulders against a slump, and forced a slight smile.

"No . . . Caroljoy . . . Not all that I would say, not all I can say. . . . Never good with words . . . Not from the heart. Guess I came to them too late. Time has passed differently for us. For all your sorrows, you have your loves, your joys, a past, a clear conscience, and memories you can treasure." He stopped, swallowed, and looked directly into her still-clear dark eyes. "I have your memory . . . your warmth . . . some hope for the future. One of the ancients said it. Miles to go before I sleep. It's a long way home. If I get there, then you or . . . Jane . . . or others from your blood will have a home . . . and I will not." His lips quirked. "Sounds too dramatic. Overdone—"

"You've never given up your dreams. That is why you will always be my lieutenant, Commander dear, why you will be loved, why you will be followed, and why you will never rest. Because you cannot surrender."

Caroljoy, his lover and Her Grace, one and the same, young and old, stood. She took a step toward him, and a second, until her hands reached for his. Her fingers were cold within his already cool hands.

"You came to ask for something, and you will not. You cannot."

He nodded, unable to deny the truth as she looked into his eyes, unflinching.

"You are too direct, still, to deceive those whom you love. That is why you love so seldom, my Lieutenant. Because you care, you will not use me, though I used you." She laughed, gently. The sound echoed sadly in the study lit only by the glimmer of the glowstones and the dimness of the twilight. "And I, the more fool, for all the same reasons, will ask you to tell me."

Gerswin told her. Told her about the need for the arc-dozers, about the only way he could find to get them for Old Earth, and how both the Duchess and the Duke could help without personally being involved.

"All you want is the opportunity to borrow one of Merrel's yachts on its way for a refit?"

"Steal," corrected Gerswin, smiling wryly. "And it seems like a great deal to me."

"I suppose it would, but for the stakes for which you play, and the price you have already paid, how could I refuse?"

Gerswin looked down, but squeezed her hands in his, feeling how cool and smooth, how strong, even after all the years, they seemed in his.

"A foolish old lady. But more fortunate than you know. Far more fortunate, and some day, when the stars have dimmed, and you look into your own twilight, you may see why. I have loved, and been loved, three times, and that was almost too much, even though I treasure each of you."

He looked up to see her smile.

"You will have the yacht, of course, but the Duke will offer it to transport you and your man back to your duty station. Would that suffice?"

Gerswin nodded, unwilling to speak. The lump in his throat made it difficult even to swallow.

"Consider the arrangements made, Lieutenant. Consider them made." She tightened her fingers around his.

His arms slipped around her, and his lips brushed hers, and, cheek to cheek, two sets of tears mingled while the twilight flowed into night, and while a younger woman watched the embrace on a screen while her own tears streamed unchecked, unknown to the two who had loved only once, yet always.

LXVIII

Crimra, Communications Technician Second, frowned and studied the comm board again. Had there been a flicker on the lavender band?

He peered at the register plate below the indicator light, but no signal strength was registering, even if there had been a flash a moment before.

The *Sanducar* was loaded, except for the small priority and security items that would come aboard when the captain returned. The old lady was planetside, along with the third section, and wasn't scheduled back for another twenty standard hours.

Crimra glared at the offending light that refused to glow lavender, but it remained dark.

"Lots of luck, Crimra," he muttered aloud. "No Imperial comms for your watch."

Tomorrow, after the captain came back and delivered her usual rivet-scouring inspection, Crimra and the *Sanducar* would push away from New Glascow to cart their load of combat decon dozers off to New Hades, where the Imperial engineers would use them to train the latest crew of planet busters and clean-up troops.

The comm tech shook his head. He was not totally thrilled with the thought of all those deactivated fusactors in the holds. If even one was operating—Crimra didn't want to think about that, not that it would matter one milli-second after the *Sanducar* began to jump-shift. The return trip would be more dangerous, since they would doubtless be carrying busted dozers for rebuilding, and Crimra wondered if the field engineers were as scrupulous as the factory types. There wasn't much of an option, since New Hades was not exactly conducive to large scale on-planet repairs.

Crimra leaned forward in the standard ship swivel and looked at the seamless gray deck beneath his feet.

From the corner of his eye, he thought he saw the same lavender flicker, but when he stared at the board and the register, there was no indication on any transmission.

He licked his lips and scanned the entire board, indicator by indicator. Next he checked the cube board, to insure the fields were holding for all the E-mail the *Sanducar* was carrying.

Everything was as it should be.

Slowly, slowly, he leaned back into the swivel and waited.

Cling! Cling!

As the communicator chimed twice, both the green and lavender lights above the blank main screen lit.

Crimra pursed his lips.

Cling! Cling!

Finally, he leaned forward and tapped the acknowledgment stud.

"*H.M.S. Sanducar*, Communications, Comm Tech Crimra."

The officer in the screen wore a uniform similar to the standard Service undress blouse, but in lavender, with cream piping and no rank insignia.

"Tech Crimra, this is the *Sindelar*, ducal flag of His Grace, the Duke of Triandna. I am Commander Carlesir, commanding for the Duke. His Grace would like to make a courtesy call, if that would be possible. After that, His Grace would be pleased to have the captain and the senior officers as his guests."

"Yes, ser, Commander. Would you hold while I patch in the exec? Captain Cortalina is planetside."

The sharp-eyed yacht-master nodded.

Crimra's fingers danced across the panel.

"Sindra, there's a Duke's yacht out there. Came in on the lavender. Can you locate and verify?"

Another flicker of fingers.

"Niter. Crimra here. Yacht out there that claims it's a Duke's boat. Sindra's trying to find it. Want to put a turret on the tracer?"

"Crimra, take it easy. If it's small enough and far enough out not to trigger the screens, it can't be a danger yet. Besides, who'd dare to impersonate a ducal boat, and who'd have the equipment to come in on a reserved Imperial band?"

Crimra's eyes glanced from one screen to another, from the frozen image of the yacht-master to Sindra in navigation, to

Niter in gunnery, to the fourth screen where he was calling the executive officer's rating.

"Fores, Crimra here. Yacht blasted in on the lavender. Duke of Triandna, or so the yacht-master claims, would like to pay a courtesy call, then return the favor by having the exec and senior officers over for grub."

"Gerro will love that. I'll get him ready. Not really started on this run, dozers yet, and he's grumbling about the mess."

Ping!

The navigation screen indicator lights blinked.

"Get back to you with the details, Fores."

"Yes, Sindra? What's the gather?"

"According to every single code, outline, and verification, you have indeed the *Sindelar*, number two yacht of the Duke of Triandna, and she's statted one and a half screens out, precisely, just like protocol says. No heavy weapons or energy concentrations."

The gunnery screen indicators blinked, and Crimra switched to Niter.

"Yes?"

"We've put number two on the yacht, but it wouldn't matter."

"Wouldn't matter?"

"Crimra, yachts can't carry weapons. Emperor's edict. So they got screens like battlecruisers. Accel/decel like corvettes. We're a big fat freighter. She'd be gone before we could even put a load on her screens. Anyway, her screens are the genuine article. Codes and all in the energy warp."

"Thanks."

Crimra paused and wiped his suddenly damp forehead with the back of his left hand before switching back to the executive officer's screen.

"Fores, we've checked and comm, nav, and guns all say it's the genuine article, one certified Duke's yacht. So Gerro can play gracious host and get a decent meal in afterward . . ."

He paused and wiped his forehead.

"Still . . ."

"Still what?"

"What's a Duke's yacht doing here off New Glascow?"

"Blast it, Crimra. Those boys go anywhere. Sometimes just on a bet. And remember, half of them hold reserve I.S.S.

commissions as commodores or admirals. Anyhow, even if it weren't a Duke, who'd want a couple hundred dozers? For anything?"

"Admirals?"

"Right. They never really get to command except in practice games out in Gamma sector once a year. So they run around in their own little boats. Who knows, maybe this Duke will punch old Gerro's ticket."

"He wouldn't!"

"Never know what can happen, Crimra. You never know." The exec's screen blanked.

The comm tech cleared the board, except for the still-frozen image of the yacht-master, waiting in his lavender uniform for the response from the *Sanducar*.

Somehow, the cramped comm center seemed to constrict around Crimra. He shook his head, wiped his forehead again with the back of his hand, and tapped the panels in front of him.

 LXIX

"Shuttle's heading back," Crimra observed, simultaneously notifying the gunnery section so they could drop the screens.

"Got it. Screens down. If five isn't enough, Sindra, let me know." Crimra monitored the exchange between guns and nav.

"Five's plenty, Niter. The little boy's almost clear now."

Crimra checked the board. The homer was clear, the green light showing the near-empty shuttle was locked on.

He checked the board again. All clear. With a sigh, he leaned back in the anchored swivel so that the air flow from the vent could dry the remaining dampness from his forehead.

From the outside, the *Sanducar* was huge, but the habitable space was not much more than in the ducal yacht. Most of the *Sanducar*'s space was devoted to drives or cargo, and the ship could have been handled easily by a third of its thirty crew members, as was routinely the case with the handful of commercial freighters equivalent to the *Sanducar*.

Crimra stretched his legs and watched as the screen light indicators blinked amber twice, then settled into the green to show the screens were back in place.

The faintest of clinks and a nearly infinitesimal shiver occurred as the shuttle entered the receiving locks and clicked into place.

The homer signal beeped once, and the light switched from green to the amber of standby.

The comm tech relaxed further now that the shuttle had returned. Stand-down watches weren't half bad, with one section gone. Now, with the exec and his two tag-alongs over playing with the Duke, all he had to worry about were any incomings, not that there were likely to be that many.

He straightened in the swivel and brushed a strand of hair back off his forehead.

Then he shook his head. He'd only seen pictures of the Duke before, but, in person, he seemed thinner, more military than the faxers had shown him. The Duke and the yachtmaster had really looked at the *Sanducar*. They'd been quick, but they'd asked questions, almost like an inspection.

Crimra didn't see Gerro getting his ticket punched by that Duke. He acted like he knew more than the exec, not that that was any great surprise to any of the *Sanducar*'s crew.

Crimra yawned. He shouldn't feel sleepy.

He stretched again, trying to stifle another yawn, aware that the breeze from the vent was stronger, with a faint scent of . . . something. He shrugged.

And yawned again. Blast! He shouldn't feel that sleepy.

The comm tech concentrated on putting his feet in exactly the correct position in front of the swivel. Next, he grasped the arms and concentrated on lifting himself out of the seat.

His arms wouldn't lift him, and he was yawning again, his mouth so far open that his jaw ached.

From somewhere, the blackness came up and hit him.

 LXX

Gerswin bent his forefinger in the odd configuration required to seal his suit, and the faceplate slid closed.

He hoped none of the onboard crew of the *Sanducar* had been suited, not that there would have been any reason for them to have been, not while in orbit and on stand-down.

He raised his hand. The shuttle was sealed into the hold, both locks opened. Gerswin and his crew of ten were outside the shuttle itself, hidden behind the more than man-tall driver shields from the vid scanners and from the direct vision of the tech who was in charge of the hangar and lock operations.

Gerswin was betting that there would be a single tech on duty, two at most.

If not, he was prepared to employ more direct means.

Nitiri, wearing the shipsuit of the shuttle's pilot, went through the power-down procedures, locked the shuttle onto the mesh, and exited from the forward shuttle hatch. He stepped out, turned to look over the shuttle as if to give it a cursory inspection from outside, then turned back and took careful steps toward the interior lock.

The single on-duty tech looked up as Nitiri appeared, suit still sealed.

"Hey! You—"

Thrumm!

The tech crumpled across the console. Nitiri lifted him off the board. Carefully, because he was wearing the heavy suit gauntlets, he made a number of changes to the status board, the last of which unlocked the interior lock for Gerswin and the nine others.

Gerswin clumped in last and manually sealed the battle locks to prevent anyone from surprising them in turn. By the time he had finished cranking the heavy bolts into their jackets and entered the hangar lock control room, Nitiri was stretching out the unconscious tech in the only vacant corner. The others had

318

split into three different parties, each group with a small gas cannister.

The commander traced a question mark in the air, unwilling to use the suit radio, since most suit frequencies would trigger the automatic defense alarms of Imperial ships unless accompanied by the ship's own carrier code.

Nitiri stood, straightened, and shrugged, both gray gauntlets held palm up.

Gerswin motioned to the nine to go ahead, then took a thin cable from his suit pouch, along with the tool pack, and began to work. With three movements and the use of two tools, he was plugged into the console.

The odds were against their completing the changes to the ship's air systems before someone stumbled across the intruders, and Gerswin wanted to know when it happened.

He switched from frequency to frequency, from console station to console station, but picked up nothing on the first sweep.

Ideally, he would have preferred the comm center, but that was obviously impractical. Any alarm would show on the common channels within seconds, in any case.

In the interim Nitiri placed himself, stunner still drawn, to cover the now-closed portal from the main access corridor into the cargo control lock center where they waited. The room was so small that anyone who entered would see them at once.

Gerswin plugged to the lit stations on the comm panel.

"Sindra, Niter here. Do you know if Weryon is pushing dust again?"

"Negative, Sindra. Could be. Fores said that the exec's cabin was getting air that smelled oily. Thought they'd fixed it."

"Just thought I heard some noise below in the vent system. . . . Oh . . . ohhh . . . Wish Peres would get here."

"Why? You said she doesn't like you."

"Doesn't. Sleepy, and she's my relief."

"Got a while. It must be the waiting. Feel the same way."

"Dorfstuff! Hurry up and wait. Exec's off. Captain's gone. We're here. Who's in charge?"

"The senior lieutenant . . ."

Another light blinked, and Gerswin shifted frequencies.

"Fores! Fores! Get the O.D."

BRING! BRINGG! BRINGGG!

The piercing ringing of the general quarters alarm shook Gerswin even through his suit's armor.

He tabbed his own transmitter.

"Blue team. Blue team. Interrogative status."

"Blue team to Captain Black. Status is green and sealed."

"Commence clean-up. Commence clean-up."

"Affirmative. Commencing."

Gerswin tabbed his transmitter the second time.

"Green team. Interrogative status."

"Green team to Captain Black. Status is three plus until green."

"Split. Plan beta. Plan beta."

"Stet. Affirmative plan beta for green team."

Gerswin hit the button, then dropped behind the console as he saw the disruptor preceding the big tech barreling into the lock control room.

Crack!

Thrummm!

The intruder dropped under the stunner, but not before his disruptor left what had been the right corner of the lock control board as a molten chunk of metal and plastics.

Gerswin stayed low behind the console.

"Red team. Interrogative status."

"Red team to Captain Black. Shunts complete. Communications blanked. One plus to green on seals."

"Red team. Commence plan beta."

"Stet. Commencing beta. Good luck, Captain Black."

Gerswin looked across the small room to Nitiri, who by now had shifted the stunner into his left gauntlet. He held the disruptor he had recovered in his right.

Gerswin returned to monitoring channels. While several lights continued to blink, indicating keyed or open channels, no actual communications were on-going. Either the crew had succumbed to the sleep gas or stunners, or there was a fight going on somewhere, and the Imperial freighter's crew was not talking because they knew their communications were being monitored.

Gerswin glanced across at Nitiri, but could only see his own reflection in the other's face plate.

Belatedly, he unholstered his own stunner and leveled it in the direction of the portal to the main corridor.

"Captain Black, red team leader. Area is now secure. Area three now totally secure. No casualties. I say again. No casualties."

"Captain Black, blue team leader. Area one is secure. No casualties."

"Captain Black, green team leader. Area two secure with one exception. No casualties, but one exception. Armored and at location level three, frames 192 and 193."

"Green team leader, Captain Black. Interrogative weapons status of exception."

"Captain Black, exception has no standard weapons, but has officer's sword."

"Green team leader, Captain Black is on the way. On the way."

Gerswin unplugged from the console and handed the jack to Nitiri.

"Watch the inboard freqs from below."

Nitiri nodded.

Level three, frame 193, was the space armor locker.

Only Lostwin waited for Gerswin. The rest of the team continued to work.

"Every one of those suits has a disruptor, Captain."

"I know. I know." Gerswin surveyed the area. "Is this place saturated under full atmosphere?"

"Yes, sir."

"Have a medic standing by. Hope I can do this without too much damage, but . . ."

"What—"

Gerswin cut off the exchange with a downward chop of his hand. If the Imperial officer were any kind of fighter, he'd be on Gerswin's frequencies already.

"Blue team leader, this is Captain Black. In one point zero from mark, pull your board for one point zero. Do you understand?"

"Captain Black, blue team leader. Pulling my entire board for one point zero. That is one point zero from your mark."

"Stet. *Mark!*"

"We have mark."

Gerswin gestured to Lostwin, pointing to the space armor locker portal and to the controls box.

Lostwin got the idea and nodded, using hand signals to move his team out of any possible line of fire, then moved to the controls. He began to operate the manual overrides of the internal locks. As the portal began to iris open, a beam of red energy flared against the inside of the portal once, then again.

Gerswin smiled. The officer inside was trying to fuse the portal shut.

He moved closer, waiting.

The grav generators went off, and he launched himself to the overhead. In three quick mincesteps he was by the edge of the portal, crouching low, and throwing the knives.

One!

Two!

A silent flare of red energy died with the second knife.

Captain Black was through the half-open portal like a streak, plowing into the Imperial officer from above and knocking the disruptor away.

As the other dropped to the deck more easily than Gerswin expected, he had a sickening suspicion.

"Lock guard, get medic here on straight line full accel/decel. Casualty may need immediate medical attention."

"Affirmative, Captain. Affirmative."

Gerswin didn't see any blood, but both knives had hit the holdout officer, one in the right shoulder, and the other in the left thigh.

"How could he throw it through armor cloth?"

That came through the suit intercom. Gerswin didn't recognize the speaker's voice.

"Ever seen his knives? Ever seen him throw?"

"Yeah, every year or so he takes up a new weapon. Keeps him alert."

Gerswin ignored the background chatter, and hoisted the faintly struggling figure over his shoulder and headed for Nitiri and the lock control center. The last thing someone who was bleeding needed was a full dose of sleepgas, and until he could unsuit, there wasn't a thing he or anyone else could do.

As he reached the hangar locks he felt the vibrations of the *Sindelar*'s boat locking in with Winsters.

The young officer was limp by the time Winsters and

Gerswin had her unsuited in the yacht boat, the single place aboard the *Sanducar* not permeated with the gas.

Winsters began working, and without glancing at his commander, observed, "She should be all right. While you pinned the one in the thigh pretty deep, you missed about everything you could miss. Shoulder wound's mostly muscle. She'll be laid up for a while, but it doesn't look like any permanent damage."

Gerswin sighed, followed it with a frown. One casualty wasn't bad, but why did it have to be a female officer? On some planets that wouldn't set well at all, if it ever got out.

"Remember, Winsters, no names, and no treatment once she's conscious without privacy gear and an armed guard."

The former shambletown kid nodded with a grim smile. "Understand, Commander. Understand."

"You take her back with you. We'll go on as planned. Have Dewart bring back the officers when you get the signal."

"Need more support?"

"We're set, unless something changes. We're securing the crew, and we've got the supplies for the jump. If they have any spare torps, I'll send them back when you send over the exec. Best we break before someone sends out a corvette."

Gerswin sealed his suit and headed back into the *Sanducar* and the command bridge, leaving Nitiri to outlock the *Sindelar*'s boat and lockseal the outer doors as well.

On the bridge, he began the checks.

"Interrogative drives."

"In the green. Power up sequence at minus fifteen to touch point."

"Navigation, interrogative screens."

"Up and in the green. Course feed input on schedule. Will have break point computations adapted in twelve plus or minus two."

"Gunnery?"

"Captain, for our purposes, no guns. Permission to divert to screens."

"Go ahead, if you can reshunt without leaving traces after arrival and downloading."

"No problem."

Gerswin wondered how small that diversion problem really was, but extra power to the screens certainly wouldn't hurt.

"Drives, interrogative governor status."

"Plan to reset at plus point two. Enough to throw off the Impie computers, but not enough to hurt our passengers."

"Navigation, interrogative visitors."

"Captain Black, no visitors in sight. None anticipated."

So now all he had to do was wait . . .

He needed one quarter of a standard Imperial hour, one quarter hour before His Imperial Majesty's freighter *Sanducar* could vanish from orbit for an unknown destination.

At that point, the *Sindelar* would also vanish to deliver a few messages, and to send out a raft of message torps, before being returned to its rather surprised refit crew.

Then—Gerswin shook his head, violently, and refocused his attention on the screen before him. One thing at a time.

First, his teams needed to finish securing the crew. Second, they had to bring the freighter from stand-down to full operation. Third, they had to recover the exec and two officers and leave orbit without discovery and attack by Imperial vessels.

"Captain, incoming from yacht."

"Stet. Lock in and recover."

"Captain Black? Incoming on standard comm net. Interrogative response."

"Respond without screen. Explain you're doing last minute maintenance. Ask to feed back in three to five."

"Affirmative. Will do."

Gerswin checked the read-outs. Minus ten until full power-up sequence was complete. He hoped the *Sindelar*'s boat was clear by then. He jabbed the engineering stud.

"Interrogative drive status."

"Minus nine until green."

"Report when ready."

"Yes, ser."

"Navigation, interrogative status."

"Minus seven until course feed complete."

Gerswin sat watching the screens, looking at the flow of information on the status of the ship, watching the green panels light, watching the red shift to amber, and then to green.

Another thought crossed his mind, and he tapped the tight beam back to the *Sindelar*.

"Landspout, this is Captain Black. Interrogative status of messengers."

"Captain Black, messengers ready to depart within one plus of your completion."

"Affirm one plus."

"Stet."

He turned back to the unfamiliar bridge board.

"Captain." This time the voice did not come from a distant channel, but from the suited figure to his right, from the opening portal where Lostwin stood.

"Crew totally secured and unconscious. Ship will be flushed and clean within twenty."

Gerswin nodded, part of the tightness in his gut subsiding.

Lostwin settled himself into the O.D.'s swivel, trying to match what he'd studied and the board of the freighter against the smaller ships he had piloted.

"Captain, red team leader. Estimate thirty plus for unsuit time. Nav indicates after first jump point."

"Stet."

"Navigation to bridge. All systems green. Course feed complete."

"Stet."

"Engineering to bridge. All systems green."

"Stet."

"Hangar deck to bridge. Transfer complete, and visitors clear."

"Screens dropped for departure?"

"That's affirmative."

"Guns to Captain Black, diversion complete and green."

"Stet."

Gerswin took a deep breath within the confines of the suit, exhaled, and began to move his gauntleted fingers across the board.

At last, he touched the pulsing green stud that would mesh the inputs and boost the *Sanducar* from orbit to the first jump point.

"Landspout, this is Captain Black. We are green and departing. Green and departing."

"Stet. See you later."

Gerswin watched the screens, the course line display that represented where the *Sanducar* was headed, and the real-time monitor that showed the blackness outside, punctuated with unwinking stars. He watched the screens, the familiar displays in unfamiliar positions, his face blank, expressionless behind the suitshield.

As the outward velocity of the *Sanducar* mounted, he saw a spark break from the small circle captioned "New Glascow" on the representational screen.

"Comm, any interrogatories?"

"Standard inquiries from planetary ops and from the geosynch high ops, but we're farside. Not much they can do. We're maintaining full-band silence."

"What's the breakway?"

"Breakway is high speed shuttle. Has the *Sanducar*'s C.O. Guess he's afraid of being left."

"Any combat ships?"

"No other energy concentrations."

"Navigation, interrogative closest approach of shuttle."

"He's already past CPA. We're clear to jump point."

"Stet."

Clear to jump point meant clear to Old Earth, and clear to unload nearly two cohorts of dozers and get them operating before they could be easily reclaimed. But Old Earth would be exactly where his real troubles began, Gerswin reflected.

Lerwin had protested being excluded, but there had to be someone officially innocent should things go wrong, someone who could pick up the pieces.

Gerswin shook his head, still watching the screens, still waiting to insure that no untoward Impie combatant appeared from nowhere, waiting until the real battles began.

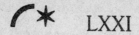 LXXI

"Commander Gerswin to the Ops center. Commander Gerswin to the Ops center."

The senior commander under summons swung his feet off the narrow bunk and sat upright, pulling his boots onto his feet.

Buzzz! Buzzzz!

He ignored the harsh noise from his console. He had no doubt about the reason for the summons, none whatsoever.

He smiled and took a deep breath. After all the years, the room—and he had never put in for a suite, which he rated—still smelled like a mixture of wilted trilia and machine oil. It always would, he supposed, not that it was likely he would be the one worrying about it for much longer.

As he finished fastening the undress black tunic, he was through the portal and into the main corridor. It was empty, unsurprisingly, since it was just before dawn local Old Earth time. Then, the Imperial Interstellar Survey Service had never operated on anything other than New Augustan Imperial District time, and by that clock, it was mid-morning.

Lerwin, wearing his new linked diamonds of commander, met him at the Operations portal.

"They're here, Captain. Upset, too."

"Did they announce it?" asked Gerswin with the same disinterested smile.

"In their own way. Arrived with five corvettes, two destroyers, and a battlecruiser. That's a full battle group."

"Lunar pick-up?"

"Right. No comm link yet."

"Open a link with them. Welcome them and ask innocently what we can do for them."

"What?"

"No sense in acting guilty, is there? Or giving them an excuse to use all that firepower?"

Lerwin nodded slowly.

"And . . . Lerwin . . ." the senior commander added slowly, "hope those dozers are well dispersed and very actively reclaiming the land."

"We already did that. They can't get them without destroying everything we've reclaimed, and then some."

The dark-haired executive officer with the eyes like an eagle smiled. Both his smile and that of the commandant were like sun over the northern ice, like the moon above winter tundra.

The two turned together wordlessly and strode through the portal and into the Operations section.

"Captain, there's an admiral out there!"

"They wouldn't send less, would they?" Gerswin cleared his throat. "I'll speak to him. Put him on the main screen. That way everyone in the base can see. Make sure you catch a cube of it. We might find it helpful . . . later."

The image on the central screen in front of Gerswin flickered blue once, then focused on an officer with iron gray hair, a man wearing the drab gray of ship battle dress, distinguished only by the silver stars and joining bar on his collars.

"Welcome, Admiral," offered the senior commander, his vagueness deliberate since he hadn't the faintest idea which of the Empire's several dozen admirals he was addressing.

"I appreciate the courtesy," returned the I.S.S. functionary, "and would appreciate the opportunity to speak with Senior Commander Gerswin."

"Speaking."

"So you're Gerswin . . . I could believe that." The admiral stiffened his already stiff bearing and lifted a single sheet of permafax into view. "Senior Commander Gerswin, by virtue of the authority vested in me by His Imperial Majesty, I hereby relieve you of your command. That command is temporarily transferred to the authority of Battle Group Delta Seven, pending outcome of the forthcoming Board of Inquiry proceedings.

"You are requested to make yourself available for interview, and for possible trial under the articles of the Service. Pending the outcome of the inquiry, Senior Commander Beloit will be acting as Commandant, I.S.S. Reclamation Base, Old Earth."

Gerswin raised his hand. "One question, Admiral. Or two. Who are you? And with what have I been charged, if anything?"

The chill in the admiral's eyes was clear, even through the screen transmission. "Senior Commander, right now, you are charged with nothing. Any possible charges will await the outcome of all phases of the investigation of the irregular transfer of two cohorts of Imperial arc-dozers from the Marine Engineering Command to the Reclamation Base, Old Earth. Under the Emperor's orders, I am conducting phase one of the inquiry."

Gerswin, while remaining at attention, smiled slightly. "You have yet to identify either yourself or the orders under which you are operating. Without such verification, I am not empowered to surrender my command, even in the face of the superior force which you have mustered."

Gerswin heard several hisses of indrawn breath around the Operations center. Even Lerwin had taken a step away from him at the last statement.

"Please be so kind, Senior Commander, as to activate your authentication system."

Gerswin nodded twice at the technician across the center. Three half-hearted jabs later, the panel blinked amber twice and settled into the green.

"Authentication on."

The admiral placed his own verifax sheet into a similar device, and waited, still ramrod stiff in the screen.

"Admiral Ferrin," whispered Lerwin, out of range of the screen focused on Gerswin.

The authenticator blinked green twice.

"Apparently your orders are genuine," admitted the senior commander. "What would you like me to do, Admiral Ferrin?"

"A shuttle will be arriving with the first members of the investigation team. They will interview every I.S.S. member in your command with two exceptions. I will interview you and your executive officer, Commander Lerwin, after all other interviews are complete.

"Senior Commander Beloit will also be arriving to take temporary command. I would appreciate it if you would remain in the general vicinity of the main base while the investigation is being conducted."

"Yes, ser. Will that be all?"

"For now, Senior Commander Gerswin. For now."

"Yes, ser."

The admiral nodded briskly, and the screen blanked.

"They're out to get you, Captain."

"Blasting inquiry!"

"Why so harsh?"

"They'll try him and never let him go."

"How many bodies do they want?"

"All of us?"

"All of us."

Gerswin stood silent until the comments died away. Waited until all those who had seen the Imperial transmission had gathered around him.

"Think," he began quietly. "Do they really want to admit to the Empire, to the whole Galaxy, that their old battered and tattered home planet had to steal dozers to reclaim itself? Do they really want to create that kind of image? Do they want to make a martyr out of me or anyone else?"

He shook his head, as if to emphasize his points.

"They can't do anything about the dozers. But they'll come down like tacheads on anyone who is defiant, insubordinate, or whom they find guilty of any easily documented transgression.

"Be polite. Be helpful. Tell the truth, always the truth, but volunteer nothing. Since it's allowed, insist on copies of your statements for your own records. That's allowed. Then send copies to Service HQ for the official hearing files. That's also allowed."

He could see the frowns, the puzzled expressions.

"Two people can sometimes keep a secret, but three never can, not about something this big."

He paused, then decided to re-emphasize a point.

"Remember, if you don't know about something from your own first hand knowledge, don't discuss it. That can only get you into trouble. If you do know, limit your discussion to the facts. The facts are our allies."

He surveyed the room again.

"Don't . . . get . . . them . . . angry," he concluded, spacing each word for emphasis. "Don't give them the slightest excuse."

He smiled, and his expression was colder than the moon's dark side.

"It's time to get ready for the temporary commandant."

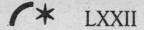 LXXII

The mathematics of purely mechanical ecological reconstruction would have been stupendous. The largest single water purifying or recycling unit ever developed processed five hundred cubic meters of water per standard minute. Had one million of these units been employed and had they been required to purify every drop of water on the planet, and had no drop ever been processed more than once, the process would have taken more than 50,000 years.

Beyond that, the resource drain on the Empire would have been astronomical. For a self-contained unit to be effective, an incorporated fusion power plant was required, with all contaminants processed either reduced to basic elements or elemental hydrogen.

While nature's natural processes, given time, are also effective with the most critical areas of land and water pollution, neither nature nor the puny mechanical aids of man could have been totally effective in reclaiming Old Earth, not in the time scale in which reclamation was actually accomplished.

Viewpoints
Accardo Avero
New Avalon, 5132 N.E.C.

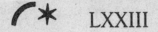 LXXIII

The admiral picked up the executive summary, waved it once, and dropped it on the long green table.

"You know what this is worth? That's what it's worth."

None of the other Service officers around the table spoke. Not one opened his or her mouth.

"I take it that you all agree?"

Vice Admiral Boedekkr nodded her head slowly up and down.

"Admiral Boedekkr. Your thoughts?"

"The same as yours, Admiral. We know the *Sanducar* was diverted. We even have solid evidence in some cases. We could probably prove it in a court martial. But what would we gain? We would prove to most of mankind that we care nothing about Old Earth. It isn't true, but that is what such a trial would indicate. We could make the Emperor look foolish by denying all the press reports of his good will and largess toward our parent planet. And, also to be considered is how foolish the Service would look."

"Foolish?" questioned a white-haired admiral.

"Foolish," repeated Admiral Boedekkr. "First, the ease with which a heavy Imperial freighter was diverted would have to come out. Second, we would look like we were trying to punish some idealistic officers for making us look foolish and for doing what most people think was right. And last, to the Imperial Senate, we would look as if we were trying to weaken the Emperor's position.

"Then, too, by issuing denials of the press releases that were circulated to the major media in who knows how many systems, we would end up making the media look as silly as we would. All in all, prosecution seems unwise."

"Why?" demanded a commodore from the end of the table, as if he had ignored her entire argument.

"Because, Commodore," and her flint eyes bored into the

man, "in addition to the entire argument you have apparently ignored, I would not wish to put the Emperor in the position of denying reclamation efforts on Old Earth. Nor am I terribly anxious to admit that a handful of Service personnel managed to divert a major amount of Imperial resources and a freighter without our even knowing about it until the ship disappeared for an unknown destination. Furthermore, we could not even follow up until they kindly returned both our ship and a Ducal yacht with the crews unharmed."

"Almost unharmed," corrected the commodore.

"Thank you, Admiral," nodded the senior admiral at the head of the review board. "Most important, it would be difficult to prove other than circumstantially exactly who was responsible for what. Not one of the ship's crew saw any of the pirates. Nor can the Duke's personnel identify whether or not their passengers were associated with those who took over the yacht. We have conflicting reports of someone impersonating the Duke, and the Duke, of course, is most reluctant to press that charge unless we can prove it beyond any doubt whatsoever.

"All we have are two cohorts of arc-dozers which are busily reclaiming sections of Old Earth, and demonstrating to the Empire that Emperors keep their commitments."

"So we're going to hold a court martial to prove it's all a hoax and return those dozers to a training hell-hole in Gamma sector?" he asked rhetorically.

"Wrong," he answered himself quietly. "But we won't let the guilty get away with it, either. The Service takes care of its own, one way or another."

"How?" asked the vice admiral to his left, the vice chairman of the review board.

"Thank you, Virl, for asking the question on schedule."

The two grinned at each other.

"We have a solution. One that will give the Emperor great credit for taking an important step toward reclaiming Old Earth. One that will remove the financial burden of Old Earth from the Service and return it to the Senate and the Court, and one that will send a clear message to everyone in the Service who knows without alerting anyone else."

His voice became matter-of-fact. "Obviously, you must approve the solution, but, if approved, the whole incident becomes a lesson learned relatively cheaply. We got the ship back. The Emperor will get the credit, and our budget will benefit. And we have a chance to change shipboard procedures so this cannot happen again."

"Might I ask you to outline the solution?" That was Vice Admiral Boedekkr.

"Shortly, the Emperor will announce that Old Earth needs a special effort. He will declare the formation of the Imperial Reclamation and Reconstruction Corps—Recorps, for short. Recorps personnel will be recruited locally from Old Earth and from volunteers throughout the Empire. Any officers and technicians now at Old Earth Base may transfer without prejudice, and with good recommendations to Recorps in order to take advantage of their experience and dedication."

"In effect, it becomes a lifetime tour on Old Earth?"

"Assume those who don't elect to transfer will face some 'prejudice,' if you want to put it that way."

"Will it work?"

The admiral waited, then cleared his throat.

"Those who choose not to volunteer, in order for the Service to avoid 'conflicts of interest,' must elect another home of record and will sign a release acknowledging that they will never be stationed in that quadrant again. Further, because of various Service-related difficulties, they will have to accept a marginally satisfactory rating for their last Old Earth tour. If they remain in Service, unless they truly accomplish a heroic deed, they will probably never be considered for promotion beyond captain or their present rank, if they are already above the rank of captain."

"Clever."

"Very neat."

"Marvelous."

Vice Admiral Boedekkr did not join in the comments. She alone smiled faintly, and leaned back in her swivel.

Admiral Roeder observed her silence and made a mental note to follow up. He wanted to know what her reservations were. In the meantime, he tapped the gavel.

"Follow-up briefings will begin after lunch."

The flag officers filed out on each side of the long green table, most with their shoulders high, as if an enormous weight had been lifted from them.

Roeder refrained from shaking his head. Most still didn't understand how they had been maneuvered, and he didn't know whether he was glad they didn't, or appalled at their density.

He twisted his lips in a thin smile before he set down the gavel and left to follow the others.

"The dozers are only a symbol, as are the promises of pumps and purifiers."

The senior commander frowned at the screen a last time before blanking his calculations. What would they say, those for whom he had made the choice? Those who would be forever grounded or forever exiled?

He took a deep breath and exhaled it slowly, letting it out with the sigh of a hot flitter touch-down.

He could only hope that the few young and Imperial-born officers who had elected to remain in the Service would be quietly re-reviewed once they left Old Earth, since he had made sure that the record showed they had had no part in whatever had occurred.

If the Service was inflexible enough not to . . . he shook his head.

None of the choices were easy, and even the best of dreams sometimes faded.

He stood and took a step toward the portal, his eyes flicking from one corner of the commandant's small quarters to the other, from the pale gray of the right, with its built-in locker, closet, and console, to the pale gray of the left, with bunk and flat walls.

His own decision had been made before it had been offered, for he had no other choice. Already he had stayed too long, and it was time for change. He could not come home until it was no longer home for him, but for all men and women.

If he stayed, the Service and Imperial hatred would focus on Recorps. At least, it might, and that he could not risk.

"Hope is so fragile, and for now, the dozers will help . . ."

He picked up both packets off the console, then slashed a line across one, the one with the new symbol at the top, and placed his signature across the bottom of the second.

Two kit bags—all that he intended to take—stood by the portal.

His fingers found their way to the console, which lit and focused on nothing as he tapped out the codes he wanted.

The commander's face snapped into view.

"Captain."

"Just Commander Gerswin, Lerwin." He paused. "It's all yours. Your command will take effect immediately, and you'll have to work out the reorganization plan to get the best out of what you have. You know who they are."

The other nodded, his hawk-green eyes never leaving Gerswin's.

"Don't say I understand, but if that's it, that's it."

"Some day, it will become more clear. Lived with it so long I never bothered to explain. Little late now."

Neither said anything as the moments stretched out.

"You're the captain now. Make sure you are."

"And you?"

"Just say that I had no choice. They know whose idea it was. For me to stay would cost everyone too much. So I have no choice. Besides, my work's not done."

"No choice. That's the best way to put it. Keep them on edge against the Empire, and they'll need that to begin with."

The senior commander agreed, but did not nod this time.

"You're the captain," he repeated. "Whatever you think best."

"Now?" asked the new captain.

Even through the screen, Gerswin could see the incipient signs of age, the faint lines around the eyes, the heavier muscles. Lerwin would outlive the Imperials, had already outlived some before showing any age, but he would not see the rebirth for which he worked. Even Corwin might not see that, assuming Corwin followed in his parent's footsteps.

Corwin . . . Gerswin scarcely knew the child, and had seldom even seen his sister Ellia. With the growth of the children, while she did her job well, Kiedra had turned her personal side inward to Lerwin and Corwin and Ellia. Like all devilkids, reflected Gerswin sadly.

"Now?" asked Lerwin again.

"Shortly. I leave on the next shuttle." Gerswin frowned. "Afraid I left you in the lurch. My file keys are on the commandant's console. Everything's there. Try and do a better job for your successor, Lerwin."

"You did fine, Captain."

"Thanks, but we know better. I'll be down in ten plus."

Gerswin tapped the console once, and the image of the commander who would be listed as the first Commandant of Recorps faded from the screen.

Gerswin was ready to go, but he stood shifting his weight from one foot to the other, waiting. Lerwin needed the time to round up the remaining devilkids. They all needed to see him enter the shuttle, needed to see the departure, to understand that he could no longer stand behind them.

Lerwin needed the visual image of his departure also. While there was no ritual such as a change of command, because the old Command had been abolished, and the new one was not in place, they all needed some sort of ceremony to mark the end of the old era and the beginning of the new.

The senior commander, his short and curly blond hair untouched with silver, his hawk-yellow eyes as fierce as ever, his face unlined, smiled at the blank wall. The sole imprint of the years had been the slight sharpening of his features—that, and the hint of blackness that lingered behind his eyes like a reminder of eternity itself.

He picked up the kit bags himself, though he could have had them carried to the shuttle, and tabbed the portal. As it irised open, he stepped through into the main corridor and the omnipresent but faint scent of ozone.

He half-shook his head. Someday, sometime, the closed buildings would not be necessary. Nor the fortress-like or half-buried construction. Already, the new town construction was halfway there, though the residents were far hardier stock than the average Imperial. The landspouts were less frequent in the reclaimed areas around the base. Elsewhere, they raged scarcely abated, and those "elsewhere lands" comprised the majority of the globe.

Gerswin's steps did not resemble those of a senior commander with more than eighty years' service. Quick and light, his feet, even at a walk, scarcely seemed to touch the pale and milky gray of the plastone floor tiles.

He slowed as he approached the last turn in the corridor before the Operations center.

Had Lerwin had enough time?

He shrugged. If necessary, he could prolong good-bys and remarks until they all straggled in.

The portal stood open. Inside the center, the entry console was vacant. Only a single technician manned the duty console, and the corridor leading down to the departure portals was also vacant. So was the tunnel to the hangar-bunker that served the shuttle.

The shuttle from the *Relyea* was grounded in beta two, and Gerswin picked up his pace as he entered the sloping tunnel. After about fifty meters the tunnel slope flattened before beginning the gradual ascent toward the hangar-bunker.

As he stepped through the last portal into the hangar, he straightened.

"Ten'stet!"

Crack! Crack! Crack!

The ceremonial volley of the ancient long guns caught him off guard as it continued.

All eight of the remaining devilkids, four on a side, in full-dress Service uniform, stood at attention. They formed an honor guard between him and the open port of the waiting shuttle.

Behind them, also in full dress, was Lerwin, and it had been Lerwin's voice that had given the commands.

Gerswin stood, waiting.

"Captain," began the new commandant, "there will be a commandant of Recorps here on Old Earth who will succeed you. And he will have a successor, as will his or her successor. But there is only one Captain, and there will be only one Captain from Old Earth. Either here, or out among the Imperial stars."

"Ten'stet!" another voice barked.

Crack! Crack! Crack!

"Any words, Captain?"

Gerswin swallowed. Hard. Waited.

Finally, he cleared his throat.

"You all understand. Remember what we did. More important, remember why. Time will make it easy to forget. I'll be back, one way or another, but it may be a long cold trip. It's all in your hands, and you have a big job. The biggest ever tackled." He paused. "We know it can be done. I did what I

could, but the biggest part is up to you, and I know you're up
to it. You can do it. You just have to forget the past and get on
with it."

He turned to Lerwin and saluted.

"Your command, Commander. Your command. Permission
to depart?"

"Your command, Captain. Always your command. We may
hold it for you, but it will always be yours. Good luck
. . . from all of us . . . for all of us."

Lerwin returned the salute.

Crack! Crack! Crack!

Gerswin waited until the last volley died away before
bending to retrieve the two kit bags. He lifted them and
marched through the eight devilkids and across the plastarmac
toward the shuttle.

Once inside the lock, he set down the bags, turned and gave
a last salute before the shuttle ports closed.

A long trip so far . . . and a longer one that was just
beginning.

THE DRAGON REBORN

Sequel to *The Great Hunt*

Book Three of *The Wheel of Time*

by

Robert Jordan

Praise for *Eye of the World*

"A powerful vision of good and evil...fascinating people moving through a rich and interesting world."   —Orson Scott Card

"Richly detailed...fully realized, complex adventure."
—*Library Journal*

"A combination of Robin Hood and Stephen King that is hard to resist...Jordan makes the reader care about these characters as though they were old friends."   —*Milwaukee Sentinel*

Praise for *The Great Hunt*

"Jordan can spin as rich a world and as event-filled a tale as [Tolkien]...will not be easy to put down."   —*ALA Booklist*

"Worth re-reading a time or two."   —*Locus*

"This is good stuff...Splendidly characterized and cleverly plotted...The Great Hunt is a good book which will always be a good book. I shall certainly [line up] for the third volume."
—*Interzone*

The Dragon Reborn
coming in hardcover in August, 1991

SCIENCE FICTION FROM
L.E. MODESITT, JR.

SCIENCE FICTION FROM
GORDON R. DICKSON

☐ ☐	53577-4	ALIEN ART	$2.95 Canada $3.95
☐ ☐	53546-4	ARCTURUS LANDING	$3.50 Canada $4.50
☐ ☐	53550-2	BEYOND THE DAR AL-HARB	$2.95 Canada $3.50
☐ ☐	53544-8	THE FAR CALL	$4.95 Canada $5.95
☐ ☐	53589-8	GUIDED TOUR	$3.50 Canada $4.50
☐ ☐	53068-3	HOKA! with Poul Anderson	$2.95 Canada $3.50
☐ ☐	53592-8	HOME FROM THE SHORE	$3.50 Canada $4.50
☐ ☐	53562-6	THE LAST MASTER	$2.95 Canada $3.50
☐ ☐	53554-5	LOVE NOT HUMAN	$2.95 Canada $3.95
☐ ☐	53581-2	THE MAN FROM EARTH	$2.95 Canada $3.95
☐ ☐	53572-3	THE MAN THE WORLDS REJECTED	$2.95 Canada $3.75

Buy them at your local bookstore or use this handy coupon:
Clip and mail this page with your order.

Publishers Book and Audio Mailing Service
P.O. Box 120159, Staten Island, NY 10312-0004

Please send me the book(s) I have checked above. I am enclosing $ _____
(please add $1.25 for the first book, and $.25 for each additional book to cover postage and handling.
Send check or money order only—no CODs).

Name _____
Address _____
City _____ State/Zip _____
Please allow six weeks for delivery. Prices subject to change without notice.

THE BEST IN
SCIENCE FICTION

☐	54310-6	A FOR ANYTHING
☐	54311-4	*Damon Knight*
		$3.95
		Canada $4.95

☐ 54310-6 A FOR ANYTHING $3.95
☐ 54311-4 *Damon Knight*   Canada $4.95

☐ 55625-9 BRIGHTNESS FALLS FROM THE AIR $3.50
☐ 55626-7 *James Tiptree, Jr.*   Canada $3.95

☐ 53815-3 CASTING FORTUNE $3.95
☐ 53816-1 *John M. Ford*   Canada $4.95

☐ 50554-9 THE ENCHANTMENTS OF FLESH & SPIRIT $3.95
☐ 50555-7 *Storm Constantine*   Canada $4.95

☐ 55413-2 HERITAGE OF FLIGHT $3.95
☐ 55414-0 *Susan Shwartz*   Canada $4.95

☐ 54293-2 LOOK INTO THE SUN $3.95
☐ 54294-0 *James Patrick Kelly*   Canada $4.95

☐ 54925-2 MIDAS WORLD $2.95
☐ 54926-0 *Frederik Pohl*   Canada $3.50

☐ 53157-4 THE SECRET ASCENSION $4.50
☐ 53158-2 *Michael Bishop*   Canada $5.50

☐ 55627-5 THE STARRY RIFT $4.50
☐ 55628-3 *James Tiptree, Jr.*   Canada $5.50

☐ 50623-5 TERRAPLANE $3.95
☐   *Jack Womack*   Canada $4.95

☐ 50369-4 WHEEL OF THE WINDS $3.95
☐ 50370-8 *M.J. Engh*   Canada $4.95

Buy them at your local bookstore or use this handy coupon:
Clip and mail this page with your order.

Publishers Book and Audio Mailing Service
P.O. Box 120159, Staten Island, NY 10312-0004

Please send me the book(s) I have checked above. I am enclosing $ _____
(Please add $1.25 for the first book, and $.25 for each additional book to cover postage and handling.
Send check or money order only—no CODs.)

Name _____
Address _____
City _____ State/Zip _____
Please allow six weeks for delivery. Prices subject to change without notice.